Julia Stephenson was [illegible] leaving the Lucie Clay[illegible] College she had stints as a professional cook, a chalet girl and a housewife. She is now a full-time writer. When she is not working she enjoys travelling and moving house, and is a student of Buddhism and *feng shui*. This is her second novel.

Praise for Julia Stephenson:

'A nineties Nancy Mitford' *Harpers & Queen*

Also by Julia Stephenson

Pandora's Diamond

Chalet Tiara

Julia Stephenson

HEADLINE

First published in hardback in 1999 by
HEADLINE BOOK PUBLISHING

First published in paperback in 1999 by
HEDLINE BOOK PUBLISHING

10 9 8 7 6 5 4 3 2 1

ISBN 0 7472 6163 6

Typeset by Avon Dataset Ltd, Bidford-on-Avon, Warks

Printed and bound in Great Britain by
Mackays of Chatham PLC, Chatham, Kent

HEADLINE BOOK PUBLISHING
A division of the Hodder Headline Group
338 Euston Road
London NW1 3BH

www.headline.co.uk
www.hodderheadline.com

With grateful thanks to my mother, for reading as I wrote, laughing at the right bits and correcting my awful spelling – this one is for you.

Acknowledgements

Many thanks to the Soka Gakkai, the lay organization of Nichiren Daishonin's Buddhism, for its support and inspiration, and especially to the UK Express Buddhist magazine, for stretching, encouraging and inspiring me as a writer. To all at Headline for continuing expertise, tolerance and patience! Jan Cisek for his excellent *feng shui* advice. Nigel Pendrigh, computer genius. Gay Annand, health practitioner extraordinaire. David and all at Corona travel in Woking, for creative expertise in solving my increasingly obscure and complex travel requirements. The girls at the Ritzy Marina Club, may all our dreams come true! To Allan Butters, for his invaluable advice, kindness and generosity of spirit. Nantucket Accommodations for always finding me lovely places to stay in dreamy Nantucket. Sylvia Earle, authoress and distinguished marine biologist, whose eloquent plea for the preservation of the ocean inspired so much of this book. Dr Wayne Dyer and Dr Deepak Chopra for explaining everything. And to Switzerland, Hawaii and Nantucket whose loveliness gives me time to dream and space to write.

Your future is generated by the choices you are making in every moment of your life.

Deepak Chopra, *The Seven Spiritual Laws of Success*

I think of a writer as a river: you reflect what passes before you.

Natalia Ginsburg

Chapter One

My sister Siena is four years older than I am and used to be very beautiful. My equally beautiful mother named her after a trip to Italy, which she had visited on a modelling assignment during the sixties dolce vita period. This was when voluptuous women were jumping in and out of fountains, and swaying from the ocean clutching sea shells and Sean Connery, not joining Weightwatchers as they would be in the liberated nineties.

Anyway, my mother was probably thinking of Rome as she never got to Siena. I've never been to Siena either, but glorious colours like amber, ochre, and the sight of ancient churches burnished dusty gold spring to mind whenever the place is mentioned. For Siena was a golden child who was born into her sun-washed name.

When we were very young we used to go on cruises with our glamorous parents and their sophisticated friends. Cruises were quite smart then and I don't remember any excitable elderly ladies playing slot machines, shell-suited lovers or the mass gluttony you think of when cruises are mentioned now.

Then, ship life meant slim upper-middle-class couples playing deck quoits and ladies wearing bathing hats doing leisurely breaststroke in the pool. Anyway, my parents liked the ship so much they named me after it. Thank goodness they didn't care for the *QE2*, I wouldn't have made a good Elizabeth. No, Oriana suited me very well, even though from a numerology point of view it's not very good, but you can't have everything.

Siena and I adored shipboard life and the world adored Siena. At eight years old, with her sunny smile, golden hair and light-green eyes, she held the world in the palm of her hand. She used to trot around the ship with a tin asking for donations; people thought it hilarious. I trailed along in her wake, a small pale, elfin figure, lacking her charm, picking up the rear with my empty tin. My parents were livid when they found out but that wasn't till the end of the fortnight. They'd been pretty occupied themselves. Mummy had rather fallen for the Italian purser and Dad was apparently having a thing with the croupier.

Nanny, who was meant to be keeping an eye on us, was doubly torn between the cooking masterclasses and one of the waiters, so Siena and I had plenty of time to ourselves. We used to spend hours looking out for dolphins, once we were even convinced we saw a mermaid but, of course, no one believed us. Anyway, by the end of the holiday Siena had collected a fortune in her tin. Mine was embarrassingly empty. Our parents tried to give money back to everybody but it got too complicated so they gave it to the lifeboat charity. When it comes to money, both of them are dead honest. I really admire that.

I don't know when the tables turned exactly. Probably around the time of the divorce. Attractive people are much more likely to split, there's so much more temptation. And everybody fancied them. I'm surprised they stayed together as long as they did. Mummy went blonde with grief and ran off with the deputy MD of one of Dad's companies and Dad ran off with his secretary. It was all ghastly so Siena and I were shunted off to boarding schools. She was very bright and got into Benenden, while I scraped into a funny little place in Hastings that catered for dyslectics. Not that I was dyslectic, just not particularly 'academic'. Fortunately I wasn't sent to the local comprehensive where I would have just been labelled thick.

I thrived there. Away from Siena's shadow I found my share of the sun. I was quite good at English and cooking but was hopeless at everything else. But I blossomed. I can't say my hair got blonder or anything, that came later courtesy of John Frieda, but I began to feel – the French have a great expression for it – *bien dans ma peau*, at home in my skin.

It was about this time that Siena, her seduction of the world complete, began to fade. Her lustrous hair, so thick and golden, lost its sheen and began its inexorable slide into mouse. Even her huge almond shaped eyes changed colour quite noticeably, I thought. The lovely green changed to an indeterminate hazel and her glowing skin and pink cheeks grew pale.

Our parents didn't seem to notice anything, or if they did they didn't mention it. Neither of them was much around and at fourteen and twelve we were old enough to look after ourselves anyway.

I think the worst thing was that Siena, having absolutely worshipped our father, took against him quite suddenly. He had made a lot of money from a wastepaper tub-making company that he had started up from nothing and as a sort of altruistic gesture sometimes advised companies that were in trouble.

Every time he was mentioned in the business pages of newspapers I cut out the story and pasted it into a huge scrapbook. I was looking forward to showing him it when he returned. Siena just laughed at me, called him a capitalist bastard and developed an unhealthy obsession with the Sex Pistols. She also changed her name by deed poll to Sin and dyed her mousy hair black. The transformation from golden child to grim punk was complete. I discovered Clairol, dyed my hair blonde rather messily and learnt how to apply make-up.

I was always aware of the value of beauty. An ugly duckling for so long in the presence of my glamorous mother and exquisite sister had given me first-hand proof of how it eased its gilded bearer's passage through life. I always feel irritated when stunning actresses and models complain about the 'burden' of beauty. Some burden!

By the time I was sixteen my eyes had shifted from an undetermined hazel and settled on a striking sea green. People often commented on them. My nose was small and straight and I had inherited my mother's full wide mouth. Siena had effortlessly sprouted to a willowy five foot eight whereas I had stopped quite suddenly at five foot four, which was odd because my parents are quite tall. My father used to console me that at least I was taller than the Queen which made me feel much better. Fortunately Siena and I had both inherited our mother's slim ankles. She was big on ankles, after all, you can change the colour of your hair and eyes, but bad ankles are bad ankles, you can't do anything about those.

After years of fading into the wallpaper people started to pay attention, to tell me I was pretty. The first time a man turned round to look at me in the street I thought I must have my shirt tucked in my knickers. But I hadn't. It began to happen a lot. It felt strange but wonderful.

Like I said, Siena was clever. She sailed through masses of O and A levels and was offered a place at Oxford which she turned down in favour of Sussex. Sussex! I got As in cookery and English but failed everything else so I couldn't get into a polytechnic let alone a university. How I envied her!

Mummy, by this time married to an Argentinian banker (an odd combination, I know, but they can't all be polo players), had arranged for me to go to her old finishing school but I bottled out at the last minute (odd, because I wasn't remotely rebellious), and ran away to London where I got a job in the pet department during the Harrods sale.

I was very involved in an animal charity that protested against wild animals being smuggled into England, so I thought this would be a good place to persuade customers about the iniquities of this trade. But they didn't sell anything live, just diamond-encrusted poop-a-scoops and things like that, so I was completely unable to do any agit propping at all.

But one useful thing came out of it. I met Pandora who was 'working' in the lift. I use the term 'working' quite loosely. She used to have great parties in her lift, stopping between floors for hours, so it was a good opportunity for me to meet all sorts of interesting people.

She was soon sacked from her lift (it used to shake terribly and I think she ended up breaking it), and moved to the country with her 'first husband', as she likes to call him. Not that she's had any others. But she feels that 'first husband' gives her a sort of Elizabeth Taylor cachet.

We hadn't seen each other for years then we bumped into each other at a wedding, and, united by our dysfunctional singleton status, she invited me to share her palatial penthouse flat off Sloane Square.

I was living in Notting Hill in a desperate bid to appear bohemian, but failing miserably. I just couldn't get into the swing of it at all, I couldn't rip my jeans right or wear those wispy silk dresses. The only thing I did like was that I kept bumping into old school friends and long lost cousins. Unfortunately they'd moved to Notting Hill hoping to get away from old school friends and relatives, so the streets were full of irritable trust fund hippies leaping behind bins in a futile bid to escape from each other. As you can imagine, I literally *jumped* at the chance to leave. I mean, Pandora's flat was in Draycott Place, practically next door to Peter Jones. The *relief* of returning to the Mother Ship was indescribable.

Anyway, Pandora wrote this great novel about her sex life which didn't sell at all and now she's taking a sabbatical from writing and doing up flats.

Fortunately I had at last found my *thing* in life, and was working as a professional cook, doing dinner and lunch parties for friends and friends of friends. As a non-practising vegetarian I had decided right from the start that I would only cook free-range meat and use organic vegetables. I worried a bit that the extra expense might put off potential clients, but not a bit of it. There were plenty of people who loved the idea and as no one else was doing it, I was soon booked up to my eyeballs.

It was when I was catering for someone's cocktail party that I met my ex-boyfriend, Tom Gold. If you read the business sections you may have read about him, he's one of those swashbuckling entrepreneurs that the papers have a love-hate relationship with. We only went out for six months, but I was crazy about him. The trouble was he was travelling most of the time and very unreliable when he wasn't. I think that's why I liked him so much really. Same old story. I compensated by working all the time, just to play him at his own game, so it turned out that I was never available either. The times when I was available I pretended to be unavailable (like it says in The Rules, I'm convinced it works, I just did it wrong).

When I couldn't make it to his firm's Christmas party he took his secretary, and that was that. But you know, you live and learn. Next time I meet someone nice I'll still be unavailable, but unavailable in a more positive alluring kind of way, if you see what I mean.

Anyway, Tom and I broke up *two years* ago, and since then I haven't had a sniff of excitement in any shape or form. Mind you, I wasn't really looking; after a man like Tom everybody else seemed completely colourless. But I do think the theory that you're more likely to meet someone when you're not looking is rubbish. After all, I hadn't been looking for ages and I still hadn't met anyone.

As you can imagine, after squashing my pheromones for so long, they eventually began to leak and I couldn't help thinking it might be nice to have some divine man to get dressed up for again.

The turning point came one evening when I struggled into the flat laden down with bags of food for a lunch I was cooking the next day. My hair was lank and smelt of cooking fat, my feet ached and I was exhausted. I had spent the day cooking an elaborate lunch for a group of exquisitely manicured American women who didn't look as if they had ever seen inside a kitchen, let alone washed up a plate. Yet here was I, ten years younger, considered pretty (if one scraped away the layer of cooking fat), supposedly in my prime, with my head inside an oven most of the day. I was feeling particularly disaffected because I'd had to do all the washing up because my assistant had just got engaged and been whisked off to Paris.

Dumping my shopping bags onto the floor, I banged the kitchen table in utter frustration and demanded out loud: 'I'VE HAD ENOUGH, I DEMAND EXCITEMENT!!'

Pandora happened to be coming in the front door at that moment and came into the kitchen. She and I both have blonde hair and are both five foot four, but that's where the resemblance ends. She has wide set blue eyes, a sweet snub nose and a mouth which turns up naturally at the corners. She's got this lovely luminous skin which glows all the time because she drinks lots of water. But she has a thing about her hair which she thinks is too fine and the bathroom is full of every hair thickening lotion known to man. I'd swop her silky fine hair in a shot because my hair is thick and completely ungovernable. It costs me a fortune to have it straightened and highlighted to ash blonde. It's my greatest indulgence. I'm growing it and at the moment it's halfway down my back, which is a bit of a fag to look after but worth the trouble.

'What's wrong? You look really cross.'

'Um, yes, well, I am a bit, actually.' I hoped she hadn't heard me banging the table. It came from the Conran shop and was very expensive. 'I've been slaving away for the last year and I'm . . . I'm worn out, like an old rag! I'm going off! People are going to start describing me as an exquisite plate of food that's been left out overnight—'

'Well, what do you expect?' Pandora interrupted, sitting down and whipping off her red beret. She ran her fingers through her fine shoulder-length blonde hair and fixed me with clear blue eyes. 'If you get asked anywhere you never go. Take Julia's party last week, everyone asked after you, James wondered if you'd emigrated. He's got a big crush on you, you know. I think he's quite attractive.'

'No you don't. You can't bear merchant bankers.' But Pandora was right. I hadn't been out for weeks. I just didn't have the time.

'What you have to do is make a strong determination for whatever it is you want, and the universe will automatically support you.'

'Have you been reading Deepak Chopra again?'

'Well, it's your book. Besides I think it was Nietzsche who said that. Or maybe it was Wayne Dyer. It was one of that lot, anyway.'

'But I tried doing that just now, and nothing happened!'

Both of us were increasingly turning to exciting New Age philosophies in a vain attempt to make sense of our chaotic personal lives. It was a bit too early to say if it was working but we liked Deepak Chopra because he made everything very simple yet very complicated at the same time. I particularly liked the law about becoming rich by giving all your money away but I didn't quite have the confidence to try it out just yet. Besides, I didn't have much to give away, unless you count buying the *Big Issue* every now and then.

'Haven't you been asked to something very dressy tonight?' asked Pandora.

'Yes, but I don't think I can go. I'm doing this big lunch tomorrow and I really ought—'

'To go out and have a break,' interrupted Pandora firmly. 'Why don't you wear that fabulous gold lurex fifties dress with the mermaidy tail. You haven't worn it for ages.'

She was referring to a slinky dress that had belonged to my mother which had been a great hit on cruises. I had only worn it twice before, but each time it had been a huge success.

'You don't think it's a bit much?' I asked, doubtfully.

'You can carry it off. It'll have all the chaps drooling, it'll do you good.'

'Okay, why not.' I smiled gratefully. It was nice having a flatmate to run things by. 'Maybe it's time to make an effort.'

One hour later, having bathed, washed and blow-dried my hair, re-applied my make-up and slithered into the dress, I surveyed myself in the full-length mirror. Sometimes, when I'm all done up, I can hardly believe what I see there is really me.

The shimmering gold dress fitted like a sheath, clipping in my narrow waist while the high neck flattered my breasts, which are normally swathed in practical sweatshirts. I have to admit the dress is pretty impractical and so narrowly cut below the hip that it might have been designed for a woman with only one leg. Still, who cared. Tonight I would just have to shuffle. I'd been looking a bit pale lately, but the rich gold drew out my green eyes and made my skin glow, and while I normally tied my hair back tonight I'd blow-dried it so it hung straight and gleaming halfway down my back.

The dress had quite transformed me and the effect was stunning. Tom, you don't know what you're missing. Then I frowned. He obviously did know what he was missing and had quite happily come to terms with it, judging from grapevine gossip that he had suddenly left his secretary for the gorgeous German über model, Skye Spratt. Skye had sprung to sudden fame in a mould-breaking advert for Tampax, in which she was photographed jumping out of planes naked, jumping into planes naked, swimming in shark-infested Hawaiian lagoons naked, hanging upside down on a mountain naked (what was she? A bat, for God's sake?) – but only when she had her period of course. The rest of the time she was laid up in bed eating grapes and reading magazines like an invalid. Huh, some girls get all the luck.

None of the rest of my family are any better at the love thing than I am. Sometimes I think we must have a missing chromosome when it comes to relationships. It's like we've been beamed down on earth and given some sort of secret code for accumulating money and building up successful businesses, but they left out the relationship manual. You can't have everything on a plate – unless you come to one of my dinners, of course!

I was just putting a final coat of mascara on when something made me think of Siena, the sister I hadn't seen for so long, whose green eyes and natural beauty had once been the talk of strangers. I remembered the mousy sister who had trailed behind her for so long and smiled at my reflection. 'At last,' I murmured. 'At bloody last.'

Chapter Two

The party was in full swing when I eventually arrived, my *toilette* having taken an hour longer than anticipated, and full of glamorous braying people I didn't know. I suddenly felt horribly self-conscious. I had felt smart and sophisticated when I left home but now wondered if the dress wasn't a bit over the top and flashy. This was Belgravia after all, not a racy cruise ship.

I pasted on an approachable expression and practised some open body language (pointing your feet towards a person you wanted to talk to and not crossing your arms over your chest, you know the kind of thing), hoping someone might talk to me. But though I noticed several men looking, nobody approached and I decided to finish my glass of champagne and leave. If I went home now I could at least make the meringues for tomorrow and let them dry out in the oven overnight. They'd be much crisper if I did that than if I left making them till the morning.

I was just edging my way to the door in a confident and meaningful manner, as if I was returning to a riveting conversation with someone by the door, when Victoria, the hostess, came bearing down on me with a large tray of devils on horseback. That reminded me, next week was National Prune Week. Good old Victoria. You could always rely on her to be at the culinary cutting edge.

'Oriana, I'm so glad you could make it. You're looking absolutely gorgeous, all the men are asking who you are.'

'Are they?' I glanced around the room doubtfully and

caught sight of a tall, broad shouldered man with rumpled sandy hair and an equally rumpled blue shirt looking at me. With his ravaged sunburnt face, heavy lidded eyes and big nose, he wasn't at all good-looking, but he had a certain presence. I guessed he must be what the French call *beau laid*, beautiful ugly. Then, to my embarrassment he winked at me. I blushed disconcertingly.

'Who's that?' I whispered to Victoria casually, secretly flattered.

'Oh that's Dan, he's a marine biologist, American, frightfully clever. I wouldn't go near him looking like that, his wife is ferociously jealous. It would cause a frightful scene.'

'But I don't want to go near him. He's not my type at all.'

But Victoria was barely listening. 'Now, as a special treat because you're looking so glam I've seated you next to Peregrine Skye-Rocca. Now don't say I don't look after you,' she continued sotto voce. 'That seat is worth thousands, if not *millions*!'

I got her drift. Peregrine was one of the most eligible bachelors in the country, having inherited a substantial sum from his parents, the original dolce vita couple, Lord Rufus Skye-Rocca and the sultry screen goddess Sophia Sloane, who had died tragically in a lift at the Palace Hotel in St Moritz. It had plunged to the ground, apparently weighed down with jewels, leaving Peregrine and his confusing number of siblings tragic orphans.

Victoria scuttled off, balancing precariously on a pair of Manolo Blahnik fluffy mules, and began chivvying people into dinner while I retired to the ladies' and applied a bit more slap. I wanted to look my best. After all, it wasn't every day one dined with a micro celeb.

The dinner table was vast and seated at least twenty people. I made my way over to my seat, glancing at Peregrine nervously. He was unthreateningly handsome in a very English way. His hair was thick and sandy coloured, and brushed into smooth wings over very clean ears. He was lightly tanned from a recent holiday and his pink cheeks gleamed with good food and comfortable living.

As soon as he noticed me making my way towards him his blue eyes lit up and he stood to attention. He must have been about six foot and his well-cut, double-breasted suit flattered his ample though not overweight figure. 'You must be Oriana,' he said. 'Victoria told me to look out for a green-eyed goddess in a gold dress. I must say, she didn't do you justice.' I blushed at the delicious flattery. 'Here, let me help you to your seat,' he continued smoothly.

My nerves soon evaporated and we immediately relaxed into easy conversation. He was terribly nice to talk to and seemed genuinely fascinated by my life behind the green baize door. I was just explaining that I shouldn't have any more to drink because I had to get up at the crack of dawn to make individual strawberry pavlovas when he suddenly picked up my hand with his rather soft, well manicured one and kissed it, then just sat for a moment gazing at me. I was flattered but a bit embarrassed too, so I just kept on talking, spilling out how fed up I was with my penurious existence and asking him what I should do about it. He kissed my hand again (I'm afraid not in that nice, dry, barely touching you sort of way foreign men do, but in the slightly slobbery manner of Englishmen when they're trying to emulate Continentals), and exclaimed flatteringly, 'But a girl like you shouldn't *have* to toil in subterranean kitchens for a measly remittance! It's an outrage!'

'But I love cooking! Besides, I'm educating people about the benefits of organic food and the iniquities of factory farming, it's too awful what happens to pigs.'

He ignored my outpouring and leaned towards me again. 'You have the most amazing green eyes, Oriana. Has anyone ever told you how incredible they are?'

Many people had but I remained modestly silent.

'I have always longed to meet a green-eyed girl with long blonde hair and racehorse ankles.'

'Well, now you have.' The champagne was beginning to kick in and I was enjoying the flirtation. Besides, it wasn't every day that one met the son of one of the country's most memorable and glittering couples.

Yes, Peregrine was quite a man about town and knew everybody. Meeting him changed everything for me. The Skye-Roccas were one of Scotland's premier Catholic families and Peregrine was a key member of the exclusive and glamorous Catholic mafia. He recommended me to all of his grand recusant friends, insisted I treble my prices, and my culinary career took off. Because I was a friend of his they all treated me like a friend who just happened to enjoy cooking. And some of them remembered Mummy from the sixties, when she was quite a famous model, and they'd all heard of Dad of course – well, the ones that read the business news had. I loved it all for a time. The problems started when I decided to take on more staff regularly to help me out. It got so complicated keeping track of them, and the more money I made, the more paperwork there seemed to be. So I'd be on my feet cooking all day and most of the night then have to come home and do all this maths.

One awful evening I cooked dinner for a cabinet minister and his wife. The wife was Jewish and everything had to be kosher. I was a bit tired and muddled up the chopping boards so that the meat touched the cheese or something like that. She was really nice about it, but she hadn't been able to eat a thing except the bread rolls.

I staggered back home to Pandora's flat, ran myself a hot bath and fainted getting out of it. I smashed a vase as I fell and she came rushing in to see what the noise was. I was probably only out for a few seconds but she was very worried and packed me off to bed with hot sweet tea laced with brandy. I stayed there for a week.

Peregrine came round the next day, took one look at me

and sent for his doctor. The doctor said I was exhausted, prescribed iron tablets and told me to get some sun. That was what my mother advised too, but he charged Peregrine £150. Peregrine wouldn't tell me that of course but I found out because I saw the bill on his desk a few weeks later.

Everybody kept on saying I should go out with Peregrine. He was besotted and we got on brilliantly. The trouble was I had never really fancied him. But lying in bed that week surrounded by the flowers he had sent and the magazines he had brought I gave it some serious thought. He was pleasant looking, we got on, he was very kind and he thought I was the bee's knees. I decided that the next time he made a pass I would Give In. He hadn't really ever made a proper pass, thank goodness. There had been a bit of inebriated grappling after Victoria's party but that was all.

He must have realized I was mellowing because one morning he dropped in with two first-class plane tickets to an unknown destination, leaving the next day. The only clue he would give me was that it would be very hot.

'My dear girl. The doctor says you need some sun, so sun is what you shall have.' I melted on the spot. You'd have to be mad not to try to love a man like that.

Peregrine had arranged for us to stay at the Kahala Mandarin Oriental in Hawaii, a glorious light airy hotel with a view over miles of azure blue ocean. I had visited the hotel several times with my father and Peregrine knew how much I loved the place. It was so thoughtful of him.

To my relief Peregrine looked quite attractive in his bathing trunks. I wasn't quite sure about that because I'd never seen him without his clothes before. He wooed and intrigued me with stories of his famous friends and his glamorous family. I was longing to ask about his sadly deceased parents and the 'Swiss lift horror', as it was known, that had killed them. It was all a bit of a mystery and no one had ever really got to the bottom of the tragedy. Lots of books had been written about the subject, the latest asserting that Peregrine's parents were actually Palestinian spies and had been assassinated by a pro-Zionist conspiracy aided and abetted by the American President. All nonsense of course, but Peregrine had to spend quite a lot of time denying each ridiculous rumour. I don't expect we'll ever find out what really happened.

His mysterious exotic parentage certainly added to his attraction. I was longing to find out more but didn't want to appear gauche by asking too many unsophisticated questions. For the moment I'd have to rely on *Death Secrets of the Stars, Goodbye!* and all the other magazines that cater for that sort of thing.

For some reason Peregrine loved hearing about my family, perhaps because they were so crazy they made his seem almost normal. Siena was now working for the radical agit-prop environmental charity, Greens Mean Biz, and was based for obscure reasons in Chile, while my mother was divorcing my Argentinian stepfather and had taken up with the Belgian langlaufing champion. My trophy father was of particular fascination and Peregrine, who had many quasi business interests, none of which ever seemed to flourish, admired him tremendously.

'I read about your papa in the papers recently,' he said as we lunched in the open-air restaurant facing the white sandy beach. It was hot but we were shaded by a palm tree and fanned by a warm wind that breezed in from the ocean, carrying with it the glorious scent of orchids from a Japanese wedding ceremony in the distance. His thick sandy hair was slicked back from a recent swim and his face was just beginning to go brown after an unfortunate spate of peeling.

'He's done amazing things turning WTC around,' he said, munching on a large hamburger enthusiastically. WTC stood for Whoops Tobacco Company, which had suffered over a series of claims from smokers who had taken them to court, plus negative health publicity in the media. Due to some exciting manoeuvring by my father the smokers had been successfully counter-sued and pictures of him had appeared in the press chivalrously lighting his glamorous lady attorney's cigarette with a solid silver Dunhill lighter. 'You're never alone with a Whoops!' he had declared. I thought that was rather good.

Sales of cigarettes and tobacco rose incredibly, boosting the company's share price and attracting rumours of bids from Japan. A smitten journalist had described him as the Cary Grant of the business world. Of course Siena had been terribly cross and had harangued anyone who would listen with the wickedness of all tobacco companies encouraging children to smoke, etc.

'Yes, he's very lucky like that,' I replied, trying to avoid gazing at a large slice of key lime pie on Peregrine's plate. We were surrounded by a party of vast American ladies with the huge bottoms one only sees in America, and I was suddenly feeling very disciplined.

'No luck about it, he's a very talented businessman,' said Peregrine generously, pushing his now empty plate away and glancing at the menu again. Surely he couldn't still be hungry?

He resisted, and we had a long, fascinating conversation about whether luck was accidental or inherited and whether one could really create it oneself. It was one of many gripping conversations that I had with Peregrine. Maybe we were united by our eccentric backgrounds or something, but we would talk in a way I never talked to any of my other friends. He was fifteen years older than I was, though he certainly didn't look it, and had used his wealth and leisure intelligently to gain an unusual insight into his privileged world, as well as presumably to retard his ageing process.

Peregrine admired and flattered me. He would occasionally halt, mid-conversation, as if spellbound and say, 'You are so beautiful.'

He *made* me feel beautiful, admired the way my hair had

streaked gold-blonde in the Polynesian sun (I had feared it might go green from all the salt water and reveal that I was not such natural blonde after all), loved the shape of my mouth which he said was full and generous, and bought me a divine green and gold bikini with a matching sarong, because it brought out the green in my eyes. He called me his mermaid and said he was 'utterly bewitched'. By the end of the fortnight he had asked me to move in with him. I agreed, just for a while to see how things worked out.

He was over the moon and we spent hours planning guest lists for the lunch and dinner parties we were going to share. I had always loved the idea of being the hostess of a *salon*. Peregrine knew loads of fascinating people, I adored cooking and entertaining – it was a combination made in heaven.

Well, maybe heaven was putting it a bit strongly. After having flown me at considerable expense across the world after months of frustrating courtship, you might have expected him to be slathering at the bit in the sex department. The first night I settled expectantly in our kingsize bed, having luxuriously anointed myself with all the freebie lotions in the vast marble bathroom. The British Airways flight had been eighteen hours of utter luxury. We had sat in comfortable seats that, at the flick of a switch, had turned into beds, and I would have spent the entire flight horizontal if it hadn't been for the choice of fifty films on my personal video. I hadn't gone to the movies for months so sat goggle-eyed, occasionally resurfacing to eat a delicious meal, sip a glass of vintage champagne, or examine the fascinating contents of my Mulberry leather toiletry bag.

By the time we touched down in Honolulu I felt as if I'd had a week in a health farm. We had a wonderful romantic dinner that night and retired early as we were both feeling a bit jet lagged. But not *that* jet lagged. I was rather hoping he might leap on me with great passion but as soon as we were alone he began to unpack and lapsed into an anxious silence. I busied myself in the bathroom (it was a suite so we had one each), and when I returned found Peregrine still unpacking.

Then he dashed into his bathroom, to perform what turned out to be lengthy ablutions. I hadn't counted on this.

'Are you tired from the flight?' I wittered brightly when he eventually re-emerged looking much refreshed, in an attempt to fill the awkward silence between us.

'Oh, exhausted.' He yawned energetically. 'Flying always kills me.'

'But it was such a wonderful flight. I had no idea first class made such a difference, it's a holiday in itself.'

'Is this the first time you've travelled in the front?' he asked, surprised. 'Surely when you holiday with your father—'

'He travels first and I go economy – but sometimes he remembers to give me his sponge bag,' I added a touch defensively. This was the part of the trophy holidays with my trophy father I liked the least. Most people were surprised when I told them this, but Peregrine wasn't.

'It was the same with my parents,' he said. 'When we went abroad they went first and the rest of us sat in the back with our nanny. The pilot once suggested we move up with her but they said it would be wasted on us.' He sighed resignedly. 'Having therapy has really helped with that sort of thing.'

He climbed into bed beside me and switched off the light. I turned towards him as he put a hand tentatively on my breast. 'Oh, Oriana, Oriana . . .' Then he kissed me, sticking his tongue into my mouth. We'd kissed a bit before and things always started off well but soon descended into slobberyness. If only we could have avoided the tongue thing, but I couldn't possibly have suggested that. Tonight I put it to the back of my mind and concentrated on the pleasant sensations coursing through my body as his hand touched me gently. But reaching down to caress him I was dismayed to discover that my romantic overtures had been in vain.

'Kiss me down there, please, Oriana.'

I was determined to make our sex life a success so I burrowed down the duvet and made strenuous efforts to rev him up. I worked terribly hard, but whatever I did, nothing happened. It was terribly embarrassing. I'd only slept with three men, but none of them had ever been impotent. I was obviously doing something very wrong, but what? I couldn't bring myself to ask.

Peregrine was simulating little moans, but he must be faking it, mustn't he? It was all ghastly. Eventually, after what seemed like an eternity, I resurfaced.

'Oh, that was wonderful, darling, thank you,' he said, caressing me affectionately. But then he suddenly withdrew his hand, kissed me lightly and wished me goodnight. Within five minutes he was fast asleep. I lay awake beside him feeling frustrated and confused until I succumbed to the deep downy mattress and fell asleep too.

That was the pattern of our sex life throughout the holiday. Blissful chatty days followed by awkward nights, which we both pretended were normal.

Occasionally he managed a little more and I had a glimpse of how good things could be between us. I decided to be patient. Maybe the heat was affecting him. Besides, we were so compatible in every other way that things would surely get better once we returned home.

Pandora was in the flat when I returned after being dropped off by Peregrine. She was cleaning out a kitchen cupboard and had tied her straight blonde hair back in a functional ponytail.

'You look incredible,' she said, peeling off her rubber gloves and peering at me closely. 'Amazing what a bit of sun 'n' sex can do.'

I coughed and switched the kettle on.

'I adore your outfit,' she continued.

Peregrine had bought me a pair of gorgeous light-green Capri pants and a matching T-shirt he had spotted in the hotel shop as a coming home present.

'C'mon, spill the beans.' She settled down at the kitchen table. 'Have you fallen in love/lust, or are you still just good friends?'

'Well, all three really. We had a great holiday, he was kind, funny, romantic—'

'It sounds perfect,' said Pandora doubtfully. Her relationships generally veered from confusion to disaster and she was always stunned to hear of anyone else having more luck. 'I'm utterly riveted. To think,' she mused wonderingly, 'that someone I *actually* know might be on the *verge* of almost having a relationship.'

'Well, I wouldn't put it quite like that, but he did ask if I'd like to move in with him.'

'To Cheyne Castle?' This was the nickname we had given to Peregrine's palatial house on Cheyne Walk.

'Yup.'

'What did you say?'

'I said I'd give it a try. It might be fun. I feel like doing something really radical.'

'And it's such a huge place you won't be getting under each other's feet. And if it doesn't work you can come back here. I shan't get another flatmate, I'm too old to get used to someone new at my age.'

'But you're three months younger than me.'

'But I feel much older. Sometimes I feel like an old woman trapped in a young woman's body.'

We were interrupted by the telephone. It was Peregrine.

'Darling girl. I've asked the housekeeper to clean a huge room on the top floor for your study. We were wondering how many wardrobes you might need for your clothes?'

'Oh, about four coat hangers, I should think,' I replied drily. My wardrobe mainly consisted of comfortable outfits chosen because they were cool and easy to cook in.

'It looks like I'm going to have to take you shopping,' said Peregrine firmly.

'Oh, you really don't have to!' I tried to sound convincing

as a delicious scene from *Pretty Woman* when Richard Gere buys Julia Roberts, the gorgeous prostitute heroine, an entire new wardrobe sprang into my head. Not that *I* was like a prostitute or anything.

Chapter Three

Peregrine picked me up in his ancient Ford estate the next day. People were always surprised that someone with his money didn't have a Mercedes or even a Ferrari, but I thought it was the height of cool that he didn't. It was an ironic statement, which he carried off with the insouciance of a born aristocrat. Other insecure boyfriends had owned fabulous cars they could barely afford in an attempt to bolster flailing egos, but Peregrine's ego was quite healthy enough without such additions.

Today I noticed that the bumper was hanging off and asked what had happened.

' 'Fraid I drove into a wall. The sun was so bright this morning I couldn't see where I was going,' he drawled casually. 'Good job I've got this old heap, there's no point having anything else in town. Besides, I'm such a rotten driver.'

I laughed noncommittally.

'I've noticed that people never admit to two things,' he went on. 'Being a bad driver and – no, you guess the other one.'

I was about to say being bad in bed, but thank goodness bit my tongue just in time.

'Um, being colour-blind?' I hazarded as he stopped confusingly at a green light, causing a volley of hooting behind us.

'No, having no sense of humour. Everyone thinks they have one.'

‘That’s true. If you read those lonely hearts adverts, *everybody* says they have a good sense of humour – you know, they have that abbreviation, GSOH, sometimes they even put down VGSOH, which is really irritating. I mean if someone writes that, it puts you *right* off.’ I glanced over at Peregrine and knew that I had completely lost him. ‘I mean, I just read them for a laugh, with friends . . .’ I tailed off weakly.

Pandora and I had occasionally been tempted to answer some of the more mouth-watering ones written by men who sounded like crosses between James Bond, the Sultan of Brunei and Jimmy Goldsmith but had never quite been able to face it. Of course Peregrine wouldn’t know about such sad matters, women threw themselves at him all the time in the hope of becoming the next Lady Skye-Rocca.

‘Here we are, my darling girl,’ said Peregrine expansively as we parked in the private space outside his house. ‘Let’s get this lot inside and packed away. Mrs Button has done a sterling job clearing out the top floor.’

Mrs Button was Peregrine’s old nanny who lived a troglodytic existence in the basement, and ran Cheyne Castle with an iron hand. There was definitely something of the *esprit concierge* about her. One was always aware of a certain vigilant presence even when she was out visiting her medium. She was completely bald too. I knew this because I had once disturbed her when she was ironing, *sans* wig. The rather dazzling blonde bouffant confection had been carefully placed in a kind of wig container beside the ironing board. The whole thing had given me quite a shock but Mrs Button seemed unperturbed, explaining that ironing always got her ‘over’eated’, and that it was about time Master Peregrine got some ‘air con’ installed. Mrs Button picked up a lot of Americanisms from the gladiatorial American chat shows she was addicted to. Though not blessed with hair, she was nonetheless an excellent housekeeper. She and her team of industrial cleaners (Peregrine was very untidy) had scrubbed and polished two vast interconnecting rooms on the top floor so they gleamed.

When he had moved into the house three years ago, Peregrine had employed Corianda Angelica, the talented interior designer, to convert the higgledy arrangement of poky dark rooms into an oasis of light and space. Cheyne Castle was from the outside a traditional nineteenth-century Dutch-style house and part of a row of similar gabled houses fronting the Thames. Inside lay a haven of marron, café au lait, gold and cream. Upstairs, there was a wonderful view of the Thames, looking towards Battersea Park. At that height one could forget the busy Embankment that ran along the river and lose oneself in the tranquillity of the river swirling below.

I had visited many times and always felt at home. But then I had just been a visitor. I was nervous that although I was only here for a trial period I might feel awkward and spend an anxious month tiptoeing around on eggshells, but I needn't have worried.

After lugging my two suitcases up the stairs, Peregrine decided we needed a good lunch. Having had enough driving for one day, he called a cab to take us to La Famiglia round the corner.

'You're still too thin, my darling,' he said as we tucked into our delicious plates of organic liver a bit later. 'Go on, have some mashed potato. A cook shouldn't be thin, it's not natural.'

'I'm quite big enough, thank you. I put on five pounds in Hawaii, but it's all coming off with my exciting food-combining regime. So I can't have any potato with this liver. Clients don't mind what shape I am as long as I can cook them a decent meal.' I said this with some exasperation. Peregrine had an absolute thing about me putting on weight and it was very tedious.

Instead of arguing he just smiled at me indulgently. 'You have a will of iron, Oriana. You must explain this food combining to me. Is it something to do with the Hay diet? My nutritionist swears by that.'

Peregrine was fascinated by his health and had a bewildering rota of doctors, nutritionists, trichologists and therapists whose sole duty it was to help him deal with the stresses of his huge private income.

'Well, I'm going to have a pudding,' he went on. 'Does tiramisu have cream in it? My homeopath has discovered I'm allergic to dairy products. It's absolutely maddening.'

The tiramisu was indeed laden with cream but he ate it with absolutely no side effects at all. I'd never met anyone as robust as Peregrine. We'd spend hours discussing the merits of food combining, the Fat Free Diet, the Only Fat Diet, the Eat Fat Get Thin Trampoline Diet, the Some Fat But Mainly Carbohydrate Diet, the Eat Fat and Get Happy Diet, the list was endless. It was nice to find a man who was interested in this sort of thing. But although he talked about diets he never followed any of them as he was far too greedy. People always say that people who love eating love sex, but Peregrine was definitely the exception to this rule.

As soon as I moved in we began plotting our first soiree. Peregrine was all for hiring a caterer and a party planner but I insisted on being responsible for everything myself. It would save him a fortune and he'd been so generous it was the least I could do. In order to prolong our Hawaiian holiday I suggested a vaguely Polynesian theme, which I thought he might understandably reject as too naff, but he quite liked the idea.

Well, maybe I had to twist his arm a bit, but he likes me even more when I'm bossy. During her heyday in Hollywood his mother was considered impossible to work with, but her fame and beauty were so legendary that directors just had to put up with it. I have a suspicion that I rather reminded him of his mother, whom he idolizes because she died at the pinnacle of her fame and beauty. Several times he's described her admiringly as 'having a will of iron'. When he says the same about me he gets a bit misty-eyed. It's rather sad that because she died when he was so young he can't remember her. All his memories are taken from glossy film stills, where she gazes impassively into the camera, revealing nothing but perfect bone structure and exquisite dark melting eyes.

I decided to brainstorm Pandora at Starbucks. After we had put in our order, a complex business that sometimes took most of the morning, we settled down in the squishy black sofas with our lattes. Pandora likes a tall wet skinny with a dash of cinnamon; I prefer a dry, short, rich one, hold the chocolate, with a dash of nutmeg.

'Sounds like a lonely hearts advert,' said Pandora. 'I'd like a tall, wet skinny with a VGSOH. Now, I'm longing to know how life is as chatelaine of Cheyne Castle. Is it the hotbed of intrigue and excitement that you'd hoped? By the way, I adore your Kelly bag. Is it a product of the *Pretty Woman* spending extravaganza?'

'Yes. Peregrine frogmarched me to Harvey Nicks. He says he couldn't stand the sight of me wandering around carrying plastic bags wearing the same old pair of black leggings for a moment longer.'

'Yes, I see his point. The holes weren't getting any smaller.'

'I'd sewn them up. The leggings were looking as good as new.'

'Still, I expect he can afford it. I read in *The Snoop!* that he's been given planning permission for his land in Aberdeen and sold it for millions. Is that true?'

' 'Fraid so. I tried to persuade him not to because it's a site of outstanding natural beauty. They're going to completely dig it up. It seems such a shame.'

'And it's not as if he needs the money or anything. I think it's immoral. Still, at least it means you might start wearing some decent clothes. Every cloud has a silver lining.'

'I just hope Siena doesn't get to hear of it. She might come round and chuck a smoke bomb through the window.'

'Sin. You must call her Sin,' reminded Pandora earnestly.

'Yes, I must.' I banged my head, hoping the name would stick. 'My mother says she's just got back from Chile. I ought to ring her, I haven't seen her for ages.'

Pandora was scooping the minuscule froth off her tall skinny latte disapprovingly. I always had the feeling she didn't like Siena much, which was odd, because they both had similar green opinions. Pandora had even briefly flirted with Fructarianism, the radical fruit-eating dietary sect of which Siena was a leading light. But Pandora knew that throwing smoke bombs in people's faces and blowing up motor showrooms in an attempt to stop people driving alienated them rather than attracted them.

'But I really wanted your advice on next Monday's party,' I went on. 'As it's our first one, Peregrine's decided to have a big bash and invite everyone. He thought it should have a sort of Polynesian theme – well, that was my idea really. He wasn't too sure at first but I twisted his arm—'

'I bet you did,' smiled Pandora, 'You have a will of—'

'Iron. I wish people would stop going on about that. I mean, I'm not the only person in the world who has an opinion about things, am I?'

Pandora smiled tactfully. 'So is Peregrine going to wear a Hawaiian shirt and two-tone shoes?'

'You bet. He's hired a steel band too. I'm going to wear a grass skirt. But no one has to dress up. Everyone can just wear what they want.'

'I shall wear my hula-hula skirt. I knew it would come in useful,' said Pandora.

'I had a kind of brain wave that you could use the evening to drum up support for the Whale and Dolphin Ball. You know what Peregrine's Catholic mafia are like. If one agrees to take a table, the others will all flock like lemmings.'

Pandora was working flat out for the Whale and Dolphin Society and had persuaded them to have a ball. She was having trouble selling tickets as dolphins didn't have a royal patron, and consequently their fundraising events lacked a certain cachet. KwikSave, the well-known bargain supermarket chain, had kindly offered to sponsor the event, which was to be promoted with the slogan Kwik, Save the Whale and Dolphin Ball! They had offered to give away a year's supply of 'One is Fun!' vegan meals and free tins of dolphin-friendly tuna in the raffle, but Pandora felt, and I agreed, that the title lacked panache, and it was proving hard to attract the glitterati.

'That's a wonderful idea!' Pandora exclaimed excitedly. 'I was almost thinking of giving up, but if we can get some of the recusant crowd interested, it just might get things off the ground.'

'I can help you with any admin. I've got some time on my hands at last because Peregrine thinks it will be embarrassing to carry on cooking professionally for his friends now we're living together. I see his point.'

'But what will you do about money?'

'Peregrine insists on paying for everything, which is incredibly generous, and in return I've told him he can let his cook go and I'll do all the cooking. It's fine for the moment, but I've got to think about earning my own money soon. I don't want to be completely dependent on him. My allowance doesn't stretch very far.'

'Couldn't you ask your dad for some money?'

'I don't know. I still owe him some money from last year. I suppose that if I was really desperate he might offer to top it up. They say that where there's life there's hope.'

'Tell him you are desperate. You've got to start training him up.'

Another thing that Pandora and I have in common is that we both have trophy fathers. Her father is a retired rubber tycoon. He sold his business a few years ago and bought this stunning village in the West Country. I wish mine would do something like that, but he'll never retire. He's welded to his wastepaper tubs at the hip. His only outside interest is being a pikeman. They're the men you see at ceremonial occasions wearing seventeenth century helmets and holding pikestaffs. Anyway, he's got quite a collection of these pikestaffs now, and he's absolutely mad about them.

Unusually, my father never had to support my mother, Siena and me, because when he and Mum first married she had enough of her own. In those days he didn't have a penny and it was only because she sold her most valuable painting, one of a pair of Canalettos, that he was able to raise the money to buy the wastepaper tub company. But after the divorce she was badly advised and lost quite a lot to Lloyds. She still seems to have some goodies stashed away though, and managed to hold on to her extensive buttonhook collection. Every now and then she excavates something and flogs it. Luckily she's still hanging on to the last Canaletto. It's her pride and joy and she'd rather die than sell it.

I've always secretly hoped that Dad might offer to try to buy the picture back. After all, these days the business makes enough money in a year to buy twenty Canalettos. But I don't think it's even occurred to him. The trouble is, he's a great believer in poverty as an incentive to achieve things. Of course I understand his point, I just wish he wouldn't be so rigid about it.

Chapter Four

For the time being I had to concentrate on our party. We only had two weeks to organize everything so we didn't bother with invitations and just telephoned everyone. Peregrine had loads of invitations to repay, and he finally ended up asking over two hundred people. We were confident that less than half would actually come. There was so much going on in London we thought we'd be lucky if fifty turned up.

I had a great time preparing for it. Peregrine had just had a cheque from the sale of his land in Aberdeen and was feeling even more expansive than usual. He told me to charge all the food to his account at Harrods and insisted I then reward myself with 'a frock or two' from the designer room on the first floor.

I spent a heavenly afternoon, first visiting the Food Hall to order a selection of exotic Hawaiian parrotfish which had to be flown in specially, before dashing upstairs to the fashion department where I pranced around like a fifties starlet, trying on all sorts of unsuitable garments before gravitating to the lingerie, where I settled on a pair of fluffy mules in sensible navy blue and a matching satin slip nightie dress with a marabou trim.

It was odd, I thought as I queued for the powder room, a real fifties starlet's quid pro quo would have been her talents in the bedroom, whereas sadly my quid pro quo lay everywhere but. Still, maybe my exciting new ensemble would rouse Peregrine's interest. I felt a bit guilty at the price of the fluffy mules but I knew I'd get lots of wear out of them. They were terribly comfortable when I was sitting down, and navy blue went with everything. Besides, I was going to economize by ordering the rest of the food over the Internet from Safeway.

Coming out of the lavatory I bumped into an old girlfriend of Peregrine's whom I knew very slightly. She was a rather gorgeous, extravagantly groomed redhead called Araminta who wrote the witty Single Girls Diary for *Divorce!* magazine. I thought she was great fun but was a bit wary of her because Peregrine said she was still madly in love with him and would stop at nothing to get him back.

'Oriana, darling, looking *gorgeous* as usual. No wonder Peregrine is so *wild* about you. You'll have to excuse me, I'm a bit tipsy. Andre and I have just been celebrating our engagement. We're so looking forward to your party next week. I've been trying to find a grass skirt everywhere but no luck. Horrids say they've completely sold out. Are you buying something divine to wear? Do show me.'

I fished out a fluffy mule sheepishly.

'Mules! How deliciously Hawaiian. Aren't they?' She looked doubtful.

'Not exactly, but I hear they're going to be just the thing next season on Waikiki Beach,' I suggested hopefully.

Araminta giggled deliciously. 'Look, if you've got five secs why don't we grab a coffee in the juice bar?'

I agreed happily. I was intrigued to hear more about her engagement. If she was still nuts about Peregrine then she was obviously marrying this Andre chap on the rebound. I was also hoping that she could shed light on Peregrine's sex ban. I wondered if he'd been able to manage it with her. Probably, she was famously sexy, and if she hadn't been able to get him going I shouldn't think anyone could.

Ten minutes later, having squeezed our way into the juice bar only to find they didn't serve coffee and not having the strength to squeeze our way upstairs again, we settled down to gossip over a nutritious beetroot and spinach cocktail.

'I'm so glad Peregrine has found someone he really likes

at last. The *on dit* is that he's going to marry you. The whole of London is talking about it.'

'Are they?' I glanced round at the huddles of American tourists and assorted juice fanatics nervously.

'I'm so thrilled for you both. Might there be an announcement at the party?'

'I don't think so. I've only moved in for a trial period. Marriage is the last thing on my mind.' Of course I had *thought* about it. Secretly I'd love to be Lady Oriana Skye-Rocca, it sounds just like something out of *Thunderbirds*, but I dismissed the thought immediately. I knew I couldn't put up with a lifetime of the Bed Thing. 'I'm sorry things didn't work out between you and Peregrine,' I added. Under the circs, Araminta was being very generous-spirited.

'Oh, goodness. That one never got off the starter's block. We tried, but the difficult thing was that we'd been great friends, then we drifted into dating which was a big mistake.' She lowered her voice. 'You see, we didn't hit it off in bed *at all*, if you catch my drift. I'm sure it was all my fault but he didn't seem remotely interested in me in that department. But you obviously don't have a problem, judging by the sexy lingerie you've been stocking up on. Peregrine would have become terribly flustered and embarrassed if I'd returned home with something like that.' She picked up her beetroot cocktail and sighed happily. 'Thank *goodness* Andre and I don't have any problems in *that* department. No, this time I'm going to marry for sex and money like everyone else. None of this friendship rubbish. I'd snap up Peregrine if I were you. If you don't, someone else will. Girls are so *voracious* when there's a title and a bit of money about.'

'But the bed thing is a disaster with me too! We haven't had a successful attempt since we began going out. It's actually quite a relief to know you had the same problem.'

'Oh, you poor thing.' Araminta attempted a sip of her nutritious drink and gagged. 'I should never have brought it up. Excuse the pun.' She smiled mischievously. 'Tell me, does he still have all those weird libido mixtures sent over from China? He keeps them in his bathroom cabinet. I don't know why he bothers, they obviously don't work.'

I'd been vaguely wondering what the oddly shaped boxes with oriental writing on that arrived frequently in the post were, but Peregrine had refused, point blank, to discuss their contents.

I resolved to examine his bathroom cabinet when I returned home.

I had the house to myself, as it was Wednesday afternoon when Peregrine took his Anger Management Course. He always followed this with an intensive 'lymph drainage workout massage', which apparently eliminated the toxins released into the bloodstream by all the angry thoughts. Privately I thought that it was an utter waste of time. If anybody was less in need of an Anger Management Course it was Peregrine.

In fact, a bit of anger would do him good, I thought, aggressively thumping some bread dough which had been proving in the airing cupboard all morning. I was making a Hawaiian delicacy called flowerpot bread, a delicious concoction made with sweet potatoes and baked in flowerpots, which I had planned to bake tonight then freeze.

I wanted to do as much as possible in advance as I had a feeling that we had underestimated the number of guests who might be coming. It was a bit worrying that Harrods had run out of grass skirts. I had also inquired at the Hawaiian shirt department and they had been cleaned out. The Fijian Embassy had also run out. In desperation I rang the Tongan Embassy, but they were no help at all. Oh dear, the beau monde were obviously taking the theme quite seriously.

Putting the bread back in the airing cupboard to prove, I washed my hands and made my way surreptitiously upstairs to Peregrine's bathroom. Araminta was right. Inside the walk-in bathroom closet lay masses of bottles of vitamins; packets labelled Sex O Vit vied with phials of murky liquid with strange pictures of rams rearing. Bottles of something called Horny Goat's Weed lay next to syringes labelled Stallion! whose contents looked suspiciously like blood.

A wave of pity, revulsion and relief ran through me. Poor Peregrine. He had obviously had this problem for years with other women! But I knew that I could no longer share his bed in the optimistic hope that his nervous fumblings might lead to fulfilment. No, I would just have to move into the bedroom beside my study and plead an obscure gynaecological problem while I decided what to do next. It would be a relief for both of us.

When Peregrine arrived home later I cooked him his favourite snack, fried bread lightly smeared with Gentleman's Relish, and scrambled eggs. He watched me nervously as I thumped my flowerpot bread violently around the kitchen. I noted with interest that every time I threw the dough on the worktop the ceiling shook quite visibly.

'Perhaps you might benefit from my Anger Management Course, darling. I've been noticing you've been a bit irritable lately.' Great. My testosterone levels were rising while his appeared to have disappeared altogether. No wonder I was irritable. He winced as I threw the dough brutally against the wall.

'Oh, I'm fine, just a bit nervous about the party,' I lied convincingly.

'My darling.' He got up and came to stand beside me. 'You are the best cook in London. The food will therefore be exquisite. I have asked two hundred of my most amusing friends. This house is made for parties. Please don't worry.' I put down my flowerpot and snuggled into his reassuring shoulder. He smoothed back a wisp of hair from my face and kissed me on the forehead.

'Please don't worry your pretty little head about it. Now come and sit down on the sofa with me and tell me about your day.'

I smiled as I settled down next to him, then remembered the contents of the walk-in medicine cabinet. 'I'm sorry I've been irritable recently, it must be PMT. I've been having terrible stomach cramps all day. Would you mind awfully if I slept in the room upstairs for a few nights till I feel back to normal?'

'Of course not, darling,' said Peregrine happily. 'But are you sure you'll be comfortable upstairs by yourself?'

'Yes. The bed's made up and everything. I'll be fine.' I knew he was just going through the motions, and felt both relieved and offended that he seemed so content with our new arrangement. But perhaps he really did think it would only be for a few nights. At any rate, it would take the pressure off both of us. And sooner or later one of his exciting oriental potions was bound to work. After all, the Chinese must be experts at that sort of thing. Look how many of them there were. But for the time being we would concentrate on our friendship and building on our common interests.

Peregrine put his arm round me tenderly and began to discuss the guest list for Monday.

Chapter Five

Apart from a violent altercation between Mrs Button and the driver of the Safeway Internet delivery van containing most of the food for the party, events running up to Monday's bash ran smoothly. I was a bit cross with Mrs B because I had arrived back from a successful morning tracking down a supply of Maui onions from New Covent Garden market to find her shouting abuse at the poor man.

'If you're not 'Arrods we don't want nuffink to do wiv you,' she was shouting and pushing him back into his van. Mrs B could be an awful snob. And considering she was under five foot and apparently had an arthritic hip and flat feet she was terribly strong.

As I rushed over and tried to pull them apart, onions rolling everywhere, my mac falling off my shoulders, Mrs B's wig slipped off and a small man appeared from nowhere and began taking pictures. The three of us turned towards him, stunned into sudden silence, then Mrs Button, seizing the initiative, tripped the driver up so that he fell into a flowerbed.

'Miss Oriana, you tell 'im where to get orf,' she commanded, scrabbling to find her wig beneath a pile of onions as I helped the ashen-faced driver up. The photographer had disappeared and the driver handed me a screwed-up piece of paper with my order written on it.

'Delivery for Lord Skye-Rocca, miss.'

I explained the situation to Mrs B and she shuffled off down to the basement, muttering under her breath. I noticed with admiration that although she had temporarily lost control of her wig, her moth-eaten slippers had remained glued to her feet throughout the incident.

The next morning I slipped downstairs to prepare Peregrine's morning coffee – although we were sleeping separately he still liked me to wake him up in bed with a copy of *The Times* and a steaming cup of café au lait, made with a touch of chicory, in his special cup – when I caught sight of the front page of *The Snoop!* It carried a big picture of Mrs B, the Safeway driver and me wrestling, surrounded by onions. *Sans* wig, Mrs B bore a startling resemblance to Yul Brynner. It was amazing, I'd never noticed it before. To my embarrassment I was all hair and cleavage. You see, I'd got up so early I'd just thrown on an old mac of Peregrine's over my nightie and in the confusion it had gaped open embarrassingly, revealing huge amounts of exposed flesh.

If the picture made me blush, it was nothing compared to the headline: TOFF BOFFS BLOKE!! SCOOP EXCLUSIVE! 'Leggy blonde society cook, Oriana Spicer, eating man's crumpet and current squeeze of Lord Skye-Rocca, fights off the attentions of an unwanted delivery man. Spicy Oriana says, "We only take deliveries from Harrods. I've never heard of Safe Ways. Are they a security company?" '

Oh dear, I thought, hurriedly shoving the paper behind the fridge and unearthing the green organic arabica coffee beans from the deep freeze in preparation for roasting and grinding them, thank goodness none of Peregrine's friends could read.

But I was wrong. Five minutes later the phone rang, the first of many calls. It was Pandora.

'Hey, Oriana, you had a boob job or what? We're talking serious *embonpoint*.' Pandora tried to learn one new French word a day in an attempt to fend off brain shrinkage.

Peregrine was very understanding about the photos and explained that as he was a public figure of sorts it was unfortunately something I would have to get used to. 'I'm just flattered to be linked with you in any way, my darling. Please don't let it bother you.'

It didn't bother me at all. It gave me quite a thrill to think of all my parents' old friends looking twice at the picture and saying, 'Isn't that Siena Spicer's plain little sister? My goodness, how she's changed. I wouldn't be surprised if she wasn't a C cup, at least.'

In spite of this drama, plans for the party were going full steam ahead. We were so looking forward to it. Peregrine and I had gone through the guest list and I felt confident that we had invited a fascinating and sophisticated mix of people from the worlds of politics, the media, industry and the city. A good sprinkling of glamour would be provided by several well-known jet settish types (Ivana Trump had rung to say she was flying over from Aspen especially), a few minor royals plus all of Peregrine's doctors who would no doubt add a bit of gravitas to the proceedings, to say nothing of the Scottish recusants who loved a good party.

Guests were invited for 8 p.m., but when I peered out of my window at 7 p.m. wondering what the noise was, I noticed a small huddle of guests wearing grass skirts waiting to come in. It was too bad, I thought, I don't recognize any of them. They'd just have to wait until Mr Button, whom I had not met before because he spent most of the time at the Button HQ, a mobile home in Reigate, was ready to open the door.

I'd done all the cooking in advance and Peregrine had hired loads of people to serve the drinks and food and to wash up so I could relax and concentrate on introducing everyone, as well as enjoy what I'd hoped would be an evening of challenging and witty discussion.

Our guests poured in punctually at 8 p.m., unwilling to miss a moment. I was relieved to see that Pandora was one of the first to arrive. She was looking gorgeous in a flimsy hula-hula outfit, emblazoned with 'Kwik, save the Whale and Dolphin Ball' on the back and her straight blonde hair was swept back off her small face and secured with a seashell comb. She grabbed a Pearl Harbor Explosion, a Hawaiian cocktail made to one of Peregrine's secret recipes, containing brandy, vodka and topped up with Cointreau. I'd added three bottles of Tia Maria to spice it up a bit. After all, it was essential our guests relax and get into the Hawaiian aloha! spirit. Pandora took a mouthful, toppled slightly but quickly regained her balance. The room must be getting a bit hot so I gesticulated to a waiter to open a window, then dashed over to say hi to her.

'Oriana, I love your new slinky sex goddess look – and the mules. Tremendous. Isn't it wonderful that everyone's made such an effort to dress up?' We gazed around the drawing room at the mass of Hawaiian shirted and grass-skirted guests bobbing unrythmically to the steel band that had just started up in the corner. Girls carrying trays of orchids to adorn the ladies and young men wearing white starched jackets carrying small trays of exquisitely arranged Hawaiian delicacies weaved gracefully around the room.

One of Peregrine's very high-powered friends, a captain of industry and pillar of the establishment, suddenly appeared and dragged Pandora off to dance. I decided to drop into the kitchen and check how everything was going when Hugo Van Pratt, the country's leading Greek scholar and famous for his definitive translation of Julius Caesar's bodyguard's grandson's autobiography, grabbed my hand and began dancing with absolutely no rhythm at all.

'Hugo,' I yelled above the din. 'I'd like to introduce you to the Professor of Latin at Harvard University. He's only in London for a few days and he's longing to discuss . . .' but my attempts at civilized introduction were lost as the captain of industry had started to do cartwheels, presumably in a vain bid to impress Pandora, who was flirting with him shamelessly in an attempt to sell him a table for the Kwik, Save the Whale and Dolphin ball. Surprisingly, everybody was ignoring the vintage champagne in favour of the Pearl Harbor Explosion cocktail, which appeared to be having an excitable effect on all our guests. The captain of industry suddenly re-appeared, scooped me up in a fireman's lift, and carried me to the buffet table where a group of aggressive elderly men were squabbling over the last tray of flowerpot bread. I was desperately looking for Pandora, she's always saying she's looking for an older man, when I spotted her heaving a man through the window.

Looking back, I think things began to deteriorate from that moment, with the grass skirts quite possibly inciting the men to unusual and unexpected displays of macho behaviour.

After I'd separated the old men, who turned out to be Peregrine's Anger Management consultant, his trichologist, dermatologist, nutritionist, psychiatrist and urologist, I felt I'd deserved a few stiff drinks and things became a bit fuzzy. I vaguely remember dancing with the urologist and then I must have conked out.

Peregrine and I were woken by Mrs Button the next day, carrying a steaming tray of coffee. We were lying side by side in his bed, fully clothed. I hopefully felt to see if I had been interfered with, but I clearly hadn't because I was still wearing my impregnable waist-clincher knickers.

'I reckon you'll be needin' this,' said Mrs Button cheerfully, depositing the tray on the bedside table. 'Really, you young people,' she said approvingly. 'I 'ad to lift you both off the floor and put you into bed meself.'

I gasped. Peregrine weighed about fourteen stone. Mrs B must have the strength of ten men.

'Such a hoohar last night you wouldn't believe. I 'ad some copper round first thing. Said 'e was looking for the 'Ome Secretary. Sent 'im orf wiv a flea in 'is ear, I can tell you.'

'Harold!' Peregrine sat bold upright. 'Is he still here?'

'No. Sent 'im out the back, first thing. Now much as I'd like to stand 'ere chattin' all day, some of us 'ave got some clearin' up to do.' She left the room whistling the theme tune to *The Dambusters*.

'She's in a good mood,' I ventured, pouring out the coffee.

'She loves upper-class misbehaviour and chaos. It cheers her up no end. I think it must remind her of the war.' He sipped his coffee thoughtfully. 'I must be frank and admit that I can't remember a great deal about the evening.'

'Neither can I. I had three glasses of your cocktail and after that – well, things are a bit of a blur.'

Peregrine thought for a moment then exclaimed, 'It's Max! I hold him responsible!'

'Max who?' I queried.

'Max bloody Shyster! I told Mr Button *expressly* to forbid him entrance!'

The name rang a bell, I think he was a friend of Pandora's from the ecology magazine she wrote for. I cast my mind back and shuddered. I had a very vague memory of Pandora heaving a suspect-looking fellow through the window wearing an old Amplefordian tie and a grass skirt.

'Bloody Shyster! He was my fag at school before he went to work for *The Snoop!* I *thought* I saw him, or someone remarkably similar wearing an old school tie and a grass skirt, but when I tried to fight my way through the throng he'd disappeared.'

'Like a mirage,' I supplied helpfully.

'Some bloody mirage,' continued Peregrine petulantly. 'He's always writing ridiculous stories about me in *The Snoop!* and the *Daily Mail*. Max is famous for spiking drinks. He used to be a spy. He's capable of *anything*. *He* spiked my cocktail, I'm sure of it. It's a mean trick.' Peregrine slumped back in bed mournfully. 'Go and get the papers, will you, darling?'

I leapt out of bed guiltily. It all fell into place. Max was helping Pandora with the publicity for the Kwik, Save the Whale and Dolphin ball and had probably come along to help sell tickets. I was very impressed that he had once been a spy. I carefully stepped over several inert bodies lying in the hall and retrieved the newspapers.

Oh dear! Max had obviously done more than just sell tickets. The front page of *The Snoop!* carried the headline: 'TOP PEOPLE TAKE TIME OUT AT TOP TOFF'S PALACE! Turn to pages 15 and 16 for Xclusive pix!'

Page 15, really, what an insult, I thought crossly, flicking through the paper, hoping that Pandora had got her plug for the ball, and wondering if there was a nice picture of me in my fluffy mules.

There were several pictures. How Max had got them goodness only knew; he must have had one of those James Bond spy cameras attached to his grass skirt. There was an interesting picture of the Governor of the Bank of England being sick in the bushes, and another of me trying to pull apart some of Peregrine's doctors fighting over the flowerpot bread. That one was captioned: 'Miss Oriana Spicer catches up on medical matters with the Queen's surgeon, Sir Humphrey Lott-Twist OBE; top people's urologist Rupert Caveat RNMS, MSRG; and colostomy bag tycoon, Anthony Luxor-Brown KBE, DSSc.'

There was a gorgeous picture of Pandora, balancing a plastic dolphin, a tin of tuna fish and a box of vegan meals (presumably to keep the sponsors happy) on a hula-hoop. Good old Pandora! That one was captioned: 'Rubber tubing heiress, Pandora Black, raises awareness for the plight of dolphins. "Please inform your readers to ensure their tunny fish is dolphin-friendly," pleads pulchritudinous Pandora.' It continued: 'FOR MORE INFO ABOUT HOW U CAN SAVE DOLPHINS TURN TO PAGE 2!'

On page 2 there was a whole article about the Whale and Dolphin ball being *the* fashionable event of the season, where to buy dolphin-friendly tuna, and a hotline to send the Whale and Dolphin Society money.

I was thrilled. It looked as if the evening had been a success after all. I quickly rang Pandora.

'Sorry to ring so early, but I've just seen *The Snoop!*'

There was an embarrassed silence. 'Um, look, I'm sorry. I told Max to take just a few pictures, I didn't know he'd go over the top like this.'

'Don't apologize! It's great. It gave a point to the evening, without it it would have been just another posh gits get drunk and throw up in bushes story.'

'Oh, thanks, Oriana. It's really got things rolling for the ball. The phone's been ringing since nine a.m. I sold all the tickets last night to some really top names which will guarantee big coverage. I rang *Divorce!* and told them who was coming and they want to cover it exclusively for *100K*. It's just as well I booked the Grosvenor House.' Pandora had had to put the deposit down with her own money as no one thought she could possibly fill such a big venue.

I could hear her other line going. 'I know you're busy,' I said quickly, 'but I'd love to give you a hand if you need one. I don't think Peregrine is rushing to plan our next society soiree somehow so I've got lots of time.'

But I was wrong. Having a party was obviously like having a baby. You forgot about the pain very quickly and started wanting to have another one. Peregrine's hangover wore off in about fifteen minutes (he's very robust), and he immediately began talking about our next do. All his friends had been ringing up and congratulating him on a fantastic evening, how they were looking forward to the dolphin ball, and how thrilled they were to be helping such a worthwhile charity.

'I think he's secretly pleased to be associated with something worthwhile for a change,' I explained to Pandora in between fielding telephone calls and stuffing things into envelopes the next day. 'After all, he only gets publicity about his dead parents and recently there were those nasty articles about selling his land to the developers. I think he'd like to be seen in a better light. He's a very caring person deep down.'

'Yes,' said Pandora doubtfully. 'He's been good for you. It was about time you got out of the kitchen.'

'I've been thinking about writing a cookery book.'

'What a good idea!'

'I thought maybe I could exploit the celebrity society cook thing.'

'Which would guarantee loads of publicity,' agreed Pandora.

I thought for a moment. '*The Snoop!* hasn't got a cookery column, has it?'

'No. You should do it. We'll ask Max. They all know you there now, ever since you've been going out with Peregrine your picture has been in every week. They would have to be very simple recipes though.' The phone rang and Pandora reached to answer it.

'No, sorry. We've completely sold out. I can put you on the waiting list though.' She replaced the receiver. 'Yeeeees! It's a sellout! I *knew* we could do it. Wonderful Peregrine, his party has really put us on the map.' She smiled at me. 'I'm speaking to Max this afternoon, I'll run the cookery column idea by him then if you like. I think you're in with a good chance because they're trying to take *The Snoop!* upmarket at the moment and an insider column from the chatelaine of Cheyne Castle might be just what they're looking for.'

Pandora was as good as her word and to my delight I got a call from Max Shyster the next morning.

'Grite pahee,' said Max in his well-modulated estuary English accent. Pandora had told me that his real name was something like Maximillian Trestle-Table-Shyster, but a brutal early apprenticeship on the leading northern newspaper, the *Manchester Murk*, meant that he now spoke in a strangulated combination of flat As, cockney, estuary English and upper classease.

'Pandora reckons you're a cross between Mrs Beeton,

Mata 'Ari an' Marfa bleedin' Stewart. Much of a writah, are yer?'

I thought quickly. This was my big chance!

'Yes. I have a contract from Hodder and Stoughton to write a society cookbook based on my experiences cooking for all of Lord Skye-Rocca's friends, Jeffrey Archer, the Churchill family, Michael Winner . . .'

That seemed to clinch it.

'OK. We could be on to sumthink 'ere. Showuswotugot. Fax me sumthink this afternoon.'

I quickly got to work and faxed him the best of what I had. He called me the next day saying *The Snoop!* loved the idea and offered me £500 to write a monthly column based on whatever I was cooking for that week's dinner party. They wanted to illustrate it with pictures of me at the stove wearing slinky clothes, which would be credited in the magazine. He reckoned that the free publicity would mean I would be able to borrow whatever I wanted from top designers.

'Wear wotever you want, jus' keep it skimpy,' he advised helpfully before ringing off.

Like I said, I thought having a party would be the last thing on Peregrine's mind but he was such a good host and I so enjoyed the planning and cooking that we couldn't resist. And so Cheyne Castle became the setting for many wonderful parties, none of them quite as raucous as the first, but just as entertaining. Peregrine and I were frequently in the gossip columns and feted as one of London's golden couples.

I had moved back to his bedroom after Mrs Button had heaved me there after the last party. I had the feeling that she strongly disapproved of our separate sleeping arrangements and I had no wish to offend her. Besides, it would have seemed odd not to return, especially as I could not plead PMT as I had been in such a good mood recently.

Unfortunately things were no better between us in bed but I was getting used to it. After all, there are lots more important things in life than sex, if you think about it. In every other way Peregrine and I got along much better than I could have imagined, perhaps because the house was big enough for us to have our own privacy. We passed each other infrequently during the day and Peregrine usually lunched out.

I now had time to resuscitate my letter writing campaigns urging the government to take an interest in animal welfare. As if factory farming wasn't bad enough, I'd just seen a horrifying documentary showing rows of tiny cages, each containing a solitary chimp, shrieking in fear and pain every time a human came near its cage. I'd tried to persuade Peregrine to raise the subject with his influential friends, but he wasn't remotely interested. At least he was enthusiastic about me writing a cookery book. He wanted me to call it 'Lunch'.

Lunch was sacrosanct to him; I think he saw it as a kind of job. At first he tried to persuade me to join him but I always refused. We often dined out and the thought of sitting down for two long meals in one day made me faint with boredom. Besides, I loved being alone in the house. Apart from Mrs Button and her team of industrial cleaners who steamed through the house for a brief hour in the morning and again in the afternoon, I could be blissfully alone.

I realized I had been on a treadmill, so busy earning a living that my creativity had been draining away. But now, sitting in Peregrine's comfortable house, I felt it flood back, together with the freshness and enthusiasm I had felt when I had first begun cooking.

For the first time in many years I had time to dream. In my study on the top floor I moved my desk to the window and would sit and think up recipes that I at last had time to cook. In a sense Peregrine was my patron, giving me space to create and valuable criticism, good and bad. He loved restaurants and after a particularly good lunch would tell me what he had enjoyed. My head was constantly buzzing with fresh ideas for my cookery book and the *Snoop!* cookery column which Max assured me they would run as soon as they could create some space.

I soon had even more time alone. Peregrine had hired a personal trainer and was now working out at the fashionable Ritzy Marina Club most days. He had actually been a member for ten years but had only visited it once to have a massage. But recently he had been putting on a bit of weight, and had decided to do something about it. His meal routine didn't change. Mrs Button still cooked him an enormous fried breakfast, and to compensate for his increased activity, insisted he eat a double helping of fried bread before he left for the gym in the morning. Once he'd refused and she had been quite perturbed, exclaiming, 'But Master Peregrine, you'll fade away!' Peregrine had winked at me in complicity and I had tried to avoid laughing into my bowl of grapenut pellets.

Peregrine was pleased because Mrs B and I got along so well. Other girlfriends had tried to usurp her position as domestic numero uno in his life, but not me. I couldn't care less if Peregrine wanted six pieces of fried bread in the morning. It was his life. But I knew deep down that if I had really loved him I would have given some thought to his arteries. But at the time I was just relieved to be released from the domestic minutiae that had controlled my life for so long.

For the first time I didn't have to wash up, peel anything or lug heavy bags of shopping around. Peregrine had a secretary who came in once a week supposedly to take care of his high-powered business interests, but whenever I passed his study they always seemed to be playing Scrabble. Fortunately she was a computer whiz kid, and it was she who had taught me how to order everything I wanted from the supermarket on the Internet.

Chapter Six

I hadn't heard from Siena for ages. We had spoken occasionally on the telephone but our lives were so different and she had been so far away that we had drifted apart. The last time we'd spoken we'd had a ridiculous argument because I'd called her Siena instead of Sin, the horrible abbreviation she insisted on sticking to. But I was pleased when she telephoned and asked me to meet her for a coffee in Camden, an area I wasn't remotely familiar with.

She had recently moved back to London. I wasn't sure why but my mother had hinted at a broken romance and remained tight-lipped. I knew Siena disapproved of the life I led, and unwilling to face a rejection I had waited for her to make the first move. I was burning with anticipation as she said she had a surprise for me.

She was right. To be honest I wasn't in the best of moods when I eventually found the nondescript café, situated down a scruffy side street, that she had chosen for our tête-à-tête. I'd got hopelessly lost and was cursing her, wishing that just once she could eschew her principles and meet in Harvey Nicks like a normal person. But all irritation flew out of the grimy window as soon as I entered the café, for sitting on Siena's knee was a baby. I knew immediately that it was Siena's, I just knew. I saw them before Siena noticed me, and melted at the sight of my sister, normally so serious and antagonistic, so utterly softened. It was a complete transformation. The last time we had met she had been quite scrawny, but motherhood had made her put on a little weight which suited her. Thank goodness she no longer dyed her hair black and it had now reverted to its natural mouse. She had chopped it into a no-nonsense crop which would have looked frightful on anyone else, but fortunately she had superb high cheekbones so she could get away with it. Her beautiful almond shaped eyes seemed curiously faded, as if they had been bleached by the sun. Although she wasn't conventionally pretty, on a good day she could be elegant and striking, but on a bad day you would pass her on the street and not look twice. If only she would bother with a bit of make-up she would turn heads, however she'd moved beyond such frivolities years ago.

I smiled ruefully. 'You could have told me.' I extended a nervous finger towards my nephew. 'I wish you'd told me. He's really gorgeous.'

'How do you know he's a he? Did Mum mention—'

'No, she didn't. Why on earth didn't you tell me?'

'Because I knew you'd tell Dad and I couldn't face *that* particular hassle.'

'Does he know now?'

'Yes. Mum insisted. She said he had a right to know he'd got a grandchild.'

'I bet he's thrilled.'

'I don't think he could care less. I thought he'd at least be livid but he was really cool about it. He said he'd come round to see Jacob but then he rang back and said he was tied up but he'd buy him some premium bonds when he got back from Spain or wherever he was going.' The bitterness didn't disguise the hurt in her voice.

'God, he never told me! Dopey old Oriana, always the last to know everything.' I felt terribly hurt at being excluded from such a major family event.

'You're certainly not dopey and you're not old. Look, I told him not to mention it because I wanted to tell you myself. I thought that would be much fairer than hearing second-hand.'

'Yes, you're probably right,' I relented, trying to coax a smile from Jacob. 'That's a nice name. Is the father Jewish?'

'No!' she laughed. Motherhood must have mellowed her; I'd risked my life asking about the father, I shouldn't think even Mum had brought up *that* hot potato. 'Glad to see that you haven't lost your Jewish fixation,' she added.

I smiled, hoping she wouldn't start on one of her pro-Palestinian tirades, but she didn't, thank goodness.

'I'm not telling anyone who the father is. He's very young and very irresponsible, and I just want to put that part of my life behind me. OK?'

'OK,' I nodded willingly, thinking hopefully that if I learnt to be tactful we could perhaps start to be friends. I'd always wanted a sister I could gossip with and confide in. Perhaps I could help look after Jacob for her sometimes, that would bring us closer.

'He's got your fabulous green eyes.'

'Mine aren't so fabulous any more, I'm afraid, but it's nice to know I've at least passed them on.'

Siena has never mourned the passing of her beauty. In fact, one of the many things I admire about her is that, unlike most women, she's completely unselfconscious about her looks, regarding any effort spent on them as a complete waste of time and money. She judges people solely on what they're like inside, she couldn't give a monkeys what they look like. The trouble is she's an idealist and despite her intelligence just can't conceive that the rest of the world doesn't share her high principles.

'But you're looking really well.' It was true. Beneath her cropped hair, her unmade-up face glowed with a healthy tan. 'It must have been difficult being a Fructarian in Chile.' Health had always come a poor second to principles with Siena. She had been a strict Fructarian before she'd left for Chile, which had involved eating a lot of fruit and nothing else. Macrobiotic leanings made her avoid fruit grown abroad; besides, she didn't approve of food coming over on airplanes, which severely narrowed down fruit-eating opportunities. Some weeks she would live on apples from people's gardens and very little else. At that time Dad had held a brief consultancy job advising the Meat and Livestock Commission which, as you might imagine, had gone down like a pork chop at a Bar Mitzvah. It never ceased to amaze me how two people so closely related could be so different, but one couldn't help but see the funny side of it. Sadly, Siena's sense of humour just didn't run to laughing at herself.

'God, it was a nightmare. I had the shits for six months and lost masses of weight.'

'Maybe I should try that, the Chile fruit diet, it's probably a lot cheaper than a health farm.'

'Oh, Oriana, you're not still worrying about your weight, are you? Really!' Siena was exasperated at this show of useless vanity. As if sensing my unease, Jacob, who had been quietly fixing his big eyes on me as I spoke, suddenly burst into tears.

'How old is he?'

'Eighteen months,' replied Siena, cooing at Jacob in a bid to stop him crying.

'So you've kept it secret for all this time?' I was amazed that I hadn't found out somehow.

'Well, Chile is a long way from home, and I sort of wanted to see if I could cope. It was fine because I have a lot of friends out there, but I suddenly woke up one day and decided it was time to come home.' I sensed she was unwilling to talk about it any more and changed the subject.

'Shall I take him for a sec?' I asked.

'Would you? I must grab this rare moment of solitude and go to the loo.'

She dumped Jacob into my arms and rushed off. I realized that due to her radical childcare ideas she would disapprove vehemently of having a nanny. I hadn't thought a great deal about having children myself, but knew that if I did, nannies and boarding schools would feature quite highly on the agenda. But for the moment I was thrilled to be holding my own flesh and blood in my arms. I'd always felt hopelessly inadequate with children but flatteringly Jacob had actually stopped crying. When Siena came back he was snoozing contentedly in my arms.

'Hey, look at you two,' she grinned. 'Made for each other! I didn't think you were into babies very much.'

'Well, he's not just any old baby, he's my nephew! Do you have any help with him?'

'I don't have a nanny, if that's what you mean. I couldn't bear it if he thought someone else was his mother, like we used to.' Our earliest recollection had been that one of our nannies had actually been our mother; it wasn't a painful memory at all, just rather hazy and confusing.

'Yes, but what do you do if you want to go out?'

'I hire a baby-sitter like anyone else. You know we get that baby allowance. It's a godsend. Means I don't have to sign on, thank God.' Our great-grandfather had left his descendants a useful sum in trust. Sadly the trust only opened on sight of a real baby and couldn't be abused by singletons like me. I was secretly surprised that Siena accepted it, but motherhood must have inspired her with a sense of reality. After all, she could live on air and fruit, but a baby couldn't.

'It's really difficult at the moment because Jacob refuses to eat anything with fruit in it.' She frowned worriedly. This was Jacob's cue to begin wailing vociferously. 'Well, it was only a matter of time. He's probably hungry. Here, hand him over.'

Siena whipped out a mottled bloodshot breast, the shock of which shut Jacob up immediately. It shut me up too. It had the opposite effect on an elderly tramp in the corner who had been lost in a distant reverie but who suddenly sat up and began to take a lot more interest in his surroundings. I mean, Siena's breast was huge, its presence seemed to fill up the whole café.

'I hear you've got a bloke at last,' Siena was saying, ignoring the stir to the café's small clientele.

'Um, yes,' I mumbled, relieved to change the subject.

'Is it a *grand passion*?'

I thought for a moment. Peregrine wasn't the grand passion type really. 'Well, we get along well.'

'Huh. Well, Mum said he'd never set the world alight. Oh, piss *off*, you stupid halfwit!' cried Siena in the ringing tones of the hockey field. The tramp was peering over with great interest at the proceedings, but the venomous authority in Siena's voice had a chastening effect, he gathered up his musty belongings and shuffled out on painful feet. Sometimes I forgot that Siena had been captain of lacrosse for a brief period at Benenden.

'Sorry about that. I just get so fed up with being public property. When you're pregnant strangers come up to you in the street and just start prodding you. Then you get told off or peered at when you're breast-feeding. I mean, what am I meant to do? Stay at home all day and do it in the dark? I've written to the *Independent* about it.'

'Come on, Sin.' (Great, I remembered!) 'Nobody reads the *Independent*.'

'Well, you write to the *Daily Mail* about it for me.' Siena smiled.

Gosh, she had mellowed. At one time such a comment would have caused a flaming row and a stand-off period of at least six months. I smiled at her. 'Look, if you're ever stuck for a baby-sitter, count me in. I mean it. I'm staying with Peregrine in this huge house and I've got the time. I mean, I'm not much good with children, but I can read up about it . . .'

'Hey, Banana,' Siena hadn't called me by my affectionate childhood nickname for years and I was strangely touched. 'Don't always put yourself down. I'd love you to baby-sit sometimes. I can't tell you what a relief it would be to have some help. It's really difficult being a single mother. Mum's offered to help but it's difficult getting about with a baby.'

'Couldn't you buy an old banger just to get around a bit?'

I asked tentatively. Siena had learnt to drive but had sold her car for moral reasons once she had started to work full time for Greens Mean Biz. Now she went everywhere by public transport, which must have been exhausting. 'It must be hard getting about with Jacob without a car.'

'Not really. Someone gave me an old bike, and I bung him on the back of that.'

'But isn't that a bit dangerous?'

'No more dangerous than driving that heap you call a car. Have you at least had a catalytic converter put on it yet?'

'Of course, ages ago,' I lied.

Siena looked at me irritably. 'I do think that my own family could make *some* kind of effort to support my work. Do you know how many children are knocked down every day, all round the world?' I shook my head. 'No, neither do I, but a lot. And I suppose that rich boyfriend of yours has got some whacking great petrol guzzler?'

I thought of Peregrine's horrible old Ford estate, which stalled at green traffic lights and hadn't been cleaned for four years because Mrs Button refused to go near it. What had once seemed like an amusingly ironic statement now seemed a bit irritating. If only he would buy one of those lovely new BMWs, in fact anything that went from 0 to 6 in less than thirty minutes would be an improvement.

'No, he hasn't. He goes practically everywhere by taxi.' I decided to change the subject and reached into my capacious leather rucksack and pulled out two jam jars. 'I brought you some homemade quince jam – with honey, not sugar.' We both had an aversion to white sugar. Me because it was unhealthy, Siena because it came by air from horrible places that underpaid their workers. 'I stayed with some of Peregrine's friends last week who own a quince farm and they let me pick some.'

Siena fingered the pots reverently. Even in the grimy cafe they glowed a rich honey-brown. 'Oh, Oriana, they're far too beautiful to eat. I shall put them on my window ledge so the sun catches them. Ummm, they smell of honey,' she sniffed them appreciatively. 'Thank you. Are you still cooking professionally? Mum said you'd given it up to become a glorified housewife.'

'Oh, did she?' I was rattled and the brief moment of intimacy disappeared. 'I'm still cooking but not in the way I used to. Oh, Siena, it's great fun, Peregrine and I have this salon every Monday night and all sorts of different people come. Why don't you come next week? Bring Jacob. Mrs Button, the housekeeper, would look after him.'

Siena smiled pityingly. 'I don't think I'd fit in really.'

'But we have all different types of people. The leader of the Green Party came last time.' I didn't mention that a fight had almost broken out between him and Father Hubert, a Neanderthal priest chum of Peregrine's, who was a leading member of the Quorn hunt.

'No, but thanks for thinking of me. If you're serious about looking after Jacob one day I'd really appreciate it.'

'Just name the day. I can be free any day except Mondays.'

'Well, some friends are going to sabotage the Countryside March in Hyde Park this Saturday. I didn't think I'd be able to go—'

'This Saturday will be fine. Peregrine is, um, doing something or other. I'll be at a loose end.' Thank goodness I didn't mention that Peregrine was also planning to attend the march, but for the other side. 'It'll be great looking after him. It might be the closest I get to having one myself at this rate.'

'I should work on Peregrine. He sounds the perfect candidate.'

I smiled noncommittally. Unless one could get pregnant from eye contact, my chances of becoming a parent were decidedly slim.

'But he's probably not that interested in sex, is he? In my limited experience most aristocrats would rather do almost anything else. Of course, the South Americans are the other extreme, they don't think about *anything* else. It's terribly tiring.'

I grabbed my bag excitedly. 'When's the next plane to Chile!'

'Christ, Oriana, don't even think about it, they'd eat you alive.'

Yes, I thought optimistically, after we'd arranged for Siena to bring Jacob to me on Saturday, perhaps Jacob would bring Siena and me closer together. After we had said goodbye I caught the bus back to Chelsea. Gazing idly out of the window at the grubby streets of Camden that my sister was so attached to, I tried very hard to think of more optimistic descriptions like 'colourful' and 'excitingly bohemian'. It was time I became more open-minded about life, I decided. I admired Siena's strong principles so much but spending time with her was exhausting. One had to be so careful not to say the wrong thing. And so many things were the wrong thing.

On a whim I decided to ring my mother on my mobile to gossip about the news. I was hoping she might invite me down for a night so I could pick some of her vegetables and discuss the Jacob excitement.

'Hello, darling.' She sounded distracted.

'I'm sorry, is this a good time to talk?'

'Well, I was just about to listen to *The Archers* but . . .'

Oh dear. I should have been familiar with my mother's habits by now. 'Sorry. Shall I call you back in twenty minutes?'

'Oh, darling, would you mind awfully?'

'No, of course not. 'Bye.' I remembered there was a ten-minute window between *The Archers* finishing and the beginning of *EastEnders*. One day I'd get used to taking second place to the plethora of soap operas that filled my mother's life. One day I supposed it wouldn't hurt any more. I wondered when.

I tried to think rationally. I knew from experience that

tomorrow she would ring me back and we'd have a lovely chat. I was just being over-sensitive as usual. Thank goodness I had Peregrine to talk to. He would understand.

I let myself into Cheyne Castle, crossing my fingers that Peregrine was back and bursting to tell him about the day's dramatic excitements. I found him in the kitchen, munching some leftover fried bread from breakfast and reading the *Catholic Herald*.

'Guess what?' I cried excitedly. 'Siena's had a baby!'

'Bit sudden, isn't it?'

'No, no. She kept it a secret from the family, well, from my dad and me. He's called Jacob and he's gorgeous. I'm going to baby-sit for him this weekend!'

'What a surprise. So you have a nephew. Who's the proud papa?'

'I did ask, but it's a deadly secret.'

'Well, I think this calls for a celebration. Let's have a glass of champagne.'

I smiled fondly at him as he went to the fridge and took out a bottle of vintage Moet and Chandon that he had been given for his birthday months ago. He uncorked it without spilling a drop and poured it with great ceremony into two antique flutes.

'Here's to young . . . what's his name?'

'Jacob.'

'Here's to young Jacob, and may he grow up to be as lovely and talented as his beautiful aunt.' My eyes filled with tears. The events of the extraordinary day were beginning to catch up with me.

We clinked glasses. 'Hmm, Jacob. Was the father Jewish?'

I laughed. 'That's just what I asked! I think it's very unlikely given my sister's strong anti-Zionist feelings.'

'She doesn't take after you then,' smiled Peregrine.

' 'Fraid not.' I thought for a moment about Peregrine and his mysterious maternal origins. The Skye-Roccas could be traced back beyond William the Conqueror, but his mother's family were shrouded in obscurity. 'It would be interesting to be half something, half Jewish or Norwegian or something, don't you think?'

Peregrine sipped his champagne and munched a piece of fried bread abstractedly before sitting down on the large sofa. He patted the seat next to him.

'My mother used to pretend she was Jewish to annoy my father who was a great Mosley supporter. It used to make him awfully cross but because she was adopted he couldn't be certain that she wasn't lying. If she wasn't lying it would make me Jewish.'

'Gosh. What an exotic thought.' I gazed at him in shock. Peregrine with his sandy hair and pink complexion could not have looked more Celtic. 'Why didn't you say before?'

'Well, my mother used to change her mind so often nobody was ever sure. Her origins used to change depending on what movie she happened to be making. Once after a particularly good holiday in Hawaii she informed the press that her grandmother was a Hawaiian sorceress with magical powers. Another time she claimed she was descended from Anastasia, the youngest daughter of the Tsar. But sadly the reality is a little more prosaic because she was actually born in Alaska and then she was adopted by a couple who lived in Cheam. She hated people knowing that. You must promise not to tell a *soul*. My real grandparents are probably Alaskan lumberjacks.'

'Well, maybe Jewish lumberjacks,' I said, trying to cheer him up. The Cheam connection was obviously quite traumatic which might have been why he'd waited this long before telling me. 'Though that's a bit unlikely, I suppose, as there can't be many Jews in Alaska.'

'Oddly enough there are. They call themselves the Frozen Chosen.' He sighed dejectedly. 'Anyway. That's the story. Tomorrow some biographer will probably claim she's descended from the last of the remaining Incas or something.'

I snuggled up to Peregrine, anticipating a cosy chat. I liked him best when he was like this, witty and self-deprecating. We were staying in tonight and had settled on the sofa in the kitchen. Peregrine put down his paper and put his arm round me. I frowned, thinking of the brief conversation with my mother. Peregrine was very good on this sort of thing. If he went on *Mastermind* I would put him down for people foibles.

'I'd just be interested to know when it stops hurting,' I said, after I had explained the brief exchange with my mother. 'I mean, I'm twenty-eight, I physically left home when I was sixteen but emotionally I'm still dependent on my parents. I have a feeling it shouldn't be like this.'

I knew Peregrine's parents had barely seen him from his birth until the age of six, when they had been killed. The things he had told me about his family life made one's hair stand on end. And yet he showed no bitterness and had completely forgiven them. I really admired that.

'So how old were you when you stopped minding?' I asked.

'Oh, about forty-one.'

'But you're forty-one now. What happened?'

'Can't you guess?'

I racked my brains. It must be something very obvious but my mind was completely blank. 'Um, no, I can't.'

'*You*, my darling, are the most unromantic girl I have ever known.'

'You don't mean meeting me?'

'Of course I do!' He looked at me with soft blue eyes and my heart melted with the love spilling out of them. He took my glass gently from my hand and kissed me softly. Dizzy with champagne and affection I responded passionately, making the most of it before he began the tongue thing.

'Oh, Oriana, I love you so much,' he murmured into my hair. 'You do love me, don't you?'

'Of course,' I replied, hypnotized by his hand stroking my

hair. If I had been a cat I would have purred.

'Shall we go to bed?' he inquired gently.

'Hmmm,' I replied as he pulled me to my feet. I reached for my champagne and held it up briefly against the window, mesmerized by the tiny golden bubbles dancing in the glass. I glanced down at the Thames, its ripples lost in the inky blackness of the night and shivered.

'It's hypnotic, isn't it?' Peregrine drained his champagne and put his arm round me. 'I could watch it for ever.' This said a little impatiently as he turned and walked to the door. I stood there for a few more minutes, lost in thought, before going to join him.

He was already in bed and glanced up from his magazine when I entered, his eyes following me around the room with a lascivious dog-like devotion. He did this every night and it was very irritating. I could understand the dog-like devotion, but considering his impotence I found the lasciviousness bewildering and faintly disturbing.

I slipped into bed, longing to be left alone with my thoughts, but knowing he wanted, needed to consolidate our intimate evening. If only he could accept the physical deficiencies of our relationship as I was prepared to do. It was the constant efforts, the prodding and the fiddling that were so trying. It made me feel like a radio. Against my will I would get excited but would be left high and dry. It was most unsatisfactory. We were so in tune in other ways; maybe we had used up all our intimacy allowance mentally.

Peregrine turned towards me, cupping my breast carefully and seeking out my mouth. 'Oh, darling, I do so love being with you,' he murmured then stuck his tongue in my mouth where it wavered around desperately, possibly looking for loose fillings. I suddenly remembered that I'd forgotten to clean my teeth and longed to get up. Peregrine manoeuvred my hand downwards. 'Oh, my darling, you turn me on so much.' To my surprise there was a sign of tenuous activity. Peregrine hurriedly positioned himself on top of me, but sadly things soon collapsed. He began to caress me rhythmically, which he knew would get me very excited. It drove me mad with frustration.

'Please, Peregrine, let's go to sleep, I'm terribly tired.'

'But I thought you liked this.'

'I do, but you don't seem to,' I said brusquely, brushing him away irritably.

'Of course I do. You don't seem to realize how much stress I'm under at the moment. I wish you wouldn't put me under so much pressure, you're so impatient.'

I shifted away crossly. 'It's a bit rich blaming me for everything.'

'Oh, darling, don't be cross. It's just that I like you so much it puts me under a lot of pressure. Be patient. When I've managed to sell mad Uncle Rupert's zoo I'll be much more relaxed.' Peregrine had armfuls of strange excuses on which he blamed his flailing libido. I was 'too thin', (ridiculous, I had put on weight since living at Cheyne Castle), too 'tight', sometimes I was even 'too attractive' and he liked me 'too much'. But recently he had been 'too stressed out' and had blamed his spurious business interests, which mainly seemed to involve selling things he had inherited at a huge profit. Members of his family seemed to die fairly frequently, often leaving him land, art collections, and most recently a zoo. He was presently involved in intriguing negotiations with a reclusive Hollywood film mogul I privately thought was more interested in doing business with a real life English lord than in buying what appeared to be an elderly collection of Manx cats, three kangaroos, six incontinent sloths and a wallaby who romped chaotically around mad Uncle Rupert's castle and garden.

'I know you will be,' I said soothingly, bored with the conversation, versions of which I had heard many times before, and longing to go to sleep.

'Darling,' said Peregrine. 'Have you ever thought about having your breasts enlarged?'

Chapter Seven

That Saturday Siena cycled over from Camden with Jacob swaddled in her bicycle basket. It seemed rather a terrifying arrangement but I didn't dare say anything. Fortunately she just missed Peregrine who had left for the march ten minutes earlier, looking quite handsome in tweeds, flat cap and plus fours. His cheeks were pink and his blue eyes gleamed with anticipation. He was looking forward to the march, though he preferred to describe it as a 'rally'. I was surprised at his enthusiasm as up until now he had always been utterly indifferent to the countryside, had never been hunting, loathed horses and was neutral about foxes. Although he accepted invitations to shooting weekends, lack of co-ordination meant he never managed to shoot anything.

I persuaded Siena to come in for a cup of tea (fortunately I always had plenty of soy milk because Peregrine occasionally remembered he was allergic to dairy products), and to discuss Jacob's arrangements. She had been very organized and had packed everything Jacob might need inside her enormous backpack, and had even expressed her own milk into a bottle, which was very impressive.

Should things get beyond me, Mrs B, an expert having raised eight children of her own, was on standby downstairs and longing to be of assistance.

Siena was wearing full combat gear, Timberland boots and khaki jacket, and was very excited about sabotaging the march. I had thought she might support the protest of country dwellers, united in their irritation at being told what to do by townies like us and who seemed drawn from all different classes, but she was rabidly anti all country sports, having recently witnessed a fox being torn apart. As she described the process in gory detail, I must say I began to sympathize with her.

'It's utterly revolting, and we've got to stop it.'

'I see your point, of course,' I said. 'But hunting seems to be one of the few things that brings people together in the country. They've lost their village shops, they have minimal public transport. People just sit inside and watch their TVs and videos and play with their computers. At least the hunt gets them out and about and talking. And trapping foxes is much worse.'

'You don't know what you're talking about,' said Siena mildly. 'Now watch me while I change Jacob's nappy.' I paid close attention. Jacob had been quite sleepy but began to wake up. He seemed to love the attention and waved his arms about and gurgled quite happily. But the whole nappy business looked a bit complicated. Still, Mrs B would help me. 'I've no objection to drag hunting,' she went on. 'What I can't understand is how people actually enjoy the killing bit so much.'

'Yes, that's always flummoxed me too,' I said, relieved there was something we could agree on. 'But then we are townies, of course. And you have to admit that a lot of hunt saboteurs just hate toffs. If they were that mad about animals they'd protest about factory farming, which is far more horrible than fox hunting.'

'That's true,' agreed Siena, itching to be off. 'But once we've banned fox hunting we can mobilize the troops against that. Now, are you sure you'll be OK? I'll be back in five hours. If you're lucky he'll sleep most of the time.' She briefly ran through some complicated baby physiology, explained some even more complicated educational games that I couldn't figure out, and departed.

I breathed a sigh of relief. Jacob began whimpering a bit

so I picked him up from the nest we had made on the sofa and took him upstairs to watch the Teletubbies which I'd got out on video. I hadn't mentioned this to Siena, feeling she was bound to disapprove. 'What the mind doesn't know the heart cannot grieve over,' I said to Jacob as we settled down in front of the TV. When we were tired of watching it I would read to him from Beatrix Potter's *Tales of Squirrel Nutkin*, which I'd discovered in Peregrine's library.

I didn't know much about eighteen-month-old children but Jacob seemed very bright and enjoyed being bounced energetically on my knee in time to the Teletubbies theme tune. Mrs B appeared with some Mr Kipling cream buns, which were pounced on with great enthusiasm. Peregrine returned early having been unable to track down Father Hubert and his country chums and was quite taken with Jacob, even though by this time he was covered in cream and becoming quite noisy. But I think Peregrine found half an hour about enough and had to go for a lie down. Mrs Button then disappeared to prepare Mr Button's tea, but not before I had dragooned her into changing Jacob's nappy which was probably a bit overdue if the damp patch on my leggings was anything to go by. Jacob fell asleep quite suddenly and I thought I'd take advantage and have a five-minute snooze myself.

I conked out for an hour and was only woken up by Siena and Peregrine chatting as they came up the stairs. They seemed to be getting along surprisingly well, I could hear them quite clearly as they both had very carrying voices.

I hoped to goodness Peregrine wouldn't mention the video or the buns or the rally, but they seemed to be chatting quite animatedly about Peregrine's mother's latest role as feminist icon – rather odd, as she had always hated women. However, one of her first films, the classic, *Kiss Me Before I Kill You*, in which she had played an erotic Turkish belly dancer who was really a spy, had just been re-released to rapturous critical acclaim.

I quickly kicked the Teletubbies video box under the sofa and picked up an educational toy, which I began waving at Jacob enthusiastically. He started wailing and only stopped when Siena gathered him up in her arms and began cooing at him. Her cheeks were flushed and her eyes were bright from being outside all day, but there was something else, she had an inner radiance that came from fighting fairly for what she believed in. My mind flickered back to the cruise we had attended as children where she had rattled her collecting tin to such great effect and then to the present as she held her child close. I saw that her beauty hadn't disappeared. Her hair may have been shorter and darker but as she stood beside me in the failing light I could see that the sparkle and glow was still there, and given the right catalyst would reappear.

Peregrine was smiling beatifically at the domestic scene. He'd never seen Siena and me together and he was probably surprised, I'd given him the impression that Siena was a real old battleaxe.

'Thanks so much, Oriana, you've no idea how great it's been to have a whole day out without having to worry about Jacob. It's done me the world of good.' She turned to Peregrine and smiled. 'I really appreciate you letting him stay the afternoon. I hope he didn't make too much of a racket.'

'Not at all,' replied Peregrine suavely. 'It was a pleasure. I hope he'll come again.'

'Yes, please bring him soon. I've had such a lovely day looking after him.' It was true, even though I had spent most of it asleep. Besides, I was looking forward to watching all my favourite childhood TV programmes again. All the Narnia books were now available on video and it would be nice to have an excuse to see them.

'Peregrine's not a bit how I expected,' said Siena as I let her and Jacob out. 'He's absolutely charming – whoops, that sounds really rude!'

'No, it's not,' I laughed. 'Give me a ring if you need me to look after Jacob next week. Perhaps he could stay over for the night if you want to get out one evening.'

'Well, maybe Friday? That brilliant new Hungarian film is showing at the Camden Playhouse. It's only on for one night and all my usual baby-sitters go out at the weekend. I haven't been to the cinema for aeons,' she said wistfully, packing the sleepy Jacob into her bicycle basket. 'Though we'd better be careful, Peregrine was looking a bit misty-eyed in there. You don't want him getting broody . . . or do you?' She peered at me closely.

'No fear!' I replied vehemently. 'I think I'll just stick to cooking for the time being.'

Siena shrugged her shoulders, kissed me on both cheeks and pedalled off into the night. I hugged myself tightly as a great wave of affection rolled over me. It was great to feel part of a family, to be needed. I was right, Jacob was bringing us together. And who knew, I might never have children of my own, Jacob might be the closest I'd ever get. I shut the door quietly and went to have a quick bath before joining Peregrine in bed.

Siena was right; witnessing the domestic scene had made him very misty-eyed.

'I never knew you were so good with children, darling. You have such a natural way with them.'

'To be honest, Jacob is the first child I've spent a whole day with. I don't know if I'd be as patient if he hadn't been my nephew.'

'Have you thought about having children?' Peregrine asked gently. He'd touched on this before but I'd always evaded the subject. It was very tricky.

'Oh yes,' I replied blandly. 'One day.'

'Would you have my children?' Peregrine persisted.

'Um, yes.' I mean, what else could I say? I had thought about it, and even gone so far as to make up names in my head for them, but given Peregrine's sex ban it would be a challenge. And though I adored him and he was my best friend I didn't really *love* him. And I wasn't really over Tom. I often succeeded in putting him out of my mind but I couldn't help comparing Peregrine's fumbles with Tom's expertise. Besides, I wanted to write my cookery book first. But of course it was immensely flattering to be asked. I decided to play along with the idea. It was fun to dream.

'I think Davina Skye-Rocca sounds nice. Or Jack if it's a boy?'

'Oh, not Jack. It would always remind me of that rough diamond friend of Pandora's.' He had met Jack Dudley once but they didn't have much in common. 'I started reading her book the other day. It's very *graphic*, isn't it? Odd, she looks so innocent.'

'She said when she was writing it she never really thought anyone would ever read it, but they did. It caused such a fuss she rather regrets it now. Everyone thought she was writing about her boyfriends but she made most of it up.' I didn't add that the most exciting scene in the book, involving a tin of treacle, a pair of handcuffs and a self-propelling shiatsu massage bed had been based on one of my own experiences with Tom. But all that was a long time ago. Another life really.

Funny, people made such a big deal out of sex when one could so easily get used to living without it. Other things were probably much more important. Being with Peregrine was a lesson in learning what was really impotent in life; there was nothing like the security of living with a man who really loved you. I could see that very clearly.

Peregrine snorted disapprovingly. 'I thought it was all utter tosh. Lights out, darling?' I nodded and put my book down while he switched off the light. 'Goodnight, darling. Sleep well.'

'You too.'

Five minutes later we were both asleep.

Chapter Eight

I was getting despondent because *The Snoop!* were dragging their feet about my cookery column. But I soon cheered up when out of the blue my career took a turn in another direction.

Naff Ovens, an obscure Bolivian kitchen company, had seen a picture of me in *The Snoop!* wearing my satin slip and mules and asked if I would appear in a glossy brochure they planned to enclose in *Tatler*. They were trying to take the company upmarket and had already approached several society figures who had all refused.

My mother advised against it, but she's still haunted by some knitting patterns she did when she first started modelling. She was persuaded to wear a crocheted bikini, which revealed *everything*. When she became well known they would resurface with terrifying regularity until my father got back the negatives and destroyed them. He had to break the photographer's kneecaps to do it and ended up in prison for three months. He said it was the only way he could think of getting my mother into bed. Of course my mother succumbed the moment he got out and they married soon after. It's *such* a romantic story. The newspapers ran thrilling headlines. The *Express* wrote: 'Working-class hero saves model's honour!' While *The Bugle* screamed: 'Hero Wacks Woofter!' You couldn't imagine a paper getting away with that sort of thing now. Apparently *The Bugle* was terrifically politically incorrect and the government ended up banning it.

But I was old enough to make my own decisions. In the back of my mind there lurked a secret hope that it might lead to an exciting and glamorous modelling career. I was only five foot four admittedly, but look at Kate Twig, she was short too. Besides, Peregrine thought it sounded like a good idea.

The photo shoot itself started off quite well. I had a special person to do my hair and make-up and a stylist had brought some gorgeous, albeit rather flimsy negligees which we had decided in advance would be just the thing to go with my sensible navy-blue fluffy mules. Naff had provided us with several bottles of delicious champagne, to make us all as relaxed as possible, but sadly there was no food and I was soon feeling very light-headed and extremely relaxed indeed.

I told the make-up lady to make me look as much like Ivana Trump as possible, envisioning a sort of hair-sprayed-up-in-the-air kind of look, and after hours of prodding, backcombing and spraying, the resemblance was indeed quite striking.

I quickly slipped into a negligee, which annoyingly was a size too small. I was sure I'd told the stylist I was a 10, but it was too late to get any more by then.

Tristram the photographer was famous for his avant-garde shots and persuaded me to climb into an industrial-sized oven. I couldn't bend over because the negligee was too tight, and my head was spinning a bit because of the champagne, so when he suggested casually that I take it off, no one would see anything as I'd be all curled up, it seemed like a very sensible idea. He took some very tasteful shots of me naked in the oven then suggested I climb out and stick my head inside it so that just my legs were showing. The stylist draped a J-cloth over my bottom so it was all quite proper. Besides, Tristram said he would airbrush out anything 'too revealing'. The shots were bound to be just like the ones David Bailey had taken of Marie Helvin where she wanders around naked except for the odd tea towel over her head.

Frightfully avant-garde. I was following in fine footsteps.

Then I got back into my negligee and Tristram asked me to get onto a huge gas cooking range where I lay with all the spiky hob things digging into my flesh. And then they lit all the hobs that I wasn't lying on. I was trying to get into the spirit of things but was just getting hotter and hotter.

Eventually I asked Tristram if he could turn the flames down (everyone else had gone out to lunch), but he kept saying, 'Baby, baby, just one more shot. You're bootiful. Reely bootiful. D'ya know that?' My hair caught fire, but even then he kept taking pictures. Thank *God* the stylist then returned and chucked her iced latte over my head, otherwise anything could have happened.

By now the champagne had completely worn off and I was beginning to feel slightly worried about some of the shots, in particular the ones with my head inside the oven. Had the J-Cloth covered *everything*? And would the picture come with a warning not to try this at home? It was so irresponsible. I voiced my concern to Tristram but he appeared shifty and uncommunicative. Oh dear. If only I had listened to my mother after all.

Peregrine was in the kitchen when I returned dishevelled, my hair singed, and red weals all over my body where the gas hob had serrated my flesh. He was quite concerned.

'Darling, have you been in an accident? You look frightful.'

I told him about the shoot, exaggerating slightly. I didn't actually *say* that Tristram had drugged me then forced me to take all my clothes off against my will, but I may have given that impression. Peregrine was quite influential in the recusant world (Naff was a Bolivian company and Bolivians are Catholics, aren't they?) and I was hoping he would leap to my defence and have Tristram arrested or go and beat him up or something. But it was Wednesday, the day of his Anger Management Course, and he was feeling extremely loving and peaceful.

'Oh, darling. I'm so sorry you've had such a frightful day, but do try and put it out of your mind. It's in the past now and we must look to the future.' I gritted my teeth. He always came out with this sort of ghastly mumbo jumbo on Wednesdays. By Thursday he had normally quite recovered. 'I've just had some news that might cheer you up a bit. I went to see my trustees this afternoon. You know I mentioned ages ago that some people in Hollywood want to make a movie based on one of my father's books? Well, the auction was yesterday and they appear to have raised a considerable sum.' He mentioned a huge figure, which made me gasp.

Although Lord Rufus had had many other children, most of them were illegitimate or, if legitimate, had upset the old man in some way. Even though Peregrine was the youngest of the sizeable brood, he was the main beneficiary of his father's will. Media experts had occasionally speculated on why this was, and come to the conclusion that as he was only six years old at the time his father died and hardly saw either of his parents, he had no opportunity to cause offence.

Lord Rufus had had loads of illegitimate children. He must have been quite a chap. I secretly wondered if he might have been so over-used when Peregrine came along that he was unable to pass any sperm on at all. Although we bumped into his siblings occasionally at parties, Peregrine didn't seem to know any of them very well.

'Let's have a—'

'Party to celebrate!' I finished his sentence excitedly.

'My darling girl. You take the words straight from my mouth. Oh, I forgot to say that one of my half-brothers rang from Munich, he's one of the Finnish lot.' I remembered vaguely from my intensive studying of the *Mail* Diary over the years that Lord Rufus had enjoyed a thrillingly brief affair with a former Miss Helsinki which had presumably resulted in a son. 'He's in London next week and wants to come and stay. He's frightfully libidinous, like all Finns, but extremely amusing.'

‘Well, let’s be ultra hospitable and have a Finnish theme this time,’ I suggested.

Peregrine hugged me affectionately. ‘What I *most* love about you, my darling girl, is your infectious enthusiasm. Compared to my friends you are like a breath of fresh air. I’m sure Magnus will be charmed.’

‘I’ll get onto Harrods straightaway and order some reindeer. I think I’ll do a smorgasbord, followed by a cloudberry soufflé. I wonder where I can find cloudberries at this time of year,’ I mused excitedly, all thoughts of the photo shoot driven from my mind.

Chapter Nine

I was soon given a grim reminder. Two days later Mrs B came steaming into the kitchen clutching *The Tit*, a paper so low it made *The Snoop!* look like the *Economist*. She pretends she only gets it for the crossword but I know she reads it from cover to cover.

''Ere, Miss Oriana. 'Ave you seen this?' She shoved some grimy newsprint under my nose. I could just about make out a naked woman's bottom sticking out of what might have been an oven. My heart sank as I read the accompanying article which was in the infamous 'Toff's Slot'.

The Tit was rabidly left wing and had single-handedly managed to abolish what was left of the House of Lords by discrediting as many peers as possible. Several of Peregrine's recusant chums had recently appeared.

'Toffs used to send kiddies down the mines, now they send their birds into ovens to make a few bob! Lord Peregrine Sky-Rocket has a fortune of *twenty million pounds* (I gulped, that was news to me!) yet according to a close friend his fiancée is so short of readies she is reduced to stripping to earn a living. Another disgusting example of how our lords and masters behave . . .'

I couldn't bear to read any more. The bottom of the page was lined with a series of smug pictures of spuriously discredited aristocrats.

I ran into Peregrine's bedroom clutching the rag. 'Will you go and duff Tristram up and get the negatives back for me?' I pleaded hopelessly. 'To save my reputation?'

'I can't just "duff him up" as you put it. We should use the proper channels, not the laws of the jungle. Besides, I doubt anyone will even notice the pictures. If you pursue the matter, everyone will be sure to see them. Now do simmer down.'

'If you really loved me you'd *do* something!' I snatched the paper out of his hands and stomped back to the kitchen. From the basement I could hear distant sounds of cackling. It was too awful, the industrial cleaners had obviously found out about my misfortune.

In the kitchen I took a deep breath. To be honest it wasn't so much the pictures that upset me as Peregrine's feeble attitude. I was longing for him to raise a sword in my honour. If only he would get his testosterone levels checked. I was just about to change the message on my mobile phone saying that I had gone to New Zealand until further notice when my trophy father callcd.

'I've just seen a picture of you in the paper. It's not very flattering, is it?'

It was too bad nothing got past him. He didn't even take *The Tit.*

'How on earth did you find out? I thought you were in Norway.'

'I am. Mrs Sprout told Bridget and Bridget faxed me first thing.'

Marigold Sprout worked in my father's factory canteen and was a frightful old gossip. She was just the sort who would read *The Tit* from cover to cover. She probably got it on subscription so that she wouldn't miss a copy when she and Mr Sprout took their summer holiday.

'It says here you're short of a few bob. Is that right?'

I thought of Pandora and her advice about training him up. 'Um, yes, I am a bit.'

'Well, I'm coming back this afternoon. Why don't we meet for dinner at the Savoy and discuss it tomorrow evening.'

Maybe this would be a good opportunity to get Siena

along. I knew she hadn't seen him since she'd got back from Chile.

'Why don't we invite Siena?' I suggested. 'She's not a Fructarian any more so she can eat in restaurants.'

'No fear. She'll insist on dragging Jacob with her and we'll have to put up with all that breast-feeding nonsense. I couldn't stand that.'

I remembered the huge bloodshot breast and shuddered. The Savoy Grill probably wasn't ready for such excitement just yet.

I hurriedly began to pack up some things as I'd arranged to see Jacob and Siena in Camden. We were getting along so well and I was really beginning to build up a relationship with Jacob. I'd made him organic sugar-free carob muffins as he wasn't allowed any sugar, except when he came to Cheyne Castle and Mrs B tempted him with Mr Kipling cakes. Of course, Siena didn't know anything about that and Jacob wasn't giving anything away.

I was looking forward to going round today because Siena said she wanted to introduce me to 'someone'. Presumably she had met a man; it must be quite serious because she had lured Mum up from the country for the occasion.

When I rang Siena's bell, an attractive woman with silky chestnut hair pulled back in a sleek ponytail, opened the door clutching Jacob. She was wearing tight jeans and a colourful tie-dyed T-shirt and possessed an air of calm authority. There was a hell of a din going on upstairs, it sounded like ten children were playing cowboys and Indians with the sound turned up.

She smiled at me pleasantly. 'Sorry about the noise. You must be the glamorous Oriana.' She examined me closely through light blue eyes. 'You don't look a bit like your photographs, you're terribly photogenic.' This was said with such a wide sweet smile I didn't know whether it was a compliment or an insult. The inference was that I looked good in photos but not in real life. It was a bit disturbing really.

Siena burst into the room. 'Sorry, I didn't hear the bell. So you've met.'

'Well, not really, I'm sorry I don't know your name,' I said apologetically.

'I'm Mary. And the racket upstairs is my children, I'm afraid. They're still settling in.' This was the cue for three girls, aged between about five and ten, to come storming into the room shouting at once. Then the bell went and Siena went to let our mother in.

She was looking much rejuvenated after a relaxing two-week holiday in Crans Montana with her current husband, Bertie, the Belgian langlaufing champion. Her skin glowed with a light golden tan and her fine blonde hair had been slightly backcombed and set in a perfect chignon. Her small regular features were imperceptively but carefully made-up. She'd never lost the poise and grooming she'd picked up as a model in the late fifties and always looked immaculate. Next to her slight frame, Siena, Mary and I looked terrifyingly robust.

'Gosh, Mum, you're looking incredibly well. You didn't sneak off to Montreux for some rejuvenating sheep's placenta injections, did you?' I had become rather obsessed with this idea since I had overheard Peregrine's doctors discussing them at one of our recent parties. According to his urologist they were miraculous although they did occasionally have terrifying side effects. To my regret he had refused to elaborate and I was left tantalizingly in the dark.

'Good heavens, no!' she shouted irritably over the din. 'I'll tell you everything in a minute once I've met everybody.'

'QUIET!' yelled Mary firmly. The racket ceased long enough for Mummy and me to be introduced to Mary's three children. The twins Kenya and Conga had mischievous coffee-coloured faces and blonde afro hair, while India, their seven-year-old sister, was rather Indian looking. Most girls called India are pale-skinned English roses hailing from Gloucestershire, and there was something quite charming about an Indian girl being called India.

'And we all know Jacob,' I said, scooping him up and kissing his black curly head. He smiled at me, happy to be surrounded by all these new children who seemed to adore him. 'Orry,' he gurgled, reaching out his podgy arms towards me and pulling my hair playfully.

'Siena showed me an old picture of you the other day when your hair was darker. It really suited you that colour,' said Mary thoughtfully.

'Nonsense,' said my mother briskly. 'Oriana is blonde and blonde she will stay. She likes the attention, don't you, darling?' Before I could reply she continued, 'Shall we see about lunch? The children seem to be getting a little fractious.'

There was a bloodcurdling yell from India, who had fallen over, which set off Jacob. God, children were noisy.

'Good idea, Venetia. Come along into the kitchen and I'll dish up,' said Mary.

We all trooped into the kitchen where Mary served a huge delicious paella with slapdash efficiency. I wondered how old she was. When she was talking her face was so animated and her full lipped sensual mouth was so expressive that she looked quite young. But in repose the large mouth seemed to almost sag, dragging her small nose and light blue eyes downwards with its weight, giving her a sad crumpled look. She could have been any age between thirty and forty. I guessed that she hadn't had an easy life.

'Help yourself to salad, Oriana,' Mary was saying, handing me a plate of aromatic rice. 'How much would you like, Venetia?'

'Oh, I'll just have some salad,' said Mummy firmly, helping herself to a small tomato.

'Don't take any notice, Mum stopped eating twenty years ago with no visible side effects,' explained Siena. It was true. Some days the only thing she ate all day was a green tomato from the greenhouse.

'People make too much fuss about food these days,' she said, picking at her tomato indifferently.

'Huh, you should try saying that to Peregrine. It's all he really cares about.'

'That's not a good sign, darling,' said Mummy. 'You know what they say about men who are obsessed with food.'

The three of us turned to her expectantly, then the twins started fighting over the paella and the moment was lost.

'QUIET!' yelled Mary and there was a temporary silence. 'Get your coats on, we're going to the park.'

'But I haven't finished, Mummy,' complained India.

'You can finish it later. The grown-ups want to talk quietly,' explained Mary.

There was much disgruntled moaning and groaning amongst the children as they shuffled out. It was drizzling outside so I couldn't blame them.

'Mary's taking them out because I've got something I'd like to discuss with you,' said Siena seriously.

'You're not ill or anything, darling?' asked Mummy.

'No, nothing like that.'

'Say goodbye to Venetia and Oriana,' said Mary, standing by the door, ready to depart.

There was a chorus of muted goodbyes and kisses as Mary ushered her brood outside, slamming the door behind them. The silence was delicious.

'I think you've probably guessed, but Mary and I are sort of together.'

'Yes, darling, I did realize,' said my mother calmly. I must say I was stunned. Siena never talked about her boyfriends, but I'd never have guessed in a million years that she was a lesbo.

'You know that your father and I don't mind too much what you do as long as you don't frighten the horses. And as none of us has had much success with conventional methods I think you should give this a try.'

'And it's much less of a health risk than heterosexual sex,' I added, trying to get into the liberal swing of things.

'That's hardly the reason why Mary and I are together,' said Siena sarcastically.

I fell silent. I couldn't think of anything useful to say at all. The whole thing seemed an utter disaster. Women were behaving like men and men were turning into women. It was quite disturbing. And if you were dating another woman, who would pay when you went out for dinner? Whenever I had a meal out with a chum we often went Dutch. It would be terribly unromantic to have to do that on a date.

'Yes, I think it might work out very well,' Mummy was saying. 'And when it is time to go your separate ways –' Siena frowned. 'Don't look at me like that, Siena, nothing lasts forever – you won't have to pay any alimony.'

'Are you sure about that? In America there have been several cases where lesbians have fought each other for custody and alimony,' I pointed out sensibly. 'Remember those two actresses who sued each other for custody of their six cats? That dragged on for—'

'Anyone around here heard about love and *commitment*? Couldn't you just stop being so goddamned cynical for five seconds? Mary and I really love each other, we love each other's kids. We're in this for the long term—'

'Ugh. I wish you wouldn't use those horrid American words.' Mummy shuddered and put down her tomato.

'Yes. Commitment is an awful word,' I ruminated. 'As in she was *committed* to an institution for the criminally insane, or she was *committed* to the federal penitentiary because she had *committed* manslaughter.'

'Actually I meant the word kids,' said Mummy.

'Oh, for heaven's sake!' Siena raked through her cropped hair with a thin anxious hand. 'Why can't we have a proper discussion just for once!'

'Well, we all wish you the best of luck,' said my mother mildly. 'Now before I go I've got a bit of news of my own. Bertie has left me!'

'Oh.' Siena and I looked concerned. We weren't quite sure yet if this was a Good Thing or a Bad Thing.

'We were in Crans Montana and we were just finishing our breakfast—'

'Can you get green tomatoes in Switzerland?'

'Don't interrupt, Oriana. Anyway, Bertie said he was just going off for a spot of langlaufing. We said goodbye amicably and I watched him langlauf perfectly happily off into the distance from the balcony. But when he hadn't come back four days later I started to get a bit worried. He only had a small packet of dried bananas on him. But I thought I ought to wait another week or so, there's no point worrying the police unduly. And then, as luck would have it, he called from Austria; it turned out he'd langlaufed all the way there, and said he wanted a quickie divorce, if I was amenable. *If* I was amenable! Does the Pope pray! Of course I didn't say that. So, isn't that good news, girls?'

'Um, yes,' we agreed in unison. I hadn't known Bertie very well as he spent most of his time attending langlaufing championships in obscure places like Liechtenstein, but he'd always seemed a perfectly decent fellow.

'But I'm slightly concerned about our divorce settlement. Bertie was quite comfortably off but he became rather attached to my Canaletto. He also happens to have a brilliant lawyer. What I propose to do is sell my lovely picture and put the proceeds in trust for you both.'

'But Mummy, you swore you'd never sell it!' I protested weakly.

'I know. But I'm nearly fifty,' she was in fact fifty-five, 'and there have been so many burglaries in the village. It's probably someone else's turn to enjoy it now and I'd feel safer without it. It's funny how your priorities change as you get older. And as they say in Israel, I've decided to "just take the money".'

'But they don't stop at the money, do they?' said Siena bitterly. 'They want all the land as well.'

'Figure of speech, darling,' said my mother quickly. 'I've had it valued by Sotheby's and they think it will fetch about two million pounds, which I shall split between the two of you.'

I sat stock still, unable to breathe. It was a dream come true for me.

'I don't know. Maybe you should donate it to the Tate so everyone can see it. It's an awful thought that it will be bought by someone and locked away for years and years,' said Siena compassionately. I bit my tongue. Really, she could be tremendously irritating.

'No, I've thought it through and I want you both to have the money. You may think it is the root of all evil, Siena, but it's not. It brings independence and freedom, and that is worth its weight in gold. Besides, you'll only have the income from the trust. The actual capital will be tied up until you are both forty.' *Ancient!* 'By that time one might hope that you'll both be settled with someone who can support you.' She looked at me meaningfully. The last time we'd spoken I'd mentioned that Peregrine had been murmuring about children and making our relationship 'more permanent'. It had seemed like an interesting idea, but I knew realistically I was deluding myself. 'Or perhaps making a living of your own.'

'Maybe my cookery book will make me a fortune!' I joked.

'Hardly, I think there are already far too many cookery books.'

'And books are an incredible waste of paper,' added Siena.

'Yes, but the trees come from self-sustainable forests, surely,' I said.

'Of course, but the amount of energy used to chop them down, pulp them and make the books that people really don't need is incredible. And the chemicals used are so toxic—'

'Can we please not start an argument. I was also going to add that your father will probably leave you something. Remember you still have your shares in the business.'

'Huh, blood money,' huffed Siena.

'Anyway, nothing will be happening immediately. The sale won't be for ages, but I just thought I'd let you know.'

She glanced at her watch. 'Heavens, is that the time? I must fly to Hatchards. *The Buttonhook Compendium* has just come out and they're keeping a copy for me. If I leave now I might just get home in time for *The Archers*.'

She packed up her things and slipped into her camel cashmere coat. It was twenty years old, but you'd never know it, she looked after her clothes so beautifully. She kissed us both goodbye and was gone, leaving Siena and me to ruminate on our good fortune.

'Mary seems nice,' I ventured. I didn't really mean it, her comments about my hair colour had really put my back up. 'And she seems devoted to the children.' At least this appeared to be true.

'Yes, she's a brilliant mother. Much more patient than me.'

'So are the children all by different fathers?' I asked conversationally. The twins seemed an interesting mixture; they had quite an African look about them. Mary had mentioned during lunch that she was an enthusiastic traveller, murmuring something about the Congo, but she'd seemed reluctant to go into any more details.

'I don't think that's really any of our business,' said Siena worthily.

'No. Well, I'd better leave you to it. I'm seeing Dad tomorrow night for dinner. You should come along, he'd love to see you.'

'Yes, amazingly he actually rang yesterday and asked me, but I couldn't possibly leave Jacob behind. I still have to feed him every four hours.' I didn't dare ask when that would stop; I knew that in many parts of the undeveloped world and in fashionable left-wing circles in the developed, some mothers continued breast-feeding until the child was quite old. It seemed remarkably economical. 'I thought the best thing was for him to come here and then he could meet Mary and the kids. He'll have to find out about the situation sooner or later.'

Chapter Ten

The following evening I made my way to the Savoy where my father was waiting. He was a powerfully built, robust-looking man with dark hair that was greying around the temples. Even sitting down minding his own business he had an air of natural authority. All my school friends had been a bit scared of him, which was ridiculous because he's very fair minded and easy going, except on the rare occasions he loses his temper. That's like a volcano exploding. Tonight his mouth was set in a thin line, his square jaw looked particularly determined and his shrewd blue eyes were weary. He was drinking glumly from a large gin and tonic.

'I've just been to see your sister.' He fell silent and drained his glass.

'So you've met Mary and her brood.'

'Christ, yes. It was like the United Nations in there. I kept expecting some African chieftain to come swinging in to claim one of them.' He sighed wearily. 'It's all come as a bit of a shock, I can tell you. She said you'd been round with your mother yesterday. What did she make of it?'

'Oh, she took it in her stride.' A waiter materialized, Dad ordered a steak and chips while I skimmed the menu quickly, settling on a seaweed salad. He shuddered. 'I don't know how you can eat that rabbit food.'

'Rabbits don't eat seaweed,' I pointed out mildly.

'I don't think Mary thought a lot of me. We had quite an argument about how I could justify the fact that one per cent of the population owned eighty per cent of the world's wealth.'

'What did you say?'

'I said it was a disgrace. Which was why I voted Labour at the last election. What I can't stand is people like what's her name—'

'Mary.'

'Mary, whingeing on about the iniquities of capitalism when they're quite happy to live off its proceeds. I mean she doesn't work, she gets free health care, schooling, you name it, and where does she think the money for it comes from? Idiots like me, that's who. It's as plain as a pikestaff. They live in a dream world, these people.'

'Besides, who else would employ Ted Sprout?'

'Yes! Who indeed.'

Ted Sprout was married to Marigold Sprout, the terrible gossip who worked in the canteen. Ted was the company union leader and spent his life unsuccessfully trying to persuade the other workers to join the union.

'Has anyone joined his union yet?'

'Well, he called a general meeting last Thursday but nobody turned up.' He chuckled.

'What did you do to them, break their legs at the knee with one of your pikestaffs?'

'Nothing like that. They know what side their bread's buttered. There've been a lot of layoffs in the industry, exports are down, and the pound is too strong. I pay the best wages in the county, they get free health care, car insurance, meals. They don't get that on the dole, I can tell you. The trouble is now that the company's got so big I don't know half of them any more.' He sipped his claret absently.

'But why do you do so much consultancy work?'

'Christ knows. It's not for the money, that's for sure. No, I've been lucky and it's a way of paying my dues. But I'm cutting down on all that now. I've been busy setting up a fund for the company employees. I won't be around forever and I want to make sure that whoever takes the place over when I'm gone looks after our people. The last thing I want is one of these corporate raider fat cats coming along and getting rid of my best workers.'

He pulled out a scrumpled photo from his inside pocket and pushed it towards me. A beaming family were being hugged by Minnie Mouse at Disney World. A little girl wearing a baseball hat was carrying a sign which said 'Thank you' in large letters. They looked as if they hadn't a care in the world. I glanced at Dad for an explanation.

'You probably don't remember Mr Robinson who works in the print room?' I nodded vaguely, the name rang a bell. 'His daughter had leukaemia and the company gave him a few months off so he and his wife could stay at the hospital with her. Then we sent them off to Disney World.' I looked at the picture more closely. Beneath her smile and sassy baseball hat the young girl did indeed look wan and pale.

'She wore that cap all the time because most of her hair came out,' he said brusquely. 'They're a super family, the Robinsons. Nice people.'

I handed back the snap and he put his knife and fork over his half-eaten steak. I felt choked with emotion. The gesture was wholly altruistic. Peeling back the tough exterior one found a marshmallow interior, but the guard was dropped so rarely one sometimes forgot it existed.

'Robinson said that some employers sacked parents with ill children at the hospital because they had to take so much time off work.' He shook his head in bewilderment.

'That's very kind of you, Dad,' I said quietly.

'It's nothing. They're a great family.' He changed the subject briskly, but I could see his eyes were watery with tears. 'But enough of all this. What's going on with you and these photos?'

'Wasn't the photocopy Bridget sent you very blurred?' I asked hopefully.

'Mrs Sprout very kindly left an original copy of it on my desk yesterday evening.'

I cursed Mrs Sprout inwardly. 'It was all above board,' I explained. 'Naff Ovens asked me to model for their catalogue—'

'Not that dodgy Bolivian kitchen company? Really, Oriana! How much did they pay you?'

'Um, nothing yet. When I rang up yesterday to ask them for the money, I couldn't get through and the operator said the line had been disconnected.' I was feeling a bit churned up after the Robinson thing and I began crying, my tears falling onto my seaweed salad which began to glisten horribly. I put my fork down, my appetite had completely disappeared.

'Don't cry, Oriana,' said my father anxiously. He hated displays of emotion. 'We'll sort it out. That's what I'm here for.'

This was a very satisfactory answer and my tears dried up immediately.

'But what about this boyfriend of yours, Lord Skyrocket?'

'Skye-Rocca,' I corrected.

'Damn silly name. Anyway, what's he doing about it?'

'Nothing. He doesn't like trouble. He's Catholic,' I added uselessly.

'What is he, some sort of pansy? I had the same sort of trouble with your mother years ago. It took a bit of sorting but I got back the pictures all right. But I'm too old for that sort of caper now. At least you weren't completely in the buff like she was.'

I stifled a sob. 'There are some pictures of me naked in an oven,' I admitted. 'I don't know where they are, or who's got them. They could be *anywhere*!'

'Oh, Oriana. You always were so scatty. Ring me with all the details in the morning and I'll get the firm's lawyer to deal with it. Just don't do anything like this again, all right?'

'Well, I've given up work for the moment as I've become the chatelaine of Cheyne Castle.'

'Does it pay, this chatelaine business?'

'No,' I said frankly. 'But it's good experience for the cookery book I'm writing.'

'That'll be the day,' he laughed. 'You were never much of a writer. I'd stick to what you know.'

I shrunk into my chair. He lit a cigarette and sipped his coffee. 'I think you should give up this chatelaine nonsense and find something that pays a decent wage. You were doing all right before with your little cooking business, weren't you?'

'Scraping a living.'

'Well, we've all got to start somewhere. I'll say one thing for your mother, she was a good cook. You must get it from her.'

'Did you hear? Bertie langlaufed off so she's single again. She's thrilled about it.'

'She won't be single for long. She's a good-looking woman.'

'And she's selling her Canaletto. She's worried it might get stolen or that Bertie will try and claim half of it in the settlement.'

'Wouldn't put anything past that little Belgian bugger,' he said, examining the bill and removing a wedge of notes from his wallet.

'I was thinking that when it goes for auction you could buy it anonymously and give it back to her. It would be really nice, considering she sold the first one to buy the business for you.'

He stared at me with amazement; this sort of thought would never have occurred to him naturally, but now I'd mentioned it, surely he couldn't fail to see the poetic justice of such a gesture.

'I don't know about that,' he said. 'It must be worth a fortune.'

'Maybe a couple of big ones. But the arts market is depressed at the moment, it might not go for very much. Oh, go on, Dad. It would be tremendous gesture. And you're always saying you've been lucky and that you feel you should repay your debts.'

I could see that a seed had lodged and that it was best to leave it to germinate undisturbed.

It had been an odd evening, I reflected as the cab drove me back to Cheyne Castle. Unfortunately the cheque I had been anticipating had not materialized, but instead I had a lovely warm glow in my stomach every time I thought of the beaming family carrying their thank you banner. That was worth far more than money. Siena used to joke that our father was tighter than two coats of paint; if she knew about this sort of gesture I'm sure she would change her mind. I made a note to tell her.

My father was such a curious mixture of kindness and cruelty. Just when you thought you had him sussed he did something to take you off guard. Often I felt bewildered, sometimes I felt hurt, but tonight I felt proud. So very, very proud.

It was nice to think the best of people. It made everyone feel so good.

Despite my improving relationships with my family and the fact that I'd reached a contented modus vivendi with Peregrine I was aware that something was missing from my life. I didn't feel it fundamentally had anything to do with him or the deficiencies in our relationship, it was to do with me. I was just coasting along having a comfortable time. It was nice but it wasn't enough.

Up in my study I had reams of recipes and detailed notes about all the dinners and parties we had thrown, interspersed with amusing stories and gossip relayed. I knew I could somehow weave it all together into a novel cum recipe book but I wasn't quite sure how. I knew it was possible, and the fact that everybody said I couldn't do it was just firing my determination.

I've often read that if you put your full force behind an

idea, the universe will do all it could to see your dream come true. If that was the case, it was just a matter of time.

Chapter Eleven

All these family dramas seemed to make me feel even more creative, and I was determined to create a wonderful evening for Peregrine's brother Magnus and all the ambassadors who were coming. It would be a real challenge to see if we could get the Norwegians along to the dolphin ball.

Peregrine was taking more interest than usual in the proceedings because Magnus wanted to involve him in a business venture he was starting up in London. When I'd asked what sort of business, Peregrine had mumbled something about 'business and blubber', and remained tight-lipped. I hoped it wasn't anything unethical to do with whales that might conflict with Pandora's and my secret agit prop mission, but suspected it might be.

We decided on a dinner party for twenty people and Mr Button was furnished with a strict guest list on the door. The press always found out about bashes at Cheyne Castle and often passed the information on to Shmooze Associates, London's top PR agency, who had access to the world's A-list celebs.

Occasionally, if a luminary was at a loose end in London he would be informed by Shmooze about the most happening events that evening in Cool Britannia, and as Cheyne Castle rated along with the Met Bar and Annabel's, some very interesting people dropped in. So we rather liked gate-crashers. The only drawback was that because our first party had descended into chaos very quickly, with members of the public being sucked in off the street in the tidal wave of bona fide guests, we had had to operate some kind of door policy. That meant Mr Button was always very much *in situ* at the door. The trouble was that the TV in his mobile home was permanently programmed to the Ivana Trump Shopping Channel and he wasn't a great reader, so celebs had to be very famous indeed to pass the Button Celebrity Door Test.

More than once the morning after I had fielded angry telephone calls from the terrifying Petronella who ran Shmooze Associates, complaining that the obscure door policy at Cheyne Castle had ruined her life. She was particularly livid when Mr B turned away Liam Gallagher. Mr B said he'd 'never 'eard of the bloke'. Besides, Liam Gallagher was wearing an anorak, which is something Mr B would never tolerate under any circumstances, unless they were worn by one of his heroes, like Engelbert Humperdinck or someone.

I was looking forward to meeting Magnus, who was flying in from Munich just before dinner. As he was a Finn and very well connected within the Scandinavian contingent we had invited the Finnish, Swedish and Norwegian ambassadors who had all accepted with surprising alacrity given their hectic schedules. But then, as I said, invitations to Cheyne Castle were much sought after.

I had discussed the dinner with Pandora at length and we were determined not to let this opportunity to help the Cause pass us by. We planned to do some gentle but none the less persuasive lobbying. It would be the perfect opportunity to agit prop the Norwegian ambassador in a luxurious environment. We planned to seduce him into a sense of false security with Peregrine's finest wines, my most delicious food and witty and urbane conversation. He would feel he was amongst friends. Pandora would be seated at his left, I at his right.

After the smorgasbord our charm offensive would begin. We were going to invite him, as Lord Skye-Rocca's personal guest, to attend the Kwik, Save the Whale and Dolphin ball. But of course we wouldn't mention the dolphin connection, it would just be a charity ball we were planning.

He would then be photographed by the media, who would be out in force that night. Pandora had instigated petitions and a letter-writing campaign (I had written to my MP under fifteen different names), and organized a boycott of Norwegian and Japanese products. The appearance of the ambassador might not actually change anything but at least it would stir up controversy and create publicity.

Pandora had discovered from her chums at the charity that Magnus really was a big wheel in whale blubber manufacturing. I expected him to be a dark saturnine figure, his hands practically stained with the blood of innocent mammals, but he wasn't like that at all. In fact, he was utterly charming. He arrived just before dinner and strolled into the kitchen where Mrs B and I were busy putting the finishing touches to the smorgasbord.

Mrs B visibly melted as a huge, dark man with thick unruly black hair and a wicked smile materialized in the kitchen.

'You must be the gorgeous Oriana that my brother cannot stop talking about,' he said, raising my hand to his lips and barely brushing it with dry lips. Thank goodness I'd taken the precaution of removing my rubber gloves as soon as he'd come in. Mrs Button wasn't the only one with a beating heart around here.

Surprisingly, he wasn't laden down with blubber products as one might have expected, but boxes of cloudberries and a bag of elk steaks. If I could have asked for two things from Helsinki these were what I would have asked for. Mrs Button sniffed suspiciously at the elk steaks as she put them in the fridge.

'And for you, Dorothy, I have brought your favourite thing.' I was shocked. Nobody ever addressed Mrs B by her first name. It had never even occurred to me that she had one. She gazed at him adoringly as he produced several large jars of pickled herring from his huge black bag.

'Ooh, Mr Barteskidonshin, you shouldn't!' she squealed girlishly, her small blonde head shaking with excitement.

Mrs B had a bit of a pickle fixation. She seemed to get through a jar of pickled eggs a day, and as for Branston Pickle, she and the industrial cleaners got through so much of the stuff that they had it delivered directly from the pickle factory at a substantial discount and kept it in sinister steaming vats in the basement.

'You're very kind,' I said coolly. I had to remember, this was a man who had made his money out of the suffering of innocent mammals. 'But we mustn't keep you. I'm sure you're longing to freshen up after your trip.'

'Not particularly,' said Magnus, lounging casually against the fridge. I felt myself flush disconcertingly. Luckily the industrial cleaners suddenly appeared (I often roped them in for waitressing and kitchen duties), and I was able to hand things over to them and flee upstairs.

I had half an hour before the guests were due to arrive and quickly re-did my make-up. I was unsure about what to wear but decided on my flimsy satin slip nightie dress with the marabou trim and fluffy mules. I wanted to be taken seriously and it seemed to be a lucky outfit, always heralding an excitingly successful evening for all concerned.

Tonight was no exception and things ran seamlessly apart from Magnus who had rearranged the placement so that he was sitting next to me. I could have changed it back, but I was the last one into the dining room and it would have meant reseating everyone. Plus it was terribly important that I agit prop him on the whaling issue.

I'd made elkball soup, the famous Eskimo specialty, for our starter. For once the industrial cleaners didn't trip or spill any of it on the guests – they were a bit unpredictable about soup – and this lulled me into a state of delicious calmness.

Peregrine had provided his best champagne, the conversation was urbane and civilized, it was the kind of evening we had planned meticulously and so enjoyed. Looking back, so many evenings had descended into wild revelry and drunken behaviour. Of course I enjoyed it when our guests let their hair down but it was also pleasant to enjoy sparkling conversation with cultured and educated guests. Pandora and I planned to begin our charm offensive during the cloudberry soufflé, but till then we were lulling our victims into a state of mildly inebriated contentment.

'My wife and I haven't been in London long,' said the Norwegian ambassador, politely inclining his head towards me, 'and we are amazed at the hospitality of the English.' He drained his glass gratefully.

I knew that alcohol was very expensive in Scandinavia and he was obviously catching up on lost drinking opportunities. We hadn't accounted for how much Norwegians drink and I noticed that Peregrine had to send Mr Button (who was acting as the sommelier for the evening), twice down to the cellar to replenish stocks during the soup course alone.

I had gone to tremendous trouble with the smorgasbord and spent all afternoon arranging it on the sideboard in the dining room. Trays of finely sliced sturgeon, marinated herring and smoked reindeer vied with a stunning display of home-cured gravadlax, which lay succulently on a thick layer of dill. I asked the guests to help themselves but everybody was so involved in conversation that I had to repeat myself several times. That was when the ambassador leaned over and asked if I knew that he had once been the Norwegian lap dancing champion. I didn't want to lower the tone of the proceedings so I pretended not to hear. Pandora had overheard this titbit and presumably thinking he meant tap dancing, not lap dancing, leant over flirtatiously and demanded a demonstration. I didn't think that Nars would take her up, but he gave a small roar, pushed his chair back, breaking several glasses, and began tap dancing (thank goodness I had misheard!) right there.

Everybody began clapping appreciatively and very large toasts were drunk. So large, in fact, that Peregrine had to send Mr Button downstairs *again* for more replenishments. It's always a pity to let good champagne go to waste and it's important for the hostess to get in the swing of things so I drained my glass and allowed Magnus to replenish it for me. It was then I noticed his huge wrists – they looked as if he'd spent a lifetime chopping down trees! Our eyes locked for a second, then I glanced down at my empty soup plate and remembered no one had had any smorgasbord.

'Magnus,' I pleaded helplessly, 'no one will listen and the smorgasbord will be getting hot, could you make an announcement?'

'For you, anything,' he said chivalrously, getting to his feet and telling everyone to help themselves. There was much backslapping amongst the Scandinavians and another toast, then everybody got to their feet and made their way unsteadily to the buffet table.

The Finnish ambassador, overcome at the sight of reindeer antler stew, an obscure Finnish delicacy, took the opportunity to do an impromptu Finnish folk dance, which would have been fine but he was still carrying his plate full of stew. Of course he dropped it, but no one noticed. Luckily the industrial cleaners were still downstairs so I dashed down to tell them. They're awfully good on stains, and provided they get to them early enough can remove just about anything.

I was rushing upstairs from the basement, still wearing my mules, when I caught sight of a dark, hulking figure on the stairs. It was very dark but I knew who it was.

'Phew, I just caught them before they left. That's a stroke of luck,' I wittered nervously, squeezing past him deliciously on the narrow staircase. This was difficult because he took up most of it and there was a definite sizzle as my nightie dress brushed against his black jacket. I don't think any woman could have resisted when he grasped both my wrists and pinned me against the wall, separating for a tantalizing moment as the industrial cleaners steamed up the stairs between us, laden down with buckets and bottles of their obscure homemade stain-removing fluids.

'Oh, Oriana, I have been longing to make love to you since I first saw you in the kitchen, so cold, so cool, so English . . .' He pressed me against the wall and kissed me and for a moment I was lost, my head spinning with lust, fear, and the pungent aroma of the stain-removing fluids which had a tendency to linger for many hours. It was an intoxicating combination.

There was a sudden crash above, as if someone had had an accident. I wriggled away from Magnus, my duties as chatelaine temporarily in the ascendant.

'I better go and see what's wrong,' I murmured, extricating myself regretfully. I knew from experience that things might develop into anarchy at any time. The signs were all there. And Pandora would be waiting for me to begin agit propping the ambassadors. They might never be this mellow again.

I couldn't resist looking back at Magnus over my shoulder. He had raised his hands in an irresistible gesture of gentlemanly defeat but there was no mistaking the distinctly ungentlemanly look of pure lust that passed between us. For a split second I remained motionless as a frisson of excitement and guilt flooded through me, then I escaped up the stairs and into the dining room.

The cleaners had done a sterling job on the reindeer antler stew but their stain-removing fluids, though magical in their ability to remove even the most deeply embedded stain, were even more odorous than usual. Either that or the drains were playing up. I had once asked what the magical ingredient was, but they had just cackled and said it was for them to know and me to guess. But luckily one of the ambassadors was smoking some exotic-smelling cigarettes, which soon covered up the smell.

Pandora was busy winking at me so I sat down next to her. Nars appeared to be experiencing a Nordic gloom and was staring intensely at the ceiling in between frantic puffs of one of the Swedish ambassador's cigarettes. I glanced over at Peregrine. He was having an animated discussion with one of the lady ambassadresses, who bore a spooky resemblance to the blonde girl in Abba. Catching me glancing at him he toasted me with an empty glass

'Darling, you'll never guess. Eva is the leading authority on Elias Lönrott, Finland's greatest playwright. It's an amazing coincidence.' He turned to her. 'You see, I studied Finnish nineteenth-century literature at Cambridge.'

'Ask her if she sings too,' whispered Pandora. 'She looks just like the girl in Abba.'

'She can't be, can she?' I whispered back.

'No, it's impossible. Anyway, all Swedes look the same. Look at Arne.' We glanced at the Swedish ambassador. 'He's a dead ringer for Björn Borg.'

'My God. So he is.'

Nars suddenly shifted out of his reverie. 'We Swedes are very physical people,' he said confusingly. A moment ago he had been Norwegian. What was going on?

'Ahem.' Dear oh dear. Was I the only person around here thinking any sense? 'Mr Ambassador,' I inquired politely, 'I'm probably being a little obtuse, but I was under the impression that you were from Norway.'

'Yes, we thought you were the Norwegian ambassador,' said Pandora, looking worried. I knew she was concerned that she had wasted the evening schmoozing the wrong man. Having softened him up with drink (the strange cigarettes were a bonus), she was probably preparing to agit prop him any moment.

'Yes, yes, it is all the same,' he said mystically, taking another puff.

'So you are the Norwegian ambassador?'

'YES, I AM THE NORWEGIAN AMBASSADOR! WHAT DO YOU WANT? A MEDAL?' he bellowed crossly. Phew, that was all right.

'OK, I was only asking,' said Pandora.

'I'm sorry, girls. I've just had a difficult day with the

anti-whaling protesters. They stormed the Embassy at five p.m., and one of them threw a herring on me.' Oh dear. Our approach would have to be subtler. He resumed his sad gaze on the ceiling.

'Peregrine is organizing a ball in two weeks,' I plunged in. 'We'd love it if you and your wife would join our party. We're going to meet here for champagne, then go on to the Grosvenor House for dinner and dancing—'

'Then we'll go on to Annabel's for more dancing. And Magnus is going to come too,' said Pandora hopefully. Magnus had edged his way round the table and was squeezing into the elegant Louis XVI chair. I hadn't noticed till now but his legs were like tree trunks too!

'Where Pandora goes, I shall follow,' he said, reaching beneath the table and stroking my stocking tops with his big hand.

'So we can take that as a yes then,' said Pandora firmly.

'But of course.'

I was lulled into silence as Magnus had put his hand between my legs. I really thought I was going to faint with desire. Then Peregrine, dragging himself away from the discussion on Finnish nineteenth-century literature, stood up.

'I'd like to make a toast to Oriana, for her charm, her beauty, and her loyalty in standing by me in what has been, by anybody's standards, an extremely stressful period in my business life.'

I smiled in what I hoped was a loyal sort of way as Magnus continued his exploration of my inner thigh. I couldn't understand the bit about the business stress. OK, selling mad Uncle Rupert's zoo had run into a few complications when the Hollywood mogul who had wanted to buy it had discovered that the tailless cats were not in fact Manx cats but stray cats who happened not to have tails (not surprising when you think about how many Chinese restaurants there are in the area), but Peregrine's brilliant lawyer, Mr Houdini, had sorted everything out most satisfactorily, even managing to offload the incontinent sloths, which was a stroke of genius. I couldn't understand what he was banging on about at all.

Everybody drained their glasses then started thumping the table, while Mr Button rushed round refilling glasses. Pandora shouted, 'Speech, Oriana, speech!'

I took a deep breath for strength and surreptitiously removed Magnus's hand. I was going to say something profound about Anglo-Norwegian relations – you know, mention the Christmas tree they put in Trafalgar Square, that sort of thing, but it suddenly seemed a bit complicated. Instead I asked, 'Anybody for some cloudberry soufflé?'

This caused some serious table banging. Nars began whooping with a kind of drugged excitement, Magnus made a toast to cloudberries in general, and the ambassadress who looked like the girl in Abba began reciting an ode to cloudberries by Elias Lönrott. It seemed like a good moment to slip downstairs to check on the soufflé.

Delicious smells were wafting upstairs and I crossed my fingers that it was going to be a great success. I'd folded in the egg whites earlier and instructed Mrs B to put it in the oven at 9.45.

'It's risin' nicely, Miss Oriana,' said Mrs B as I rushed into the kitchen. 'I was just coming to fetch you.'

I peered into the oven at the frothy mixture rising inside. It was *à point*.

'OK, Mrs B, we're ready to go. You take up the rear with the hot plates.' Mrs B and I were a great team when it came to soufflés; we'd done so many that we had it down to a fine art.

'Righty-ho.' She quickly peeled off her Marigolds, re-adjusted her wig and scuttled over to the hotplate where the fine Limoges china plates were warming up. I whipped open the oven door and grasped the soufflé dish and dashed upstairs to the dining room.

The room was literally shaking with revelry. I pushed the door open with a flourish. No one took a a blind bit of notice, they were all singing Finnish folk songs very loudly while Magnus was somehow balancing on the table pretending to conduct an orchestra using a cigar as a baton. Nars had collapsed into the remains of his smorgasbord and Pandora was discussing important matters earnestly with the Finnish ambassador.

'Ahem,' I coughed pointedly.

' 'Ere! PAY ATTENTION, YOU LOT,' cried Mrs B, steaming up behind me and chucking the plates onto the table with a crash. There was silence.

'Ah. It's Oriana with the soufflé,' said Peregrine. Rather stating the obvious, I thought.

Things got a bit calmer after that with the Scandinavian contingent ooing and aahhing over the soufflé, which had risen beautifully. Nars poured freshly whipped cream, lightly scented with vanilla and lavender honey, into the frothy concoction and took a mouthful. He sighed happily. 'Ambrosial. It melts in the mouth like a warm body in the snow.'

After coffee Magnus dragged everyone off to Annabel's. I quite wanted to go but Peregrine wanted me to stay and analyse the evening with him. We always loved mulling over our parties.

'I think Eva rather fancied me,' said Peregrine, looking at himself contentedly in the mirror. 'It was all a great success, but it always amazes me how much Scandinavians drink. When they next come round I shall have to get some plonk in. They don't taste it, you know, they just swallow it.' He sighed. 'The cellar's utterly depleted.'

'I was surprised that they can all make it for drinks next week.'

'Oh, Scandinavians are terribly flexible. They have an ability to make themselves free whenever they choose. They probably have six dreary cocktail parties on that evening so they'll send a consul and just come to ours.' He combed his hair carefully and examined himself in the mirror. 'Not a bad head of hair for a forty-year-old.'

'Forty-one,' I pointed out helpfully. Really, Peregrine could be so self-satisfied.

'I must just ring the States and find out how negotiations are getting on. You don't mind, darling? Touch of the Bill Spicers . . .'

I shrugged irritably. How Peregrine could possibly compare the sale of his stupid cat zoo with my father's multimillion-pound business, I couldn't begin to understand.

'It's Lord Skye-Rocca. I'd like to talk to Mr Doppelganger. Yes, well, do try. He'll take my call, I'm sure.'

Sadly he didn't.

'Idiotic secretary. She didn't seem to realize who I was,' said Peregrine, putting down the receiver crossly.

'Magnus was very helpful.' I was eager to dissect the evening and talk about Magnus. 'Mrs B absolutely melted when he gave her those pickled herrings.' I wondered if Peregrine had noticed the flirtation. Maddeningly, he was so self-absorbed he hadn't.

'Yes. Women love him. I told him to stay away from you, though.'

I remembered the feel of Magnus's big hand on my thigh and shivered with frustration, remembering that I hadn't had normal sex for six months. I had thought my drive had disappeared, but Magnus seemed to have reawakened it. It was too maddening.

Peregrine got into bed beside me and caressed my breast. Against my will I felt a great surge of desire. I put a tentative hand on his thigh, which I'd learnt was an occasional erogenous zone and massaged it gently. To my shame he pushed away my hand and scrabbled beneath his side of the bed for his eye mask and earplugs.

'Damn, I can't find my earplugs, I'll have to sleep with my shooting helmet on.' This was a set of headphones that one wore to reduce the noise on shoots. Occasionally when we were on a shooting weekend and Mrs B had forgotten to pack his earplugs he would sleep in this contraption. It wasn't very attractive but he has a horror of any kind of noise pollution. (I know it's odd, OK, but we all have peculiar habits.) But tonight, with champagne and lust swilling unsettlingly around my aroused body, I could take no more.

Jumping out of bed I stormed over to the chest of drawers, picked up the shooting headset contraption and dumped it on the bed.

'Here, keep your bloody shooting helmet thing, I hope it gives you more pleasure than I do!' I began picking up my clothes from the floor and flinging them on in the order I had taken them off. Unfortunately I had acquired Peregrine's messy habits, and the industrial cleaners were so efficient that they tidied everything up after us.

Peregrine sat up wearily in bed and watched me for a moment. He seemed utterly bemused.

'Darling, what on earth are you doing? You can't go out now. It's too late.'

'It's not too late. I'm only twenty-eight. I'm going out, you can't stop me!' I stood for a moment fully clothed in my flimsy dress and mules, clutching my evening bag and car keys, wishing he would forcibly restrain me. I had no desire to go out and had nowhere to go.

'Well, if you must go out remember to lock the door behind you. I can't hear a thing with my headphones on.'

'I'm going to find Magnus!' I shouted desperately, longing for a display of jealous energy, longing for anything but this awful bemused indifference. I wanted him to pin me against the wall and say, 'You're not going anywhere!'

'Please, darling, don't be irrational. I've never seen you behave so childishly. It's rather worrying.'

'Oh, bugger off!' I stormed out of the room and into the kitchen to pick up my car keys, catching sight of a large cauldron of congealing moose stock on the sideboard. That would be just the ticket. I picked it up with both hands and staggered back into the bedroom. Peregrine was lying on his back wearing his headphones and eye mask. Without further ado I tipped the murky brown liquid all over him. Pieces of moose bone, reindeer antlers, carrot tops, wizened leeks and other obscure bits and pieces that Mrs B, the industrial cleaners and I had added throughout the week embedded themselves in Peregrine's hair and floated horribly on top of the crisp white linen sheets.

Peregrine shot into an upright position in panic, bits of meat and jellified liquid draining off him into the bed. He tried to pull off his headphones and his eye mask at the same time but just succeeded in getting very tangled up.

'What the hell is going on?' he yelled after me, presumably unable to see or hear anything, but by that time I was slipping out of the house and into the night.

I unlocked my car and glanced into the basement. The sounds of Barry Manilow wafted upwards and I could see shadowy figures dancing around within and candles flickering. An occasional cackle of laughter emanated from the gloomy interior. The industrial cleaners were obviously having a late night.

I sat in my car and heaved a sigh of relief. Freedom at last! It was over with Peregrine, there was no *way* he'd take me back after my behaviour. I had burned my boats, but I regretted nothing. '*Je ne regrette rien*,' I cried dramatically out of the window, causing two old men trysting happily on the Embankment to look up in shock and scuttle off nervously.

But where to go now? Perhaps I should go round to Pandora's flat; I still had my key. I sat and thought for a moment then glanced at my watch. It was 1 a.m. Magnus, Pandora and the others would still be at Annabel's. I would drive over and meet them.

I quickly re-applied some make-up, brushed my hair and dabbed some scent on my wrists. I thought of Magnus, sitting at the bar and smoking one of his huge illegal cigars and shivered. I was ready to go and the night was still young!

Chapter Twelve

Annabel's was throbbing when I arrived fifteen minutes later. Standing for a moment outside I heard several glasses smash and distant strains of the Finnish national anthem wafting up from the basement. Thank goodness, it sounded as if the Finns were still very much in situ.

I tripped downstairs past the doorman who doffed his hat politely. Good evening, Miss Oriana.' I was grateful that he didn't ask where Peregrine was. The staff here were very discreet. I had come here often with Peregrine so people knew me. I had an overwhelming surge of gratitude. Peregrine had literally opened so many doors for me. I hoped the moose stock wouldn't leave a frightful smell. The industrial cleaners would certainly have their work cut out, but I wasn't too concerned. It was the sort of challenge they relished.

I bumped into Pandora coming out of the cloakroom. The agit propping was obviously having a stimulating effect on her and, despite the lateness of the hour, her blue eyes shone and her silky blonde hair gleamed in the subdued lighting.

'Oriana,' she said, taking in my wild hair and uneven make-up. 'You're looking excitingly dishabille. Have you been caught in a fire? I thought you and Peregrine were going to have a romantic evening.'

'His pills just aren't working. Look, can we go back into the ladies'? I need to talk to you before I greet the Finns – top secret.'

Pandora went pink with excitement. 'Of course,' she

whispered. I glanced around to check we weren't being followed as we scuttled to the sanctuary of the ladies' loo.

'I've left Peregrine!' I whispered dramatically.

'Where?'

'At home of course! I just couldn't stand it any more, he treats me like a sister—'

'Without even a glimpse of any incest at all?'

'Not a glimmer. I thought tonight because he was in a specially confident mood, admiring his hair and trying to make tycoony phone calls, that the new pills he's been taking were renewing his vigour, but they didn't seem to make any difference at all.'

'So what did you do?'

'Emptied a vat of congealed moose stock on his head and came here. I did something else too, I snogged Magnus on the stairs. I just couldn't resist. I've got this awful feeling that he's my type.'

'Sort of foreign, brutal looking and smokes illegal cigars type?' said Pandora. 'I rather thought he might be. He likes you too.'

'Does he?' I asked breathlessly. 'In what way?'

'Well, I don't think he's interested in you for your mind.'

I could have danced for joy.

'But, of course, he's against everything we believe in.' I said, nervously.

'All's fair in love and war. Maybe you can succeed where others have failed. You'll have your work cut out though, he seems to be on intimate terms with most of the women here.'

'We'll see about that,' I said firmly, rearranging my embonpoint to maximum advantage and spraying myself liberally with Lust, Pandora's heavily pheromone-laden scent that she had specially imported from China.

We made our way past the attendant, who was fortunately asleep, and into the bar. Half-finished bottles of aquavit and obscure Finnish liqueurs lay dotted about. I spotted the ambassadors and some of their cronies collapsed on the sofa, while the barman was slumped on a stool behind the bar with his head in his hands. The poor fellow looked quite worn out.

'But where is Magnus?' It would be too disappointing to have got myself pheromoned up for nothing.

'Let's see if he's dancing,' suggested Pandora.

We peered into the next room where in the louche scarlet gloom we could just make out Magnus's brutal form in the distance. He was deep in conversation with a small swarthy man, possibly of Middle Eastern extraction. The swarthy man was handing Magnus a large box of cigars when he must have sensed us looking at him. He glanced up and waved us over. We threaded our way nervously across the crowded room until we reached their table.

'Pandora and Oriana. What an unexpected pleasure.' His lips brushed my hand and a volt of electricity surged through my body. 'We all thought you had gone to bed. I'm so glad you decided to get up again. I would like you to meet a very special friend of mine, Ahmas, who is in London very briefly. Ahmas has very kindly given me a superb present for my birthday.' Ahmas smiled cagily and went through a complicated routine with one of the cigars before lighting it, while Magnus poured us some champagne.

It seemed rather surreal to be sitting with this probable Lebanese arms dealer and my boyfriend's half-brother, whom I had snogged hours ago on the back staircase at Cheyne Castle, as if nothing had happened. The mellow aroma of the cigar and the delicious champagne instilled a sort of dream-like reality. I wasn't feeling my sensible self at all and it seemed the most natural thing in the world to slip my stocking-clad foot between Magnus's massive ankles and rub them seductively.

'And what line of business are you in?' Pandora was politely asking the diminutive Lebanese arms dealer.

'Import export,' he replied gruffly, his face totally obscured by cigar smoke. In fact, an unkind person might have said that the cigar was bigger than he was. He didn't seem in the mood for elaboration and fortunately at that moment 'Dancing Queen' by Abba came on and Pandora was whisked off to dance by one of the ambassadors. It was hard to tell which one it was, in the louche lighting the Scandinavians all looked like Björn Borg and were utterly indistinguishable. All apart from Magnus, who didn't look remotely like Björn Borg, with his thick dark hair and olive skin. I remembered what Peregrine had told me about his mother's possible exotic Alaskan lumberjack ancestry and shivered. Magnus would make a great lumberjack.

'And so what have you done with my poor brother?' Magnus was murmuring in my ear.

'I left him at home. We had a bit of a row,' I explained gingerly. I had no desire to explain why, it wouldn't do my *femme fatale* image any good at all.

'Well, I shall just have to make sure that you come to no harm myself.'

'Yes, Berkeley Square is horribly dangerous at night,' I murmured, snuggling up to him, thinking that nothing would be nicer than being rescued by him from a crowd of marauding strangers and being whisked away to a luxurious hotel. Then he reached over quite suddenly and kissed me lightly. His skin smelt deliciously of cigars and aftershave, and some indefinable masculine scent that has yet to be bottled.

'I've wanted to do that ever since I saw that picture of you in the paper spilling out of your dressing gown.'

I was dimly aware of the Lebanese arms dealer shuffling off in a cloud of smoke, presumably feeling a little *de trop*. Magnus kissed me again passionately. My head was spinning so much that I rested it against the scarlet banquette, loving the feel of his huge thighs pressed against mine.

'Come back to my hotel for a drink,' he said hoarsely. I pretended to consider this option when I knew that it was a foregone conclusion.

'Um . . .' I paused, feigning some doubt and confusion.

'Oh, come on. You haven't lived until you've tasted a Don Julia.'

'All right then. Just the one.'

Magnus got up surprisingly steadily considering how much he'd drunk and led me firmly out through the dark crowded interior and into the night. It was freezing cold and beginning to drizzle. Berkeley Square was deserted. It was a relief to be with someone as the bleakness of my situation was beginning to seep through the haze of champagne. I was completely homeless on this dank cold night and I didn't think twice about going back to Magnus's hotel. Besides, I had always wanted to see the Humple.

The Humple was rivetingly minimal. In fact, it was so mimimal that the taxi had considerable trouble finding it, despite being set in its own square, Humple Square in throbbing Notting Hill.

The lobby was completely white with a splash of green cleverly provided by the picture of a little green man on the fire escape sign. Apparently Corianda Angelica had spent months making sure the right shade of white was used and her trouble had obviously paid off as the Humple was now a mecca to the chic and fashionable. I was very impressed that Magnus had secured a room.

When we eventually arrived, Magnus cracked open a bottle of champagne from the mini bar and poured it smoothly into two glasses. Tilting my face towards his he kissed me passionately. It seemed the most natural thing in the world when he shrugged off his black jacket, peeled off my stockings and pulled me beside him onto the bed. It had been so long since I'd been with a man who knew what he was doing, it felt absolutely wonderful.

I was getting blissfully carried away when he suddenly began fiddling around my back passage. I removed his hand firmly. I was a little drunk, but not *that* drunk.

'Please let me, Oriana. You'll love it, it's wonderful.' The only time I'd given this part of my body any consideration was to vaguely wonder if colonic irrigation led to serious weight loss. Besides, wasn't it illegal?

Realizing this was a no-go area he thankfully gave up and we resumed our blissful rolling around while Magnus murmured exciting ideas in my ear. I was a bit shocked by some of them; the Finns obviously made exciting use of their long, dark nights, that was for sure. Eventually, exhausted, I sank limply into his arms while he stroked my hair gently and kissed my forehead. Thus entwined, reassured by the feel of his strong arms wrapped around me, I soon fell into a deep sleep.

I woke up horribly early the next morning, longing to go to the loo and feeling dreadful. I wished I could just slip out; I had no desire to be caught dishevelled and hungover in the brutal early-morning light. Unfortunately, to get out of bed I had to disentangle myself from Magnus and climb over him as the bed was against the wall.

I successfully extricated myself and was hotfooting it into the bathroom when I fell into a table, cunningly positioned by a door. Flailing, I accidentally flicked a light switch, which activated the floor to ceiling television screen next to the bed. I appeared to have tuned into some sort of horrible Finnish or Hungarian (I can never tell the difference, the two languages sound identical to me) porn channel; judging by all the unintelligible guttural grunting going on.

I flung myself desperately towards the remote control button hanging from the ceiling, pressing the first digit I could find, and a giant-sized Larry King beamed into the room. CNN! Too horrible for words!

The din had woken up Magnus who reached out and pulled me towards him and kissed me passionately. But it was impossible to concentrate with Larry King cackling away right in front of us.

'I must switch him off,' I mumbled between kisses.

'No, I like him,' murmured Magnus.

'No, I must go! I've got to give a friend a lift to the airport!' I cried desperately, scrambling off the bed and searching for my clothes, retrieving bits of unappetizing underwear from beneath the bed. My waist-clinching knickers, though most effective, had a depressing utilitarian wartime look about them and I stuffed them surreptitiously into my mac pocket. But I could only find one of my self-propelling stay-up stockings – I didn't want Magnus's last impression of me to be white goosepimpled legs. Luckily he found the other one beneath his jacket and handed it to me. It was inside out and the rubber tubing round the top which gripped the thigh preventing it from falling down was clearly visible.

'What's this?' He fingered the rubber curiously.

'It's my self-propelling stay-up stocking,' I explained, wishing that I'd worn the sexy lingerie that Peregrine had been so indifferent to.

He insisted on escorting me to a taxi. Outside on the quiet street he placed a big hand on my neck, steering me towards the Brompton Road. I was feeling dreadful and just longing to get back to Pandora's flat and have a bath.

'You seemed to enjoy yourself last night,' said Magnus.

'Oh yes. It was wonderful,' I replied, skimming the road for a taxi.

'I love the noise you make when you come,' he went on.

I shrank into myself. The last thing I wanted was an in-depth analysis of last night in the brutal light of day.

'I can't wait to come in your mouth,' he continued. The line the conversation was taking was making me extremely uncomfortable. 'Would you like that?'

'Yes, it sounds very nice.' I was squirming inside. The cheek of it! I hardly knew the man.

At last a taxi appeared and I began jumping around waving my arms about in a desperate bid to flag it down. I now knew what it felt like to be stuck on a desert island and see a plane fly past. I couldn't bear the thought of talking about blow jobs for a second longer. It was horribly sordid. The taxi stopped and Magnus handed me in.

'Will you ring me at the Humple this afternoon?' he asked.

'Yes, of course.' I smiled politely and kissed him goodbye. 'Thank you for a wonderful evening, Magnus. I had a great time.' He slammed the door.

Ten minutes later the taxi dropped me off at Pandora's flat and I hobbled miserably upstairs clutching my mules. I was beginning to feel a bit sore, my parts had probably shrunk from lack of use. Also my ankle was a bit painful from falling into the table, but I didn't think I'd done any lasting damage.

It was good to return to the Mother Ship, I thought, letting myself into the flat. There was something very soothing about the view of Peter Jones from my window. Of course I'd miss the river and Mrs B, but the bliss of sleeping alone again! I was obviously destined to be single forever.

I had probably blown it with Magnus (not literally, you understand). I should never have leapt into bed with him, he couldn't have had any respect for me at all, otherwise he wouldn't have bombarded me with unsavoury suggestions. No, to him I was just another good-time girl, another notch on his well-worn bedpost.

The flat was silent and Pandora's room was closed. She must still be sleeping, hopefully alone; it would be too embarrassing if she had brought one of the Scandinavians back.

It would have been out of character, admittedly; Pandora didn't usually get up to that sort of caper, but last night had been a full moon in raunchy Scorpio (according to yesterday's *Evening Standard* which she had left open at the horoscopes) and, like me, not fully in possession of her faculties. Maybe I could blame this astrological aberration for my potentially raunchy experience last night. Anyway, the Scandinavians were all married, though they seemed to have a very *laissez faire* attitude as far as that sort of thing went.

I made myself a mug of hot water and lemon juice to

flush away all the alcoholic toxins rushing around my body (shutting the stable door after the horse has bolted, I know), and ran myself a long, hot Badedas bath. It was a blissful relief to feel clean again.

I thought about last night. The numbness was wearing off now and worry was seeping in. We hadn't used a condom! Had I caught something? I would have to go to the doctor for a test. I made ripples in the water with my hand nervously. Reality was beginning to seep through the hangover and asking sensible questions that I would have to answer.

I got out of the bath feeling very sleepy. Clutching a towel round me I made my way to my old room. I decided to have a quick nap then go round to Peregrine's to pick up my stuff. Lying down on the comfortable and familiar double bed, I sighed contentedly and immediately fell into a deep, exhausted sleep.

I woke up several hours later feeling depressed after a horrible dream where I'd had indifferent sex with an anonymous stranger who insisted on wearing a plastic bag over his head. It reminded me horribly of the Magnus episode. If only he had worn a bag over his balls not his head, I would be spared this ghastly worry.

'I'm never ever going to have sex again,' I muttered grimly, jumping out of bed, eager to share my angst with Pandora. I was feeling increasingly confused and worried. Weren't anal excitements enjoyed exclusively between homosexuals? Was Magnus a switch hitter? It was all most disturbing.

The telephone interrupted my miserable musings. It was Pandora.

'Oriana, thank goodness you're back. I've just remembered that Georgie's coming round in a minute to give me a valuation of the flat. Could you let her in for me?' Georgie was a friend of ours who had just set up her own estate agency after eight years working for the ache-makingly exclusive Lucreforole-Rope.

'Of course. I had no idea you were thinking about selling the flat, though.'

'I hadn't until yesterday, but I was flicking through *Condé Nast Traveller* and I suddenly got this urge to unfetter myself and push off. But I haven't decided anything, I just want to see what Georgie thinks the place is worth.'

'I see. OK, I'll let her in,' I replied weakly as the impact of Pandora's worldly goods disposal flickered around my hungover brain uncertainly. I retired back to bed feeling even more depressed. I was homeless, manless and careerless. What on earth was I going to do? Pulling the bedcovers over my head I shut my eyes, trying to blank out my fears. A few minutes later the doorbell rang and I leapt out of bed, pinched my cheeks and ran my fingers through my hair in a desperate attempt to appear with-it and let Georgie in.

'Oriana, how are you? I wasn't expecting to see you until the Whale and Dolphin ball. Did Pandora tell you, I'm taking a whole table,' said Georgie as she burst through the door, a mass of dark curls and energy, talking nineteen to the dozen. Georgie was a great supporter of the cause.

'Pandora's not back yet but she just rang to say she won't be long,' I explained, leading us into the hall. 'Shall I whip you round the flat and then we can have coffee?'

'Sounds perfect, I'm longing to hear your news.'

I showed her round the flat but I didn't do a good sales job. Georgie strode about purposefully, making efficient notes and enthusiastic noises. I could see she wasn't putting it on, the flat was stunning. A lump came into my throat. We'd had such good times here. If Pandora really did decide to sell, it would be the end of an era.

'So what's the market like at the moment?' I asked casually, rather hoping that she would say it was on the verge of collapsing. That would put Pandora off.

'Absolutely booming,' Georgie replied cheerfully. 'Pandora couldn't sell at a better time, I've got loads of people looking for just this sort of thing.'

'That's great,' I said, showing her the squalid broom cupboard under the stairs.

'I can't tell you how relieved I am to have left Lucreforole-Rope,' she said, moving on to the bathroom. 'Can you believe that three of the other agents were called Rupert? None of them was very bright so it caused absolute chaos. Then one of them left, which made things a bit easier, but then the boss goes and employs *another* Rupert who was even dimmer than the last one. The only qualification one really needed to work there was to have a triple-barrelled name or be called Rupert or be extremely stupid. And most of them scored on all three counts.'

'You're well out of it. You're so good you'll wipe the floor with them. So what do you think Pandora will get for the flat?'

'Half a million, no sweat. It'll walk. I can't believe that she wants to sell.'

'No, neither can I.' I felt choked with emotion. Life suddenly seemed very unstable and insecure. I led us into the kitchen and busied myself with the kettle in a vain bid to hide a tear slipping pathetically down my cheek.

'Ummmm, what's that lovely smell?' asked Georgie, glancing around the streamlined Bosch kitchen with an experienced eye.

'It's a freesia-scented candle by Jo Malone. It's meant to lighten your spirits,' I said heavily as we settled down with our coffee in the kitchen.

'Well, it doesn't seem to be working for you,' said Georgie softly, flicking back a strand of curly dark hair and fixing me with piercing grey eyes. 'What's the trouble? Have you split up with Peregrine?'

'Yes, but that's not the problem. I'm actually in a bit of a quandary because I've done something dreadful. You see, I left him after a drunken dinner party last night and then I jumped straight into bed with his brother. I only slept with him because I wanted to see the inside of the Humple. I can't even pronounce his surname!'

'So, what's the problem?'

'I was so drunk we didn't wear a condom. And he wanted to do it up the backside like a woofter and now I'm terrified he may have contaminated me with a dreadful disease!'

'Who wants to do it up the backside?' It was Pandora staggering through the door laden down with shopping.

'Magnus.' I slumped in my chair and tried to take deep breaths of the mood-enhancing candle scent.

'Ugh, how horribly traumatizing.' She shrugged off her red cashmere jacket and pulled up a kitchen chair. 'I'm so sorry I'm late, Georgie. Have you had a chance to look round?'

'Yes, Oriana's given me a full guided tour. I told her it's fabulous, we're desperate for this sort of thing at the moment. I could sell it ten times over.'

'Could you?'

'Oh, definitely.'

'Mmmmm.' Pandora stirred her coffee thoughtfully and looked at me. 'So, Oriana, where were *you* last night?'

'I was just explaining to Georgie. I had a one-night stand with Magnus at the Humple, but I have to admit that I now feel deeply ashamed.'

'So you were humping at the Humple, big deal. After all that fiddling around with Peregrine you were entitled to some action.'

'Yes I know, but I've been analysing some of his suggestions and I'm getting very worried.'

'But lots of men like doing it up the bum,' said Georgie sensibly. 'Especially single ones.'

'No surprises for guessing why *they're* still single,' I retorted.

'I've heard that Finns and Hungarians are particularly keen on it,' said Pandora.

'How do you know all this?' The subject had never been

of any interest to me before and I was amazed everybody had all this information on a subject that no one ever really talked about openly. Maybe it was time for an article in *Cosmo* about it, but if there had been one recently I wouldn't have bothered to read it. It just wasn't a subject that had really crossed my consciousness before.

Pandora shrugged. 'Just do. But I do think it's a bit of a cheek asking to do it on a first date.'

'Yes, so do I,' agreed Georgie staunchly.

The last thing I wanted was to be the object of their outraged pity. It was very demeaning. Obviously none of my other boyfriends would even have dreamt of suggesting such a thing, to them I had been a princess. This was what happened when one neglected to play by The Rules and slept with someone after four hours.

'So you don't think he's a bum bandit then?'

'Not necessarily.'

'Not necessarily? You mean he might be?'

'Well, if you're worried, go and have an Aids test.'

I stared at them both glumly. 'There's more. I examined his sponge bag and I came to the following conclusions.'

'Go ahead, Miss Marple.'

'He had this Aramis hair-thickening gel in his sponge bag. I can't see why because he has loads of hair, much more than me. And he had this delicious-smelling bubble bath that is so exclusive you can only buy it in Italy, Parma—'

'Ham?'

'No! Acqua de Parma.'

'And what else? Come on, spill the beans, old girl.' Pandora wasn't taking my concerns seriously, I could tell. It was quite reassuring.

'He didn't seem to be carrying any condoms. At least not in his sponge bag. So he obviously has a casual attitude to unprotected sex and a strongly developed female side to his nature as revealed by the selection of exquisite grooming products.'

'Oh puhleese,' said Georgie witheringly.

'Say that again,' demanded Pandora.

'What?'

'That sort of puhleese thing. I've seen it written a lot but I've never heard anyone say it.'

I wasn't in the mood for discussing phonetics. 'I'm never going to have a one-night stand ever again. It takes all the anticipation out of things.' I could see they were less gripped by this whole issue than I was and reluctantly changed the subject. 'Anyway, Pandora, the good news is that Georgie thinks the pad is worth a packet.'

'Yes, I love the way you've done it up. It's just what people like. I've got several people looking for just this sort of thing. Mainly men,' she added temptingly. I shuddered. Pandora was trying to look nonchalant.

'What sort of men exactly?' she asked casually.

'Rich ones,' replied Georgie crisply.

'Well, I was on the verge of giving Hopeless-Smug-Parker sole agency but I think you sound much better. It's so important to help one's girlfriends in their new ventures – jobs for the girls and all that.'

'And it'll be such a relief not to have Tristram Hopeless and his cronies bursting in without making an appointment when one's in the bath,' I said sensibly. I never wanted another man to see me naked ever again. Either it led to complicated sexual encounters or it didn't and that was even worse. Basically the whole relationship issue was a hornet's nest of complicated problems and best avoided.

'Oh, gosh, don't worry, I'll give you plenty of time to tart up before I drop round. You want to – I mean you want the flat to be looking its best.'

Pandora was literally shivering with anticipation so I left them to it. My hangover had faded now so I decided to slip out and refuel at Starbucks.

Chapter Thirteen

Leaving the flat, I felt my spirits lift as a brief burst of sunshine illuminated the empty street, shiny and clean after a recent downpour. Most of the neighbours disappeared to unknown destinations at the weekend, presumably to give their massive Landcruisers some purpose in life, leaving the streets safe for die-hard townies like Pandora and me.

I meandered along Sloane Avenue towards the Fulham Road shopping frenzy that surrounds the half-mile radius of the Conran Shop. I paused for a moment in front of Sam De Teran's ski-wear shop. The window display consisted entirely of a huge colour poster of a stunning girl skiing down a mountain, her blonde hair streaming over her shoulders, glancing behind her nervously as a man pursued her in the distance, balancing a box of Milk Tray chocolates on a ski pole. She was obviously longing to be caught and was just going through the motions of escape. Perhaps she had read The Rules too. I bet she wouldn't leap into bed with a man after four hours, I thought sadly.

Lured by the poster, I wandered into the shop. It was a haven of escapism. Blue fir trees had been sprayed with snow and huge pictures of snow-covered chalets nestling in alpine forests lined the walls. I fingered a skin-tight pastel-blue ski suit reverently and tried on the matching furry blue hat.

'That's our Lady Penelope range,' said the svelte assistant. 'D'you want to try it on?' The Lady Penelope link was just too much. It was karmic. I couldn't resist such a direct association with my heroine from childhood. I bet her admirers didn't ask to do it up the bum, I thought mournfully, they'd have more respect. Tears pricked behind my eyelids. Maybe if I tried on the suit I would absorb some of her sang froid.

The suit fitted like a glove, transforming me into an expert skier and *femme fatale*. The Milk Tray man just wouldn't stand a chance. I slipped the hat on. It complemented the suit perfectly, as I knew it would. The ensemble begged me to take it away to Gstaad where it would fly down mountains and sit elegantly in the most chic mountain restaurants from Verbier to St Moritz. Such an outfit would, I was sure, utterly change my life and lead me to new and exciting destinations.

'Wow!' said the assistant flatteringly, peering into the changing room. 'You look fabulous! Do you want to see yourself in the big mirror?'

I sashayed out into the shop and she led me to a large mirror embarrassingly near the window.

'Are you a model?' she asked kindly.

'Gosh, no!' I laughed, then remembered the Naff Ovens experience. 'Actually I have done a bit, but not for a while.'

'I just ask because the *Daily Mail* are running a piece on chalet girls tomorrow and they suddenly decided they wanted to take a picture of the shop. They say they haven't got time for us to call in a professional model, but as you're here looking fabulous he's bound to take some pictures of you.'

'What fun!' I said excitedly.

'I'm afraid we couldn't pay you, but we could do a deal on the ski outfit if you wanted to buy it?'

It was fate. I was meant to own it. The only trouble was that I could barely ski, so where on earth could I wear such a divine creation?

At that moment the photographer appeared in a tearing hurry.

'Sorry to rush yer, love, but I've just had a tip-off from Heathrow. The Spice Girls are flying in this afternoon.'

'No probs,' said the assistant confidently. 'We've organized a model wearing something from our exclusive new range. I suggest we take some pictures of – what's your name?' she whispered, giggling.

'Oriana.'

'Of Oriana, outside next to the fir trees.'

The photographer looked me up and down and grinned. 'You any good at climbing trees, love?'

Oddly enough I had been a leading member of the Tree Climbing Group at school and well known for my ability to shimmy up and down trees at a moment's notice. 'Well, yes, actually, I used to be a member of the Tree Climbing Group at . . .' but they had lost interest and had dashed outside the shop to set up.

Of course my vanity was immediately punished when the two of them insisted that I climb into the tree so just my face was peeking out. Luckily the branches were quite strong so they bore my weight but the pine was very scratchy and dug into my stomach very painfully. Still, it would make a lovely shot.

A crowd of interested onlookers had gathered to watch and people in cars were slowing down and pointing at me. It was quite disconcerting.

'Smashin',' said the photographer, getting quite carried away. 'Now, love, we're going to need to get you a bit higher in the tree. The editor's gonna love this,' he said to the assistant who, thrilled at the possibility of increased coverage, was jumping up and down in her fashionable wedge heels.

They both helped to peel me out of the tree.

' 'Ere, love, you get on my shoulders and I'll give you a leg up.'

'Yes, you're terribly slim, you can sit on top of the tree like an alpine fairy!' suggested the assistant, looking at the spindly branches hopefully.

'Um, well, I'm not sure that's a very good—'

'Can someone give us a hand?' the photographer interrupted, appealing to several tall men who had come to gawp at the proceedings.

Before I could protest several had shot out to be of assistance. Carried away with the spirit of the thing and inspired to ridiculous attempts of courage by my new outfit, I climbed onto the shoulders of the tallest man who propelled me into the top echelons of the tree. Feet balancing precariously on two branches, I clung on grimly to the trunk, baring my teeth in a fun-loving expression.

'Cheer up, love, it'll never happen!' called a wag in a passing car.

'Hah, hah,' I replied, trying desperately to get into a jollier frame of mind. I imagined Magnus spotting me in the newspaper, modelling London's most fashionable ski wear, and felt a bit happier. Huh, then he'd feel sorry for making his horrible suggestions. But then again perhaps he wouldn't.

'Fabulous, darlin',' called the photographer. 'I jus' need to see a bit more of you – can you lean out of the tree and unzip the top a bit?'

I did what I was told, smiling cheerfully and dreaming about becoming the next Kate Twig when I was distracted by a sudden crash of metal.

Looking up, I noticed a middle-aged Bentley driver who, over-stimulated by the commotion from my tree, had been craning from his car window for several minutes and had crashed into an older, humbler vehicle which in turn had crashed into several recycling bins.

The impact had caused the driver of the Bentley to become painfully embedded in his electric car window, which must have been activated on impact. The other car had been completely written off and its owner was now waving his fists around in a very agitated state.

The crowd on the pavement, bored of my tree antics, had turned their attention to the road where the promise of fisticuffs loomed excitingly. I had a feeling that the branch I was standing on was about to crack and I called for assistance but nobody was listening. The Bentley driver had managed to wriggle out of his car and the two men were throwing punches at each other in a most alarming manner.

'Help me!' I called. Luckily I caught the attention of an elderly dowager drifting past and she somehow helped me down before the whole tree collapsed.

'Dreadful show,' she complained, dribbling slightly as I landed on her shoulder, and nodding towards the commotion. 'One doesn't expect this sort of carry-on in Chelsea. One might expect it in a distant suburb – Acton, or Guildford . . .' She drifted off and was soon absorbed into a cloud of incense wafting out of Chech and Speake next door. I gazed after her, feeling vaguely insulted. What had she meant by her inference that Guildford, the reassuring green belt gin 'n' Jag haven where I had grown up was on a seedy par with grimy and menacing Acton?

But I was distracted by the arrival of the police who with effective use of their truncheons soon managed to drag the combatants off to the police station, conveniently just round the corner. The assistant rushed over to me as I was disentangling bits of pine cone from my hair and was very apologetic.

'Um, gosh, what did you say your name was?'

'Oriana.'

'Oriana, thank you so much for being such a good sport. Why don't you keep the whole outfit as payment? The pictures are going to be fabulous and it was so brave of you to climb into the tree.'

We were interrupted by a reporter who had been tipped off about the commotion by the photographer.

'I hear the accident was caused by a naked girl hanging out of a tree.' He looked around lasciviously.

'It was me. But I most certainly wasn't naked,' I volunteered primly.

'Were you a *bit* naked though?' He salivated hopefully.

'No, I most certainly wasn't.' I pursed my lips. There seemed to be far too many pictures in the world of me naked already and in my sensitive frame of mind I had no wish to get a reputation for exhibitionism. Besides, I lived in constant fear that any more media debacles would result in my father's wrath. I had promised that after the Naff Ovens episode I would lie low for a while.

'I'll just get a few more pix of you at the scene of the accident, if you don't mind,' said the photographer who seemed to have completely lost interest in the Spice Girls' imminent arrival at Heathrow. 'We're running a road safety campaign next week and this will tie in nicely.'

My spirits rose. Here was a chance to associate myself with something really worthwhile, maybe even save lives!

We crossed the road and surveyed the accident. The Bentley was wedged into the side of the small car which was embedded in three recycling skips on the pavement. Waste paper, old bottles, jam jars and other unsavoury items of waste lay spewn about the road.

'Now, luv, I'd like you to drape yourself seductively over the Bentley with a little smile.'

'But surely I should be looking sad and concerned.'

'Nah, we're lookin' for more Sharon Stone meets Mother Theresa,' advised the photographer. 'A pretty girl like you will get the campaign off to a good start. Think of the kiddies.'

I thought of the kiddies which made me think of unprotected sex with Magnus. I might be pregnant! Would that be better than catching a sexually transmitted disease? If I had a choice, which would I choose? I didn't know what would be worse. Magnus was so dark and hairy; if the child was a girl it might have a moustache. At best she would be doomed to a lifetime of painful hair removal, although I had heard that there was a new laser machine that literally banished unwanted hair forever.

'Can you look a bit more cheerful and unzip your top a

bit?' called the photographer in between frenzied snapping. I edged the zip down a bit – it was constricting my chest anyway – and smiled happily.

'That a girl.' He finished his film, winked at me and dashed off to his car.

I wandered back to the shop and changed into my clothes. The assistant was on the telephone recounting the recent dramas in great detail but she broke off to ask me to leave my number in case they needed to get in touch. Clutching my booty I made my way down to Starbucks for a restorative latte and a muffin. I was starving. I would have liked to sample a minimalist breakfast at the Humple, their small but perfectly formed quail's egg omelette was famous, but I don't think I could have managed to eat in front of Magnus. I didn't really know him well enough for that sort of thing.

Really, it had been quite a morning so far. Sipping my coffee meditatively, I reflected that though life was often painful and always confusing, at least it was never dull.

I skipped out of the cafe feeling quite merry, my mood artificially enhanced by the rapid caffeine ingestion. I imagined the photo caption. Oriana Spicer, face of responsible road safety! My family would be so proud of me for once, especially Siena who was always going on about children being run over.

The morning's contortions had left me a bit sore and a tree bristle had somehow made its way into my pants, making it difficult to walk properly. I caught sight of Georgie in the distance, letting herself out of Pandora's flat. She waved at me and started laughing to herself. I tried to speed up, looking forward to sharing the joke, but walking fast exacerbated the sharp pricking of the fir in my pants. I couldn't wait to dig it out.

'Hey, Clint Eastwood – where's your horse?' she called once I was in hearing distance. 'This Finnish chap must be quite a boy!' She was rolling around now, clutching her sides with great amusement.

'Hah, hah!' I laughed sarcastically. 'Very funny. I've got a piece of fir cone wedged down my knickers if you must know and it's been rubbing away between my legs quite painfully. You see I had to climb into a tree and have my photograph taken for a road safety campaign and . . .'

Georgie was by now quite hysterical with laughter and not making any sense at all. At last she stopped and clutched her sides. 'Youch, I've got a terrible stitch. Oriana! I was just remembering that picture of you with your head in the oven with a J-Cloth over your bum! It could only happen to you! Hah, hah-hah!' She unlocked her car door and collapsed inside, tears rolling down her cheeks. 'And do you remember that picture of you and that bald cleaner fighting that delivery man! Aaaahahhh.'

Her laughter was drowned by the roar of her car engine as she blew a kiss and drove off, still laughing like a demented creature. Really, Georgie was terribly eccentric sometimes.

I dived into my bedroom and removed the fir cone from my pants then went to join Pandora who was sitting at the kitchen table making a list.

'Phew, am I glad today's over,' I said, slumping in my chair. 'I was planning to go round to Peregrine's to pick up my stuff but I don't have the strength.' I explained the day's traumas and excitements as Pandora shook with laughter. What on earth was wrong with everyone today?

I glanced at her list, which was headed, selling flat, pros and cons. There was a long list under pros and nothing under cons.

'So what have you decided to do about the flat?' I asked.

'I've been thinking that it's time for a change. What would you say if I put the flat on the market?'

'But you're so comfortable here.'

'Exactly. I've been getting *too* comfortable, treading water, going nowhere.'

'But comfortable is a nice thing, most people spend their

lives arranging things so that they are comfortable, it's not a bad word!'

'I know, but I want to pull the carpet from under my feet and create some chaos in my life. Things have been getting too secure.'

'How can things be secure? Neither of us is married!' I wailed.

'Hah hah, very droll.'

'It's impossible to be really insecure when you have a private income,' I huffed. Really, it was OK for Pandora, she had a huge private income from the sale of her father's rubber factory to live off.

'How would you know?' she replied sarcastically, stomping out of the kitchen. If there was one thing she hated it was the assumption that because she had money she didn't have a proper grip on reality. I wished I'd kept my mouth shut. She'd been incredibly generous to me and was always telling me to forget about paying rent. I had always insisted, though; it was good to keep things businesslike. But even so, it was very low and if she decided to move I'd never be able to afford anything as nice.

I'd lost Cheyne Castle, I thought with a sinking heart, now it looked as if I might lose Pandora's flat. I'd be utterly homeless. Pandora was such a loose cannon she might do anything, go anywhere.

She came back into the kitchen looking guilty. 'I'm sorry, Oriana. That was below the belt. Especially as you've just walked out of Cheyne Castle. But don't worry, it might take ages to sell this place. There's no rush.'

'But it might not take ages. It's so fabulous, you might get an offer straightaway. What will you do then?'

'Well, I'm rather itching to go travelling. It's only been the ball that's really kept me here for the last few months. Ideally, I'd sell this quickly, find something that needs doing up and get the builder to start gutting it. Then I'd be free to push off. I'm sorry I didn't discuss all this with you before, you might not have walked out of Cheyne Castle so fast.'

'Oh yes I would. I couldn't have gone on staying there. Anything would have been better. You know what it's like once you make up your mind to leave somewhere.'

'You're preaching to the converted. But I'm worried about you. What will you do?'

'Haven't a clue. Everything has changed so suddenly, I need a few days to think, really. I wonder how long it'll be before you get an offer for the flat.'

'Not long if we follow a few simple rules. People aren't just buying a flat when they buy a flat, they're buying a lifestyle. The trick is, when the punters roll in, we must seduce them with our dream lifestyle.' I grimaced. 'From now on we can't hang our tights to dry on the sofa, leave boxes of Tampax in the bath, abandon our washing up for days in the sink or invite smokers to dinner. And no dumping in the loo, we'll have to go out for colonics.'

'You're joking, aren't you?'

'Herons do it. There's no reason why it shouldn't work equally well for humans,' she explained.

'Well, I'm not a bloody heron, am I?' Really, sometimes it was tough being a tenant; the sooner I got my own pad the better.

'I'm going to buy a job lot of scented candles and beeswax polish, have white lilies on tap and keep a vanilla pod and a coffee bean ready under the grill to infuse the kitchen with homely scents. We'll have to recycle all our grandest invitations and stick them on the mantelpiece and I'll leave my Ritzy Marina Club membership card prominently displayed. It's a scam but it works every time. Can I try on your new hat?' She snooped around the exciting contents of my chic Sam De Teran bag enviously.

'OK, imagine some punters are about to come through the door. Talk me through it, what d'we do?'

'Ideally it would be better not to be here at all so they can snoop around a bit and soak up the lifestyle. But if we are caught on the hop, it's best to let Georgie do all the talking. We should stay friendly and elegantly mute, and refrain from following them around pointing out the energy-efficient boiler and the exciting amount of storage space. People get intimidated by overenthusiastic owners.'

'If it's not raining perhaps we could recline languorously on the roof terrace eating peeled grapes and sipping martinis. That would give the flat a nice ladies-who-lunch feel.'

'That's a good idea. I'll peel some grapes and keep them in the fridge so we're always prepared.'

'OK. Let's do a dry dummy run. The doorbell's just gone, get into position!'

I waited while Pandora fiddled with the key to the lovely terrace overlooking the gardens. We never used it, neither of us being particularly interested in outdoor life. Once outside, we reclined seductively pretending to eat peeled grapes and read glossy magazines.

'OK, dummy run over now.' I tried to heave myself out of the chic but agonizingly uncomfortable garden chair but gave up.

'You know what I've decided to do this winter?' said Pandora, similarly unable to move. 'This is something we could do together and would be great fun *and*,' she paused for effect, 'the ultimate *pièce de résistance*, you could wear your lovely new furry hat every day and not be laughed at. Promise me you won't laugh if I tell you.'

'Course not.'

'I rang up the chief chalet girl recruiter at Jolly Holidays this morning, they were the company I worked for in Val d'Isere a few years ago, to see if they had any last-minute vacancies and they have! So I'm off to spend the winter in the Alps. Oh, do come, I'm sure they'd take you on like a shot.'

I stared at her open-mouthed. 'Us! We're too old surely! I thought you had to be twenty-one and horribly jolly cheerful all the time.'

'Am I a jolly person?' Pandora asked grimly.

'Not really. I mean neither of us are natural grinners. And besides, we're both very good cooks. I've never met a chalet girl who can cook, have you?'

'Course not. But things have changed. They expect them to be able to cook a bit now, and they like them to be older too.'

'Like air hostesses?'

'Exactly. Remember I told you about that seventy-year-old who still works for United Airlines? She refuses to leave because her doctor says she's addicted to flying and stopping would kill her. Anyway, we can lie about our age. If they ask to see our passports we can say we dropped them in a puddle.'

'Good thinking. But you're a good skier, I haven't skied since I was eight, and even then I was hopeless. There was a race and I came tenth.'

'That's not bad.'

'Of course it's bad. There were only nine other entrants and—'

'They were all legless, armless and blind.'

'They were the lucky ones,' I replied darkly. 'Siena came first, of course. It was all very embarrassing because I had a temper tantrum and our nanny was really cross because she had to be prised away from this divine ski instructor she'd fallen for madly. And we went for a sleigh ride with our parents and the chap got lost. We ended up in his parents' restaurant in the middle of a wood, forced to eat a horrible cheese fondue at vast expense. It stayed in our stomachs for weeks afterwards and that's when Siena became a vegan.'

'But things have changed now,' said Pandora. 'Besides, you must be a dab hand at langlaufing. Didn't your stepfather give you lessons?'

'Yes, he did actually. He had this langluafing machine at home that he used to practise on. It looked quite hard work.'

'See, you're a langlaufer by marriage. It's quite mystic.'

'What's mystic about being a pair of elderly langlaufing chalet girls, for heaven's sake?'

Pandora was stumped but not for long. 'OK, some diehards still ski, but no one who is anyone skis after lunch any more. It's simply not chic.'

'But why are Sam De Teran ski suits so popular if no one is skiing?'

'One needs something to keep the snow out during the short dash from luxury hotel to cappuccino café heaven, of course.'

'Of course.' It was all getting a bit confusing and I decided that it was better to bow to Pandora's experience in these matters. 'I think I'll think about it. I just want to absorb everything that's happened over the last two days before I make up my mind about anything just yet.'

'You're probably right. You need a few hours to take stock. Anyway, I'm off to chat up Corianda Angelica. I'm really pleased because she's agreed to do all the decorations at the ball for nothing provided she gets a credit in *The Snoop!* and *Divorce!* magazine. I've persuaded Max to do a feature on her too so she's feeling pretty happy about it. I just need to make sure she's not going to do anything too minimal. Left to her own devices she's likely to paint the ballroom sixteen different shades of white and plonk a Zen sandpit on the dance floor.'

'Sounds rather nice.'

'I know it does. I was thinking of getting her to do a sort of Zen look for my next flat, with a fountain . . .' Pandora's voice faded as she drifted into the hall to put on her coat. I caught the words 'fish tank' and 'feng shui', and 'round the world trip' before she drifted out of the door, letting it slam behind her.

Pandora always goes into this dreamy mode before she takes off somewhere. Once she has made up her mind to go, she is gone in spirit, if not in body. The only question was, did I want to go too?

I switched off the chattering radio and stood for a moment in the blissfully silent flat that only a moment ago had been so full of chaos and laughter and tried to make up my mind what to do. Of course Siena and I would have a bit of money from the sale of the Canaletto, but we had no clear idea how much and I didn't want to count my chickens before they were hatched. Besides, the sale wasn't for ages.

I looked around the flat, loving its stillness and the contrast of the cool ash floor with the white walls which had been painted a shade of white from Corianda Angelica's range of white paints, which all looked identical. This shade was called Picket Fence White and was quite a white shade of white.

Pandora had got quite friendly with Corianda since her divorce and in return for free paint and interior advice had helped Corianda dream up enticing colour descriptions which had proved to be the key to their popularity.

Pandora had christened the collection 'Corianda's Paint Palette', and they were the fashionable urban equivalent of the National Trust paint collection whose sickly yet apparently authentically aristocratic colours were so beloved of wannabe squires in the countryside.

Chapter Fourteen

I woke up the next morning in very low spirits. I was dreading seeing Peregrine and was feeling increasingly horrible about the Magnus episode. I'd always thought that I was one of those people who could quite easily shrug off a meaningless sexual encounter but I now realized I was probably far too morbidly sensitive. How on earth did people have one-night stands on a regular basis? It was utterly soul destroying.

I took my time getting dressed. I wanted to ring Peregrine and ask him if I could come round and pick up my things, but it was only 8 a.m. and he wouldn't be awake for another hour.

I was dreading returning to Cheyne Castle. If the moose stock had left a frightful stain and ruined the Italian bed linen he had imported at huge expense from Rome I would be in seriously bad books. I was hoping we could still remain friends, it was all we had ever been really, but I would miss him dreadfully if we parted on bad terms.

I rang him at nine and he answered the phone very blearily. Oh dear, I'd obviously woken him up.

'Hello, Peregrine, it's me.' I half expected him to put the phone down – I might have – but luckily he didn't go in for histrionic behaviour. He sounded peeved, though.

'I was wondering what had happened to you,' he replied curtly.

'I just wanted to apologize for ruining your duvet cover.'

'Oh, don't worry about that. The cleaners took care of it.'

'Oh, good. Perhaps I could come round this morning and

pick up my stuff? I've moved back to Pandora's.'

'Oh, all right then. I'll see you later.'

I drove round to Cheyne Castle with a heavy heart and rang the bell with some trepidation. Normally I would just have used my key but now I was no longer the chatelaine I would probably not have the same privileges. After a long wait of several minutes Peregrine answered the door. He looked very calm and relaxed and I thanked my lucky stars that I had caught him just after he'd had his Anger Management lymphatic drainage massage.

'Oh, Oriana. I'm relieved you're all in one piece. Magnus and I have been extremely concerned.' Magnus, concerned? What was going on?

'There was no need. I joined Pandora at Annabel's for a quick drink and then I drove us both back to her flat. I had a very restful night's sleep.' I took a dcep breath to stop myself gabbling. It was a sign of guilt to give away too much information. I hoped to goodness Magnus hadn't revealed our unfortunate night together. It was too awful. Peregrine would never forgive me for sleeping with his half-brother!

'And how was he?' I asked casually.

'In very good form. We had a very amusing lunch at my club. He said he saw you at Annabel's and kept a brotherly eye on you.'

'Yes, I was feeling a bit low and he was terribly kind. I think he was rather keen on Pandora.'

'Most probably. Like I said, the Finns are a very libidinous race.' Phew. Magnus obviously hadn't spilled the beans. Good chap. 'I said I didn't mind who he set his cap at as long as he stayed away from you. Luckily he does have some morals.'

I felt a blush spread over my face. I don't know what it is but as soon as I know it would be really embarrassing to blush, what do I do? I go and blush. I hadn't blushed for months. Luckily Peregrine didn't notice as he was staring at himself in the mirror with great concentration.

'You don't seem to realize how much stress I've been under recently, I've got a touch of the Bill Spicers – your father would understand. My urologist says I'm one of the worst cases he's seen for years. He's suggested I go to The Mayr Clinic in Austria and take a rest cure for three weeks.'

'What a good idea.' There was an awkward silence. 'Well, I'll just go and pack up my things.'

'You don't have to do anything rash, darling. You could come to the Mayr Clinic with me if you liked. People rave about the place. It's extremely rejuvenating.'

'Um, I don't think so. The doctor's right. You need to get away for a good long rest and put all your business stresses behind you. I think I ought to pack up my stuff and go back to Pandora's for a bit.'

'All right, darling, if that's what you'd prefer. But I hope you'll permit me to take you out for dinner before I go?'

'Of course.' I thought quickly. I had to persuade him to stay long enough to entertain the ambassadors before the ball the following week. It was our only chance of getting them there.

'But you won't go before Wednesday, will you?' I said firmly. 'Remember, Magnus and the ambassadors were going to come round for drinks before that ball they've been asked to.'

'Oh, yes,' said Peregrine vaguely. 'We'd better stick to that arrangement. Nars had a business idea that Magnus and I were interested in. It would be a good opportunity to discuss it further.' He sighed, once more overwhelmed by the strains of business.

I tried to look suitably concerned. I'd heard a rumour that Magnus's company wanted to use Peregrine's name in an advertising campaign for a new brand of pickled herring to give it an aristocratic appeal. Having murdered and banished their own aristocrats and with no royal family to speak of, the Finns were oddly class conscious, and they adored movies. A range of Lord Skye-Rocca pickles detailing Peregrine's illustrious dynasty on the back would go down a storm, especially if Peregrine could be persuaded to appear on Finnish TV discussing some of his mother's more seminal movies.

It was with regret and relief that I packed up my suitcase quickly and lugged it to my car. Peregrine had nipped out for a quick confession with Father Hubert who lived round the corner when he wasn't hunting. Peregrine only saw him when he was suffering from stress overload and I felt very guilty for my contribution. But he'd get over it. He was very robust.

I glanced down to the basement, noticing that it was shrouded in darkness. Mrs B was obviously not at home. It was probably just as well; I would have burst into tears if I'd had to say goodbye just then and she hated displays of emotion. Besides, she was bound to give me a real telling off about the mess on the bedspread. I accelerated quickly into the Embankment, careful not to look back.

'I'm glad you're back for good. I've really missed your juicer,' said Pandora, helping me unpack my few indispensable kitchen gadgets when I returned. 'I could have got one myself of course, but I had a feeling you'd be back sooner rather than later. How was Peregrine?'

'Oh, Peregrine-like. Luckily he had an emergency lymphatic drainage massage yesterday so he was feeling quite relaxed.' I collapsed in a chair. 'Phew, I'm knackered. It's been quite a day. I suppose Magnus hasn't phoned, has he?'

''Fraid not,' said Pandora sympathetically. 'It's such a cheek. Men should always phone afterwards, it's such bad manners.'

I detected more than a whiff of *Schadenfreude* in her outrage on my behalf, which depressed me far more than Magnus not ringing.

'The odd thing is that I'm not really very interested in him but it's an ego thing really. I'd like him to be mad about me.' I ruminated deeply from the depths of my kitchen chair.

'If I hadn't leapt into bed in five seconds no doubt he'd still be pursuing me. But I don't really regret it, it's sort of helped me make a clean break from Peregrine. Magnus must think I'm a right old slapper, but I couldn't wait for our tenth date like it says in The Rules because he doesn't have ten dates, at least not with the same person.'

'I would have done the same, anyone would,' said Pandora. 'After six months of Peregrine's frantic fumblings anyone would have been utterly desperate.'

'Yes, it's funny, I've been without sex before for much longer but it wasn't so bad. The trouble is that the fiddling sort of keeps you just below simmering point.'

'It's like Quentin Crisp's housework theory. After four years of never doing any cleaning one's house reaches a point of filthiness that never gets any worse. I think sex is like that. After about a year of not glimpsing any, your hormones sort of hibernate and you lose interest. But if you see a decent-looking man on the telly or you're interfered with, they come back.'

'Exactly.'

'It's awfully good to have you back in the flat, Oriana. I've had no one to talk to since you've been away. And you can help me with the last-minute bits and pieces for the ball if you like.' She frowned anxiously. 'I've just thought, now you've done a runner from Cheyne Castle, what shall we do about the pre-ball agit prop soiree with the ambassadors? It was rather our plum to lure them to the ball.'

'Oh, don't worry, I reminded Peregrine and he's still on for it.'

'Thank goodness for that. By the way, when did he start his Anger Management lymph drainage therapy?' she asked thoughtfully.

'I think he said he began it around last December to cope with the seasonal stress of having to employ a company to do all his Christmas shopping for him. He said that although that meant he didn't have to do any shopping himself, he still had to cope with the stress of dealing with everybody else doing theirs.'

'I knew it!' cried Pandora triumphantly. 'Last Christmas was when the first incident of trolley rage was reported at the Waitrose in the Kings Road. That's round the corner from Cheyne Castle. I knew there had to be a connection.'

'I think that's a bit of a red herring,' I said. 'You see, Peregrine's anger levels are naturally very low so any excess anger secreted into the water system would be minuscule. Certainly not enough to start a violent altercation on that scale.' This particular incident at Waitrose had resulted in a group of pensioners from the nearby World's End housing estate setting upon random Jane Asher lookalike housewives, and anyone they felt had a yuppy look about them who might be responsible for putting up prices in the area.

The *Daily Mail* later discovered that they weren't all pensioners but prematurely aged members of the radical anti-toff organization Class War, who were using several bona fide pensioners as 'stooges', I believe that is the correct term. I couldn't tell any of my friends but Siena had been a member before she went to Chile and I recognized several of her more rabid chums in the blurred 'wanted' pictures in the paper.

Thank goodness she was now A Mother and more sensible these days, although the jury was still out on Mary, whom I considered a little spooky.

'I'm amazed he didn't notice the chemistry between you and Magnus. He must be terribly self-absorbed.'

'Just a bit. I'll miss him though, and the house, the river, Mrs B—'

'The industrial cleaners. Don't forget them.'

'The bedspread must have posed a real challenge to their considerable skills. I think they should write a book.'

'Yes. It should have a short snappy title, something like *Stains*.'

'An everyday guide to the refurbishment of *soiled* items.

I never did find out what they put in those huge boiling cauldrons they kept in the basement. I have a feeling they may take their secrets to the grave with them.'

'Perhaps we should try some unguent espionage. I'm game if you are.'

'It's no use. I did try to find out what they use, but they guard their secrets very closely.' I sighed.

'When you write your cookery book, perhaps you could include a chapter on them?'

'I love the way you say "when" you write your book. You're the only person who hasn't said there are far too many cookery books already.'

'You've got to follow your heart. If you want to do it you'll do it, I'm sure. Once you get the bit between your teeth you can be quite determined, you know.'

'Peregrine often says that. I think he sees me as a cross between Elizabeth I, Maggie Thatcher and the River Café,' I said mournfully. 'But at least lots of men fancied Mrs T. I think Peregrine only put up with me because he saw me as a walking restaurant. Huh, someone else can jolly well grind his coffee beans for him now.'

'I think you should go for it. I wasn't going to tell anyone because it's a bit of an ego bash, but I just had a letter from my publisher saying they were going to pulp the rest of my books due to "cessation of demand". *Pandora's Gold* is going to be mashed! It'll probably end up as recycled bog roll.'

'I'm so sorry. Is it very upsetting?' I asked gently.

'No. The days of weeping in bookshops that didn't stock it are over. Just as well, there were rather a lot of those sort of bookshops. I had to stay out of them for months.' She smiled wryly. 'But I'm much more relaxed about it these days. What's the spiritual law for that?'

'Law of Least Effort?'

'No, no, the other one.'

I thought hard. 'Law of Detachment?' I suggested.

'That's the one. Rolling with the punches, enjoying the

journey, and not worrying about the end result too much. That was my mistake, I got too obsessed with the thought of writing a bestseller and it became a sort of life or death thing.'

'At least you learnt something valuable from the experience,' I hazarded.

'But I did cry a bit when I heard they were going to be mashed, so I guess I'm not a completely pure spiritual being after all.'

'We're only human. We can't eradicate all our desires. Desires are very powerful. If we didn't have them we'd be living in caves.'

Pandora nodded sagely.

'And having a much easier life and definitely not having one-night stands,' I added.

'But I'm sure you'll do better,' she continued. 'You'll generate loads of publicity. Max will give you lots of puff, I can just see it. "Gorgeous Oriana Spicer, daughter of ex-sixties supa model and sausage skin heiress Venetia Mowbray and wastepaper tub tycoon, Bill Spicer—" '

'Ugh, it sounds absolutely revolting. I don't want to be associated with sausage skins or wastepaper tubs unless it'll really help. At least going out with Peregrine was a bit more glamorous. I don't know what I'm going to do with myself now I've left Cheyne Castle. I can't face going back to cooking. All my clients are Peregrine's friends – it would be too embarrassing. If only *The Snoop!* would get back to me about my cookery column, but they seem to have shelved it. It's maddening. Something like that could open so many doors for me.'

'I know. Those two sample articles you showed me were great. Maybe you could show them to someone else.'

'Yes. I really must do something about it. I sent a synopsis to a publisher friend of Peregrine who mentioned that he'd be interested in seeing something, but now he says they're not looking for cookery books at the moment. I'm sure that if I got a cookery column I could interest someone though.'

'Hmm. It's so difficult coming up with the right thing at the right time. So much of it is down to luck.'

The doorbell rang.

'Oh God, that must be the Bermudan tycoon who's coming to see the flat. Quick, get into position!' Pandora hissed.

I dashed onto the verandah and eased myself carefully onto the agonizing garden chair with the exclusive Ritzy Marina Club glossy magazine and a box of Charbonnel and Walker chocs, while she raced to open the door.

'What a heavenly smell,' I heard Georgie say as she came into the flat. 'Is it all right if I go right ahead?'

'Yes, help yourselves. Oriana and I will be on the roof garden if you need us.' Pandora raced upstairs and joined me. A few minutes later Georgie appeared with a rather small, very rich-looking man. Pandora and I smiled at him winningly. I couldn't have staked my life on it, but I was sure I saw Pandora subtly hitch her skirt up. I popped a peeled grape into my mouth and sighed languorously.

'Quite a pad you've got here, girls,' said the Bermudan tycoon smoothly. 'I'm looking for something for my daughter, she'd absolutely love this.'

'Yes, we've been terribly happy here,' whispered Pandora in a breathy voice. 'It's a very secure flat.'

'And it's such a safe neighborhood,' added Georgie, steering the tycoon back into the drawing room where he paused for a long time at the mantelpiece admiring our invitations, assorted Ritzy Marina membership cards and glamorous photos of Pandora and me with our dysfunctional families in glossy locations around the world.

Pandora sat with crossed fingers for a quick sale, while I clenched my fists tightly. Please let Georgie show him the leaking broom cupboard beneath the stairs and the squalid make-up cupboard in the bathroom. It would be for the best in the long term, I knew it would.

Chapter Fifteen

Pandora and I were kept very busy in the run-up to the ball, showing glamorous potential buyers around the flat.

Thankfully the Bermudan tycoon had been revealed as a Walter Mitty type character and was actually a chiropodist from Cheam *posing* as a Bermudan tycoon. Selling a flat, it seemed, was full of unforeseen pitfalls.

We weren't bothered though, being far more concerned about last-minute arrangements to ensure that the ball went without a hitch. The Whale and Dolphin Society had decided on a completely dolphin-friendly, animal-free meal in the hope of stirring up controversy. We thought that an entirely meatless do might stimulate the jaded partygoers and give the evening a bit of oomph.

By exploiting our various connections we had secured the attendance of E.E. Lung, London's most vitriolic and feared food journalist. He was the founding member of Real Men Eat Pig's Trotters, a rabidly anti-vegan group. Siena had once tried to blow up their HQ in South Kensington but hadn't had much luck.

E.E. Lung was also a social commentator, and no glossy was considered complete without his witty and frighteningly incisive comments on the London scene. He had offended so many chefs in recent years that he now had to travel everywhere with an armed guard. It would be a real coup if he did appear, as recent threats against his life had become so extreme that restaurants had to use Security Corps to bus his meals to him because they could not be insured if he was on the premises. He now had an elusive Salman Rushdie appeal and was invited to simply everything but rarely came.

Max Shyster had also invited lots of his rabid journo chums who similarly prided themselves on their political incorrectness, gleefully writing endless columns extolling offal, pig's trotters and beef bones. They adored sending up caring vegetarian celebs like Paul McCartney and Sting and would no doubt complain about the no choice vegetarian stance and give the charity a bit of puff. After all, bad publicity was better than no publicity at all.

Fortunately the Grosvenor was quite happy to cook delicious recipes from the Linda McCartney cookery book so that was fine.

The only potential fly in the ointment was that we hadn't told them that the ball was being partly sponsored by the American Herbal Tobacco Corporation, and *Whoops!* who were trying to launch their new 'slimming cigarette' in a barrage of bad publicity. It had been a great success in America, achieving record sales with the exciting slogan: 'You've gotta die, so why die fat?' It seemed that people would rather risk a slow, lingering death than obesity, and who could blame them?

In return we were going to show a short film detailing the delights and health benefits of smoking and auction off some stunning stills of glamorous smokers like Lauren Bacall, taken from various steamy Hollywood film noirs. Nobody was quite sure of the ethics of all this, but so much money had been offered (not surprising when you considered that many of the world's leading movers and shakers were attending the ball) that the Whale and Dolphin Society had decided quite sensibly not to quibble. They needed to raise many thousands of pounds to release Willy the orc from his disease-infested swimming pool in Mexico and, quite rightly, that was their priority.

Whoops! had donated thousands of packets of cigarettes for our guests, and Corianda Angelica had cleverly incorporated the chic silver packets into her minimalist table decorations. Things nearly came a cropper when the manager saw the cigarette arrangements the day before and said cigarettes were out of the question as they had just instigated a no smoking policy in the hotel. He said that if people insisted, they could stand outside in Park Lane and smoke there.

'But they'll all get run over!' protested Pandora when she heard this exciting survival-of-the-fittest hotel policy. It was quite a blow. It was too much to impose vegetarianism *and* non-smoking on our fashionable guests, many of whom had travelled many continents for the occasion.

'And if people aren't allowed to smoke they'll stop coming to London altogether,' I added, thinking of Magnus and his dangerous cigars sadly. I was longing to hear from him. My many gynaecological examinations had put me in the all clear and I thought that I had probably over-exaggerated some of his more outlandish suggestions. I remembered how handsome he was, and how masterful. What if I had thrown away my one true chance of real and abiding love?

'We'll just have to lie and say that we're going to announce that they're imitation cigarettes and not to be touched,' said Pandora.

'And conveniently forget to make the announcement,' I added.

On the night of the ball Pandora and I made our way to Cheyne Castle in good time to greet the ambassadors. The charity wasn't thrilled at our subterfuge but agreed it would indeed be a coup if we could get the Norwegian ambassador along.

Our devotion to the cause had been strengthened by several gruesome documentaries exposing the brutal and unnecessary whaling trade shown recently on TV. The British government had been strongly pressurizing the Japanese and Norwegian governments to observe restrictions without much success, so anything that kept the whaling issue in the news would be a bonus.

Pandora was to ring the *Daily Mail* as we left Cheyne

Castle when we had locked the ambassadors firmly into the limos. The *Mail* had been running a campaign to release Willy the captive orc for several weeks and was planning to cover the ball anyway. The arrival of the ambassadors and their glamorous wives, who had taken the diplomatic corps by storm, would just be the icing on the cake. Of course, the ambassadors wouldn't know where we were going. Just to be sure, I had flattered Peregrine into concocting one of his dangerous cocktails which would ensure that everyone would leave Cheyne Castle as ignorant as when they had arrived and quite possibly on stretchers.

I had hired several limos with tinted windows and planned to use the back entrance of the Grosvenor. Peregrine didn't know about any of this subterfuge. He'd asked vaguely where the ball was and I'm afraid I lied and told him it was to be held at the Paddington Palace, a rather bohemian mansion belonging to an old boyfriend of Pandora's. The chances were he would forget immediately. He liked to think he was too high-powered to remember grungy facts like that, but if he did ask why we weren't going to the Paddington Palace, I'd just say I'd made a mistake.

Pandora and I were in a state of great euphoria, the ball was a sellout and had already attracted huge amounts of publicity in the press. Dolphins and whales looked like being this week's cause amongst the glitterati and photogenic weather girls and gorgeous *über* models had been begging to become the charity figurehead.

I had a feeling that the beau monde were becoming tired of worthwhile but disfiguring charities like Aids and land-mines, and were longing to lend their support to something with a little more physical appeal.

Ulrika Temptation, ex-meteorologist and the current Lottery presenter, had graciously agreed to do the raffle. Max had just exposed her clandestine affair with a minor royal and in a desperate bid to cultivate a more serious image, as she harboured dreams of marrying the minor royal, she had agreed to give an exclusive interview in which she talked exclusively about her charity work. As she hadn't actually done any charity work yet I imagined it would be a very short interview, but you couldn't have everything.

'It will be great,' I reassured Pandora as we drove to Cheyne Castle. I watched nervously as she lit up her twentieth 'ginseng' cigarette of the day. I didn't like it when she took both hands off the wheel when she was driving, but I knew better than to back-seat drive.

Just recently she had taken to chain smoking ginseng cigarettes in a frantic bid to stay awake. As a main organizer she had been working sixteen-hour days for the past fortnight and was horribly sleep-deprived. It hadn't done much for her driving and I was crossing my fingers we would arrive in one piece.

'The wheels are set in motion,' I continued. 'There's nothing more we can do now except confuse the ambassadors and enjoy ourselves.

'Turn off here!' I reminded her sharply. It was easy to miss the turning into Cheyne Castle from the Embankment if one wasn't being especially vigilant. Pandora turned suddenly into the drive, causing a volley of hooting behind us and narrowly avoiding two of the industrial cleaners who had to jump into the flowerbed for cover.

'I'm glad they're about. I must ask them how they managed to clean up the bedspread.' I got out of the car and caught a fleeting glimpse of them limping into the basement, and shutting the door firmly behind them. Pandora had obviously given them a bit of a scare and they weren't in the mood for conversation.

I still had my key so I let us in, breathing in the familiar scent of Mrs B's homemade beeswax polish and fresh lilies. The world outside might be buffeted with change but Cheyne Castle always stayed the same. It was very reassuring. Mr Button was standing to morose attention in the hall, holding a tray of champagne.

'Evening, Miss Oriana and Miss Pandora. It's good to have you back. The place hasn't been the same without you.' It was the longest speech I had ever heard him make and I was very touched.

'It's only a fleeting visit, I'm afraid, Mr B,' I explained sadly, as Pandora and I helped ourselves to a glass and went into the kitchen.

Mrs Button was busy thinly slicing a loaf of brown bread with a hot knife, the way I'd shown her. She grimaced cheerfully when she saw me. I think we both felt a little moved. I would have hugged her but she wasn't a great one for displays of emotion.

'So you're back then,' she said irritably as I deposited my glass of champagne and slid my large tray of devils on horseback into the oven.

'Only a brief pit stop, Mrs B.' I helped her butter the bread while Pandora laid a thin piece of glistening smoked salmon over each slice.

'Master Peregrine hasn't been the same since you left.' Mrs B shuffled off to the fridge grumpily.

'What, you mean he's not impotent any more?' whispered Pandora deadpan.

'Master Peregrine will always be important.' Mrs B shuffled back bearing several lemons. ' 'E's a peer of the realm, 'e is, like his father was 'an like his *son* will be. You don't get any more important than that.' She stared at me meaningfully. Mrs B rather saw me as Peregrine's last great white hope when it came to continuing the Skye-Rocca line. I remembered the way she had dragged me several times into his bedroom when I had been unconscious after one of our drunken parties. She had hated it when we slept in separate bedrooms. I squeezed lemon juice over the smoked salmon while Pandora ground over a little black pepper.

'Right, let's get upstairs and wait for our guests,' I said firmly, changing the subject. 'Mrs B, perhaps you would keep an eye on the devils on horseback and bring them upstairs when they're ready.'

'Righty ho, Miss Oriana. I'll just go an' wake up Master Peregrine. 'E said to call him as soon as you both arrived. 'E's been sleeping more than usual since you left,' she added pointedly.

'More than usual must mean he's sleeping all the time,' I said irritably. I'd heard of sloths that were more energetic. Really, he led such an unnatural life for a man. I was amazed I had stuck it for so long.

Pandora and I busied ourselves anxiously setting down the plates and lighting the candles. There seemed to be some sort of march going on in the Embankment; the sounds of inebriated singing and laughing drifted up to us.

'Don't tell me Chelsea are playing at home tonight. I can't bear it if they throw up hot dogs on my car again,' muttered Pandora.

'Too maddening,' I agreed. We both started, as there was a screech of brakes followed by a resounding crash. We rushed over to the window just in time to see the ambassadors weaving an unsteady path across the road, blithely unaware of bringing the entire Embankment to a standstill. Several cars had piled into the back of one another, and several small and vicious-looking men had sprung out of their vehicles and were waving their fists about in a menacing manner.

'Quick! We've got to save the Scandinavians from the brutal British public!' cried Pandora as we dashed downstairs to the sound of hammering on the front door.

'Mr B, let them in quickly, then bolt the door firmly!' I cried as Mr B rushed to open the door. The ambassadors toppled in chaotically, singing Finnish football songs at the top of their voices.

'Busy old road that. Made it by the skin of our teeth. Beat the Brits by a whisker, what?' Nars was reverting to his RAF lingo in the excitement of the moment. 'Come on, chaps. Upstairs!'

They all piled upstairs to the drawing room, Mrs B

bringing up the rear with a steaming tray of devils on horseback. There was much hammering on the door – the hoi polloi had obviously found out where the perpetrators of the multiple pile-up had escaped to. It was too scary for words. Then Peregrine burst out of the bedroom.

'What on earth is going on?'

'My dear chap,' began Nars. 'We've come straight from lunch and we're so looking forward to this evening.'

The hammering was getting louder and louder. Mrs Button rushed downstairs. ' 'Ooever you are, you can PUSH ORF. WE'VE CALLED THE POLICE, PISS ORF!'

'We are the police,' came the gruff rejoinder.

The ambassadors straightened up, glanced at one another and reached into their dinner jackets for what looked like some kind of pass.

'Diplomatic immunity!' whispered Pandora as Pils, the Finnish consul, strode purposefully towards the door.

'OPEN UP BEFORE WE BREAK DOWN THE DOOR!'

Pils opened the door calmly, ushering two small, sweating policemen inside.

'They barely look a day over fifteen,' I whispered nervously to Pandora.

'Do be quiet. Noticing how young policemen are is the first sign of premature ageing.'

'Good evening, officers,' said Pils smoothly. 'Perhaps you would care to follow me upstairs.' It was an order not a suggestion and the policemen followed him obediently to the drawing room. We all trooped in after them, riveted by the drama.

'Allow me to introduce the ambassadors of Norway, Finland and Sweden.' The ambassadors bowed elegantly. 'And our secretaries, Miss Spicer,' I inclined my head in an efficient, secretive Miss Moneypenny sort of way, 'Miss Black, and Lord Skye-Rocca. I am the Finnish consul, Pils Munississten. We are awaiting the arrival of Mr *Hhhhhhhammas*,' I was impressed at how sinisterly he rolled his hhhhs, 'the Palestinian second-in-command, and the Israeli ambassador for an informal meeting. It is essential that this information is not leaked to the press. There was an unfortunate incident outside as we were coming in, but I trust that you will instruct your men to take care of things with their usual efficiency and discretion.'

The policemen glanced at the diplomatic passes nervously. I could barely see them as they were both dwarfed by the Scandinavians who were all well over six foot four.

'Everything seems to be in order, gentlemen,' said one of the policemen, obviously eager to be off. I couldn't blame him. The ambassadors could look quite alarming in a sinister Baltic sort of way when they tried. 'All that remains is for us to disperse the disorderly element outside the premises. Goodnight.'

'Miss Spicer will show you out, gentlemen,' said Nars, patting my bottom in a lingering sort of way. I remembered Magnus's unsavoury suggestions and shivered nervously. Were Finns really interested in that sort of thing? I hoped Magnus hadn't let our disappointing encounter out of the bag. It was very worrying.

After showing the policemen out I bolted the door firmly and rushed back upstairs, unwilling to miss a moment of the intrigue.

Mr Button had reappeared from inside the cupboard that he had shot into when the police arrived and was handing around a tray of Pearl Harbor Explosion cocktails. The ambassadors were knocking them back with gay abandon and considerable relief.

'Are your wives coming along tonight?' I asked Nars hopefully. It would be impossible keeping them in check without some restraining influence.

'Wives? What wives?' asked Nars, looking blankly at me.

'Now, now, Nars,' said Pandora. 'We met your wife last week. She's very pretty, has blonde hair and blue eyes and wears bright blue spangly eye shadow.'

'Oh, you mean my *wife*, Agnetha,' remembered Nars

suddenly. 'I don't know where she is. I am not her keeper.'

We drained our cocktails quickly. They were even more delicious than usual, Peregrine had surpassed himself.

'Skull,' I toasted the assembled group cheerfully. My limbs were warming up nicely and I felt overcome with a sort of wartime camaraderie. The police had added a most welcome *frisson* of danger to what already promised to be a very exciting evening. Pils sucked in his cheeks, giving his face a skeletal expression.

'Not skull. Skol.' He laughed uproariously and I blushed becomingly.

'Skol.'

'Skol.'

Backs were thumped and glasses raised. Everyone smiled mistily in a haze of Baltic bonhomie and friendship.

' 'Ere we go 'ere we go 'ere we go.'

It was the Swedish ambassador, presumably letting off steam and overcome with relief at surviving his near death experience on the Embankment outside.

We all joined in vigorously; even Mr B, who was tone deaf, managed to mutter something tunelessly under his breath.

'This is all very jolly, I must say', said Peregrine who had come to stand next to me. 'I'd like to take this opportunity, Oriana, to tell you that you look,' he paused for a moment, 'you look absolutely beautiful. That dress suits you so well. You remind me of an exquisite ocean goddess.'

I was wearing a slinky greeny-blue dress that I adored because whenever I turned, the skirt swirled around my thighs like water. The tender moment was interrupted by the ambassadors who were attempting to do headstands against the wall.

'We Swedes are very supple,' Nars was explaining from his inverted position.

'I thought he was Norwegian,' whispered Pandora nervously.

'I don't think it really matters, they all seem quite interchangeable really.'

'It's frightfully good for the hair,' explained Peregrine. 'Yehudi Menuhin swore by it.' I hoped to goodness Peregrine wasn't going to try, he could barely touch his knees. Attempting to do a headstand might finish him off altogether.

Pandora glanced out of the window. 'Thank goodness, the limos are here. Oh gosh, do look, the ambassadresses have arrived!'

We peered out of the window where the three glamorous blondes, clad in shiny silver catsuits, matching crocheted caps and shiny silver platform boots were being mobbed by a cordon of admiring police officers. Agnetha, who appeared to be the gang leader, was shouting and wielding her spangly gem encrusted handbag with considerable skill, causing several policemen to retreat with quite severe injuries. Thank goodness for diplomatic immunity.

Pandora pulled open the window and yelled down, 'Girls! Get in the limos and lock the doors, quick! We'll be down in a sec.'

'Come on, everybody, time to go!' I shouted, gathering up my bag and coat. Mrs B did a sterling job shooing everyone out of the door and into the two waiting limos. I sat with the ambassadresses in the first limo while Pandora took up the rear with the chaps.

'I'm so glad you made it,' I said to the ambassadresses, once we were sitting comfortably in the luxurious car which was replete with television, champagne bar and several chaise longues. This was the life! I quickly poured everyone some champagne. The ladies appeared to have been drinking all day, which was just as well. Hopefully they would be too tanked up to notice that they were attending an anti whaling ball until it was too late.

'We never miss a party at Cheyne Castle,' said Agnetha re-applying some of her glittering blue eye shadow. 'It is such a relief to let our hair down like we do at home.'

'Yes, we're fed up with stuffy parties at stupid embassies,' said Eva. 'We Finns are very free-spirited. Our lives are *torture* in our gilded cages.' She sighed dramatically, peered out of the window which was tinted so dark that no one could see in or out. 'I can see nothing. Where are we going?'

'I'm not quite sure,' I lied, 'but the driver knows where we're going. Magaretha, I love your coat, it looks terribly warm,' I gabbled, changing the subject.

'Yes. Nars gave it to me. It's sealskin.' I frowned. Wasn't Nars Agnetha's husband?

'So chic, so comfortable,' said Agnetha admiringly. 'Is it from last season's kill?'

'Oh yes,' replied Magaretha. I shivered. Johnny Foreigner had a very different way of looking at these things, that was for sure. It had been ages since I'd seen anyone wearing a fur coat, I'd assumed Magaretha's was a very realistic fake.

The limo pulled to a halt at the back entrance of the Grosvenor. We had arrived. I climbed out first and helped the girls out. We were suddenly set upon by a phalanx of photographers and blinded by flashbulbs. Thank goodness, Max's photographer cronies had been waiting to record our arrival. The ambassadors' limo was just pulling up behind ours and the ambassadors piled out unsteadily, walking straight into several huge dustbins. The photographers stormed over to snap them as Pandora and Beatrice rushed across.

'It's too exciting!'

'Yes, good old Max. The pix should be all over the *Mail* tomorrow!'

The Scandinavians were very flattered at the attention, hovering expectantly, hoping presumably to be asked profound questions about the state of the nation. Thankfully nobody asked them anything and we were whisked past the bins and into the gilded interior.

Dinner was just being called, so we made our way to our table. Corianda had done a stunning job with the interior, the silver cigarette boxes had been cleverly juxtaposed with grey lilies and the huge room was softly lit with masses of cigarette-shaped candles. Cigarette smoke was billowing softly out of the air conditioning vents, giving an exhilaratingly illegal feel to the proceedings. The beau monde were out in force and I recognized several glittering society figures as well as masses of celebrities.

At a nearby table I recognized the tall broad-shouldered man who had winked at me at Victoria's party. Amongst the well-groomed oleaginous playboys he looked as deliciously rumpled as ever. He was actually quite attractive, odd that I had thought him *beau laid*. It would have been nice to go and talk to him, about marine conservation and that sort of thing, but he appeared to be chatting up Anoushka Bird-Whistle, aristo It girl, with considerable energy, while she was hanging onto every word. Huh, in her last interview, Anoushka had been boasting about her pony-skin mules and her latest gastronomic discovery, penguin steaks, specially imported from Greenland. I bet she wasn't telling him about *that*.

I was squeezed next to Nars and Peregrine. Nars had ignored the seating plan and had elected to sit next to his wife whom he appeared not to recognize at all. He was asking her where she lived and whereabouts in Sweden she was born. It was obviously some sort of spooky game to keep their marriage alive.

Luckily all the ambassadors were too bombed by the Pearl Harbor Explosion cocktails to notice the anti-whaling theme, which was just as well. I turned to Peregrine who was shovelling food into his mouth anxiously. 'Have you heard from Magnus recently?' I asked hopefully. 'I thought he was coming along tonight.'

'He rang to say he couldn't make it because he'd been unavoidably detained,' explained Peregrine, wiping his glistening mouth with a napkin. 'I say, when I heard this meal was vegan I thought it would be inedible nut rissoles and lots of brown food, but this is actually rather good.'

I replaced my fork feeling sick. Detained? Was he ill? Was he dying of some appalling sexually transmitted disease that I was now contaminated with? It was too horrible to contemplate!

'Lost your appetite, old girl? Shame to let it go to waste. Can I?' He took my plate and tucked in hungrily. 'Yes,' he went on. 'He rang from Helsinki to say that he's completely lost his sense of smell and that his passport has been withdrawn.'

'Oh dear.' I was right! Losing your sense of smell was a symptom of a frightful disease, I was sure, I just couldn't remember which one.

'Not really. He got into a fight with some girlfriend's husband and had his nose broken. The trouble is that the husband is now in intensive care fighting for his life and Magnus is up for GBH. When the police caught up with him he was dancing naked in a fish tank. The man's a complete savage. I don't know what women see in him.' He wiped his plate clean with a piece of bread. 'He even had the cheek to ask me to stand him bail.'

'You didn't refuse, did you?'

'Of course I did. It'll serve him right. He had it coming to him. As far as I'm concerned they can lock him up and throw away the key.'

Poor Magnus. He hadn't had his fingers chopped off or immediately died of a mysterious sexually transmitted disease after all, he was incarcerated in a Finnish prison, presumably unable to make phone calls. The fact that he hadn't rung didn't mean I was terrible in bed after all!

'He wasn't bothered,' Peregrine went on. 'Finnish prisons are the most luxurious in the world. He had a marvellous time last time he was banged up in Helsinki.'

'But it must be an appalling deprivation, not being able to make phone calls . . . and things.'

'Not make phone calls? The man hasn't been off the phone since he was arrested. Because he's a diplomat, hah! That's a joke. The government pays for him to have his own private line. Anyway, he'll be out soon enough. Too soon if you ask me.'

Our pudding arrived, a lemon syllabub, a delicious frothy concoction made with soya cream. Peregrine dived in as soon as it was placed in front of him. He had always been keen on food but he seemed to be becoming a bit obsessive about it. I hoped it wasn't a relationship substitute.

'Mmm, this is really rather good.' He was already scraping his glass clean by the time I was having my first mouthful. 'You should try making this.' He glanced at the menu card. 'Amazing. It says here it's got no cream in at all just a cream made with tofu. Extraordinary.'

'Yes extraordinary.' I cheered up as I noticed Pandora making her way to the stage.

'Ladies and gentlemen,' she said clearly into the microphone. 'It gives me great pleasure to introduce marine biologist, author, lecturer and scientific consultant, Dr Dan McCloud, our guest speaker tonight. Tonight Dan is going to talk to us about being one of the first witnesses on the scene when the *Titanic* was discovered in 1985. Will you please welcome . . .'

Dan clambered on to the stage with a creased sheet of paper and a half smile playing around his ravaged face. He reminded me of a rumpled lion, with his hair gleaming bronze in the harsh stage lighting and his powerful body that seemed too big for his restricting black tie. He looked incredibly relaxed given the fact that he was about to address hundreds of people whose interest in matters marine probably extended to worrying about where they were going to spend their next beach holiday.

'I was going to talk about the *Titanic*,' Dan began, in a mellow American accent which was music to my ears after the strangulated well-bred English tones I was used to, 'but as the movie went on longer than the ship actually took to sink – ' laughter – 'I figured you'd probably know more about it than I do. I thought I'd talk about lunch instead.' Peregrine immediately perked up. 'This time last week I was visiting the largest fish market in the world, Tsukiji, in Tokyo,' Dan continued. 'Over a million tons of seafood are sold there every day, it's an incredible place. I like sushi. D'you like sushi?' The audience nodded.

'Absolutely,' said Anoushka clearly. Really, the girl was such an attention grabber.

'But that's just a fraction of the ninety million tons of fish that are sold in fish markets throughout the year. Staggering quantities of life are trawled from the ocean every day and aren't being replaced. We're talking about huge nets being trawled on ships so big they're called factory ships. But it's not just fish they scrape up off the ocean floor, it's whole ecosystems that have taken billions of years to evolve, gone in a split second. I've lost count of the thousands of seals, sea lions, horseshoe crabs, dolphins, whales and birds I've fished out of those nets. And nets aren't the only hazard, there's a mountain of plastic down there, too. Once I found a turtle in the Seychelles that had suffocated on a plastic shopping bag. Some garbage rots, but the bags, they just keep piling up.'

I thought of the amount of plastic I threw away in a week and cringed as Dan went on to describe the unexplored magical world beneath the sea. I glanced around noticing that he held the audience in the palm of his powerful hand. But no one was listening more attentively than Anoushka who was staring at him with rapt attention, her fluffy platinum head nodding at everything he said. I wondered what his jealous wife would say if she was there.

'Last week,' Dan was saying, 'I was standing on a cliff overlooking a coastal whaling station in Japan. You may have seen pictures, even films, but nothing prepares you for the stink of those places. We humans are so clever, we can reduce these huge creatures many times our size to small chunks of meat and buckets of oil. But have you ever thought how much more clever it would be *not* to destroy something so magnificent that we don't understand or know how to replace?

'I mean, who the hell decides that it's all right to consign these miraculous creatures to cookpots without even listening to what they might have to say? Doesn't anybody want to know how they manage to find their way to destinations thousands of miles away that have no apparent signposts? What do they know? Might they have a sense of humour? Enjoy the feeling of warm water flowing over their skin? What might we learn from them alive, that makes them so much more valuable than barrels of oil? I guess I'll never know. But one thing I do know. There's no such thing as a free lunch.'

'You can say that again,' said Peregrine. Apart from this interruption there was a rapt silence from the audience for a long moment. I glanced at the rest of the table. The ambassadors seemed to have taken the speech in their stride, while the ambassadresses seemed quite taken with Dan. Eva was ferreting around her undergarments. I had a bizarre notion that she was going to rip off her knickers and throw them at him. I vaguely remember someone describing Dan as the Tom Jones of the marine biology world. But she was obviously just making some kind of adjustment and the knickers remained very much *in situ*. And then the audience burst into rapturous applause.

'What a brilliant speech!' I yelled above the clapping, but Peregrine was intent on scraping the last morsel of lemon tofu syllabub from my plate and didn't hear me. Ugh, he was so annoying!

'How inspiring!' I persevered.

'Absolutely,' agreed Peregrine absently, his eye on the petit fours which were being placed on the tables. 'I must say, they're a bit slow with the coffee. Could you ask Pandora to chivvy them along a bit?'

'No I can't. Really, Peregrine, the oceans are dying and all you can think about is your stomach.' My words were drowned in the continuing applause. 'Don't you care about *anything*?' I continued crossly. Dan had disappeared from the stage and the band was setting up. People would soon be getting up to dance but that was the last thing I felt like doing. I was just longing to go home.

'I'll see you a bit later, I promised I'd help out with the raffle,' I said grumpily.

'Oh, all right, darling. See you later. Save me a dance.'

I surreptitiously gathered up my bag, pinched several boxes of slimming cigarettes, collected my coat from the cloakroom and slipped out.

It was a relief to exchange the carousing inside for the cool night air. It was a clear night and the sky was bright with stars. I shivered and pulled my coat towards me, and set off towards Hyde Park Corner. Dan's impassioned speech had opened up another world. A mysterious place of weird and wonderful creatures evolved over billions of years. If only ten percent of the ocean had been fully explored who knew what amazing secrets might be hidden within its inpenetrable depths? Perhaps an underwater Narnia of mythical creatures. Maybe even mermaids! It was a heavenly thought.

It was too easy to get caught up in day to day petty worries and forget about the bigger picture. He was right. One person could make a difference. I determined to take a more active role supporting the Whale and Dolphin Society and redouble my letter writing efforts. It wasn't much, but I was sure that if I kept my eyes open an opportunity to do something would appear in the future.

At the moment I had to make some quick decisions. Our lifestyle sales policy had resulted in several good offers for the flat and I knew that Pandora was thinking of accepting one of them. If she did I would be utterly homeless. There was nothing for me in London, no home, and no relationship. But instead of making me feel bereft, I suddenly felt full of anticipation.

According to my most recent self-help book, the universe abhorred a void and it was a law of nature that voids must be filled with something. That was my life, an empty space just waiting to be filled with new experiences! I just had to be brave, let go and trust. But should I go to Switzerland or stay in London and return to my cooking business? It was so difficult to decide.

Trying to think brave thoughts, I dashed into the underpass, wishing there were some people around; it was rather menacing at night. Then, in the distance I spotted an elderly lady tottering towards me, bearing a large basket of bits of heather wrapped in foil. A gypsy, obviously fleecing tourists who knew no better. Really, people were so gullible.

'Hello, young lady,' she mumbled as she drew within hearing distance. 'Fancy a nice bit of 'eather? For luck?' I shook my head and prepared to race off. 'I'll read yer palm for a fiver?'

I couldn't resist such an offer. After all, the magical Mrs Motley, palmist to the stars, was booked up for months and charged fifty pounds. 'Yes please,' I said eagerly.

'A tenner and we'll call it quits,' muttered the hag, not missing a trick.

I nodded and she grabbed my hand with a wizened paw.

'You'll be very rich,' she began, 'but you won't make it yourself.'

'Tell me something I don't know,' I laughed.

'And you will find great, enduring love . . .' she peered closely. 'But not here. There, I can't tell you any more. The voices have stopped.'

'Oh, please, carry on!'

She looked at me cunningly. 'OK, OK, another tenner!' I hurriedly proffered another note. 'You will find love on . . . on . . .' she shut her eyes. 'I see a cold windy place, white fences and a man who will build you a low house.'

'You mean I'm going to marry a builder?' She must have made a mistake. I was going to marry a tycoon. 'But who, where . . .'

'Nackered Island. Yes, that's the place.' A gaggle of

wobbling plimsolled American tourists had just appeared at the other end of the tunnel and were making their inexorable flat-footed way towards us. I could see she was losing interest as she prepared to ambush them.

'Nackered Island.' I racked my brains. It sounded like the horrible place off the coast in Essex that was famous for its nuclear rubbish dump. Surely I had misheard.'

'It's not that frightful place in Essex, is it?'

'I live in Essex!' the crone growled menacingly. 'Don't you say anything about Essex, otherwise I'll put a curse on you!'

'No, I didn't mean to cause offence,' I stuttered, running off towards the exit.

'Stupid cow,' she yelled after me viciously. 'You think Surrey's any smarter? HAH!!'

Unable to bear any more insults about my esteemed birth place (home of Lutyens, Phil Collins and so many of the nation's luminaries), I scooted out of hearing range.

Goodness, she was cross. And how did she know I was from Surrey? Was that spooky or what? If only I'd had time to ask if I should go to Switzerland. Damn.

Resurfacing from the Hyde Park underpass, gasping from the dramatic encounter, I spotted an elusive number 14 bus, known as the gentleman's bus because it stopped at only a few choice destinations like Fortnum's and Harvey Nicks.

'OK, universe. I'll do a deal. If I manage to catch the bus I'll go to Switzerland. If I miss it I'll stay here.' It had started to rain and the chances of catching a taxi were slim. I wanted to catch the bus and get home. I broke into a run and jumped on the crowded bus as it was pulling off.

Hanging on to the pole, forgetting about the bizarre encounter, I leaned out, relishing the wind whipping my hair around my face and burst out laughing, the sound whisked away by the wind and lost in the gleaming wet streets of Belgravia. The decision had been made. I was free to go!

Chapter Sixteen

The next morning I woke up early with a clear head and an equally clear resolve about what I was going to do. I was going to clean out my make-up drawer. That would take several hours and by the time I'd finished, Pandora might have woken up and I could tell her my decision to go to Switzerland.

I didn't really know what I was letting myself in for but I had a feeling that I was making the right move. And once I'd made up my mind, everything started to fall into place in my head and I wondered what on earth I'd been so worried about.

I thought it would be a good idea to celebrate my new decisive personality with a brutal purge. I was going to use up all of my old make-up before I would buy any more. I'd just read a frightening article in the *Daily Mail* that revealed that the western world was being secretly polluted by dreadful toxins emanating from many tons of stale and forgotten unguents in women's make-up bags and drawers.

It had gone on to display a selection of streamlined make-up bags belonging to various luminaries like Kate Twig and Ulrika Temptation. Call me a sucker but at the back of my mind there lurked a feeling that if my make-up bag was streamlined I, too, might have a similarly streamlined easi-care life.

Yes, from now on I was going to be my own woman! Purging the planet of poisonous noxious potions that had been festering for years in my bedroom. I would be cleaning out my life just like it advised in my *Feng Shui Manual for Modern Women*.

Delving beneath my bed in my make-up overflow bag I discovered some excitingly coloured eye shadows and glittering purple mascaras that though very old were now thrillingly *à la mode*. I had already saved myself a fortune. After all, if the up-to-the-minute ambassadresses could get away with glittering blue eye shadow and green mascara, I was sure I could. I sat down at my dressing table and began to experiment.

One hour later, thrilled with my iridescent new look, I heard Pandora shuffling around the kitchen and went to tell her my news. She took one look at me and reached for an enormous pair of Jackie O sunglasses that had perched uselessly in the fruit bowl for months.

'I always felt they'd come in useful one day,' she said, continuing with her complicated morning tea ritual. 'You must have dashed off early last night. I'm not surprised, it must have taken the last ten hours to get all that slap on.'

'I heard the speech, though. Dan McCloud is the most incredible speaker. I loved the way he just got up and spoke right from the heart.'

'Yes, we had no idea he was going to give that talk. Of course the charity was thrilled, though I think the ladies on the committee were hoping for something a bit more anodyne.'

'I nearly met him once, he winked at me ages ago at a party. Apparently he has a very jealous wife, but she can't have been there because he was chatting up Anoushka Bird-Whistle last night. She couldn't take her eyes off him.'

'I think he's separated, actually. Somebody told me he's been dating Anoushka which figures. She was draped round him all evening.'

'What a strange combination. I shouldn't think they have a thing in common,' I said disapprovingly.

'Ouch!' Pandora had walked straight into the fridge, causing a clatter as several fridge magnets were violently dislodged. The glasses, while obviously *chic*, had presumably rendered the kitchen a blackout zone. Either that or my dazzling new look had caused temporary blindness.

'D'you like it?' I asked eagerly, once she had regained her composure. 'I've been using up my old eye shadows. I thought I looked very up to the minute in an Abba revival sort of way.'

'Yes, it's . . . it's . . .' She seemed to be struggling to find the right word. I didn't mind, she was probably a bit jealous. 'Very fashionable. You'll have to get a nice silver crocheted cap to complete the ensemble.' She grovelled around the floor picking up the magnets before pouring herself a bowl of grapenut pellets.

'How did the ambassadors react to the ball?' I asked. 'When I left they seemed remarkably relaxed.'

'They were still there when I left. They were having a marvellous time. Mind you, I think all the drink helped. I asked Nars if Norway was going to join the fight against whaling, but he just quoted Edward the Eighth, "Something must be done", and wandered off.'

'Huh, Edward the Eighth did bugger all about anything. He was all talk,' I said crossly.

'Well, at least lots of celebs and photographers were about. The ball should get plenty of coverage,' said Pandora hopefully. 'I was actually a bit worried when you disappeared so early,' she continued. 'I thought you might have been feeling depressed about the situation.'

'What situation?' I ferreted around the cereal cupboard hungrily. I was definitely in the mood for three shredded wheat today.

'Magnus, of course.'

'Oh, that stupid old tart.' I feigned casual indifference. 'He's banged up in some Finnish prison, according to Peregrine.'

'Lucky thing!' said Pandora enviously.

'Yes, he pinched some bloke's bird and got arrested dancing naked in a fish tank.'

'Must have given the fish a bit of a shock,' said Pandora.

'It's funny,' I continued. 'Yesterday I felt emotionally, spiritually and physically polluted by the whole experience, but this morning it's all completely evaporated.' I munched my shredded wheat thoughtfully. 'I bumped into a gypsy on the way home. She said I was going to marry a builder from a windy place with white picket fences called something like Nackered Island. Ever heard of it?'

Pandora thought for a moment. 'Perhaps she means Nantucket. It's a really unspoilt island near Cape Cod in the States. It's famous for its white picket fences and clapboard houses. People go there for whale watching holidays.'

'Hey, that's a bit of a coincidence. Considering I'd just left a whaling ball. Wow.' I was thrilled by this mystic coincidence. 'I can't wait to go there. But it won't be for a while because I decided last night to come out to Switzerland with you if they'll give me a job.'

Pandora put down her spoon in surprise. 'That's great news! You won't live to regret it, I promise.' She glanced at her watch. 'I'll ring Jolly Holidays straightaway and see if they've still got some vacancies.' She reached for the phone and dialled their number.

'Chiara, it's Pandora here. Yes, I'm all set for departure, can't wait! I was just wondering if you've got any last-minute vacancies because my flatmate Oriana Spicer is available for the whole season. You do?' Pandora grinned and gave a thumbs up. 'Yes, she's a brilliant cook and a fabulous skier too.' I shuddered at this blatant untruth. 'Yes, she's just invested in a brand new Sam De Teran ski suit.' She raised her eyes in exasperation. 'No, she's not too glamorous to be a chalet girl, it's a brown ski suit. Not flashy at all. Yes, she was going out with him but they've split up now. Three o'clock this afternoon? I'll just see if that's all right with her . . .' I nodded vigorously. 'Yes, that's perfect. OK, see you later. 'Bye.'

She replaced the receiver triumphantly. 'Yeees! They've got one vacancy left and I think you're in with a chance. You've got to fax her your CV and look frumpy. She was a bit worried that you might be too glamorous. Apparently, Melinda Mowbray—'

'The pork pie heiress?' I interrupted. 'She's a distant cousin of mine.'

'Well, apparently she was a bit of a glamour puss and she ran off with a punter in the first week. No one heard of either of them again.'

'So this year's intake have got to be as untempting as possible?'

'Looks like it.'

'But c'mon, Pandora, you're hardly a dog.'

She laughed wryly. 'Thanks! No, Chiara knows that the chances of me running off with any of Jolly Holidays' Sloane Ranger punters is very slim indeed.'

Pandora and I were as one about that, I thought. If I got the job, I'd learn to ski and also use it as an opportunity to road test all the recipes I'd dreamt up at Cheyne Castle for my cookery book. The Jolly Holidays' punters would be guinea pigs and romance most certainly would not be on the agenda. That was one thing I was sure about.

'I really appreciate the lift,' I said to Pandora, clutching my seat nervously as we raced down one of Pandora's short cuts to the Jolly Holidays HQ that afternoon.

While I did appreciate the lift, Pandora's driving gave a new dimension to the term 'wall of death'. She would have made a great taxi driver in some lawless war zone like Lebanon or El Salvador. You'd never believe that she'd learnt to drive in genteel Godalming.

'No problem. I'm just pleased you've decided to come,' she said, applying blusher while edging the car onto the pavement to give us a clear run along an inside lane. 'It'll be great fun doing it together,' she continued, shoving her blusher into the packed glove compartment and rummaging around for her lipstick.

'Let's not count our chickens, I haven't been given the job yet.' The way Pandora was driving I doubted whether I'd live long enough to be even offered it. 'What sort of egg thing d'you think they'll ask me to cook?' I asked anxiously. Pandora had explained that Chiara would ask me to cook a very basic breakfast dish to prove I knew one end of a frying pan from another.

'Probably a fried egg sandwich, or eggy bread – something very simple anyway. Definitely within your expert capabilities. My cooking test was eggy bread and it was completely inedible but I still got the job. Chiara provided me with three-month-old eggs and some ancient lard that had gone quite grey with these black bits floating about.'

'Sounds a bit like my underwear,' I muttered nervously, thinking that it was fortunate I'd had the foresight to bring six of my mother's free range bantam eggs and some freshly baked bread from the local bakery.

'You'll sail through, no probs. It'll be less eggy bread, more *pain l'oeuf cordon bleu fines herbes*. Hmmmm, that doesn't sound too good, hope she doesn't rumble us on the lingo front. I told her we'd been studying Linguaphone tapes and were completely fluent in French with a rudimentary understanding of German.'

'In our dreams. Although Magnus did teach me some useful Finnish phrases but I doubt they'd be very repeatable.'

'They might come in useful if we got Hungarian punters but I should think that's quite unlikely,' said Pandora, groping around beneath her seat. 'I dropped some of those lovely squidgy dried dates last week, I know they're down here somewhere. D'you want one?' I shook my head. 'Ah, found one!' She retrieved a small soggy brown lump, popped it into her mouth and tried to change gear with her other hand. I clutched my eggs nervously as the car jerked around the road then picked up speed.

'Really, you've got nothing to worry about, you're the best cook I know. Remember all those utterly delicious meals you used to cook when you lived with Peregrine?'

I nodded and smiled, nostalgically remembering the fight that had broken out over my flowerpot bread between Peregrine's doctors at one of our parties. I hadn't bothered to make bread for ages. I flicked down the passenger mirror and tried to rub off some of the green tinted foundation that I was using up. It was meant to even out skin colour but didn't. Unfortunately the morning's make-up experimentation had resulted in watering eyes and a blotchy complexion. Still, at least I wouldn't threaten Chiara with my glamour. But I thought I ought to do something about my miserable expression and practised some grins in the mirror. A man in a white van wound down his window and shouted, 'Careful, love, you'll frighten the horses, ha ha!'

'Oh dear, I'll never get the job if I allow my natural expression to assert itself. The trouble is my mouth turns down quite naturally when I'm not thinking about it. I'll have to stay on grin alert for the whole interview.'

Pandora wasn't listening as she was busy reversing at great speed down a one-way street, a useful manoeuvre that would knock fifteen minutes off our journey time.

I shivered and gazed out of the window, which was steamy with condensation. It was the end of November and freezing. Though only 2.30 in the afternoon, it was already starting to get dark. London was building up to the pre-Christmas panic and the pavements were flooded with irritable shoppers trying to get ahead before the festive terror kicked in properly. The newspapers were full of terrifying reports of seasonal stresses. Road rage and trolley rage, the exciting new disorder that had been discovered in the Kings Road Waitrose last year, had now spread to the suburbs, causing two hundred hospitalizations in Guildford's Sainsburys last month alone.

The incident had been the talk of the country – well, maybe that was a bit of an exaggeration, but the *Daily Mail* had run several features about it. The country was obviously on a slippery slope and it was time to leave for calmer climes before I developed a sinister stress-related hair loss disorder like alopecia. Balding women were becoming an increasing phenomenon on the London streets and I had noticed several new wig shops had sprung up in Knightsbridge recently.

'You know, I really hope I get this job,' I said. 'I wasn't quite sure at first, but the more I think about it, four months in the Alps, clean air, a bit of cooking, a bit of skiing, you never know, we might even end up married.'

'Ugh, steady on. But Chiara did say that thirty per cent of chalet girls meet their future husbands in the Alps, though I certainly didn't meet anyone worth snogging when I did it, let alone marrying. Still, every girl should do it once, or twice in my case. It's quite character building, and you learn how to cook useful things like Mars Bar sauce.'

'Yes that's tru—hey, ZEBRA CROSSING!'

'What – oh shit!' Pandora braked hard and breathed a sigh of relief. 'Phew, lucky that old lady was fast on her pins, thought she was a gonner.' She glanced at her directions. Jolly Holidays had recently downsized from Knightsbridge to an obscure part of Olympia.

'This must be it.' She slammed on the brakes, turned off the ignition and looked at me. 'I'll stay here and think positive thoughts for you. Don't be nervous. Remember, as long as you're enthusiastic, don't mind cleaning loos, your name ends in A, and you haven't got a major personality disorder, the job's basically yours. It's not nearly as competitive as it used to be. They can't give the job away these days.'

I climbed nervously out of the car and went to knock on the modest front door embossed with a ferociously cheerful brass plaque: JOLLY HOLIDAYS! JOLLY GOOD!

A secretary buzzed me in and waved me through. 'Go straight in, Chiara's expecting you.' The phone rang and she picked it up. 'Hellair, Jolly Holidays. Cen ay help you?'

I slid into Chiara's office clutching my string bag of ingredients nervously. I hadn't been for a job interview since I was a teenager and I was feeling increasingly nervous.

A robust looking girl with a face like a round friendly weathered cheese, her thick dark hair pulled back off her face in a velvet Alice band, got up to welcome me. She was wearing a pair of tight jodhpurs that revealed a strapping pair of thighs that I was sure would make mincemeat out of all but the toughest moguls.

'Oriana, isn't it? Sewper. Come and sit down.' Chiara pulled out a comfortable chair for me. 'Managed to find the new office all right?'

I nodded and grinned for good measure.

'We find Olympia so much handier than Knightsbridge, it's so convenient for Gloucestershire. That's where I keep my horse.' She grinned at me and I grinned back cheerfully, trying to disguise my confusion at her last remark. Olympia was on the road to nowhere, it's bleak hangar-like exhibition centre handy only if one wanted to attend a boat, car or obscure alternative health exhibition where one could have one's aura read at huge expense. It was on the Tube, but such was its bleakness that trains would pass through the station but rarely stop.

Chiara glanced down at a piece of paper on her lap. 'According to your CV you're perfect chalet girl material. Two O levels.' She whistled impressively. 'You must have been quite a swot. Lucy Clayton Grooming diploma, fluent French and German, and goodness me, you're an experienced cordon bleu cook too! Though that's not terribly important, people don't go on chalet holidays to *eat*, thank goodness. No, what they want from their chalet girl is an uncomplicated cheerful soul who'll brighten the place up a bit. Now, if you can follow me I'm going to take you into our *really grotty* office kitchen where I shall give you ten minutes to make a fried egg sandwich. Eggs and lard are in the fridge, the plates are in the sink . . .'

She showed me through into the kitchen, gesticulating vaguely around before suddenly brightening. 'Ooh, *there* are my ciggies, I'd been wondering where they'd got to.' She then swiped a bag of twiglets and retreated back to her office. I'd been going to declare the contents of my string bag but Chiara had seemed desperate to return to her office and have a smoke.

Once I was alone I glanced nervously around the kitchen. Grotty was an understatement. The place was littered with unwashed mugs, frying pans and plates congealed with layers of fat.

I opened the fridge gingerly and glimpsed three elderly eggs and a greying slab of lard just as Pandora had described. I shut it again quickly and began preparing the sandwich. I had nine minutes to go. It was terribly exciting! Like *Ready Steady Cook* on TV. Any moment now Fern Britten might appear with a microphone and a cameraman from behind the fridge.

I cut the fresh floury white loaf into slices (you couldn't make a fried egg sandwich with brown bread, that would defeat the whole cholesterol-laden purpose), and put them in the toaster. I quickly scoured out the office frying pan and wiped it dry with some kitchen paper, forgoing the elderly office tea towel cowering damply on the floor. Melting a knob of unpasteurized creamy butter in the pan, I cracked four eggs into the hot golden foam and flicked on the toaster. As the butter sizzled, the eggs cooked and the bread toasted, I realized how much satisfaction I got from transforming a basic set of ingredients into a delicious simple meal.

I quickly rummaged around for a plate but the ones in the sink were chipped and filthy. Luckily, right at the back of a cupboard I caught sight of a simple white plate with a gold border. It was a bit grand for a fried egg sandwich but it would do. I quickly placed it on the stove to warm up, buttered the toast and carefully lifted out the eggs when they were just cooked and arranged them on top. Chiara suddenly put her head around the door, releasing a great waft of cigarette smoke from her office.

'We're ready when you are, Oriana. Time's nearly up! It smells absolooootely delicious, the team can't wait to get stuck in!'

Oh God, I thought, hurriedly assembling the sandwich, how many of them were there, for heaven's sake? It was less *Ready Steady Cook*, more *MasterChef.* I half expected Lloyd Grossman and his foodie friends to be waiting expectantly in Chiara's office ready to jab excitedly with their forks at my fried egg sandwich and make erudite foodie comments.

I garnished it with a sprig of watercress, a quite unnecessary gesture given Sloane antipathy to garnishes in general, and I pushed open the door nervously. I was just able to make out two figures in the dense fog of smoke.

'Is that you, Oriana old thing?' called Chiara. 'Excuse the smoke, but Lucinda and I are on a stop smoking course and it's essential that we keep to our programme.'

I set the sandwich down in front of them while Lucinda waved away the smoke and coughed horribly.

'I'm going to open the window, Chiara,' she said. 'We must do Oriana's sandwich justice, it looks simply delish.' She went over to the window and heaved it open, releasing a great waft of freezing November air into the room.

Chiara cut the sandwich in half and took a mouthful. 'Ummm, this is yummy, Oriana. Jolly Holidays are famous for their fried egg sandwiches. We have punters who book with us solely because our girls still cook good simple English food. They're just not into all this foreign muck that other skiing companies seem to think people want. We've simply no truck with all that fancy cordon bleu nonsense, I'm afraid.' She prodded the watercress garnish disapprovingly.

'Yes, just keep the nosh simple – eggy bread, fish fingers, baked beans, a sponge cake at tea time, that's all they want,' added Lucinda, munching her sandwich enthusiastically. She grinned, revealing nicotine-stained buck teeth.

'So, Oriana, we'd be thrilled to offer you a job with Jolly Holidays.' Chiara glanced down at her list. 'Let's just see if I've covered everything. Cooking ability, *rather*.' She grinned at me. 'Name ends in A, yes. Cheerful disposition,' she glanced at me. 'No depressive illnesses or anything?'

I grinned brightly. 'No fear!'

'Well, you seem a sensible sort.'

I was glad I'd gone for my deeply librarian look. I knew my midi-length thick brown tweed skirt would come in handy one day.

'I know you're a great chum of Pandora's so she'll be able to show you the ropes. You're both top girls so we're going to send you to our top resort. This year we've *broken the mould*, so to speak, and taken on some rather swanky chalets in *Hssshhtaaaaaaaa*.' Her authentically guttural pronunciation ended up in a fit of coughing. When the heaving had stopped, she looked at me expectantly. I stared blankly back. Where on earth was *Hssshtaaaaaaaaaahhhhh*? It sounded Austrian. I couldn't go to Austria. In my fragile state I could only manage Switzerland. I needed neutrality and trains that ran on time. No, Austria was no good at all.

'D'you know the village? We've rented six chalets as a kind of experiment. As you know, Jolly Holidays has cornered the market in exclusive skiing holidays so we thought we would provide our clients with something really special. Our chairman has personally hand-picked six really nice chalets, quite pricey, but we're confident that this will open the market for an exclusive international clientele.'

'Um, where did you say it was?'

'*Hstaaad*,' said Chiara impatiently.

Of course, Gstaad! My heart sang! Alpine home of the world's most glamorous movers and shakers. Paradise playground for the beautiful people. How could I resist!

'We plan to put you in Chalet Tiara, which is the most recent addition to our portfolio,' continued Chiara briskly.

'We'll bus you all out on the first of December, all right?'

'Yes, that sounds fine.'

'Don't you go out with Peregrine Skye-Rocca?' asked Lucinda curiously. 'I only ask because my sister's best friend's brother's cousin used to go out with him, but I think it sort of fizzled out. She never said why, it was all rather odd.'

'I used to, but we're just good friends now.'

'That's the ticket, free agent, best way to be,' said Chiara.

'Yes, quite,' said Lucinda, fingering her lank mousy ponytail wistfully.

'Oriana, it's been a pleasure meeting you. I look forward to seeing you on the first of December, six a.m. sharp at Sloane Square. I'll write to you and Pandora with the details.'

I shook hands with them both and made a speedy exit onto the street. Through the open window I could hear distant sounds of sobbing followed by Chiara's brisk, 'Buck up, old girl. You'll feel much better once you're on your horse.'

I paused for a moment. Poor Lucinda, had she been crossed in love too? Would she really feel better when she was on her horse? Was there no respite even for the plain?

'Oriana! Stop daydreaming. Did you get it?' Pandora had leapt out of her car and met me outside the offices.

'Get what? Oh yes, yes, they've asked me to take on Chalet Tiara in Gstaad, so we can go out together. Isn't that great!'

I climbed into the passenger seat and Pandora shot off down the street. 'We're off,' she cried excitedly. 'Gstaad, here we come!' She grinned. 'Celebratory drink?'

'Definitely.'

'Ritzy Marina, first stop. We deserve some champagne! But we've only time for one, Georgie's arranged for a man to come round this evening so I need to get back and tart the place up a bit.'

'So that's this evening's entertainment sorted out,' I said hopefully. 'D'you think he'll be a dish?'

'I dunno,' said Pandora, collapsing into estuary English

as for once she concentrated on her driving. I fell silent. I had realized long ago that Pandora fell into the group of drivers who were unable to speak and drive properly at the same time and it was worse at night because her eyesight deteriorated. I glanced over nervously, wondering if I'd offend her if I got a taxi home. She had put one hand over her left eye, which didn't seem to be helping.

'Can't see a thing out of my left eye at night but I've discovered that if I cover it up things look less blurred on the left side of the road,' she explained.

'But surely it's better that things are blurred than that you don't see them at all?' I suggested nervously, thinking that perhaps we should abandon our pit stop at the Ritzy Marina Club. Though oddly enough Pandora's driving often improved after a glass of champagne.

'No, my right eye compensates. The human body is a wonderful thing when you think about it, isn't it?'

That was the last thing I remember. Neither of us saw the temporary plywood shopfront that had just been extended into the road until it was too late and Pandora had driven straight into it. Luckily we had been moving very slowly so there was hardly any damage. It was embarrassing, though, because lots of people saw the accident and we looked like a right pair of bimbos.

At least one good thing came out of it. Pandora went to the optician the next day and ordered a pair of contact lenses. So the experience ended up being quite positive really.

Chapter Seventeen

Given Pandora's bad driving karma it was just as well we could travel to the Alps on the chalet girl bus.

I was kept frantically busy until departure packing and tying up loose ends. I had to visit Cheyne Castle to pick up all my recipe books, in particular the scrapbooks in which I'd kept careful notes from our many parties. These culinary jottings would be invaluable now I was to be running Chalet Tiara.

I was terribly excited at going to Gstaad. Pandora wasn't so thrilled because she's a keen skier and had been gunning for Verbier. But I'm much more of a gold tap posing type of person and was full of anticipation at the possibility of squeezing onto a T-bar with Roger Moore or similar megawatt celeb.

I dreamt that our four months in this glitzy village would be like an elongated episode of *The Persuaders*, full of surreal glamour, mysterious, irresistibly flashy men up to no good, days of posing on the piste interspersed with the opportunity to create sumptuous and imaginative meals for my elegant guests.

I was excited at the thought of cooking for an appreciative audience again. I'd been so happy pottering around the kitchen at Cheyne Castle, organizing our wonderful parties. And it would be useful having a captive audience to road test all the recipes and handy household hints I'd been collecting. Of course, I'd have to specify organic meat and vegetables, and after Dan's speech, I'd have to think twice about fish recipes. I planned to tie in my recipes with a sort of frothy chalet girl diary cum romance. People liked reading about chalet girls for some reason, and no one had written a book about them before.

Whenever I mentioned I was writing a book, people would smile indulgently or tell me I was wasting my time, but I *knew* I was on to something. I would keep careful notes of the thrills and spills of chalet life and turn it into a novel!

On the morning of our departure, Pandora and I made it in good time to the Jolly Holidays rendezvous point at Sloane Square. It was a chaotic scene. I had already suspected that organization wasn't Jolly Holidays' best feature. And matters were complicated, as they seemed to be sharing the coach with another company called SKI CHEAPER! whose name was plastered all over the bus along with that of JOLLY HOLIDAYS, JOLLY GOOD!

The bus was parked directly outside the Tube, causing considerable traffic chaos with girls, their friends and mothers wandering around haphazardly. Several trunks had been dumped around the square and hordes of Sloaney-looking parents were calling hopelessly for porters in ringing tones.

Weeping parents were clustered around their recalcitrant offspring who were eager to be off. Slivers of conversation reached me. 'Camilla, you will ring, won't you?' 'Yah, yah, Mummy, don't fuss, *OK*?' 'Well, I told you you should borrow my Hermes puffa,' said another. 'Do remember to look up Buffy, she runs her own ballooning company in Chateâu d'Oex.'

The girls were a mixed bag. Several seemed terrifyingly sophisticated, others appeared to have led alarmingly sheltered lives and one girl was exclaiming loudly that this was her first time on a bus of any kind. I suspected that our only unifying feature might be our Christian names, which were bound to all end in 'a'.

The Ski Cheaper employees, most of whom seemed

entirely free of parental supervision, were wandering around mulishly smoking and manhandling enormous snowboards into the coach.

'Christ, it's like something out of *Passage to India*,' muttered Pandora, wrinkling her snub nose and narrowly avoiding a Salomon boot bag that an infirm parent had flung in the direction of the coach.

A harassed Chiara appeared waving a clipboard perkily, on which she was checking off names.

'Girls, girls! Order, order!! Please get on the bus immediately! And please take a copy of the *Chalet Girl Handbook* with you to read on the bus!' A Jolly Holidays minion had appeared and began handing out a book with a picture of a grinning chinless girl on the cover. 'Please read it carefully. It's packed with useful hints and recipes!' called Chiara desperately.

At last everyone seemed to be seated. But it was rather maddening because we then had to spend an hour waiting for stragglers.

'Anyone here know where Arabella Ormsby-Spore is?' pleaded Chiara, her clipboard drooping slightly.

'Probably overslept, knowing her,' muttered a voice from the back.

'Ambrosia, you're a great chum of Bella's, aren't you? Any ideas where she's got to? I've tried to ring her but there's no answer.'

A mobile phone rang. For five seconds chaos reigned as the contents of the Jolly Holidays' handbags were thrown into the central aisle. It turned out to belong to Ambrosia, a pretty plump dark girl seated in the row behind us.

'Yah, we're all waiting for you. You're bloody hopeless. See you in a sec. She's on her way, Chiara,' called Ambrosia. 'She's literally only round the corner, she lives in the GTC.'

'How terribly handy for Peter Jones,' said someone conversationally. The bus lapsed into silence.

'As long as she's not coming to Gstaad,' I whispered to

Pandora. 'Arabella Ormsby-Spore – I mean, what sort of name is that? Besides, she sounds absolutely chaotic.'

'And imagine living in the GTC. You wouldn't get much privacy, would you?' asked a muffled, unworldly-sounding person.

'She doesn't actually live in the shop, she lives in the penthouse above it,' explained Ambrosia patiently. There was a mulish tittering from the back of the coach where the Ski Cheaper employees had bagged the back seat.

'While we're waiting for our latecomer I'll put you all in the picture,' said Chiara, pushing back unruly hair with a harassed hand. 'The bus will be dropping the Ski Cheaper girls off in Val d'Isère and Les Arcs, and then taking the Jolly Holidays girls straight to Switzerland. Crans Montana, Verbier, and finally Gstaad.'

'Snobs,' muttered someone in the back, precipitating a general tittering of agreement amongst the Ski Cheaper employees, who were now all wearing baseball hats back to front and wearing sweatshirts bearing frightening messages like 'BIG AIR', and 'BOARDS ARE BEST', and 'OUTTA MY WAY FAT BOY'.

I shivered. Wasn't one safe from class warfare even on the chalet girl bus? I hoped Pandora and I would not be forced to reveal our destination and incur the wrath and jealousy of those unfortunate enough to be going to France. France was full of snowboarders. I didn't imagine there would be any of that sort of thing in Gstaad.

'It's true what Auberon Waugh says about the English hating each other,' I whispered to Pandora, sensing the possibility of a them and us situation breaking out.

'Too awful,' agreed Pandora. 'Do look,' she continued, pointing out of the window where a taxi had just pulled up. A leggy blonde with a floating cloud of hair, wearing a sumptuous purple velvet coat, falling becomingly apart at the seams (it had to be Voyage), was flapping around a vast Louis Vuitton trunk. We couldn't hear what she was saying, but she appeared to be in a state of considerable agitation.

'It must be the Arabella person. Fancy getting a taxi from the other side of the square. Her sense of direction must be even worse than yours, Oriana,' whispered Pandora.

Having dealt with her trunk – she'd obviously packed everything but her Afghan hound – Arabella climbed on the bus. 'Hello, Chiara, I'm *sooooo* sorry I'm late. I haven't kept you all waiting too terribly long, have I?' She tossed a thick skew of corkscrew curls out of her heart-shaped face and grinned at the assembled company. 'Sorry, everyone. Beastly alarm, traffic cones, usual horror, etc.' She cut such a dazzling figure that even the mulish row in the back were silenced from their rendition of 'Why are we waiting?'

'I just can't see her cleaning a loo. Can you?' Pandora whispered, riveted by the show.

'Not in a million years. Maybe she'll be able to find a cleaner when we're out there. Or maybe she's a hostess type person, or a ski guide, or something . . .' I trailed off doubtfully as the coach lurched into Sloane Square, causing a volley of hooting and mangled traffic in our wake.

The relief at finally being on our way melted the ice somewhat and we got chatting with Ambrosia who was also going to Gstaad.

'D'you know who else is going?' I asked, warming to Ambrosia, who was, well, big-boned isn't a nice description, but she was definitely what the Americans call 'heavy'. She had clear luminous skin and melting dark spaniel eyes framed by thick black lashes. She looked like the sort of girl who'd be a champion baker and good in a crisis.

'Just Arabella. She and I are working in the same chalet. I'm doing the cooking and she's meant to be my assistant, sort of doing the washing up and stuff . . .' She gazed despairingly at the back of Arabella's blonde head bobbing about uselessly in the front.

'Apparently there are only five of us going to Gstaad, it's a kind of experiment. I wonder who the other one is.'

The three of us glanced around the coach nervously.

'Oh well, we'll know soon enough,' said Pandora, yawning. That set us all off and we spent the rest of the twenty-four-hour journey semi-dozing. Most of us took one of the sleeping pills that were being offered around and within a few hours nearly all the coach was fast asleep.

I woke up briefly when the Ski Cheaper employees crashed off the bus with their snowboards in Val d'Isere and again when most of the girls got off at Verbier and Crans Montana. By that time the bus was empty except for Ambrosia, Arabella, Pandora, a noisy girl wearing tight leather trousers called Rochetta and me. It was only when we were winding our way up the narrow mountain road that led to Gstaad that we all began to sit up and smile at each other cautiously.

Entering the village I pressed my nose against the glass window, eager to drink in the glamour after our grimy journey. I shivered happily. It was absolutely beautiful, just how I imagined. It's rare that expectations coincide with reality, but Gstaad radiated warmth and festivity. The elegant fir trees lining the main street were decked with thousands of tiny white lights illuminating exquisite designer boutiques selling impractical but stunning ski wear within.

The others were similarly entranced. 'Look up there!' breathed Ambrosia, nose pressed against the frozen glass.

We followed her gaze to a Gothic building perched precariously on the top of a steep hill, bedecked in fairy lights. Could it be real? It looked more like a Jane Asher party cake.

'The Palace,' whispered Pandora. She was no doubt reliving a knee-trembling weekend she'd spent there with her then romantic interest Jack Dudley. Maybe I'd be similarly whisked away for a weekend. Maybe Magnus or my ex, Tom Gold (who had recently split up from Madison Spratt, his German über-model girlfriend), would find out I was in Gstaad and drag me there . . .

The coach came to a sudden stop, interrupting my delicious daydream. The door opened and we collected our hand baggage and shuffled out bleary-eyed into the snow. We'd been on the chalet girl bus for thirty hours and I felt like death warmed up. But a few deep breaths of the crisp alpine air soon began to have a magical effect on my sleep-sodden brain.

'Hi, girls! All in one piece?' We were greeted by a tall athletic American girl in her early thirties wearing a cropped silver anorak, a pair of sporty black ski pants and a red cashmere hat pulled fetchingly over a mop of short blonde hair. Even in the dark her face glowed with fresh mountain air and exercise. 'Welcome to Gstaad. I'm Ally, the ski guide and your rep.' She broke off to speak to the coach driver in impressively rapid German. I heaved a sigh of relief. Ally obviously knew what she was doing, thank God. I wouldn't have been surprised if the tenuous Jolly Holidays' system had completely broken down at this point.

'I've got a list of your names here,' she continued, glancing efficiently at a piece of paper. 'Pandora Black?'

'That's me,' replied Pandora, wiping sleep out of her blue eyes.

'You're running Chalet Twix just round the corner. Ambrosia and Arabella? Your chalet is in Saanen, that's the next village.'

'Saanen? I've never heard of the place,' pouted Arabella, her small but perfectly formed nose wrinkling in distaste. 'Couldn't we swap with somewhere a little more central?'

'Shush, Bella,' said Ambrosia.

'Don't worry, you'll have the Jolly Holidays car and Saanen is literally five minutes away,' reassured Ally. Bella visibly brightened at the word car. I couldn't imagine her driving any more than I could cleaning loos. What useful function could she play, poor girl?

'Rochetta?'

The tall rangy girl with the tangle of dark hair wearing

tight leather trousers raised her hand. 'That's me.'

'You're in Chalet Oiseau Bleu on the Saanen road. And last but not least, Oriana?'

I nodded, nervous with anticipation. This was the moment of reckoning. Where was Chalet Tiara, and what would it be like?

'You're running Chalet Tiara up there,' she gestured towards a distant mountain. 'It's a bit out of the way, but the views are spectacular.'

Oh God! Miles away. I'd turn into a langlaufing hermit.

'If you can stash your kit in my jeep we'll whiz over to Saanen and drop off Bella and Ambrosia and then come back and drop the rest of you off.'

We helped Ally pile some luggage into the jeep but once we had heaved Arabella's trunk on, there wasn't much room for anybody else's, so we had to leave it on the pavement.

'Are you sure it will be all right there?' asked Pandora, fingering her straight blonde hair nervously.

'Of course,' said Ally confidently. 'This isn't Val d'Isère, you know.'

'So, d'you all know each other?' she continued once we had finally piled in the jeep and set off towards Saanen.

'Ambrosia and I are kind of related,' explained Arabella. 'Our parents married each other five years ago.'

'But they're divorced now.'

'Ambrosia's mother is my father's third wife.'

'That sounds confusing,' I said cheerfully. It was nice that they came from dysfunctional families too. I looked forward to in-depth conversations in tearooms where we could mull over our unhappy childhoods in microscopic detail.

'Oriana and I share a flat together in London,' volunteered Pandora. 'I was a chalet girl in Verbier a few years ago and persuaded Oriana to come out. She's an ace cook.'

There was an awkward silence.

'Can you cook then, Pandora?' asked Ambrosia quietly.

'Oh, just the basics, enough to get by,' said Pandora.

'Nothing compared to Oriana.' Rochetta, Ambrosia and Bella shifted awkwardly but said nothing. Anyone would think they couldn't boil an egg – God, perhaps they couldn't. They certainly wouldn't be the first chalet girls who were strangers to a saucepan.

'That's good, I'll be round for dinner tomorrow then!' suggested Ally, smoothly covering the awkward moment. She paused for a moment. 'Um, maybe not tomorrow actually, the kitchen might, um, need a bit of cranking up.' Cranking up? What on earth did she mean?

'So what's the night life like then?' interrupted Rochetta energetically before Ally could elaborate. Oh God, what was wrong with the kitchen? *Was* there a kitchen?

'Well, I've only just got out here myself, it's a very social place, but I think you have to be born into it, sort of thing.'

'You mean, it's not a crazy kangaroo pub sort of place?' asked Rochetta mournfully.

'No, thank *God*,' shuddered Bella.

'The kitchen?' I inquired timidly. 'You were saying something about the kitchen at Chalet Ti—' There was a loud crash from the back of the jeep.

'Oh God, someone's dropped off!' panicked Ambrosia. 'Don't panic!'

Ally looked in the rear-view mirror and screeched to a standstill. 'It's the trunk.' The contents of Bella's vast trunk were indeed spewed out all over the road.

'C'mon, we better pick everything up before it gets run over.'

We all clambered out and dashed around the road rescuing bits of Bella's exotic wardrobe. Slithers of fine silk underwear, gauzy evening dresses and richly pattered Hermes scarves were just some of the items blowing about. Mercifully the road was quiet, apart from the occasional Swiss farmer and the odd Ferrari so we managed to retrieve most of the contents of the trunk.

It's the oddest thing, but this little contretemps proved to be quite a bonding experience. Before, we had just seemed a slightly mismatched group with very little in common. But rushing around the road clutching bits of Bella's designer wardrobe, whooping excitedly at each new discovery, really broke the ice. And just as we were picking up the final piece of Voyage, a Lamborghini came roaring towards us and screeched to a halt. A small dark man climbed out with difficulty.

My goodness, it was Tony 'the toupee' Louche, the pointlessly good-looking fifties crooner, who had had a string of hits with his band the Louche Limpets. Our first celeb!

'Ladies, can I be of assistance?'

'Rather!' said Bella, tossing her blonde curls flirtatiously and looking charmingly inept. 'My trunk has just *exploded* all over the road. D'you think you could possibly help us put it back in the jeep?'

Tony Louche, though short, somehow managed to heave the trunk into the back of the jeep. He was rewarded for his chivalry with Bella's mobile phone number, and roared off in his Lamborghini looking very cheerful.

'Tony Louche,' breathed Pandora reverently. 'I thought he was dead.'

'She's a man magnet.' Ambrosia's melting brown eyes were wistful.

'I wish,' exclaimed Bella modestly. 'He'll probably never ring me,' she added unconvincingly. 'Anyway, thanks so much for helping me pick everything up. I think we found most of it.'

'But everything you brought was so impractical,' said Ambrosia sensibly. 'I don't know what you were thinking of.'

'Oh, don't be a nag, darling. Ooh, is this it?' We had pulled up outside an elegant wooden chalet slightly off the road. A creaking looking deux chevaux was parked outside with Jolly Holidays, Jolly Good! emblazoned on the side.

'Christ, I'm not driving that old bone-shaker,' muttered Bella.

'Home sweet home,' said Ally. 'Get your kit together, Bella and Ambrosia.'

'Can we all take a recce?' asked Pandora, desperate to feed her house fetish. 'I love looking around houses.'

'Yeah, of course,' agreed Ally, nimbly swinging her long legs out of the jeep. I bet she was a stylish skier.

The chalet was immaculate inside with a huge wooden kitchen and six enormous bedrooms, one of which Ambrosia and Bella were to share.

'I'll be back at nine tomorrow morning to show you how everything works. The only thing that bothers me is that this phone only takes incoming calls.'

'*Pas de problème*. We've both got mobiles. I sleep with mine under the pillow so I never miss a call,' explained Bella checking her reflection in a handy fold-down mirror attached to her phone.

'Has anyone else got their own cell phone?' asked Ally.

We all slipped our hands into our pockets reassuringly and nodded.

'That's great, it'll be much easier to stay in touch, specially for Oriana.'

I shivered. I was being sent to an isolation unit halfway up a mountain, with no phone and no kitchen.

'We'd better exchange numbers now. And if we don't speak before, I'd like us all to meet up tomorrow at three p.m. at Pop-Ups tearoom, the café next to the tennis courts. I'll clue you all in about your guests then.'

'When are the first punters due?' Pandora had all the lingo.

'In a week, so you'll have plenty of time to get your bearings and sort out your chalets, not that that will take most of you very long. Don't worry about Chalet Tiara, Oriana, I'll be able to give you a hand straightening it out tomorrow morning. I've only glanced in through the window, I haven't actually been inside it yet as I was only given the key this afternoon.'

A thousand questions were on my lips but Ally shooed the rest of us back into the van and we headed back for Gstaad and dropped Rochetta at Chalet Oiseau Bleu. We were met at the door by the stony-faced Swiss owner so unfortunately didn't get the chance for a recce. I wondered what on earth she would make of Rochetta with her wild dark gypsy hair and tight leather trousers, but felt Rochetta could probably handle any disapproval. She seemed very confident. I doubted that she'd stick out the season though. She had 'bolter' written all over her.

'I do hope they'll all manage,' sighed Ally. 'This is my first season as a rep and I was hoping that I'd get five girls who knew the ropes.'

'Oh dear, Pandora's the only expert in our batch, I'm afraid, but I'm sure we'll all pick things up quickly,' I said doubtfully, gazing out of the window and admiring the landscape gleaming opaquely in the moonlight, the trees starkly outlined against the dark night sky. Hang on, there was something soft and pink hanging from one of them.

'Hey, that looks like something of Bella's – look, hanging from that tree.'

'God, yes, we better pick it up.' Ally braked and I slipped out and retrieved what was a soft pink cashmere shawl hanging off a branch.

'Mmmm, this must be one of those pashmina things,' I said once I'd climbed back into the van. 'Good job we spotted that, it's the only warm thing she's got, judging by the rest of the stuff in her trunk.'

The three of us silently contemplated the contents of Bella's trunk but carefully said nothing.

'So what's Chalet Tiara li—'

'And this is Chalet Twix,' interrupted Ally cheerfully. 'It's a great location, you're right by the lifts and the sports centre.' Hadn't she heard me? Why wouldn't she talk about Chalet Tiara? She must have gained some impression from peering through the window.

Chalet Twix was modern and immaculately cared for, its windows gleamed, their sills festively decorated with window boxes artfully arranged with branches of fir and purple heather.

'Oh, it's beautiful!' exclaimed Pandora, unable to believe her luck.

I experienced a small but none the less unwelcome pang of jealousy as Ally showed us quickly around the immaculate chalet. She glanced at her watch. 'We better be getting off to Chalet Tiara. I expect Oriana is getting curious.'

'A bit, yes,' I laughed casually.

'I wanted to take you to Chalet Tiara last because it might take us a bit of time to get you settled in properly,' said Ally worryingly once we were back on the road. My heart sank with dread.

'Is it, is it habitable?' I asked nervously.

'Oh, of course. Chiara said there is a caretaker, but she's been ill in hospital for three months. She says it's fine, but might need a bit of a wipe down. Like I said, I haven't actually been inside but it looks like it's got loads of character. It's apparently one of the oldest chalets in Gstaad,' she said ominously.

'How old?' I squeaked, but my voice was absorbed by the engine growling as Ally put the van in a low gear to prepare for the steep ascent.

'It's icy tonight,' she remarked absently as she concentrated on the road.

'You're very good at driving in the snow,' I said admiringly. 'Were you brought up in the mountains?'

'No, my family come from a little island called Nantucket just outside of Boston.'

'Oh, I know Nantucket.' Since the gypsy's revelation I had found out a little more about the island. 'It's famous for its cranberries and white picket fences.'

'You've got it spot on. Most English people haven't even heard of the place.'

'Actually I hadn't until this frightful old gypsy mugged me for a tenner last year, then told me I'd marry someone from Nantucket Island, though she pronounced it Nackered. She got quite aggressive when I said I hoped it wasn't some frightful rubbish dump in Essex. It was really amazing because then I found out that Nantucket used to be the whaling centre of the world in the nineteenth century and I'd just left a ball we organized to raise money for whales. It was really quite mystic.'

'She was obviously making an unconscious connection of some kind. There's always a rational explanation for those sort of things,' said Ally sensibly.

'Oh, I quite agree,' I lied. I didn't want Ally to think I was a flake just yet. She'd find out soon enough. 'I think I might have bought some cranberry pickle that came from there, that's how I know about the cranberries,' I added.

I had regretfully picked up a pickle addiction from the industrial cleaners, though I was gradually weaning myself off Branston onto more exotic pickle mixtures like pumpkin, cranberry and even parsnip. Such mixtures came in small jars, were sourced entirely from Bluebird and Harvey Nicks food hall and were therefore ruinously expensive. But now I had a proper kitchen (though I couldn't count on this) I could perhaps make my own. I wondered if one could buy cranberries in Gstaad.

'Here we are at last,' said Ally, turning off the winding road into a private drive. 'Welcome to Chalet Tiara.'

Although it was dark, the moon shone onto the bright snow, illuminating the stunning timbered chalet, beautifully decorated with sun-faded frescoes. I could hardly breathe it was so lovely. A path of mossy, snow-covered steps led up to a heavy door, above which I noticed a small wood carving of a girl with long swirling hair and a sad expression.

'What a beautiful wood carving over the door. D'you think it's an angel or something?'

Ally looked up. 'No, I think it's a mermaid. Look, her

hair turns into a kind of fishy tail. You sometimes see mermaids and angels on the front of chalets, they're meant to protect the inhabitants.'

'There's an inscription,' I said.

Ally peered up, frowning in concentration. 'I know German, but I can't make it out. The builders of these old chalets often put up a little motto; it's a very quaint custom. I think it must be in the local dialect. It's pretty impenetrable, I'm afraid.' She withdrew a heavy keyring with masses of keys attached. 'Now, let's see . . .' She tried out various keys without any luck. 'Don't worry, if we can't get you in, there's a spare bed in my studio. Here, why don't you have a go?'

I was hopeless with keys and didn't see where I could succeed where the practical Ally had failed but took them anyway. I fumbled around, putting a key randomly into the lock. It opened miraculously. Ally was very impressed. 'Hey, you're good with keys, well done.'

With more confidence, feeling that things were going to be OK, I pushed open the ornately-carved door. Though it looked heavy, it didn't seem to need very much pressure. Ally fumbled around for a light switch, I rested my hand on the wall and found it, plunging the dark hallway suddenly into dim light.

'The place obviously hasn't been touched for ages,' I murmured as we made our way through the porch into a spacious hall. Various pieces of furniture were swathed in dustsheets and the uneven floor was covered in threadbare carpets. There was a musty damp smell but I loved the place. I felt the dustsheets and threadbare carpets were just protecting a jewel. I lifted up the edge of a rug; the floor beneath, though uneven, was a rich honey-brown and set in an intricate parquet pattern. The dustsheets in the hall concealed a graceful circular table made of walnut and intricately carved chairs were backed against the wall. There was a tantalizing sense of treasures to be discovered and I felt that someone had obviously once loved this place with a passion.

'Christ, I'm so sorry about this, Oriana,' apologized Ally. 'Chiara said the owner had promised that the place was ready to go, but I guess with the caretaker being sick and all . . . Don't worry, I'll come round in the morning to help straighten things out.'

But I was barely listening, and had wandered into a large, wood-panelled drawing room just off the hall. 'Ally! Check out the fire.' I visualized the cosy room coming to life once I'd made it up.

Ally peered bleakly into the grate. 'God, it's full of ash.'

'And the ceiling, look.' The ceiling was decorated with the most beautiful trompe l'oeil of a beautiful young woman surrounded by mythical animals against a background of snow and a sparkling river. 'See, there are fawns, marmots, leprechauns, a unicorn, and look, a lion in the distance.'

'It's like Narnia,' suggested Ally. 'I wonder who the girl is.'

'Her hair and face remind me a bit of the mermaid outside the door.' We gazed at the ceiling transfixed. It was a bit smoky from the fire, but that just added to its charm.

A dining room led off the hall and beyond that lay a huge kitchen laid with uneven dark red flagstones. 'It's enormous! And it's got an Aga!'

There was indeed a huge cherry-coloured Aga, which was sadly stone-cold. Ally leaned against a large wooden dresser studded with exquisite pieces of blue and white china as I quickly pulled off the dustsheet covering a large oblong kitchen table. One end was tipped with marble.

'Wow, nice table. I wonder why they stuck the marble on the end,' said Ally.

'It's for making pastry.' I fingered the smooth cool stone reverently. I'd always longed for a marble table to make pastry on.

'You can make pastry?' Ally sounded surprised.

'Of course. Making bread and pastry are my favourite

things. I'm quite an anxious person and I find it really relaxing.'

'But if you can cook, why have you become a chalet girl?' Ally fingered a blue and white teacup curiously. 'I've worked for Jolly Holidays for two seasons now, and none of the girls has ever been able to cook. Chiara and the directors seem to think fussing about food is a bit infra dig.'

'I know, I nearly didn't get the job because I put a garnish on the fried egg sandwich. Very non-U.'

'What I don't get is that if you read the English newspapers on the weekends you'd think that the English were mad keen cooks.'

'I know what you mean, there's nothing but restaurant reviews and obscure recipes for things cooked with kumquats. But I think it's got a bit like sex, people want to read about it but they don't want to actually have to do it.'

We giggled and I felt the tension lift from my shoulders. It was going to be fun working with Ally. Pandora's rep in Verbier had sounded a complete nightmare, starting whispering campaigns against girls whose names didn't end with 'a' and turning up at unexpected times of the night to make fridge inspections. Ally, on the other hand, was a breath of fresh air.

'It's nice that you're American. It should help keep the peace a bit. I don't know if you've noticed, but English people all hate each other. Most of the time it's politely concealed, but it's started to break out more and more.' I wanted to add that throwing a colonial in the melting pot would be a great help, but I knew from past experience that colonials didn't like being described as colonials. And Ally, coming from near Boston, was bound to be quite sensitive to that sort of thing. I prided myself on my tact and kept mum.

'But the English are so polite, that's what I love about your country.'

'We can be, but there's this repressed rage simmering below the surface. I don't know if you've been reading about all the road rage and now we've invented trolley rage. People literally kill each other, and in nice middle-class places like Guildford.'

'I'd rather be killed by a trolley than a handgun,' mused Ally.

'Oh, I don't know, I think a gun is more straightforward really.'

'God, how did we get onto this topic?' We laughed and resumed our inspection.

Thank heavens Ally and I seemed to be on the same wavelength. I had a feeling I was going to make a good friend and Chalet Tiara was all I could have hoped for and more. OK, it needed a wipe down, but the only thing it lacked was someone to lavish a bit of love and attention on it.

'Look, there's even a larder.' Though dusty, this was a spotless small room and so cold it was like walking into a fridge. I imagined the empty shelves full of jams and chutneys and bowls of proving bread.

I followed Ally at a brisk pace through the kitchen, past various intriguing cupboards whose contents I couldn't wait to explore once I was alone.

Making our way upstairs, we discovered three large bedrooms and two broom cupboards on the first floor.

'They are naughty saying the broom cupboards are bedrooms,' said Ally, looking down at her list. 'I think Jolly Holidays were so desperate to expand into Gstaad that when they were offered this one they took it immediately without checking it out first. I'll ring them in the morning as soon as the office opens and tell them it can't sleep more than six.' She glanced down at her pad. 'Chalet girl's room in the attic. But they've put a question mark. C'mon, let's take a look.'

'It sounds like something out of *Upstairs Downstairs*. I used to feel so sorry for the maids as they had such grotty bare rooms,' I puffed as we climbed a small narrow staircase. I couldn't wait to see my room.

The staircase led to a short corridor with three doors. The first two were locked. I glanced at the heavy jangle of keys in my hand. 'I guess the keys must be here, it's all very intriguing.'

'Let's try them out tomorrow, when it's light,' suggested Ally.

The third door at the end of the corridor was unlocked. I pushed it open and we entered a black, airless room with shutters firmly shut.

'Oh God, Oriana, you can't sleep in here tonight, it smells so musty,' shuddered Ally, backing out onto the landing. I'm usually very fastidious about dirt, being a Virgo it's unfortunately part of the territory, but oddly enough I wasn't bothered at all.

'It'll be fine once I get the French window open. I'm longing to check out the balcony.' I felt my way blindly towards the windows and heaved back some heavy shutters that obscured them. 'Ally, can you give me a hand with this door, it's a bit stuck.'

'If I must. Ouch!' Ally, normally so agile, had walked straight into the bed. 'And how d'you know it's a French window with a balcony, you haven't seen the chalet from the garden side, have you?' She rubbed her knee carefully.

It was true, I hadn't, but some sort of sixth sense was directing me. 'Done it!' I had succeeded in opening the French windows, which indeed led to a small balcony. I stepped outside, breathing in the crisp freezing air, transfixed by the distant jagged mountains black against the indigo sky. Ally joined me. I felt a curious feeling of déjà vu, of absolute belonging, as if I was really meant to be here.

Ally shivered beside me. 'Well, you can't stay here tonight. There's a perfectly decent sofa bed in my apartment down the road. It's not luxurious, but at least you can have a hot shower.'

I really wanted to stay but my longing for a hot shower overrode everything else.

'Luckily I know a really good plumber. He costs a fortune of course, but your first lot of clients are coming out in a week so Jolly Holidays will just have to fork out. I hope they know how to light Agas. Jeez, *Agas*, I thought they only had those in Glowstershire.'

'Where?'

'You know, Glowstershire. It's where my boyfriend's mother lives. They're crazy about them.' I smiled at her mispronunciation. The smile turned into a yawn.

'C'mon, let's get out of this place. You must be shattered. Just grab your night things and you can crash at my place.'

An hour later I was tucked up on Ally's sofa bed in her tiny flat, drifting off to sleep, soothed by the thought of returning to the chalet in the morning.

Chalet Tiara had touched a distant chord, awakened a faraway memory that had been dormant for years. The heavy wooden doors and parquet floor, the atmosphere of solid reassurance took me back to my grandparents' manor house in Sussex, a refuge from the chaos of home life. It, too, had an elegant round table in the hall, and I remembered how the air was always scented with hibiscus and arum lilies from the greenhouse. It was another world, a calmer, more orderly world, where boundaries represented absolute safety and security in an otherwise unstable world.

Cheyne Castle had awakened similar memories, but I had only been a visitor there, chatelaine in name only. And despite our best efforts we'd never quite been able to hold back the forces of chaos that threatened to engulf us at every turn – well, every party at least. Even the pre-whaling cocktail party, planned with military precision, had descended into barely controlled anarchy.

Chalet Tiara was different. I'd soon get the place shipshape. I'd make it so beautiful that I would never want to leave.

I drifted off to sleep cocooned in imaginary smells of beeswax, fresh flowers, and gleaming mahogany, a kinder, softer world than the one I had left behind in London.

Chapter Eighteen

In the morning Ally woke me early with a huge cup of Earl Grey and a hot croissant. She was wearing a white bath robe and her short blonde hair gleamed in the sunshine streaming through the windows. 'Cleaning day!' she grimaced. 'I'll give you a hand this morning then I'll have to shoot round to the other chalets and see how they're settling in.'

Ally was as good as her word and spent a couple of hours with me, heaving furniture about and turning over mattresses. Although everything was dusty, it was all excellent quality. I was particularly taken with a stunning chandelier in the hall. Most of the bulbs had blown and it was dull with dust, but with new bulbs and a good polish it would look wonderful.

'Thank God we send sheets out to the laundry, I couldn't face having to iron that lot,' I observed, peering into the unexpectedly immaculate linen closet we had just discovered. Whoever had once lived here had spent a fortune on the best mattresses, duckdown pillows and eiderdowns.

'What d'you do in the summer?' I asked as we shook out some exquisite Egyptian cotton sheets and duvet covers and began to make up the beds.

'I'm writing a book about avalanche control, and I write the odd article for travel magazines,' she said.

'That sounds very scientific.' I was impressed. I had thought that Jolly Holidays was a bit of a black hole as far as intelligence went, but Ally was obviously the exception.

'Not really,' said Ally modestly. 'I did my MBA in alpine rock formulations at MIT in Boston, so this was a natural progression. When Nigel, my boyfriend, got posted to Zurich in October, it was perfect timing.' We threw an exquisite lace bedcover over the duvet and patted it down carefully. 'Right, that's the beds made up, thank goodness.'

We stretched up stiffly, allowing our faces to bask in the sun streaming through the dusty windows. 'Phew,' I wiped my forehead and flung open the window, 'this is hot work. I think I'll start on the kitchen. Hopefully the plumber will have got the Aga going by now.'

'What were you doing before you came out here?' asked Ally as we made our way down the elegantly curved staircase to the hall.

'I was cooking professionally, and then I moved in with my boyfriend, Peregrine. We had this great idea of creating a *fin de siècle* salon for all of London's most fascinating people – Peregrine knows everyone – but things always got out of control. And then we had a frightful argument one night and I ended up throwing moose stock over his head and running off with his brother to a nightclub. That didn't work out so I came out here.'

'Moose stock! I love it! Moose stock! I can just see you heaving this pot of old boiled-up moose heads over this poor guy. Peregrine you say his name is? Is he a bird or something?' Ally was leaning against the banisters heaving with hysterical laughter.

'It's an upper-class Scottish name,' I explained.

'So he's a Scottish bird? How am I going to handle you guys? First Bella picks up this . . . what did you call him?'

'Crooner. I can't believe you haven't heard of Tony Louche. He's terribly famous in England.'

'These marmots had better watch out!' She gesticulated towards the stuffed marmot heads decorating the wall. 'Guys, you better watch your backs, she'll have you in the pot in no time!'

We were interrupted by the plumber who appeared to have got the Aga going, according to Ally who seemed to make sense of his rapid and unintelligible Swiss-German.

'Oh, Oriana!' she laughed, once he had disappeared to find a stepladder so he could fix the chandelier. 'You're so much fun! You should be writing a book too, about all these crazy mooses and Peregrines and stuff.'

'Well, actually I am. It's going to be a recipe book cum chalet girl diary thing.'

'What a great idea!' said Ally enthusiastically. 'I know lots of people in the business, so if I can do anything to help you just ask. Hey, maybe we can go skiing together tomorrow?'

'Um, yes, that would be very nice,' I replied cautiously. I had no desire to go skiing. I would get cold and it would ruin my complexion. It would be a complete waste of the ruinously expensive La Prairie face creams that I had brought out. Besides, it was going to take days to get Chalet Tiara sorted out.

'Great. I thought you looked very athletic. I know where we can find some great powder.'

Goodness. Powder. I didn't think I could manage that at all.

'Um, actually, Pandora's the great skier, she loves pow . . .'

But Ally had disappeared into the hall and was putting on her sporty silver anorak.

'C'mon, let's get going, we'll be late to meet the others. I'm a bit worried about Bella, I hope she's coping all right.' I didn't want to say anything out of turn, but I shared her concern. Bella seemed such a flighty, ethereal sort of person, I wouldn't have been at all surprised if she hadn't disappeared off into the ether with Tony Louche by now. She was just his type, and I remembered reading in *Divorce!* that he was currently between wives. Arabella Louche. Yes, it had a definite ring to it.

Ally dropped me off at Pop-Ups then dashed back to her apartment to collect a fax she was expecting from head office.

The girls were sitting in the sunshine sipping cappuccinos.

'Hi, guys!' I tried and failed to order a short, rich latte from a bemused waitress.

'Ask for a *renverse*. It's the nearest thing. But forget about skimmed milk, the Swiss disapprove of it. You can't find it anywhere,' explained Pandora. 'How are you settling into Chalet Tiara? I'm longing to see it.'

'It's glorious. Needs some serious elbow grease though. By the way,' I dipped into my bag and withdrew Bella's pashmina. 'Bella, is this yours?'

'My pashmina! Thank God, I thought I'd lost it!' cried Bella. The sight of the feather light slither of cashmere caused quite a stir amongst the fur-swathed *femmes d'un certain age* who sat dotted about, observing us through impenetrable Jackie O type sunglasses.

'I was going to have to get the pashmina milkman to send another one out but I won't have to now. Thanks *so* much, Oriana.'

'Who's the pashmina milkman?' I inquired.

'Oh, he's not really a milkman. When I worked at Vogue House the *Tatler* girls used to order them all the time, so we called the chap who dropped them off the pashmina milkman. He used to come nearly every morning.'

There was a brief, mystified silence.

'Oh, so were you a Voguette then?' inquired Pandora brightly.

'Well, I just kind of made tea for everybody. I wasn't much good at it, that's why I'm here. Luckily Chiara's got a bit of a thing for my brother and he persuaded her to give me a chance in Gstaad . . .' Bella trailed off bleakly, her exquisite heart-shaped face crumpling.

'Not now, Bella, no sobbing,' advised Ambrosia briskly, adjusting her sunglasses on the back of her head and fixing me with her big brown mournful eyes. 'So tell us what Chalet Tiara's like, Oriana. It's such a lovely name.'

'It's a bit dusty but once it's cleaned up it'll be wonderful.'

'Our place is spotless,' said Ambrosia. 'I know it said in

the *Chalet Girl Handbook* that this week was for cleaning, but we don't dare touch anything in case we make it dirty.'

'Yes, my place is immaculate too,' added Pandora.

'I'm a bit worried about this cooking thing,' said Rochetta, her dark eyes frowning beneath their strongly marked eyebrows. 'I thought I might be able to wing it, you know just buy pizzas and put them in the microwave, but my chalet doesn't have a microwave. I don't know what I'm going to do.' She ran a distracted hand through her dark tangle of gypsy hair and sighed.

'Perhaps we can get meals delivered?' she suggested.

'What about hiring a cook?' asked Bella hopefully.

'Oh, Bella, don't be ridiculous.'

'Yes, but have you seen how much we have to do? I'll never learn to ski or do anything else. I've got some friends coming out next week. When will I get a chance to see them if I'm stuck in the chalet making beds and washing up the whole time?'

There was a perplexed silence.

'You see, the trouble is,' she continued, 'I was told I was going to be the sort of washer upper, or *plongeur*, which would only take a few hours a day. But our chalet sleeps twelve so we're going to be rushed off our feet.'

'Yah, I'm meant to be a plongers, or whatever they're called, too,' said Rochetta, 'but they've put me in charge of a whole chalet. I can't really cook at all. Please don't tell Ally, they'll send me home. Besides, I'm sure I can buy packets of food in the supermarket and reheat things . . .' she tailed off doubtfully.

'But how did you pass the eggy bread sandwich exam thing?' I asked curiously.

'I was tipped off about that so I bought one from Harvey Nicks food hall.'

'I ordered mine from Partridges,' said Bella. 'It's just downstairs from where I live. I buy *literally* everything there.'

'But Ambrosia, you can cook, can't you?'

'Absolutely. I did a fabulous one-week course at the Lady Amelia Sloane Cookery School.'

I'd once shared a flat with someone who'd learnt to cook at Lady Amelia's. I couldn't remember the details, but aspic had seemed to feature prominently.

'Can you learn to cook in a week?' asked Pandora doubtfully.

'Absolutely. This was an intensive course, eleven till three, like *every day* for a week.'

'Yes, Ambrosia's a real pro. She can glaze anything in aspic. Eggs, chickens, prawns, leeks. You even did a rabbit once, didn't you?'

Ambrosia nodded proudly.

'Probably looked OK,' said Rochetta, 'but just imagine what it must have tasted like. I think I'll stick with the frozen pizzas.' She glanced around the café, taking in the elderly well-heeled clientele. Diamond-encrusted Cartier watches glinted in the sunshine, and spun bouffant hairdos gleamed, obedient pekes rested under chairs, bloated with scraps of smoked salmon and morsels of creamy linguine that their besotted owners had smuggled down to them. Unfortunately Roger Moore wasn't amongst us but the possibility of one of his wives being here could not be discounted.

'God, being in Gstaad makes me feel so young,' Rochetta sniffed, tossing back her dark curly hair. 'I'm hoping that being a chalet girl will involve a bit more action than this.'

'Well, if it's any consolation, they're probably much older than they look, you know, because of the *injections*,' murmured Pandora.

'What d'you mean *injections*?' The others edged forward conspiratorially.

'There's this place in Montreux where they inject you with sheep's placenta. It's a kind of *elixir*.'

'Yes, loads of celebrities and world leaders have it, that's why some of them seem to stick around middle age forever,' I explained.

Pandora and I had still not uncovered the secret of this treatment, but I was hoping that now I was in Gstaad, the elderly alpine playground of the world's movers and shakers, I would find out more.

'That's obviously why the world's in such a mess. Our leaders are mutating into sheep,' giggled Rochetta, her dark eyes flashing with laughter.

'It must be the same sort of thing as monkey glands,' whispered Bella, horrified yet intrigued.

'No, sheep, dummy, not chimps,' said Rochetta impatiently. 'I remember when Frank Sinatra had the injections, the *Sun* had this great headline – "I've got ewe under my skin",' she sang.

I caught sight of Ally striding athletically towards us. 'Hey, guys. What are you lot plotting? Secrets already?'

'We were discussing sheep's placenta injections,' shouted Rochetta.

The café froze and twenty pairs of unnaturally stretched eyes swivelled in our direction. An elderly lady sitting at an adjoining table creaked her impregnable rock-like coiffure in our direction and glared.

'We tried to have them but they turned us away because we were too young. You've got to be over twenty-five! Like *ancient* or what!'

The rest of us looked into our cappuccinos and blushed.

Rochetta was what my mother would describe as a loose cannon. How would we contain her restless energy in this small but exquisitely formed village? I suspected she'd be much happier in Val d'Isère or Verbier, or somewhere much bigger. Well, it was too late now, she'd bolt soon enough, I was sure.

Ally sat down and ordered us another round in rapid German. 'Now listen, girls. Head office has just faxed me next week's punters. We're going to be very busy because there's going to be a feng shui convention in Gstaad, and they've block booked all our chalets!'

'Are they mad?' asked Pandora. 'Let's hope they're not hungry.'

Everybody shifted uneasily. It was essential that Ally be carefully sheltered from the looming culinary crisis. It would be too awful if the full reality of Rochetta and Bella's culinary ineptitude was revealed. And what if there was no aspic to be found? Ambrosia would be doomed! Unless there was a good takeaway in the village Ally would find out soon enough.

'It'll be wonderful. We can have our chalets feng shuied for free!' I babbled hopelessly to fill in the awkward silence. 'That'll spice things up, Rochetta. You can tell them you want to stimulate your relationship corner.'

'Huh, the only thing that's going to stimulate anything around here are the monkey glands,' grumbled Rochetta. 'I'm going to push off if things don't get a bit more exciting.'

'Feng shui sounds like a load of old cobblers to me,' said Ambrosia. 'I just hope they're not all vegans, that's all. I don't think vegans can eat aspic.'

The rest of the week passed for me in a haze of cleaning, scrubbing, cooking and getting the place shipshape.

I rolled up the threadbare carpets to reveal the stunning parquet floor. It was a bit scratched and dried out, but I discovered an old hardware shop on the outskirts of the village whose owner, Frau Perren, kept bees. She made up her own beeswax polish which smelt deliciously of honey and lemons. I don't know what was in it but it filled in all the cracks and made the floor gleam with a rich, tawny, buttery glow.

One morning I was just rooting around the chest of drawers in one of the rooms on the top floor, which I had finally managed to open with one of the many keys that Ally had given me, when I came across an old leatherbound book tucked away.

To my delight it was packed with household information, bills, recipes, lists of dinner party guests and menus. On the front flyleaf the owner had inscribed her name: Beatrice

Muller, nee Hamilton, 1938. What a find! I had been so longing to find out more about the chalet's history.

I turned over each page reverently. It was in German so I couldn't make it all out, but there was a bill for the chandelier, dated 1948. It was from the time of Napoleon III, and cost 1000SF, about £500 pounds. Goodness, it must be worth a fortune now. I must find out what year Napoleon III had been in power. I glanced at an article about chandeliers, presumably torn out of a magazine; I couldn't understand the article, but the pictures demonstrating how to clean it seemed clear enough. A beaming Hausfrau was standing on a stepladder cleaning a chandelier with a piece of bread. Maybe I should try it. For the chandelier, now with new bulbs and the centrepiece of the hallway, was filthy, emitting a grey light that didn't do it justice.

I flicked through, trying to find a more personal memento of the person who had kept such assiduous details. Luckily for nosy me much of the jottings and the recipes were in English. I guessed from her name that Beatrice Muller, nee Hamilton, must have been English and married a Swiss. But such personal details seemed thin on the ground.

Then I found a picture of Beatrice and her husband. Beatrice's husband was holding both their skis with one arm, and had draped his other arm round her, gazing down at her, while she was smiling happily into the camera. What a glamorous-looking couple. It was lovely to think of Chalet Tiara being their home.

I carried the picture towards the light to get a better look. It was hard to tell from a black and white picture, but they seemed to radiate happiness. Beatrice's hair – I think it was blonde, though it's hard to tell from a black and white picture – was loosely tied back. The man looked gorgeous, strapping and broad-shouldered. Lucky Beatrice, I sighed enviously. She had the man, the chalet, the Aga – a veritable *embarras de richesses*. I consoled myself that at least I had the chalet and the Aga. I glanced at the picture again and wondered where one found men like that these days. Surely they couldn't have all died out?

Shutting the book reverently I wondered again who the present owner was and how they could have left the place in such a state. Ally had been similarly intrigued and had asked head office, but they dealt directly with the rental agency from whom they had let it and couldn't help.

Unwilling to give up, my innocent yet persistent inquiries in the *droguerie* (which as well as selling a fascinating range of revitalizing herbal cures, poultices, locally-made essential oils and unpasteurized dairy products was a hotbed of Gstaad gossip), had revealed that the owner was called Ernst Schmitt, he was divorced, and that he was a big cheese in German car parts. He sounded just my type!

But no one knew where he was. Obviously he bought his suppositories and poultices elsewhere. And sadly, given the state of the place when I'd moved in, he obviously didn't take much interest in it. But the mystery owner only added to Chalet Tiara's romantic alpine allure and stimulated me into greater Martha Stewart type excesses.

My skinny langlaufing skis soon came into their own when I discovered a cross-country skiing track at the bottom of the snow-laden garden. This led directly into the village and was much quicker than walking.

The efficient Swiss handyman had got the Aga going and the hot water and heating, apart from the odd clanging at unexpected times, worked beautifully. I hadn't cooked on an Aga for years – this one must have been absolutely state of the art when it was installed in the forties – but once I got the hang of it I never wanted to cook on anything else. I saw it as the hub of the chalet, the steaming cherry-coloured nerve centre, providing hot water, heat, and delicious food.

I'll try not to bang on about it, but it definitely had a character. I didn't tell any of the other girls, but I even gave it a name. Orsova, that's the sister ship of the *Oriana*. Corny or what! But I felt we were a great team.

Chapter Nineteen

The day my punters were due I woke early to make final preparations for my first guests. I was a little bleary-eyed this morning as Rochetta had persuaded us to go dancing at the GreenGo, the nightclub attached to the Palace Hotel. She had been adamant that Roger Moore had definitely been spotted in Pop-Ups, and that the GreenGo was his favourite night-time haunt.

I'd been a bit disappointed because I was expecting it to be just like Annabel's; instead it was full of Le Rosey students and a small crowd of elderly ski-stiffened Euro toffs who tottered about the dance floor under the watchful air of their nurses. At least I think they were nurses. And Roger Moore hadn't appeared. In fact there weren't any glamorous tycoony types that I'd hoped to meet. Still, the village was so small, one of us would run into Roger Moore sooner or later. It was probably only a matter of time.

I opened the French windows and pushed the heavy shutters open, allowing a slew of bright morning sunshine into the room. By an incredible stroke of luck, presumably because Jolly Holidays hadn't had a chance to check out the chalet, my room, which had been described as the maid's room, was actually the best bedroom in the chalet.

Wandering onto the small balcony, I breathed in lungfuls of the bracing alpine air. I had a clear view over the surrounding mountains. In the garden, fir trees were obscured by soft white snowflakes drifting noiselessly to the ground. All around silence reigned, as if the world had stopped and I had been forgotten. It was easy to imagine this silent white world as the province of Narnia, with the White Witch, leprechauns, unicorns and other magical heavenly creatures barely skimming the ground on their way to some glittering occasion at the Palace Hotel. Maybe the lonely mermaid from the trompe l'oeil would be with them. Such an event might cheer her up a bit.

In the distance I could make out the small red bubble cars slowly meandering up the fir-lined mountain. I so wished I had the confidence to join the others. I was really crossing my fingers that the feng shui consultants could offer an esoteric solution of some kind.

'Mmm, Oriana, this is delicious.' Ally helped herself to more Saanensenf at dinner that evening. 'What is it exactly?'

'It's called Saanensenf,' I explained. 'It's a local specialty made of slowly cooked beef, alpine herbs and dried cherries. But I substituted tofu for the beef,' I added hurriedly, not wishing to upset my party's macrobiotic leanings, though they seemed quite corruptible, judging by the way they were laying into my supply of homemade pickled gherkins.

'I'd heard that chalet food was terrible, but it looks as if we've lucked out,' smiled Roberto, one of my six punters, sitting right next to me. And I mean right next to me. Roberto was Italian and had smooth olive skin and very unusual light blue eyes. His black hair curled sleekly above a beautifully cut black polo neck sweater. He was good-looking but far too smooth for me. I shifted subtly away and busied myself handing round the sour dough rolls.

I'd thought that the feng shui consultants (there were two more but they were upstairs), would be spindly and ethereal, but they seemed surprisingly robust in spite of their stringent spiritual diet. I'd been looking forward to evenings of stimulating discussion about cutting-edge developments in the feng shui world, but all they wanted to talk about was whether the other chalet girls were good-looking or not.

'Are Pandora and the other girls as stunning as you?' persevered Roberto.

'Um, yes, they're very attractive,' I said truthfully.

'So I suppose they all have boyfriends?' asked Bob. I'd thought at first he was attached to Jane, but now I wasn't so sure. Like Roberto he seemed too libidinous to have a steady girlfriend. He was wearing a very expensive looking Armani suit and a beige (although Corianda Angelica would probably describe it as taupe, pebble or ecru), shirt that toned immaculately with his fair hair and blue eyes. I wondered if he had had his colours done. He looked like an Autumn to me.

'No, they're all single at the moment, dedicated to their work, I think.' This was a complete lie, it was only the hope of alpine romance that had drawn the girls here in the first place. Pandora had said it was the skiing but I knew she was lying.

'But what about you? Are you in love? Do your wistful green eyes tell a sad story, Oriana?' said Roberto, fixing me with his strange glittering blue eyes.

'Oh no, I'm having a break from that sort of thing – so I have time to write a book,' I added apologetically. I always felt stupid talking about it, but I had to start developing as many contacts as possible.

'Yes, Oriana's got a fabulous idea, it's bound to be a big hit,' said Ally encouragingly. She was full of helpful suggestions. I loved her American can-do approach to life, it was so refreshing.

'But Ally's a proper writer,' I explained. 'She's been given an advance to write a book about avalanches from an American publisher.'

Roberto glanced around the room distractedly. I sensed the conversation was becoming a little too literary for my guests.

'The chalet has a very good atmosphere, many interesting spaces and unexpected rooms,' he said.

'Oh, you mean the broom cupboards.'

'I predict you will have many adventures here,' Roberto ran on smoothly.

'Gosh, d'you think so?' I felt that now was the right time to pitch in and get some free advice. 'Is there anything I can do to improve the feng shui?'

'Oh, definitely. I've noticed that the relationship corner downstairs is very weak. Perhaps, um, after dinner we could go round the chalet and I can advise you?'

'That would be fabulous! Though I'm really not interested in romantic relationships at the moment.'

'That will change once I re-activate your bagua,' murmured Roberto seductively.

Ally caught my eye and winked. 'Are you sure Ben and Louise won't join us? They must be starving,' she said, referring to the other guests.

'I don't think they will, Ally. Roberto was telling me that they're extremely principled breathtarians.' I was familiar with the rudimentary principles of breathtarianism as Siena had briefly flirted with the idea a few years ago. 'They don't need to eat because they live on the nutrients in the air.'

'Load of old codswallop, if you ask me,' said Roger, who seemed to have appeared by mistake. He hadn't been on the Jolly Holidays list, but fortunately seemed perfectly happy sleeping in the broom cupboard.

I hadn't believed Pandora when she'd told me that every week would bring a token male punter, often called Roger or Colin, who would drive the rest of the chalet mad with irritation, and who would as a matter of course always request a packed lunch. She called this Pandora's Law, and was convinced it was a spiritual law that Deepak Chopra was as yet completely unaware of.

I was quite relieved about the breathtarians. A few of them would help me keep within the stringent Jolly Holidays budget. I hoped Ambrosia and Rochetta had lots, then they wouldn't have to cook at all. I was dreading the Jolly Holidays nerve centre discovering that Bella and Rochetta couldn't cook and sending them home. I wasn't worried about Ambrosia because it was easy to buy aspic. The Swiss were, it seemed, mad for it and the Gstaad Co-op kept crates of the stuff round the back. Oddly enough you had to be over eighteen to buy it but none of us had been able to find out why.

Although I'd had reservations when we first arrived, to my surprise we all got along very well. Admittedly we didn't see a lot of one another as we were so spread out, but we had formed quite a camaraderie.

'I bet the biscuit tin's empty in the morning!' Roger wheezed with laughter. Everyone ignored him but Roger, presumably used to this, was unperturbed and carried on chuckling to himself.

'I hope not. Perhaps I better put a lock on the kitchen door,' I smiled at Roger. I felt a bit sorry for him in his polyester shirt and wire-rimmed spectacles. It was awful to think of him lonely and sad in the broom cupboard, ignored by the rest of the chalet and unable to even grasp the most basic principles of feng shui. Maybe this week I could bring him out of himself; maybe he would discover some feng shui tips to enhance his social life.

Roger glanced at me, blushed shyly and fiddled with the cuffs of his drip-dry shirt.

'And now he is in lerve with you,' noted Roberto, fixing me with his glittering eyes and brushing my arm with his slim hand.

'I think that's most unlikely!' I responded primly, gathering up the plates with considerable agitation. The thought of it, ugh! 'Ally, can you give me a hand getting the pudding in?'

'Don't trouble yourself, Alison,' responded Roger quickly, gathering up plates. 'I'll help you, Oriana. I'm a dab hand in the kitchen, even though I say it myself.'

I shuddered but smiled brightly.

Under the circs, meeting up with the other girls after

dinner was imperative. Ally left straight after pudding to visit Pandora at Chalet Twix and I managed to shake off the libidinous consultants by cunningly lying and saying I was just nipping out with the rubbish. I covered myself by explaining that 'I may be gone for quite some time'.

Unfortunately my Captain Oates impression was lost on my guests who had become embroiled in a violent argument about the merits of the Black Hat feng shui school versus the Flaky Free Form 'Intuitive' school and I was able to slip out unnoticed.

'One of my punters is going to feng shui Chalet Tiara after breakfast tomorrow,' I explained to the others once we were comfortably settled at the Olden, our favourite evening haunt. 'He says the romantic corners need urgent attention.'

'I don't think our chalet has any romantic corners at all, it's all strange protruding angles and circles,' mused Bella, sipping her brandy sadly. She was looking particularly fetching in a soft bluc angora jersey, and with her thick blonde hair falling in careless tendrils about her heart shaped face, she had the appearance of a soft smudged watercolour.

'You must have some, what about Tony Toupee, I mean Louche? He's not bad looking – when he stands on one of his boxes,' Pandora said consolingly.

I wondered idly if Tony's toupee ever slid off by accident. One of his ex-wives had revealed that he used a special type of toupee adhesive to keep it glued on when he was on windy chairlifts. I wondered what happened at night when he was horizontal. Surely his scalp would need a break some of the time.

'Oh, he's driven off,' explained Bella, before I had a chance to phrase my question tactfully. 'I was so excited because he said he'd written me a special song and that he wanted to come round and sing it to me at Chalet Grimm, so I asked him round to tea.'

'We spent all morning making banoffee pie from the chalet girl cookbook,' added Ambrosia.

'That sounds interesting,' said Ally. 'Is it a typical English dish?'

'It's really easy,' said Ambrosia. 'All you do is boil a tin of condensed milk for twelve hours—'

'Yah, it's absolutely amazing because it goes all solid,' interrupted Bella.

'Then you scrape it out and put it on some pastry, then you chop up some bananas and just plop them on top in a nice pattern.'

'Did you cook the pastry?' asked Pandora.

Bella looked puzzled. 'No, it didn't say anything about cooking it . . .'

I shuddered.

'You offered this guy a tin of old stewed milk and raw pastry and you expected him to stick around?' Ally roared with laughter.

'But it was really, really delicious. We ended up eating it all ourselves,' admitted Ambrosia. She obviously hadn't been named after rice pudding for nothing.

'So how are you getting on with your punters? No dietary restrictions?'

'No, ours weren't very hungry because they ate on the plane,' said Bella.

'Yah, so did mine. They didn't touch my dinner – I had to chuck my pilchard dip – such a waste, I'd been slaving away all day,' lied Rochetta energetically.

'But they flew EasyJet from Luton,' said Ally. 'EasyJet don't give you a meal.'

I shivered. Ally had been to university, she had an MA. I knew it was only a matter of time before she discovered that the girls were to cooking what Muhammad Ali is to basket weaving. Once rumbled, what would happen to them then?

'The train!' I cried hopelessly. 'They ate on the train! Roberto told me. You know how filling those train meals are!'

'Yah, that's right. Absolutely.' Everyone nodded at Ally.

'I can't wait till tomorrow morning when Roberto feng

shuis Chalet Tiara,' I cackled on.

'You be careful of this Roberto chap, Oriana. He looks like a real smoothie. He was chatting her up all night,' said Ally.

'Is he good-looking?' asked Rochetta hopefully.

I thought of Roberto's slim hands and shook my head. 'No, he's a bit on the thin side for me, I'm afraid.'

'Oriana only really likes big beefy bald beastly types,' explained Pandora.

'I thought he was very dishy,' said Ally. 'But then I've always had a weakness for Italians, so charming.'

'Well, you catch him, then pass him on to one of us,' suggested Rochetta.

'You mean like catch 'n' switch?' asked Pandora.

'Absolutely!' agreed everyone enthusiastically.

'Anyway, the great thing is he's going to tweak Chalet Tiara into feng shui perfection. Why don't you all get your punters to do your chalets too?' Really, everyone was obsessed with men, it was so ridiculous in this day and age, I thought impatiently.

'Good idea,' agreed Pandora. 'I had my flat done in London, I'm a great believer.'

'Did it work?' asked Ally curiously.

'Well, it certainly stirred things up,' admitted Pandora. 'But I think Mr Fook over-stimulated my relationship corner. Things were a bit chaotic for a time. But life certainly became more interesting.'

'Interesting in what kind of way?' asked Bella.

'Well, just after I painted my bedroom red I went to stay with my boyfriend at the Paddington Palace, then I ran away to Amsterdam with his friend, an Israeli general—'

'Who said he was in the Entebbe raid,' I interjected. 'But then we found out he was only four years old when that happened, so he must have been lying.'

'Oh, I know him!' said Rochetta.

'No, it was probably someone else,' I said. 'After all, if

everyone who claimed to be in the Entebbe raid was, you'd have the population of a small country squeezed into one airplane.'

'But that didn't work out so I married an accountant and moved to Surrey and then got divorced,' continued Pandora.

'So the feng shui had stopped working by then?' asked Bella.

'Yup. Guess so. Still, I'm game on for another go.'

We glanced around the assembled clientele which consisted mainly of Swiss farmers and elderly Greek tycoons accompanied by their 'nurses'.

'God, anything's worth a try,' said Rochetta. 'Anything.'

The following morning I cooked my guests a sumptuous macrobiotic breakfast of arame seaweed flavoured with a little lightly toasted sesame oil, sushi rice and miso soup chased down with bancha tea.

Roger's prediction re the empty biscuit tin had indeed been proved correct, and I strongly suspected the so-called breathtarians of a secret midnight raid. I would have to have a strong word with them; such irregular habits would play havoc with my housekeeping.

I was washing up when Roberto wandered into the kitchen and leaned against the Aga. His dark hair was slicked back, emphasizing his sultry Mediterranean looks. He was attractive if one went for that lean Latino type. Personally I don't, but maybe he would do for one of the other girls. I must be generous. Catch and switch!

I smiled flirtatiously. I wasn't averse to using my nearly forgotten feminine wiles to winkle out as many feng shui secrets as possible. After all, Roberto and his cronies charged a fortune, and it didn't take a rocket scientist to make some connection between the bulging brown envelopes I'd discovered under their beds and their next stop in Zurich. They were obviously smuggling money into their Swiss bank accounts, and who could blame them?

'I've so been looking forward to my feng shui lesson.' I undid my frilly apron and looked into his eyes appreciatively. I had an intuition that Roberto, a well-known figure on the feng shui after-dinner speakers circuit, would surely be able to unleash my full creative potential.

'So have I, Oriana,' he replied smoothly, fixing me with his strange glittering eyes. These were no longer quite so mesmerizing since I'd discovered they were courtesy of the bright blue contact lenses I'd spotted in the bathroom. There can be no secrets between a chalet girl and her punters.

'I think that you and Chalet Tiara have an exciting future. Your energies are connected in the most fascinating way.'

'Rairly, I mean really.' Goodness, I must be careful not to pick up too much Sloane dialect from the others.

'Yes. But we still have some work to do, especially in the relationship area.'

'Which is in the lavatory, I know, bad news. And there's a cracked windowpane and a dripping tap.'

'And the headless animal!' he cried, his agitation causing his English to become garbled. 'It 'as terrible vibe!'

'Oh. Has it?' I rather liked the marmot head on the wall. It had quite a cheerful expression for something that must have died in considerable agony.

Roberto gestured for me to join him at the kitchen table and proceeded to sketch out a rough floor plan.

'Now, if we look at all four corners of this floor, each one represents a certain area of your life. Tell me exactly what you want from your life and I shall tell you how to make it happen.'

'How exciting, you're a magician!'

'No, just a wizard,' Roberto replied. I glanced at him to see if he was joking but he was quite serious.

I shut my eyes for a moment. 'What I'd really, really like is to make Chalet Tiara into the perfect Swiss chalet, an enchanted magical place where people can unwind and recapture something missing from their lives.'

'An enchanted castle in the snow.'

'Yes, that's it. Full of laughter and romantic intrigue and lovely smells, roaring fires . . .'

'But you have made it that already.' He cast his eyes around the large cosy kitchen, the cherry-coloured Aga steaming with delicious scents of vanilla sponge and roasting coffee beans. It was the queen of multi-taskers, able to roast coffee, make cakes, soup and roast meat all at the same time.

'Yes, I'm always tweaking the place.'

At the Bahnhof newsstand, the nerve centre of the village where English *Daily Mail*-reading tax exiles mingled with Euro toff *Hola!* addicts, I had discovered an inexhaustible supply of Martha Stewart magazines that were full of useful home hints. I wasn't sure about the necessity of making my own scented candles, and rustic arrangements composed of discarded body hair and driftwood, as she instructed, but I rather felt it was only a matter of time before I tried.

'And what I'd like most of all is to be so inspired that I write a fantastic cookery book cum chalet girl diary based on my experiences here.'

'But you will. You've created it already in your mind, now you must just make it into a physical reality. It's easy. The fame area here is very strong.'

'That's the entrance, right?' I glanced at his floor plan.

'Come on, I'll show you.'

I followed him into the hall, loving the warm feeling of satisfaction and security I always felt when I walked through. I shut my eyes for a moment, inhaling the honeyed perfume of white scented lilies, and beeswax polish with their attendant lingering memories of my grandparents' Georgian manor house. The circular walnut table and roughly burnished parquet floor were nearly identical. I had re-created a blueprint of my most golden childhood memory, a realization which made me ache with pleasure and nostalgia.

'The chandelier is wonderful,' he noticed, glancing

appreciatively at the sparkling crystal glass which gleamed in the morning sunshine flooding the hall. I had tried Beatrice's bread cleaning trick and it had worked a treat. 'And a round table is very creative.' He surveyed the hall. 'Maybe red flowers would be better than the white lilies though. And make a list of your dreams and put them in the drawer. And now the drawing room. Ah, a fire in the wealth corner, excellent!'

I hadn't made the fire up yet but the ashes glowed red deep in the grate. I loved having a real fire, it brought the chalet to life; even the ritual of making it up, brushing out the dying embers, replacing them with the dry kindling and firewood from outside was soothing.

'I'll hang some crystals in the windows, then stand back and wait for excitement!' Roberto declared and strode out of the room.

We made our way to the relationship area which housed a chilly ski room and adjoining outside loo. I have to admit, compared to the rest of the chalet I had made little headway here. Despite the ministrations of the efficient Swiss plumber, the radiator continued to leak a foul, noxious-smelling fluid and there was a strange lingering smell.

Roberto sighed. 'It's terrible. Really terrible. The area isn't working at all!'

'Couldn't we just hang a crystal here as well?' I asked hopefully.

'No! That will only magnify the problem! You must fix the radiator, the dripping tap, remove this . . . this . . .' he pointed at the grinning marmot head, 'this *aberration* and mend the cracked windowpane.' He peered closely at a charming wood carving of a sad old woman wandering aimlessly through a foggy landscape. 'And who is this? Your mother? You must have pictures of loving couples here!' He sighed bleakly. 'You will never have a boyfriend at this rate.'

'Who says I want a stupid boyfriend?' I muttered mulishly at his retreating back. I'd had enough of this feng shui now.

Besides, it was time to attend to my vanilla sponge cake. My vanilla pods should be warm by now and would scent the cream and butter filling nicely. OK, it wasn't macrobiotic, but Roberto and his breathtarian chums seemed quite flexible. 'Is the upstairs OK?' I asked.

'It's excellent, but I must see your bedroom. I hope the romantic corner is better there!' I thought of the far right-hand corner in my bedroom, which housed a cupboard where I kept my dirty laundry. I couldn't face more censure from Roberto. Besides, once he was in my bedroom, would he ever leave? He had a most persistent look about him. No, I had enough information now.

'Thank you *so much*, Roberto, but I simply *mustn't* keep you from meeting the other girls, they're waiting with bated breath for your advice.'

'But I don't want to give them advice, I want to give *you* advice!'

At that moment there was a hammering at the door. Thank goodness!

Rochetta steamed in wearing her black leather trousers, a Hermes scarf tied seductively round her waist and her dark eyes glinting provocatively. Roberto's eyes were on stalks.

'Divine scent, mmm, white lilies. How d'you do, you must be Roberto. Oriana's been telling us all about you and your, um, *skills* . . .' she purred silkily, tossing back her gleaming tangle of black hair seductively. 'Ambrosia and I can't wait to find out more about this fungus spray thing. Oriana, have you been learning amazing things?'

'Yes, Roberto's going to hang crystals in my useful friends corner, but the relationship area is no-go unfortunately. I'm going to have to get the plumber back in. Anyway, don't let me keep you both.' I know it sounds anti-social but I was longing to get back to my Victoria sponge. Baking in the Alps is so unpredictable and this particular cake needed my undivided attention.

'See you later at Pop-Ups,' said Rochetta throatily, giving

Pop-Ups a rather unsavoury emphasis and enjoying a lingering eye meet with Roberto. 'We can pool our *tips* then.'

I bundled Roberto into his coat and shoved them out of the door.

'Vita Lurga.'

'Vita Lurga.' This was the only Swiss-German we knew and meant 'goodbye for now'.

'*Ciao*.' Roberta blew me a kiss.

It was with some relief that I skipped back to the kitchen, closed the door and busied myself with energetic cream whipping.

Then I made the beds (well, everyone's except the breathtarians who were apparently having a 'bed in', AKA Lennon-Ono – God, so sixties), made my unmacrobiotic Victoria sponge and sesame seed biscuits for tea and slipped on my powder blue Sam De Teran ski suit and matching fluffy hat. Perfect for Gstaad! I quickly hitched on my langlaufing skis and langlaufed down to the village to meet the others.

I was in a particularly good mood this afternoon as the post office had just rung to demand I come immediately to pick up several tubs of Branston Pickle, which had apparently begun to steam and heave quite alarmingly in the post room.

'That's nice of your mama to send them out,' said Bella as I staggered into Pop-Ups tearoom with my bounty. 'Is she going to come out and visit you?'

'She said she'd like to, but I don't know if it's a good idea because my father said he might come here when he's in Zurich on business which could be any time. I'm so looking forward to showing him Chalet Tiara.'

Bella yawned blearily. 'Sorry. I'm pooped. I went out with the Bolter last night. Big mistake. I don't know where she gets the energy. You know she skis like a maniac.' We had slipped quite easily into calling Rochetta 'the Bolter'. It suited her perfectly.

We ordered some more cappuccinos and settled down to

read our *Daily Mail* and *Daily Express* in companionable silence. We'd formed a tabloid rota and it was Bella's and my turn to buy them today. It was so important to keep in touch with current events.

I enjoyed our daily meetings at Pop-Ups. As the team was not particularly *sportif*, one could always guarantee that one of us would be taking time out and in the mood for a little diversion away from our onerous chalet girl duties.

I had thought at first I might feel a little isolated, especially as I wasn't skiing. But fortunately, after a brief burst of enthusiasm during an unseasonably hot two days (when even I had made it up the mountain on the bubble car for lunch), most of the others had lost interest when they realized how chilly the mountain restaurants were when the sun went in. Bella's pashmina, though fetchingly draped whilst seated, was less fetching when waterlogged, and her sporting enthusiasm had collapsed, according to Pandora who was trying to teach her to ski.

We were interrupted from our tabloid perusing by Pandora, wearing a slinky red ski suit, and in a state of high dudgeon, closely followed by Ambrosia who had poured herself into an unflattering pair of black salopettes and pulled her dark hair back off her round face, which was pink with exertion. Extraordinary, she looked as if she'd been skiing too!

'We've just had a terrible experience with a group of the most unbelievably foul-mouthed Finnish langlaufers,' Pandora spluttered crossly. 'They were crisscrossing the mountain as if they owned the damn thing. They just came right at me,' she complained, falling into the sofa and nursing her groin carefully.

'They skied right into us on purpose,' added Ambrosia collapsing heavily on to a chair. 'Like *so* aggressive.'

'I said to them very politely that I thought they might be happier on the *piste de fond* rather than the *piste alpin*, but they told me to eff off.'

'In Finnish?'

'Hungarian I think, though it might have been Finnish.'

We were interrupted by the Bolter, flushed and excited, followed by an equally flushed Roberto.

'We've spent all afternoon, how do I say it, Roberto, fung shwaying? Yes? All our chalets! It's so exciting.'

'Another round, ladies?' We nodded agog and Roberto wandered off to find a waitress.

'We put all these postcards of copulating rabbits in everyone's mating, I mean relationship corner,' Rochetta whispered, 'and hung crystals and windchimes and burnt incense and chanted Sanskrit incanations. And he does *love spells* too!'

'Maybe he could do one to get Tony Louche back,' mused Bella hopefully, taking a bite out of her apple tart. She draped her pashmina about her, well, I was going to say slim shoulders, but I noticed that solid was probably a more accurate word. In fact, looking at us us all now, we seemed to have expanded considerably in the few weeks we had been in the Alps. My trousers were getting noticeably tighter. I would have to start a stringent campaign of aggressive langlaufing and no puddings.

Roberto returned with a tray of calorific hot drinks which we all set upon like savages. Some people have a theory that food is a substitute for sex. Could it be true? Could Roberto, with his myriad spells and smells help the girls find love? I hoped so.

'I hear you've had a busy day,' I smiled at him.

'Yes, Rochetta says you do *love spells*,' whispered Bella furtively. 'You see, I've got this friend whose boyfriend has just disappeared, and she really likes him a lot—'

'Oh, he's hardly a boyfriend, Bella. I mean you only went out with him a couple of times,' said Ambrosia.

'I have an excellent plan for your, um, friend,' advised Roberto confidentially. 'If you are attracted to someone and you want to *draw them into your life* . . .' we leaned forward, utterly riveted. Of course this sort of thing was of no relevance to me, but it was still quite interesting. '. . . you must buy some red knickers, wear them when you are mid-cycle, take them off and *sandwich* a picture of yourself and this person face to face.' He paused for a moment to sip his espresso (goodness, he must have fallen off the wagon!), loving the attention.

'Go on!' breathed Bella rapturously.

'Put the photo sandwich inside the red knickers and leave them under your bed.'

'But for how long, bearing in mind you'd been wearing them all day?' asked Pandora. I knew personal hygiene would be her main concern in this sort of situation. 'I mean, if the spell worked and you brought the object of your desire back to your room, you wouldn't want him put off by, ahem, unnatural aromas, would you?'

'It would not be an *unnatural* aroma. It would be the aroma of lerve . . .'

'Hey, guys.' It was Ally, brandishing her daily fax from the Jolly Holidays HQ and limping painfully. 'Not interrupting anything, am I?' She plonked herself down next to me, pulled off her red hat and ran her hand through her short blonde hair irritably.

'Oh no, nothing at all,' we trilled. Ally was great, but I think we all intuitively realized that she wouldn't approve of witchcraft. Besides, she had a boyfriend in Zurich so she probably had no need for love spells.

She rubbed her foot gingerly. 'Ouch, I just got run over by some langlaufers. Jeez, those guys are real vicious. You be careful, Oriana.' I shifted uncomfortably. How could I explain the sense of agility and power that came over one as soon as one slipped one's foot into the slim, speedy, langlaufing ski? Of course I couldn't condone the spate of recent langlaufing attacks on the more cumbersome *ski alpin* aficionados, but I could understand the langlaufers' frustration.

'I've just had a fax from head office,' Ally continued. 'It's time to be serious. I've got some good news and some bad news. Which do you want first?'

'Good news, I think,' said Bella.

'OK. First of all, Chiara is thrilled with the way you're all coping with the macrobiotic vegan feng shui convention.'

We glanced at each other with raised eyebrows as she continued, imitating Chiara's ringing tones quite convincingly: ' "We here at the Jolly Hols HQ are delighted at the Gstaad gels' flexibility under this *challenging* brief, etc. etc. The clients are thrilled at the flexible and easygoing attitude of our gels." '

'Gosh, that's very sporting of them. I must say, we've really been flat out this week,' lied the Bolter blandly, brushing a cake crumb off her tight leather trousers. It turned out that she had a substantial private income which she was happy to spend on extravagant cakes and expensive pre-cooked meals prepared by Gstaad's finest pâtissiers, fish-mongers and butchers. I had run into her several times staggering out of the foie gras shop laden down with shopping bags. She always pretended she was buying birthday presents but I knew she was lying. I don't think her punters could believe their luck, though I suspected the foie gras might be wasted on the macrobiotic feng shui consultants.

'Yah, I was flat out in the kitchen the first day making stuff from the chalet girl recipe book,' exaggerated Rochetta most convincingly. 'I've really got the hang of the eggy bread now. And I put all the leftovers from breakfast into the sandwiches.'

'Um, Rochetta, was that a good idea, d'you think?' interrupted Ally. 'I know the budget is, um, challenging—'

'But look, it says here in the *Chalet Girl Handbook*, chapter two, "Leftovers". "Jolly Holidays feel that culinary ingenuity can go hand in hand with economy. Delicious but none the less economical packed lunches can be made from all sorts of interesting leftovers. Yummy fillings can be made from leftover boeuf bourguignon. Just mince up in the Magimix! Or as we say at Jolly Hols, mince'n'spread! Then pop the delish mixture into some scooped out tomatoes. These can in turn be recycled into a tasty sandwich filling." See, it's here in black and white,' insisted Rochetta. 'And there's more. "Squish up leftover eggy bread from breakfast (unlikely you'll have any of *this* left over!) to make a sumptuous sandwich filling."

'Actually, I'm making spam curry tonight, garnished with pineapple and bananas,' she boasted to Ally.

'God, no wonder they've barred you from the kitchen,' said Pandora, reading over Rochetta's shoulder. 'Oh look, here's a classic. "The sandwich sandwich. Put a slice of bread inside two slices of thicker bre—" '

'I don't think it's meant to be taken literally,' said Ally doubtfully.

'Our punters have brought their own cook,' said Ambrosia. 'He's brilliant, he's been giving Bella and me lessons in how to make this delicious macrobiotic food.'

'Bear in mind,' said Ally, 'that next week's punters might not want to do so much of their own cooking. You won't be able to ski and dance at the GreenGo every night then. And now for the, um, other news. There's a distinct possibility that you're all going to become famous.'

'Gosh, what fun!' I cried.

'Eeuo no!' Everyone else looked horrified.

'I've just had a fax from head office that the *Hello!* Trivia Channel wants to make a documentary about chalet girls. I think they were turned down by every other company and came to Jolly Holidays as a kind of last resort.' She groaned. 'I told them it would destroy business, but Chiara wouldn't listen. She thinks it'll be free advertising and turn Jolly Holidays into a sort of Thompsons for the millennium. She's mad, of course.' She sighed bleakly.

'Too frightful,' said Bella. 'My people hate any kind of publicity, what with Daddy being a high court judge and everything.'

'Awful.'

'So embarrassing.'

'What a nightmare,' I lied unconvincingly. A film crew in my chalet, filming me cooking and cleaning Chalet Tiara. I could tell the world about my book! Find a publisher! Become famous!

'My sentiments entirely,' said Ally. 'But we've just got to make the best of it. The TV crew is on their way out whether we like it or not and they're going to put cameras in all your kitchens. They suggested your bedrooms but I put my foot down.'

'Oh, bedrooms would have been OK,' said the Bolter.

'Oh really, Rocky, you wouldn't want to be filmed naked, would you?' asked Bella.

'No, it would be dreadful,' she replied unconvincingly. I knew she was lying, she would have loved to be filmed naked. She was a frightful exhibitionist. I glanced at Roberto who had been silently absorbing the news. He caught my eye and winked. He obviously felt his 'improvements' were the cause of these exciting developments.

Personally, I couldn't wait for the film crew to arrive. The sparkling chandelier and red poinsettia I had placed in the hall in my fame area had obviously had a stunning effect. There must be something in this feng shui stuff after all. And now the ball was rolling, where would it all end?

Chapter Twenty

I was sad to see Roberto and the rest of his cronies depart with their bulging brown envelopes for Zurich. I felt a bit guilty because Roberto had dislocated his arm trying to remove the grinning marmot head from the outside loo/ relationship area. He had even spent his last day trying to find a chainsaw to hack it off, but with no luck. I was secretly quite relieved. Once he started, I didn't know where he might stop.

However all talk of crystals was soon forgotten when they were replaced by a phlegmatic interviewer called Tim and a silent cameraman called Mule. Cut adrift from royal stalking duties since the tragic demise of the Princess of Wales, they were full of grim enthusiasm at the juicy prospect of following the five of us around. They spent a day wiring up our kitchens and for the next fortnight, which included a chaotic Christmas week, they trailed around after us asking inane questions. At first we were quite flattered, allowing them to buy us cappuccinos at Pop-Ups in the afternoon, but we soon got tired of their questions and learnt to ignore them wherever possible.

Bella tried the red knicker spell with devastating success and immediately became engaged to Tony Louche. This was not a Good Thing as now that she had netted a man, she was even less interested in her career as a *plongeur* and kept bolting to the Palace to drink Bellinis, leaving a harassed Ambrosia to hold the fort.

As for me, I was in seventh heaven. Being in Gstaad was

like living in a gleaming diamond bubble, a protective shock absorber against the brutal reality of other less polite places. Somewhere, if one was to believe the horrors reported in the *Daily Mail*, frightful things were happening to people, but here in our gilded alpine paradise, the living was easy, people laughed and there was an atmosphere of cheerful gaiety in the Co-op as people stopped and chatted and queued with their groceries. Even the check-out girls were speedy and full of bonhomie. It was all a million miles away from stressed yuppies in the Kings Road Waitrose, surreptitiously ramming one another with their trolleys of exotic foodstuffs like kangaroo steaks and penguin fillets.

I was enjoying cooking for my punters, most of whom were most appreciative and undemanding, happy to make their own beds if rewarded with a mini Mars Bar. I didn't get much free time, but I had just discovered an old book (in English, thank goodness), detailing the history of this part of Switzerland, known as the Saanerland, and I was fascinated by it.

It had been charmingly inscribed to Beatrice from her husband (which Ally had translated as to my darling Beatrice, another winter in paradise, all my love, Hans, 1938). I loved to think of Beatrice poring over it in front of the fire when the weather was too bad to ski.

But it was getting harder and harder to escape from Tim and Mule and their prying cameras. Whenever I was just about to sneak off for a well-earned read, they would suddenly appear with some spurious excuse. At first I plied them with delicious morsels, as they looked so thin and bedraggled. But now I feared I had set a dangerous precedent and they appeared whenever they wanted a free meal. Which was like all the time.

'Tim and Mule are driving me mad,' I confided during a hard afternoon's langlaufing with Ally. She had a rare free afternoon from ski guiding and I had persuaded her to accompany me on my favourite track from Gstaad to Saanen.

Saanen was the capital of the Saanerland, and dated back to the ninth century. I went every Friday when they had a weekly open air market, selling local cheeses, milk and dried meats. Plump farmers and their wives met to gossip with their friends before packing up their stalls and adjourning to the Landhaus Hotel to hammer out farming business. This was a tradition going back centuries and was as strong as ever. Gstaad was the glitzy icing of the region, but Saanen was where the big cheeses, so to speak, made the big decisions.

'They follow me about everywhere, watching me make the beds, polish the floor, bake the cake. They'd follow me into the loo if I let them. Anyway, I keep telling them about *Chalet Girl Secrets* so maybe if this programme is ever aired, which I doubt – I mean, who's going to be interested in us lot? – it might help me get a publisher.'

'I'm sure I can give you a hand with that, I'm speaking to my agent in Boston this week. Why don't you get something together and send it to her? I'm sure she'd put you in touch with someone who could help.'

'Gosh, Ally, that would be great. I've got enough stuff to show someone now.' I froze in my tracks. 'Careful!' A group of elderly langlaufers steamed brutally round a blind corner, mowing us down. We collapsed in a tangle of skis as they ploughed over us, singing what sounded like Status Quo hits at the top of their voices. We picked ourselves up gingerly.

'God, I wish they wouldn't do that. They're so aggressive,' I complained, staggering to my feet.

'Gee, I thought cross-country skiing was a nice gentle sort of sport. These guys are crazy. I was in the ski shop yesterday and I heard that they killed a motorist.'

'How?'

'A group of them were skiing on the road, and a motorist swerved to avoid them and crashed into a tree. Died instantly.'

'That's shocking.' In reality I wasn't shocked at all. Such an incident was only one of a number. The langlaufers were multiplying and getting way out of control. I hoped the Swiss would legislate or have a referendum about it, otherwise things would only get worse.

We mused over the vexatious langlaufing problem in silence for several minutes. It was a stunning sunny day and we could see for miles over to the Palace on our right and distant mountains beyond. A clear stream gurgled and spun clear rivulets of sparkling water by our side. The air was frosty and the snow glistened at our feet. How I loved it here! Grimy London seemed a million light years away. If only I could stay forever.

'It's so heavenly to have some peace and quiet without Tim and Mule hanging around,' I said.

I spoke too soon. 'Oh my God, look!' Like a distant hellish mirage, Tim and Mule were ploughing through the snow in the far distance. They waved cheerfully and made their way towards us. They had a hungry look about them; I feared just the sight of me now incited a Pavlovian response in their stomachs, connecting me immediately with food. It was most tiresome.

'Quick, Ally, we've got to lose them! They simply *mustn't* follow us. I haven't got enough food on me.'

We sped off at top speed.

'I've had the worst fax from head office, they've had a slew of complaints about Rochetta and Bella,' panted Ally. 'I'm going to have to be very firm with them. I certainly don't want what I have to say to be recorded, that's for sure.' Ally had arranged a top-level summit meeting at Pop-Ups tearoom this afternoon.

'Oh God, Ally, they're catching up!' Tim and Mule, still with his state of the art camera (did the wretched man never take time out?) were gesticulating at us frantically. But luckily they were no match for the athletic Ally, her short, blonde hair damp from the effort and her face glowing with high colour. I had a harder time keeping up with her, my scrunchie had fallen off somewhere and my hair was all over the place. It was halfway down my back now and way too long. I must get it cut. I was also impeded by my backpack which was full of yogurts from my hit on the Saanen molkerie. Still, it was quite exciting being on the run.

'I feel like Steve McQeen in *The Great Escape*!' I puffed. 'Except he was on a motorbike. C'mon! We've got to make it to the border before the enemy get us!'

At last we had a downhill slope. I could just let my skis do the work. Unfortunately they didn't and I lost my balance, tumbling into the snow and landing on my yogurts which oozed alarmingly all over the snow. 'Oh, what a waste!' I cried, trying to salvage my favourite coffee-flavoured ones.

'C'mon, there's no time to pick them up.' Ally heaved me to my feet and pushed me in the right direction. Luckily we were moments away from the road and the entrance to Pop-Ups.

'Ugh, God, Oriana, why have you got yogurt all over your hair?' asked Pandora as we dashed into the tearoom. Bella edged up to give us room at the small table.

'It's a long story,' replied Ally. 'Where's the Bolter?'

'She said she might be a bit late. She had to sort out some ski passes.' Bella was a rotten liar. I knew for a fact the Bolter was banged up in Gstaad clink having fallen asleep on the tracks of the railway station and been scraped off the lines by a stony-faced Swiss railway guard at 4 a.m.

'Well, I can't wait for her, I'm afraid. Is Ambrosia still ill?' Bella nodded. 'We must start before Tim and Mule track us down. They're on the scent I'm afraid.' Everybody groaned. 'Head office aren't happy,' Ally continued. 'I think you've been rumbled. There's been a string of complaints. The Grouts staying at Bella's and Ambrosia's chalet are asking for a refund.'

The Grouts from Camberley, unaffectionately known as the Groaning Grouts, had not stopped complaining since their arrival. They counted many allergies between them. Master Grout was allergic to dust which, given the standards of Bella's housekeeping, specially with Ambrosia laid up, had led to an asthmatic relapse. Jen Grout, who prided herself on her immaculate housekeeping, was horrified at the state of the kitchen, and Mr Grout complained bitterly and frequently about the state of the family's packed lunches.

'The Groaning Grouts are always moaning about something,' grumbled Bella mulishly.

'I quote from the fax,' said Ally. ' "Not since I was in the army have I been forced to eat such muck. The chalet maid's—" '

'Chalet *maid*! The cheek of it!'

' "Idea of tomato soup is to mix tomato ketchup with hot water." Is that true?' asked Ally.

'How was I to know where Ambrosia had put the soup tins?' muttered Bella crossly.

' "Instead of the tasty English breakfast we were promised in the brochure, the chalet maid made a revolting dish called Egg Foo Breakfast from the leftovers of a Chinese takeaway she had shared with her noisy friends the night before. When we refused to eat it, she put the leftovers into our packed lunch. The standards of housekeeping and hygiene are rubbish—" '

'Nanny always made me eat up my leftovers,' Bella interrupted. 'If I didn't she'd just serve them up again and again until I ate them. Eating leftovers never did me any harm.' A question mark hung over this bold statement.

Ally ploughed on. 'Chiara's not at all happy. She says that if it wasn't for the fact that your fathers were at Eton together . . .' The words 'sacked' and 'dismissed' hung obliquely in the air. Thank heavens for the old boy network. It had saved poor Bella from ignominious dismissal.

'Hi, guys!' It was the Bolter. Her leather trousers were frayed and her curly dark hair was matted and uncombed. Her eyeliner had smudged and formed black circles round her big brown eyes. Despite her sluttish appearance, she radiated an earthy sexuality and the worthy Swiss burghers who frequented Pop-Ups stared at her transfixed, the women disapproving, patisserie forks poised, the men dripping cake crumbs from mouths open with fascination.

'Sorry I'm late. I ran out of cornflour and had to rush to the Co-op.'

'I thought you were picking up ski passes?' asked Ally suspiciously. 'Oh, never mind.'

The list of complaints from the Grouts went on and on and it was many *chocolats chauds* later before we were free to leave Pop-Ups and make our way back to our chalets.

On the way back to Chalet Tiara I stopped at the Bahnhof to ring my father and find out when he was coming out. I was looking forward to seeing him as I was in low spirits because this week's punters, a crowd of gormless merchant bankers, were completely impossible. Every night they got drunk, went out (great relief), but unfortunately always came back. They would then raid the fridge, throw up and collapse in odd places around the chalet. I would frequently find remnants of my homemade soups, sauces and exquisitely marinated stews turning up in plant pots, basins and window sills the following day. And the sheets! Awful, awful stains; I mean, I tried not to look but I couldn't avoid looking as I had to make the beds.

Added to this, all the girls seemed to be embroiled in various kinds of romantic intrigue. Pandora was in seventh heaven as she had resuscitated her romantic confusion with Jack Dudley, Bella was still engaged to Tony Louche, even Ambrosia, whom I had mistakenly thought of as homely (talk about dark horse!), was being pursued by an eager ski instructor with whom she had been spotted enjoying exciting trysts in bubble cars, frequently going round and round for hours. I suspected her 'nervous exhaustion' was really only a form of travel sickness. Ally had her boyfriend in Zurich. Who did I have? Admittedly the Swiss plumber had become a little familiar of late (after many visits he had *finally* mended the leaking radiator in the relationship corner, although the strange noxious smell still lingered). No one. I didn't count Roberto, who rang frequently and appeared quite smitten. I must admit I flirted with him shamelessly but it was only in the desperate hope that one day he would offer me a feng shui tip that would really change my life. He had just sent me a wooden flute with some red ribbon tied round it, which I was to play last thing at night sitting in my relationship corner. OK, I know it sounds daft, and of course I was far too busy to think about romance really, but I thought that if it worked it might help other girls.

At the phone box at the station I dialled my father's number and was put through to Lettuce, his longserving and loyal secretary.

'Oh, Oriana, you've just missed him. He's off to London for a business dinner. He twisted his ankle skiing last weekend so he's been a bit laid up. I told him he was far too old for that sort of thing. He should have tried that long-logging thing that you do. Something nice and quiet.' I shuddered. If only people knew how vicious it really was. 'He'll be sorry to have missed your call. Shall I give him a message?'

'Oh no. Just give him my love. That's all.' I replaced the receiver heavily, trying to ignore my hurt feelings. If my own father found me too boring to look up, how could I expect anyone else to be interested? But the worst thing had been the pity in Lettuce's voice. She was used to making up for his forgetfulness but it must be one of the least pleasant aspects of the job.

I strapped my skis on numbly and made my way back to the chalet. It was dark now, the mountains etched starkly into the indigo sky. It was a clear night and the stars glistened brightly but it was very cold. I shivered bleakly and pulled my scarf more tightly about my neck. Time to prepare dinner for Crispinian and his chums. No doubt it would end up in one of my plant pots but I must go through the motions. Besides, Tim and Mule had invited themselves to dinner so it was vital I put on a good show.

Tim and Mule loved it when things went wrong. Pandora had told me that when her twice-baked soufflé had flopped twice they had become almost gleeful. I dreaded to think how excited they might become if they found out about Ambrosia's recipe for using up old peanut butter: add boiling water, cornflour and chopped sage (why sage I have no idea) to the remnants in the peanut butter jar, shake vigorously and pour over cooked pasta.

Dinner that evening was predictably raucous. Crispinian – 'Call me Crispin, old man, everyone does' – and his chums were in fine mettle, playing up to Tim and Mule with a particularly revolting farting competition. Still, I was happy because my Stilton and celeriac soup with crispy garlic and vegetable croutons was a great hit with Tim and Mule who both asked for seconds.

I was just gathering up the plates when Crispin stood up and toasted me.

'To our luscious chalet girl, Oriana, and all who sail in her.' This was followed by a loud fart from somewhere down the table.

'That's very kind, Crispin,' I replied politely. 'I didn't think you were familiar with the ship.'

'Darling girl, I'm not. I'm more familiar with your bum!' This was followed by much table thumping, farting and belching. To my horror Crispin withdrew the huge Naff Ovens advertising picture of my naked bottom barely covered by the J-Cloth. Would I never be free of this ghastly picture? And for it to fall into the Crispinians' hands was really too awful.

'Thought your name rang a bell,' drawled Rupert, a smooth-skinned young man with an untroubled expression and a mop of thick dark hair. 'So I got one of the computer nerds at the office to do a search. Turns out Naff Ovens was one of our clients before they went bust and this is what he came up with.' Crispin grabbed my bottom and squeezed it viciously.

'Get off me, you beastly poofs.' Not the brightest thing to say under the circs, as it only incited the Crispins to even greater displays of macho behaviour, roaring, table thumping, farting and belching etc. I bit my lip and rushed out of the dining room, shutting the green baize door of my kitchen behind me.

How could I ever face the Crispins again? Tim and Mule would forever see me as a pornographic figure of fun. The Martha Stewart image I had cultivated so carefully would be demolished. I sat down at the kitchen table and sobbed. It had been an utterly bloody day. And the worst thing about it was that it was all on Mule's wretched camera. You'd think he and Tim might have come to my support, but oh no. They were despicable. Anything for a story!

After a few minutes of feeble snivelling I dried my eyes and slowly got up to turn off the oven. I wasn't going to let the Crispinians ruin my delicious cassoulet which I had spent the last four days preparing. But I couldn't face returning to the dining room with it either. Oh well, it would keep till tomorrow. I was just on my knees, bottom sticking out, pulling the dish out of a distant corner of the Aga when the door opened.

'Whoever it is you can piss off!' I shouted angrily, stifling a sob and shoving the cassoulet back in the Aga and slamming the door.

'You must be Oriana. What a beautiful name. *Oriana* was a beautiful ship. I can see why you were named after her.' The voice spoke with the slow, deliberate exactitude of someone used to giving orders and being obeyed.

I pushed back a strand of hair from my eyes. Any thoughts about this stranger in my kitchen being just another punter were immediately dispelled by the voice. It was mesmerizing, deep and rich with a slight German accent overlaid with an American drawl.

Turning round quickly I saw that it belonged to a large bull-like man with broad shoulders that could have been sculpted from oak and fists that looked as though they could have been cut from granite. But horrors, he couldn't have caught me at a worse time, what with my hair scraped back off my face and secured with a pencil and my face bright red from checking the cassoulet. And I was longing to blow my nose but I couldn't because he was too sexy to do that in front of. And I must have been reeking of goose fat.

'Um, who are you?' I asked, bewildered.

He chuckled. 'Ernst Schmitt. No need to look so horrified, I own the chalet. So I guess that makes me your landlord.' He glanced around my kitchen, or I should say his kitchen, appreciatively.

'You've tidied the old place up a bit. It looks great. Mmm, and dinner smells wonderful.'

I surreptitiously dried my eyes on my sleeve.

'Here, use this.' He unfurled a large white handkerchief from his suit pocket and handed it to me. 'Go on. It's quite clean.'

I dried my eyes delicately, not daring to blow my nose on it. 'Sorry, I've got these awful punters this week. They're blackmailing me with a stupid picture I had taken by mistake inside an oven ages ago. I thought everyone had forgotten about it, but it keeps reappearing. Now it's in the Crispinians' hands I'll *never* be free of it, my reputation will be quite ruined.' I sighed dramatically and gazed hopelessly at the Aga.

'I met them on the way in. Don't worry about the picture, I'll get it back for you.'

I tried not to melt too obviously. With his broad forehead and strong jaw he inspired such confidence, I had no doubt that he would. He was definitely not the sort of man who took prisoners. 'That would be such a relief,' I gazed at him gratefully. 'You should have been here last week. We had some lovely people staying, a really quiet family. From

Manchester.' My eyes filled with tears again. If he went on being sympathetic and sexy I would break down, I knew I would. I clutched his hanky. 'And my cassoulet – it'll be wasted on them, they're English . . .'

'I'm not. Cassoulet happens to be my favourite meal. My grandmother – this used to be her chalet – kept geese. I'm very fond of them.'

'So you won't want to eat one then, will you?'

'Of course I do! I haven't had dinner yet and I'm starving. Let's have our dinner. If there's any left over you can give it to your friends next door. If there isn't, they can get a kebab from town.'

'Yes, I hear they're rather good.' According to the Bolter the recently opened Gstaad Kebab Emporium did brilliant kebabs. At least none of her punters had complained yet, and they practically had to live off the things. I dished out a substantial helping of the unctuous stew with shaking hands. I cut him a hunk of homemade bread and handed it to him.

'Go on, aren't you having any?'

I went through the motions of helping myself, but I was far too agitated to eat. This man was sex on legs. How could I possibly be interested in food at a time like this!

Ernst scooped up the cassoulet enthusiastically. 'Umm, this is fabulous, and I'm a cassoulet expert. I'm telling you, you could give those guys at the Palace a run for their money.'

We were interrupted by a racket from outside the door. Crispin, closely followed by Rupert and the others, with Tim and Mule hot on their heels, burst through the green baize door.

'Where's our dinner?' demanded Crispinian angrily. 'Christ, she's gone and fed our dinner to the Kraut. What a bloody waste of good food.'

'Don't mention the war, chaps,' called a wag. Someone burped loudly and began to hum the Dambusters tune. I was familiar with this as it was the numero uno in Mrs B's repertoire. But even she wouldn't hum it in front of a real

Krau – I mean German. That would be frightfully bad form.

Ernst deliberately wiped his plate clean with a chunk of bread (appetite under fire, how attractive!), put his fork to one side and got to his feet. I was thrilled to see that he dwarfed Crispin and all his stunted chums, towering over them considerably.

'I'm rather cross that you've been upsetting my friend Oriana here.' I loved the way he said Oh-riana. And thank goodness he was going to attempt fisticuffs on a full stomach. He had the advantage over the Crispins who ate very little, relying on alcohol for their sole nutrition generally. No wonder they were so weedy. All talk and no action, that was their trouble.

Crispin puffed out his skinny chest aggressively.

'Go for it, Crisp!' muttered somebody nervously.

'D'you know what you are?' continued Ernst. 'You're a little *putz*.'

'I say—'

Ernst picked up Crispin by the scruff of his neck and threw him down on the kitchen table, twisting his arm in a vice-like grip. Ernst's plate slipped to the flagstone floor and smashed into a thousand pieces. There was a nervous silence.

'Apologize, you little *schmuck*, and give me the picture!' growled Ernst crossly, beads of perspiration on his broad forehead.

'I haven't got it. Wupert has.' Crispin regressed into an agonized lisp. 'Wupe, give the man the picture, pleeeese.'

Rupert retreated into the dining room and returned with the offensive picture which he handed to Ernst. Ernst took a good look at it, looked at me appraisingly and returned his attention to Crispin. 'Say you're sorry!'

'I'm wairly sorry, Oriana. It was only a joke. You're an ace girl, we all think—'

'SHUT UP,' said Ernst, releasing him and chucking him towards the door. Crispin dashed out of the room, his chums following in his wake. Tim and Mule remained in a safe corner where they had retreated once the fisticuffs had broken out.

'And you two putzes can piss off too.' Ernst's knowledge of English and Yiddish expletives was most impressive. He made to grab the camera but Mule, who'd I'd noticed before was oddly flexible for a man, scooted out of his range and into the hall.

'Shit. What does a man have to do to earn a meal these days?' Ernst collapsed on a chair and rolled up his shirt sleeves, revealing big hairy wrists. 'Have you got any pudding?'

'Homemade eighty per cent cocoa solid chocolate ice cream with hot arabica coffee bean sauce?'

'Only if you've used Starbucks coffee beans.' His dark eyes were deadpan, I couldn't tell if he was joking or not.

I laughed. 'How did you guess? I brought them out with me.'

'Why? You can get perfectly good coffee in Switzerland.'

'I know that now, but I didn't want to take a chance on it.'

'Control freak, huh?' He was smiling now. 'I was teasing you.' He brushed my shoulder lightly and I shivered. 'I only tease people that I like.'

'Oh.'

'But I would love some of your ice cream.'

Relieved to have something useful to do with my hands, I busied myself warming up the sauce.

I placed a melting mound of ice cream topped with aromatic coffee sauce beside him. 'Oh dear, you've got some blood on your shirt.'

'If I'd known I was going to be involved in a punch-up I wouldn't have worn my best suit. I drove straight from a meeting in Zurich. Should have changed into my combat clothes on the way.'

'You weren't to expect fisticuffs, not in a place like Gstaad,' I said consolingly.

'You'd think that but I was held up in the village because

some girl was attacking a group of policemen. Quite an attractive girl.' He noticed my face fall as I had a realization.

'She didn't have dark curly hair, possibly wearing leather trousers, quite tall . . .'

'Yes, that sounds like her. Is she a friend of yours?'

'Um, yes. She's kind of a political activist, she was protesting against the Swiss rubbish policy.' This was a grandiose way of explaining that the Bolter was over budget again and was trying to save money by throwing the chalet's rubbish into a bin outside the Co-op. The Swiss cleverly encouraged people to recycle as much as possible by charging a fortune for rubbish bags in the supermarket. If you were found using other types of bags you were sent to prison.

Oh dear, this wasn't the first time the Bolter had been caught trying to dispose of rubbish illegally, and together with her recent arrest after falling asleep on the railway line I hoped she wouldn't be deported.

'Jeez, I feel sorry for the Brits, they're always getting caught siphoning off rubbish where they shouldn't. Times must be really hard in the UK, ja?'

'Yah, what with exports taking such a hammering from the obscenely strong pound,' I rattled off, mesmerized by his amazing fists. Even his fingers looked as if they had biceps. God, he was attractive.

'That shouldn't be bothering you, the strong pound is working in your favour. More money for shopping,' he said indulgently, his eyes momentarily diverted to my fat-splattered frilly apron and too skimpy T-shirt. Too much birchermuesli and rösti consumption had caused an increase in my *embonpoint* and I was bursting out of all my clothes, a fact that seemed to go down well with him, judging from the approval in his dark eyes.

'You're obviously a bright girl, and you're a fabulous cook, so what the hell are you doing working as a maid for a bunch of *putzes*?'

'I'm not a maid, I'm a chalet girl. In England it's

considered quite a smart thing to be,' I explained defensively.

'Ja, in England it's considered amusing to bang on about something that happened over fifty years ago. Still, it's been an interesting evening. I needed some exercise after sitting in the office all day.' He glanced at his watch. 'Damn, I'm going to be late. I'm meant to be going out to dinner. Thank God I've had a decent meal already. Their cook's lousy.'

'What do you do in Zurich?' I asked, intrigued.

'I run a company that makes rubber caps for car wheels. We've just opened a branch in London.'

Hurrah! A man who made things!

'My business partner has a chalet here. Come back and have a drink with us.' I was conscious again of what I must look like, mascara dripping, blonde hair trailing, and spots of goose fat on my apron, and no deodorant! I had just read a terrifying article in the *Daily Mail* about the carcinogenic effects of blocking up sweat glands, and I had thrown it away. I just hoped my *embonpoint* and pheromones would cover up any aromatic shortfall.

'Um, I'm not really dressed for it . . .' Oh please, please suggest tomorrow, when I have time to spend four hours getting ready.

'Oh, all right then. But will you be OK staying here tonight with that lot?'

'Oh yes. My room's right at the top. It's quite self-contained.'

'You've nabbed the master bedroom! Smart girl. But take my number, call me if you have any problems. Promise me? I'm only down the road.' He scribbled his number down on the back of his card.

I nodded solemnly. Could I call if I didn't have problems? Could I create a problem perhaps? Would a leaking radiator count? I knew Crispin and his cronies were unlikely to break my door down. I had been nervous at first and had pushed the bed, chests of drawers and heavy tables against it but I soon realized that despite their posturing, none of them was particularly interested in women in that way. Even if they were, after the amount of alcohol they consumed, they would be unable to do very much about it.

As he handed me his card our eyes locked and I felt myself drowning, hypnotized, like a rabbit caught in headlights. I hated it that he was the one who looked away first.

'I enjoyed my dinner. You're a great cook. And you don't take a bad photo either.' He picked the photo up from the table and slid it crisply into his wallet. I blushed and looked down. The atmosphere in the kitchen had become quite electric. He paused for a moment. 'Johnny Ruritania has asked me to a party tomorrow night. Would you come as my guest?'

'The Prince of Ruritania?' I asked casually. The *Prince of Ruritania*! *Hola!* staple and king of the Gstaad Euro toffs? Would I? Just try stopping me! The Crispins could starve for all I cared. 'Um, it depends what time it is. You see I have to cook dinner . . .' I didn't want to appear too keen. After all, he probably had women throwing themselves at him all the time, being one of the few obviously heterosexual man in the western world. Besides, after a dodgy start it was essential I begin playing The Rules to the hilt.

I got up and began piling the plates into the sink efficiently. 'I'm sure I can get away after dinner. What time can you pick me up?'

Chapter Twenty-one

'God, Oriana, I can hardly believe it!' Pandora and Ally were in fits of laughter as I regaled them with last night's adventures.

It was a stunning day and we were basking in the sunshine on a chair lift, trundling slowly up the mountain. The sky was strikingly blue and dotted with colourful hot-air balloons that had drifted over from the Chateau d'Oex ballooning competition.

This was the second time this week I'd been skiing with the others, and to my surprise my nerve was flooding back. And today, full of excitement from Ernst's thrilling appearance in my kitchen, the warm sunshine and perfect snow conditions, I suddenly realized what I'd been missing.

'So was he *snogtastic*?' asked Pandora.

'I don't know. Crispin had more physical contact with him than I did, lucky man.'

'I'd have given anything to be a fly on the wall,' said Pandora enviously.

'I think Tim and Mule filmed some of it.' I sighed. 'Like a real movie. With good guys, bad guys, Steve McQueen hero type rescuer—'

'Does Ernst look like Steve McQueen then?'

'Um, no, he's quite dark, at least he probably was.'

'Sounds like a sad bald git. Your usual type.'

'He's not a sad git, he's a tycoon. And he's only a bit bald. Look, here's his card, Ernst Schmitt, Managing Director, Car Fahrt.'

Pandora sniggered.

'Gee, I've heard of Car Fahrt,' said Ally. 'That's a big company.'

'Anyway, I'm glad he's not blond and hairy, blond men leave me quite cold,' I continued.

'But you're always talking about Steve McQueen and he's blond and hairy,' reminded Pandora with Virgo-like precision.

'Yes, but only because he played a fireman in the *Towering Inferno* and I have a thing about firemen.'

'Is Ernst a fireman?'

'No, he's far too busy making the rubber caps that you screw on wheels to stop them dropping off. I think that's what he said he makes.'

'Ugh, that doesn't sound very glamorous.'

'At least he's making something useful. Unlike the Crispinians. I mean, what are they putting back into society? Nothing.'

'They're keeping us lot employed, that's something,' said Ally sensibly. This was true. If the Jolly Holidays team were not trying to organize holidays I couldn't think what else they could possibly do.

'It's a shame you only fancy dark men,' Ally continued. 'I thought I had the perfect man for you. I have this old friend who used to live near us on Nantucket. Dan's a really smart guy, went to MIT in Boston, now he's a marine biologist. He used to date my sister when they were at high school. I just thought of him because she called me yesterday and said he was back on the island for a few weeks. He just loves English girls, especially blondes.'

'Dan McCloud?' asked Pandora.

'Yeah, d'you know him?'

'Dishy Dan McCloud, you remember, Oriana, he gave that brilliant talk at the whaling ball.'

'How could I forget? He gave this fascinating lecture about whales and the ocean being the last unexplored frontier, Ally. It made me look at the sea in a completely different way. It's amazing to think we have better maps of Venus than we do of the world's deepest oceans.'

'I just read in Nigel Dempster that he's dating Anoushka Bird-Whistle, which seems an unlikely combination,' said Pandora.

'I know you upper-class English are into that hunting thing in a big way, but do you still hunt whales?'

'NO! We were trying to raise money to save them, not kill them. What do you take us for?'

'I know. I was only kidding.' There was a small cultural impasse.

'What a coincidence that we all know him,' I said. 'I mean I don't know him at all really, but I met him the same night I met Peregrine. Actually I didn't meet him, but he winked at me. It really cheered me up. But I wasn't allowed to meet him because apparently his wife is very jealous.'

'That would be Madison,' said Ally coldly. 'Thank God they've split up now. She was pathologically jealous. Gee, I can't believe you've met Dan. Don't you think he's great-looking?'

'I'm afraid I'm the wrong person to ask, there's only one person I've got eyes for at the moment. You see, I have a particular crush type and Ernst is it,' I replied simply. 'Besides, I don't know anything about marine biology.' I didn't add that a marine biologist didn't fulfil any of my wife of tycoon type dreams.

'But you went out with Peregrine, and he's not your type,' Pandora pointed out.

'Peregrine caught me at a low moment. Besides, we were just friends.'

'Well, don't get too caught up with this Ernst boxer tycoon person. Remember, you haven't even snogged him yet. Besides, ever since you've been here you've said you needed a boyfriend like a hole in the head.'

'Perhaps it's the feng shui improvements. There must be some connection between Ernst's mysterious appearance, mending my leaking radiator and getting the outside lavatory mended, what do you think?'

But released from the chair lift, Pandora and Ally had set off in the direction of Chalet Twix where Ally was dining that night.

' 'Bye!' I yelled at their rapidly retreating backs. Pandora raised a ski pole in response as they disappeared round a corner.

Humming the Dambusters theme tune cheerily, I set off in the direction of Chalet Tiara which, due to radical snowfalls, it was now possible to ski back to. In the distance I spotted an elderly man skiing gingerly with a ski guide. On closer inspection it turned out to be none other than aka James Bond, yes! Roger Moore himself. My goodness, he was an even worse skier than I was. I couldn't wait to tell the others.

On the downward schuss, speeding through the fir trees, the wind whistling through my ears, I smiled secretly into the setting sun. I couldn't *wait* till this evening.

Ernst's brutal attack on my behalf had bolstered my confidence with the Crispinians dramatically. On my return I took a deep breath outside the drawing room, slipped on an imaginary pair of jackknife boots (to get in storm trooper mode) and stormed straight in to collect the tea things, wielding my outsize tea tray for moral support.

I needn't have worried as the startling display of fisticuffs had left them quite subdued. They were dotted about the room in various stages of alcoholic stupor, but rather than producing its usual euphoria, the alcohol had exerted a curiously depressing effect upon the assembled company.

To my disappointment they hadn't touched my sachertorte chocolate cake or crumbly buttery flapjacks. Brandishing my tray vigorously I crashed the plates and empty teacups violently together, eliciting nothing but a small maudlin groan from the comatose figures dotted about the room and a feeble attempt to throw a bread roll at me.

As they hadn't had any tea I made sure that dinner was as enticing as possible. After all, I had no desire to add to Jolly Holidays' increasingly long punter complaints list.

To my surprise the chaps were as good as gold, treating me rather like a feared nanny, presumably terrified that any misdemeanour might result in my releasing my brutish German genie once again.

'But you must eat something,' I cajoled as the boys picked listlessly at their golden crispy roast chicken. Tonight their excessive drinking seemed to have taken on a more desperate note than usual, and I wondered if they might be alcoholics.

'If you don't eat your dinner I'll serve it up again and again until you do!' I commanded fiercely. After all, sometimes one has to be cruel to be kind, and I was starting to feel a bit sorry for them.

There was a visible brightening up at my unusual display of firmness and they began to tuck in obediently.

Relieved that I had somehow gained the upper hand, I abandoned them to their hot toffee apple crumble and hotfooted upstairs to make rapid preparations for the party.

I was so looking forward to meeting the Prince of Ruritania and his fragrant wife, Princess Poppy, scioness of an old Monegasque family. The Prince's chalet was bound to be wall-to-wall Euro royalty and staples of *Hola!* magazine. I never buy *Hola!* because I can't speak Spanish, but I enjoy looking at the pictures in W.H. Smith's. What I like about it is that it goes beyond *Hello!* into a distant exotic realm of obscure foreign royalty. I don't know about you, but I think ours have been done to death, but if you read *Hola!* you'll discover a whole new strata of foreign princelings and Euro toffs to be intrigued by.

Perhaps I would meet the Aga Khan, Roger Moore, Julie Andrews or even Taki. He was building a grand chalet nearby; Pandora would be interested to find out if Swiss builders were more reliable than their British counterparts.

I had wanted to wash and blow dry my hair but there was only time to rub some mousse in and do a bit of backcombing, slap on some foundation to even out my cheeks which were still pink from the hot kitchen and slip on a little greeny blue cashmere dress. A little black dress would have been appropriate, but I didn't want to look like a waitress (which is what I was, I know) and due to my minimal packing I did not possess such a thing anyway.

I dashed downstairs, hoping to avoid the Crispinians who would only ask nosy questions if they caught me dolled up, but fortunately they were dotted about the chalet in various states of unconsciousness and didn't stir when Ernst barged in as if he owned the place, which I guess he did really.

'My little hausfrau, you're quite transformed.' He circled me admiringly with a panther-like predatoryness, like a cat playing with a mouse. His skin was even darker today, it gleamed a rich dark brown from skiing, and his eyes seemed black in the dim candlelight. He emanated a potent mix of power and sexual charisma. Spellbound by fear and lust I was quite unable to move and stood impassive as a statue, longing for him to touch me. But he didn't. He continued, more absently, less enraptured, 'You should wear that colour more often, it brings out the green in your eyes.'

There was a muffled groan from the drawing room. I tensed. Oh God, the Crispinians were waking up! It would be too awful if they reappeared now and ruined this crucial romantic moment by inciting Ernst to fisticuffs!

'Come on,' I gabbled, grabbing my bag. 'I'm longing to get to the party!'

Ernst's black Mercedes was parked outside and smelt expensively of cigars and new leather upholstery. It was reassuring to know that all the nuts and bolts were obviously in good nick, Ernst being the nuts and bolts gaffer, so to speak. And after the Jolly Holidays' deux chevaux, which was constantly weighted down with chocolate wrappers and rotting pieces of forgotten fruit (besides being on its last legs since Bella had crashed it into Tony Louche's Lamborghini in a successful bid to gain his attention), Ernst's car seemed like something from a sleeker more orderly world.

'You speak fantastic English, have you spent time in America?' I inquired.

'Well, my grandmother was from Boston and she was very keen I went to Harvard, so I did.' Ernst had a connection with Nantucket! I must find out more!

'Was your Grandmother Beatrice Muller?'

'Yes.' He looked at me curiously. 'How do you know her name?'

'I found her diary in a drawer. I must show it to you. But I assumed she was English. It's a bit of a coincidence that she was from Boston, Ally, our rep, comes from there – well, Nantucket, actually.' It was extraordinary, the gypsy's prediction was coming true! I wondered if Ernst had building skills.

'Ugh, that awful place. I went there once with some friends and I'm never going back. It was bloody freezing!'

My heart sank. 'But didn't you like the white picket fences and the windswept beaches?'

'No, too twee for me, I'm afraid.'

'Yes, it does sound awfully twee,' I agreed quickly in a desperate bid to incur empathy. 'I've never been, but Ally raves about it.' Stupid gypsy, what did she know! 'So, d'you get to Gstaad very often?' I inquired casually as Ernst skilfully negotiated the narrow icy road that led to the Prince's chalet.

'Hardly ever. I've been too frantic the last couple of months with work, I'm afraid my social life has taken a battering. It's not really a priority at the moment anyway. In my company we have a saying: dinner at home is a wasted sales opportunity.' He turned to look at me with black brooding eyes. My heart flipped.

'So why is work so busy?'

'I'm floating my company, but you won't want to hear about that, it's very boring really.'

'Oh, I'm sure it's not.' I was just phrasing an intelligent question in my head about PE ratios (that would shock him), when we pulled up in front of a huge chalet, lit with flares.

A sullen factotum, smartly dressed in a red jacket with gold buttons, came smartly to our assistance, helping us out of the Merc. This was the life! Dinner at the Prince of Ruritania's chalet! Pandora would be green with envy. Actually, she probably wouldn't be green with envy as Jack Dudley was driving out this weekend so she was probably trysting with him at Chalet Twix.

'Ernst! Dahhhling! It's such a treat to see you.' A very tall, lean ex-model (don't ask me how I knew, I just knew) pounced on Ernst as we walked through the door. 'And thrilling!' she purred in attractively accented English. 'You've brought a little friend!'

Hey, string bean, I wanted to shout, I may be only five foot four, but I'm still two inches taller than the Queen of England, and no one's called *her* a dwarf yet. But I just smiled in an agreeable Lilliputian fashion as another, equally disaffected factotum, disappeared with my jacket while the Euro toff ex-model disappeared with Ernst.

I wandered into the drawing room which was heaving with gorgeous-looking people and helped myself to a glass of pink champagne. What a treat! Surprisingly, I didn't feel in the least bit nervous. I was more intrigued than scared, I was so out of my milieu I could have been in a film set.

I noticed with interest that I was the only women not wearing a little black dress. Ernst suddenly appeared solicitously at my side with another drink. I felt even more unreal. This gorgeous man with his delicious granite-like fists was my date. All the other men looked like South American polo players and had bright white teeth and identical blazers. Ernst with his boulder-like arms, and well-worn though undoubtedly well-cut black business suit, looked like the only man in the room who had ever done an honest day's work in his life.

'Come and get some dinner.' He propelled me into the next room where more factotums were ladling out plates of delicious foie gras. I have a bit of a love-hate relationship with foie gras. I love it, but what about the geese? Still, I accepted a plate and followed Ernst to a small round table, at which were sitting three gorgeous *femmes d'un certain age* and one little man, his dark hair slicked sleekly back, whose function I immediately surmised was to be 'amusing'.

'Ernst! Too delightful,' chortled the amusing little man. 'I was just telling the ladies that you work so hard these days that we never see you. People always tell me that hard work never killed anybody, but I'm not taking any chances!' Everybody burst out laughing.

'Ernst, do introduce us to your friend,' murmured the most gorgeous of the gorgeous *femmes d'un certain age*, as one of the sullen factotums refilled our glasses with the ambrosial pink champagne.

'This is Oriana, who happens to be working in my chalet. I rented it to an English skiing company over the winter, and it's all worked out very well. She has restored the chalet to its former glory. And as well as her considerable culinary skills, she is also writing a book.'

I gazed down modestly and blushed.

'A book!' trilled the amusing man. 'You must be frightfully intellectual. Most of us never read books, so the thought of writing one is quite beyond us!' Everyone laughed delightedly.

'Ahh, Chalet Tiara is so beautiful,' the gorgeous one continued. She had the most beautiful, slightly singsong soft voice, a honeyed mixture of European accents melted down into a harmonious whole. 'We're so pleased to know that people are living there again. I knew Ernst's grandmother very well.'

'But, darling, you were only a child, you could hardly

remember her, surely?' interrupted the amusing man.

She didn't reply but just gave a small sphinx-like smile. Maybe *she* would know about the sheep's placenta injections. Dare I ask?

'Beatrice gave such wonderful parties, such wonderful food. She had the best cook in Switzerland you know, her dinners were quite famous. It was such a shame, what happened, poor lady.'

There was a brief silence when even the amusing man looked quite sad.

'What happened to her?' I asked, agog.

'She was madly in love with my grandfather, but he left her for someone else,' said Ernst. 'She never returned to Geneva where they also had a house, and just stayed here in Gstaad. She became a bit of a recluse at the end.' I thought of the leaking radiator in the relationship corner and the sad, solitary wood carving, which I had covered with a gorgeous picture I'd torn out of *Tatler* of Liz Hurley dancing with a bottle of scent, wearing a beatific expression and a tulle frock. If only Ernst's grandmother had heard of feng shui, maybe her life would have been less of a romantic disaster.

'You look familiar, my dear,' noticed a well-preserved stony-eyed lady. 'Haven't I seen you at the club?'

'Um, what club?' I hazarded.

'Our club,' she said impatiently. 'The Eagle.'

Fortunately we were interrupted by a factotum clearing our plates away with gritted teeth. I realized I'd been so riveted I hadn't touched my foie gras.

'Oriana,' interrupted the honey-voiced lady. 'You haven't touched your foie gras. Don't you like it?'

'Oh yes. But what about the geese?' I blurted out.

'Oh, they love it,' reassured the amusing little man. 'You know, at our farm they come running out when it's time to be fed. They're so frightfully greedy.'

'The English are so amusing about animals,' smiled the stony-eyed lady to the others. Someone stopped by the table and there was much cooing and air kissing and babbling in French and German. I didn't understand a word but just smiled beatifically, sipped my champagne (delicious!) and nodded, frowned and gasped with the others. Through a haze of multilingual bonhomie I was aware that Ernst had laid a heavy hand on my knee whilst dexterously managing to munch his veal (really, Johnny Foreigner had *no* idea!) and truffle casserole.

'Not nearly as delicious as your cassoulet,' he murmured as the Euro babble reached a crescendo at our table. I felt the thin-faced lady's pebble eyes bore into us. Oh dear, did she have a crush on Ernst too?

'So, Oriana, are you the only one from England doing chalet work?' she interrupted.

'Oh no, there's five of us. Well, we're down to four at the moment because we think Rochetta's got arrested.' I paused, realizing I'd said too much. I had no desire to reveal the cause of the Bolter's sudden disappearance to this august crowd. How would they understand the constraints of keeping within a chalet girl budget and the stresses this might lead to?

The stony-eyed lady seized on my discomfort. 'Arrested! In *Hstaaad*?'

Desperate for diversion, the table briefly stopped Euro babbling and turned its eyes to me.

'No one is ever arrested in *Hstaaad*,' stated the amusing man, unamusingly. 'There isn't even a police station, is there?'

'Was it drugs?' asked someone standing nearby.

Ernst looked at me, amused, and said something in rapid German. Everyone burst out laughing. The amusing man said something and everyone roared with laughter.

'It was rubbish not drugs,' I replied hotly. 'She wasn't throwing away anything illegal, she's tremendously honest. We're terribly worried about her. The police say they let her out with a warning but we haven't seen her for two days.'

'Probably just run off for a few days with a ski instructor,' said Ernst. The amusing man said something in French, causing everybody to laugh delightedly.

Bored with the subject, everyone went back to gossiping in rapid French and German and Ernst disappeared to get me a pudding.

'Speak in English!' commanded the honey-voiced lady for my benefit, but everyone ignored her.

'Have you known Ernst very long?' she inquired gently.

'Um, about a day,' I replied, 'but it seems like a lot longer.'

'He's a brilliant businessman. He takes after his grandfather in many ways. The resemblance is quite striking.' I followed her gaze towards Ernst, who was standing chatting earnestly to another man in a corner. 'We know his family, of course, but we never see Ernst these days. I fear we bore him.'

'You, my dear, could not bore anyone,' interrupted the amusing little man gallantly, raising her hand to his lips chivalrously. I was shocked to see that she had the hands of an old woman; they contrasted bizarrely with her plump vitamin-enriched face and thick mane of lustrous blonde hair.

'My friends and I have been really wondering about this place in Switzerland where they do these rejuvenating sheep's placenta injections,' I blurted out suddenly, 'but we can't seem to find out where we can get them.'

There was an embarrassed silence, the amusing man was for once lost for words, the stony-eyed lady's eyes narrowed alarmingly, and the honey-voiced lady's voice became decidedly less mellifluous.

'I have never heard of such a place but it sounds most interesting.'

I knew they were hiding something, there was some kind of conspiracy going on. It was unfair. Why should the Euro toffs have sole access to the font of eternal youth and the impoverished Brits have to make do with Oil of Ulay? It just wasn't fair. But I could have cut the *froideur* with a knife.

'My goodness, is that the time?' The table covertly

checked their Cartier watches and discreetly snapped shut their Hermes bags. 'My dear, such a pleasure to meet you,' and then they all just melted away.

Ernst reappeared at my elbow. 'The party's breaking up, I better get you back home.'

'Oh, I'm not too worried, the Crispinians don't get up till midday, though the way they were when I left them I'm worried they might not get up at all.'

'Well, I just hope you lock your door at night,' said Ernst, steadying me protectively as I wobbled to my feet. The unaccustomed champagne had left me unusually light-headed.

'Oh, there's no need to worry, they're not interested in that sort of thing. They haven't got the strength,' I explained, allowing a factotum to help me on with my jacket. We got in line to say goodbye to the Prince and Princess who were air-kissing their guests goodbye with vague bonhomie. 'So glad you could make it.' 'Such a delightful evening.' 'See you tomorrow at the club.' Slivers of Euro gossip wafted towards me. 'The Aga *promised* he'd fly in.' 'Yes, Sally's still in Geneva, all too shocking.' 'Such a shame Taki couldn't come, you know he has Bill Buckley staying?' 'Bill who?' 'Some sort of writah chap.' 'Never heard of him.' 'Member of the club?' 'Don't think so.' 'No wonder.'

'What an interesting evening,' I trilled, once back in the dangerous confines of Ernst's sleek car. 'Everybody seems to be part of a secret club. It's really nice . . .' I tailed off doubtfully. I knew this was one club I'd never be asked to join.

'Thank God it broke up so early. Normally these things go on until four a.m.' He paused to light a cigar with a steady hand. It was amazing that the Swiss drink driving laws were so lax. Everybody had been consuming vast amounts of booze all night and quite happily climbing into their cars and driving themselves home, but it was illegal to throw away rubbish and for men to pee with the seat up after midnight. And yet the Swiss had a lower drink driving accident rate percentage than the English, who were quite obsessive about it.

I had a feeling that my innocent sheep's placenta query had caused the party's early break-up but I said nothing.

'The Prince's servants looked a bit grumpy.'

'So would I be if I had to dress up in those ridiculous uniforms. Johnny Ruritania's a decent enough guy, but he's still living in the eighteenth century.'

'Yes, you can just imagine them ripping off their tunics for a long night of tricotosing, plotting the downfall of the Euro toffs,' I laughed.

'One wouldn't want to be in the Ruritanians' shoes come the revolution, that's for sure,' agreed Ernst in his deep gravelly voice, taking his hand off the wheel and laying it softly on my knee. I shivered. Come the revolution I wanted to be sitting in Ernst's car, with his hand on my knee. Just like this. I shut my eyes for a second, willing this moment to go on forever. But after an electrifying minute, Ernst replaced his hand on the wheel and the moment was lost.

'This Eagle Club place, have you been there?' I asked conversationally to fill the charged silence.

'Yes. The food's bad and the service is worse. They've been threatening to close it down for ages, the ski lift up to it's on its last legs. But I guess some idiot will fork out the money. God knows why, it's nothing special.'

'Oh, I know, but my friend Pandora's simply longing to go. She loves all that sort of thing. It's very sad really.'

'Well, I shall take you both there for lunch next weekend. Now here you are, back safe and sound.' He had stopped outside Chalet Tiara and switched off the engine. It had started to snow heavily and noiselessly. For a moment neither of us moved, hypnotized by the heavy stillness, such a contrast with the noisy twittering of the evening we had just left.

He turned towards me, caressed my face with a big gentle

hand and kissed me. The scent of cigars, leather and the memory of the unreal evening we had just spent, the long-awaited thrill of touching him at last and the soft noiseless snow falling outside made me drift seamlessly into his arms.

'God, I've been wanting to do that ever since I saw you heaving that thing out of the oven with your backside in the air last night. You're going to be quite a distraction to me, Miss Oriana, I can see that.' He stroked my hair back from my eyes and kissed me again.

I was just about to ask him in for an Armagnac (the Crispinians had brought a sizeable bar with them from duty free), when I noticed stealthy movement in the pine tree in front of the chalet. I drew back from Ernst suddenly.

'It's the Crispinians! They've come back to life!' Dammit. Under the circs, smuggling Ernst back to my room would be quite impossible.

'I must escort you back to the chalet. I don't trust that lot,' growled Ernst crossly.

'Hang on.' I peered at the bushes. 'It's not the Crispinians. It's Tim and Mule! Oh God, they might have filmed us through their spooky long-distance lenses. They love doing that.'

I was right. Tim, blinking owlishly through his bifocals, closely followed by Mule, wielding his omnipresent camera, shuffled towards the car.

Galvanized by the prospect of yet more fisticuffs, Ernst leapt out of the car. So protective! He made me feel like a gangster's moll all the time!

'Who the hell are you, bloody stalkers or what?' He lunged towards Mule's camera, but Mule, with his many years of stalking experience, was too quick for him.

'Break it up! Break it up!' I cried. 'It's OK, Ernst, they were here last night, remember? They're quite harmless.' But were they? Who knew what incriminating footage they had of us?

'Everyone's been trying to get hold of you, Oriana,'

explained Tim in his carefully modulated estuary tones. 'There's been an accident at Chalet Grimm.'

'Oh my God! Is it Bella?'

'Oh no. *Bella's* all right. It's her guests, they've been rushed to Montreux hospital. Suspected food poisoning, but they were dead on arrival. We just thought you ought to know. Ally tried to ring you, but your phone was switched off.' He looked pointedly at Ernst who bristled aggressively.

'Um, Ernst, I'm going to have to ring Ally and see what's going on. It sounds serious.'

'Of course you must.' He clicked his heels in a deliciously Germanic manner and strode off towards his car. I cast a longing look at his retreating back. There was silence but for the crunch of snow beneath foot. 'I spread my dreams beneath your feet, tread carefully for you tread on my dreams,' I whispered, then started. I'd forgotten Tim and Mule, who were standing so quietly I'd slipped into a dream world and completely forgotten them. So embarrassing!

'Ernst is an old family friend. He's been telling me about his grandmother who used to live in the chalet. It's fascinating unexplored material that I shall be able to use in my book *Chalet Girl Secrets*.' I continued in this efficient manner for several more minutes, it was essential that I was not seen as just another snogging chalet girl. My charged grapple with Ernst wasn't just a snog anyway, it was something far more important. I knew for sure he was *the one*! 'I am just going to write up my new findings.'

Tim concealed a yawn. 'Yes, thank you, Oriana. This is all fascinating but we mustn't keep you up any longer.'

As they shuffled off into the bushes I heard them whispering, 'Got some great stuff . . . the boss'll be thrilled, fabulous evening's work.'

I shut the heavy wooden door behind me and leant against it for a moment. The chalet was in darkness and silent apart from the sounds of snoring emanating from the drawing room and under the table. I glanced at my watch and saw it was past 2 a.m., too late to ring Ally, I'd have to wait till the morning now.

I was just about to make my way upstairs when there was a knock on the door. I took a deep breath and pulled the heavy door open. In the light of the reflected snow Ernst's dark eyes bored into me. 'I thought you'd gone,' I said uselessly, dizzy with champagne and desire, reaching out to brush the snowflakes that were settling on his black jacket.

'I'm afraid I don't give up that easily,' he smiled, catching my hand and following me up the curved staircase to my room.

'I'm glad you came back,' I murmured, shutting my bedroom door quietly, oblivious to everything but the feel of his big hand slipping beneath my cashmere dress and pushing me gently towards the bed.

Chapter Twenty-two

The next morning I woke early as the first shaft of light seeped into the room. Before I opened my eyes I knew that I was alone. I could almost have believed that I'd dreamt the whole evening but the presence of Ernst was still so strong. Burying my head in the dent of his pillow the smell of him brought the passionate encounter back with painful clarity. It was considerate of him to leave before the Crispinians emerged but I wished he'd woken me up to say goodbye first. Then the phone rang. Yes! But it was Pandora.

'Oriana! I was trying to ring you all night. Have you heard?'

'Yes, Tim and Mule –' why was it always Tim and Mule not Mule and Tim? I wondered pointlessly – 'broke the news last night. Is it true?'

'Yup, the Grouts were dead on arrival at Montreux hospital. Apparently they think it was probably a virulent type of botulism caused by an old French egg.'

'Are we sure it was a French egg?' I asked.

'I think that's the only thing we can be sure about,' said Pandora morosely. 'It was hardly likely to be a Swiss egg.'

'No, of course not. Silly of me. Sorry.' I thought of the fridge at Chalet Grimm and shuddered. Ambrosia was a natural hoarder and took the *Chalet Girl Handbook* to extremes, recycling everything until it had quite dwindled away. Bella was in charge while Ambrosia was laid up with her 'travel motion sickness', but I knew that Ambrosia had developed a fiendishly complicated recycling policy which I suspected Bella had not yet fully grasped.

'Oriana, are you okay? You sound a bit slowed up.'

'Oh, I'm fine, just a bit tired. Ernst stayed over last night.'

'God, I'm sorry, I didn't mean to interrupt you . . .'

'No, you didn't. Don't worry, he's just left. So what're we going to do about the Grouts?' I had no desire to discuss Ernst's silent leave taking with the girls just yet.

'Ally's called an emergency summit meeting at Pop-Ups at two,' explained Pandora. 'She was trying to keep it secret from Tim and Mule but they've obviously found out. I've got a feeling they've tipped off the papers because Ambrosia said she caught some little men with estuary accents going through the rubbish at Chalet Grimm. Ally says we might have to go home, Oriana! I can't face leaving, not when things were going so well for us . . .'

Go home to England. It didn't seem like home any more. Where would I live? A hotel? A boarding house for dispossessed gentlefolk? It didn't bear thinking about. The only thing I could really focus on was the heavenly night I had just spent with Ernst. Still, it was getting late and I had to prepare the Crispinians' breakfast. That would distract me. I'd brought my juicer out from London and tried to revive them every morning with freshly squeezed blood-orange juice which they enjoyed with a packet of Marlboro Lites and strong black coffee.

Today it did the trick; at 9 a.m. they were sitting to attention around the dining room table looking suspiciously perky. I suspected they had been taking their 'homeopathic medicines' again which always exerted a curiously stimulating effect on the group. I know what you're thinking, but I don't think even the Crispinians would risk smuggling *that* sort of thing through customs. Anyway, it was none of my business. Anything that got them up and out of the chalet before midday had my full support. I was desperate to finish my duties as quickly as possible so that I could write up last night's adventures while I was still in a delirious state of numb optimism. After all, even if I never saw Ernst again, I would always have the wonderful memory. After all my bad experiences I was beginning to think that real passion was just something that happened to other people.

By 11 a.m. I'd made the beds, hosed down the bathrooms and was busy peeling apples for tonight's apple crumble. I knew from the last time that the 'homeopathic medicines' stimulated the boys' appetites and I was doubling up my usual quantities just in case.

I was just stewing the apples on top of the Aga with some cinnamon, cloves, Frau Perren's alpine honey, and a sliver of orange peel when I heard the door slam and the familiar heavy footsteps making their way to the kitchen. I gripped my wooden spoon tightly.

Ernst! Luckily I was prepared for his arrival, wearing my most fetching apron with my freshly washed hair piled artfully on top of my head. I'd also taken particular care with my make-up. I wasn't being caught on the hop again like the first time he saw me. No, from now on I was going to be on red alert all the time. I pinched my cheeks and bit my lips, patting my hair nervously.

'So how goes it, my little hausfrau?' Ernst cupped my face in his big hands and kissed me lightly on the cheek. 'All your guests still in one piece?'

'I think they're still hanging on, thank you,' I said briskly, returning to stir my fragrant fruity mixture. I had no wish to be tainted with Bella's bad luck.

'I'm afraid the news is all round the village. I've just come from the Bahnhof newsstand and it was quite a topic of conversation. The general consensus was that the English have many talents, but that cooking isn't one of them.' He delivered this deadpan and I couldn't resist smiling.

'It wasn't Bella's fault, it was a French egg. Besides, she's not English, she's Scottish.'

'Whatever. We're all Europeans now.' He walked away and leant against the fridge, staring at me with watchful dark eyes. My cheek was burning where he had kissed me, and I longed for him to scoop me up in his arms, or at least mention last night, but there was a calculated coolness about him, which, despite the frequent collapse into fisticuffs, inhibited impetuous displays of emotion. I had the feeling that most of his actions were well thought out and controlled and I was just a pawn, albeit a diverting one, in his well-structured emotional life.

'The Swiss aren't members of the EU, are they?' I babbled pedantically to hide my confusion. 'Frau Perren says that's why she's allowed to sell unpasteurized milk. It's illegal in every other country which is just so ridiculous when you think you're far more likely to die from—'

'A French egg?' asked Ernst dryly.

'Quite.' I concentrated hard on my stirring. He was so deliciously droll!

'So what are you cooking for your undeserving guests tonight?'

'Apple crumble with crispy oatmeal topping and home-made vanilla and orange blossom ice cream, and perch from Lake Geneva with a light Béarnaise sauce, with lots of spinach, because I think they need the iron.' I'd grown almost fond of the Crispinians since Ernst's attack. I think it was an English thing about feeling sorry for the underdog or something. 'I want to send them back to Parson's Green stronger than when they arrived,' I explained.

'And how long are you staying in Gstaad?' asked Ernst, gazing at me with impassive brooding eyes.

'We're all meant to be here until the beginning of April, but I've got a feeling we might be deported sooner than that because of the . . . the . . .'

'Egg?'

'Yup.'

'That's a shame. I like to think of you here, stirring things up . . .'

I stopped stirring for a moment and glanced at him, unable to tear my eyes away, relinquishing control of my apple puree and standing limply, wooden spoon poised, hardly daring to breathe. The air between us seemed charged, spicy with apple and sexual chemistry. How could he bear not to touch me, grab me, especially after the passionate night we had spent together?

'Well, I'd like to stay. We haven't been here very long but I feel I've been here forever. The thought of going back to London makes me feel quite ill.'

'But you have to go back some time to publish your wonderful book. Have you got anything you can show me?'

'If you promise not to laugh.' I slipped over to the large kitchen dresser, knelt down and pulled open the bottom drawer. 'I love this china, was it your grandmother's?'

'Yes, she was fond of blue and white. Her family were actually Quakers way back and she liked all that simple Shaker style stuff.'

'So do I, it's huge in London now.'

'You're a bit like her, you know. She was a great beauty in her youth before she went . . . um . . .'

'Off?'

Ernst looked bemused.

'It's an English expression that people use about women,' I explained. 'Going off, like when food goes off. A friend of mine, well, she was actually much older than me, was once described as an exquisite plate of food that had been left out overnight. Ah, here it is.' I pulled out my manuscript and laid it on the kitchen table.

'So you've brought your computer with you?' asked Ernst.

'Pandora's lent me her laptop. I don't need a printer because I can fax out from it direct to Ally's fax and get a hard copy that way.' Ernst looked suitably impressed. 'I've been so inspired since reading your grandmother's diary. I've even tried out some of the recipes she recorded, everyone raves about the rösti with crispy sage. And her watercolours are so pretty.'

'So you're writing a recipe book?' asked Ernst, flicking through my manuscript, intrigued.

'Kind of. I've been cooking for years but I've interspersed the recipes around stories I've heard, or things that have happened to me. And the girls have lots of good stories about their punters and romantic disasters. I've only been here a month but I've had loads of ideas, just living here has been so inspiring. Frau Perren in Rougemont keeps bees and makes her own beeswax polish and all these different types of organic cleaning things made out of lemons and vinegar and stuff. She gave me all these recipes, not that people in England are going to rush out and do it, but it's interesting.'

'I haven't seen old Frau Perren for years,' mused Ernst. 'She must be in her nineties.'

'I just think that people feel they have to travel to places like India and Africa to find interesting tribal customs, whereas Switzerland is only an hour away from London and the people in the mountain villages have been living in the same way for centuries.'

'Because the villages were cut off from one another for months at a time. It's only relatively recently that people have managed to get to the next door village easily at all.' He pulled me out a chair and we sat down at the table together. 'Have you been to Chateau d'Oex?'

'Where they have the ballooning competition? Yes, I went there a few years ago.'

'It's only fifteen minutes away but the people there speak a completely different language and don't look a bit like people in Rougemont or Gstaad. They look more like goats.'

'Yes! You're right! They all seem to have limps, and everyone is incredibly short.'

'Christ, if you think they're short they must be bloody midgets.'

I laughed delightedly.

'Will you put me in it?' asked Ernst lightly.

'Oh no, I wouldn't dream of embarrassing you,' I lied. I

now knew that Ernst's thrilling punch-up would be a focal point of the book and give me a wonderful opportunity to share my cassoulet recipe specifying free-range geese, of course. The victory of man over mouse and the perils of drinking would be another interesting theme I could explore. And the evils of nationalism, for if the Crispins hadn't started their Dambuster tirade, maybe Crispin would still have the use of his spindly arms and not been embarrassed in front of all his friends. 'Oh no, it'll be very loosely based on real life,' I explained.

I imagined showing the first copy off the presses to Ernst; by that time we would probably be married. How he would laugh at my amusing description of his heroics. 'And that was when I first fell in love with you,' I would say, curled up in front of the roaring fire at Chalet Tiara. He would run his business empire and I would be writing eco-friendly cookery books. It was all so perfect, and so possible!

'Well, I think you're really on to something,' said Ernst. We were sitting so close that I could almost feel the bristles on his broad cheek burning into my soft skin. The smell of him, his enthusiasm for my small dream, so small compared to his kind of empire building, just took my breath away. I don't know who moved towards the other first, perhaps my longing drew him close, and when we kissed I felt myself utterly dissolve into his arms. My dreams, the accident at Chalet Grimm, everything was forgotten.

'Oh God, I'm sorry!' We started apart to find Ally standing by the door, pink cheeked with embarrassment. 'I did call! I'm sorry to butt in but the door was open.'

'Ernst, this is Ally, Ally this is Ernst. He owns the chalet, I was just showing him my etchings, I mean book,' I explained quickly.

'Isn't it just the greatest idea?' smiled Ally, holding out her hand. 'I think she's really on to something.'

I smiled at Ally appreciatively. I was always running ideas by her and she'd been terribly patient and helpful. If anyone had to interrupt us, it wasn't so bad that it was her.

'I was just driving by and I thought I'd drop in and give you the lowdown on what's going on. I've arranged the meeting here, if that's OK. We'll be able to talk more freely. You may have heard, one of our girls has had a bit of an accident,' she explained to Ernst. 'I'm afraid the place is crawling with creepy journalists from London. You see, Bella's father is a really well-known judge, and she used to go out with that obscure royal guy a few years ago. I'm afraid it's going to be big news.' She shuddered. 'Some guy from the *Daily Mail* has already collared me this morning. Anyway, I'll love you and leave you, I've got to get back and phone Chiara. Nice meeting you, Ernst.'

'It was my pleasure.' He got to his feet and did his heel clicking thing. I could see that Ally was very impressed – at least she would have been if she hadn't been so worried. Ernst turned to me. 'Well, I better be making tracks myself.'

'Back to Munich for more empire building?' I said lightly.

'You and your empire building. I make car parts, I'm not Alexander the Great, you know.' The slight irritability in his voice was so unexpected, it hit me like a slap in the face and I didn't quite know how to respond.

'Would you like to take some oatmeal cookies with you for the journey?'

'You're such a sweet girl. I'm not a cookie man, but thanks for offering.' He twisted a piece of my hair round his finger, reeled me in and then stood back, gazing at me. He gave me a long look. 'I wonder what sort of man will make you happy, Oriana . . .' I gazed back at him, wanting to say a man like you of course. But I said nothing. He released me, picked up his briefcase and made for the door.

'I'll be back next weekend. I'll come and see you, take you and your friend to the Eagle for lunch.'

'That would be lovely, if we haven't all been deported by then,' I replied.

'No one is going to deport you in a hurry, Oriana.' He

lifted a big hand, clicked his heels and left the kitchen. I had a sudden urge to race out after him, kiss him passionately in the hall and wave him tearfully goodbye, but thank God I didn't. Instead I stood by the window, clenching my fists and hardly daring to breathe as he reversed his car silently and expertly out of the drive.

Chapter Twenty-three

I made my way numbly to the larder to fetch some oats and flour in preparation for making my crumble. I set down my big china bowl on the cool marble table and concentrated on rubbing chilled unpasteurized butter into the oaty mixture. The hypnotic repetitive job had a soothing effect on the muddle of conflicting thoughts that were racing through my head.

I thought of Ernst, and the way he had played with my hair and how I was molten putty in his hands. How could he even ask who my ideal man was when the answer was as clear and obvious as the jagged mountains etched so clearly against the sky outside my window? He was perfect for me, he was what I'd always dreamt of. I was utterly, completely smitten.

I had just put the crumble into the bottom of the Aga when there was a screech of brakes outside. I glanced out of the window to see the deux chevaux come to a spluttering halt in front of the chalet. Ambrosia, Bella, the Bolter and Pandora piled out, looking ashen-faced, talking in worried, low voices. It reminded me of a convention of world leaders meeting to discuss some impossible situation like Northern Ireland or Bosnia or somewhere.

I ran to the door to welcome them in, and returned to the kitchen where I busied myself making our favourite hot drink, melted chocolate slowly mixed with foaming milk.

'Oh, Oriana.' Bella burst into sobs as I led her into the kitchen. 'It's all a nightmare. Mummy rang me this morning to say it's in all the papers.'

'Just *The Snoop!* darling,' consoled Ambrosia soothingly.

'It's the same thing. I'll never work again, I'll never get married . . .'

A tear slid down her perfect peachy cheek and she reached into her sagging purple coat for a sodden handkerchief. 'Hey, has anyone told you you've got an enormous piece of snot right at the end of your nose?'

'What?' I dashed to the mirror hanging above the Aga (so handy), where I was horrified to see an offensive blob perched on the end of my nose. 'Hang on, it's not a bogey. It's apple puree! Look, from the saucepan.' I lifted up the pan for them all to see.

'What were you sticking your nose in it for?' asked Pandora. 'It's far more likely to be a bogey.'

'It's not. Really it's not!' Oh God. Was the blob pre Ernst or après Ernst? If it was pre then no wonder he hadn't snogged me. 'I just hope it landed on my nose after Ernst left. D'you think I should ring him and tell him it was apple puree, not some sort of horrid infection?'

'NO!' shouted everyone.

'Look, if a chap likes you, he likes you, blobs or no blobs,' said Pandora sensibly. 'C'mon, hurry up with the hot chocolates, we're dying here.'

'Sorry.' I busied myself with warming up the milk as Bella resumed her sobbing. I felt like joining her but remained silent. Plenty of time later to obsess, analyse and fret about the nose incident.

'Here, drink this, it'll make you feel better.' I handed round blue and white china mugs of the steaming chocolate brew with a hint of vanilla.

'Mmm, this is delish, Oriana. I tried to make it the way you said, but it wasn't nearly as good,' said Pandora.

'The secret is to let a vanilla pod steep in the warm milk, and to let the chocolate melt really slowly. But it's Frau Perren's bio-dynamic unpasteurized milk, it's quite delicious. She's happy to deliver if you're interested.'

'Is that the same old crone who makes the beeswax polish and lemon cleaning fluids that you rave about?' asked Ambrosia, sniffing the air appreciatively. 'That must be what that gorgeous smell is when you come in. You should bottle it.'

'I've had to double up on fluids this week because of the Crispinians. They have absolutely no control over any of their orifices. But luckily the lemon scouring jelly is very powerful,' I explained.

'God, don't get Oriana onto her cleaning fluids,' warned Pandora. 'She could write a book about them – whoops, you *are* writing a book about them.'

I was longing to discuss Ernst's perplexing leavetaking with the girls but it seemed a bit tactless, what with Bella and Ambrosia in such a state. Bella sucked up the last of her hot chocolate and blew her nose desperately. Her thick blonde hair was a mass of matted corkscrew curls and mascara had run down her cheeks, giving her the appearance of a broken doll splattered with mud. Her purple velvet Voyage coat wasn't the only thing falling apart at the seams. My heart went out to her.

'Come on, Bella,' insisted Pandora, patting her arm. 'We haven't had complete confirmation that they're actually dead yet. Let's at least wait for Ally till we come to any conclusions.'

'Hey, guys.' Ally steamed in purposefully, clutching a handful of faxes. 'It's not looking at all good. I've had confirmation from Montreux hospital that they did everything they could but the Grouts passed away unpeacefully at three a.m. this morning. Some of the papers have already run the story. Christ, you couldn't have picked a better person to poison, Bella. It turns out that Mr Grout worked at the BBC.'

'Yes, Mrs Grout was always boasting that he was a big cheese in the media,' said Ambrosia sadly.

'I think big cheese might be a bit of an exaggeration,'

commented Ally. 'He used to collect the trays in the canteen.'

'That must be why he always refused to help stack up the plates after dinner. He was quite obsessive about it,' remembered Bella miserably.

Ally handed her a fax. 'You better see this. Chiara saw it in *The Snoop!*.'

' "Judge's daughter poisons punter!" ' read Bella in a small voice. ' "Party girl, ex-Voguette and chalet girl, Arabella Ormsby Spore, daughter of controversial right-wing judge Lord Ormsby-Spore of Specklefield is suspected of poisoning three unfortunate guests staying in her chalet. Arabella is a former girlfriend of the Queen's cousin, the talented watering can designer, the Earl of Rococo. The relationship, expected to end in marriage, collapsed soon after the engagement was announced in *Hello!* magazine. Arabella is currently being romanced by ageing crooner Tony 'the toupee' Louche, who had a string of hits in the 1950s with the Louche Limpets." '

There was a blurred photograph of Bella and Rufus Rococo standing in a large watering can and smiling cheesily. Bella groaned.

'Look, we've got to hit the ground running on this one.' Ally spoke efficiently and fluently, like a commander-in-chief. I knew she was a fan of CNN and was a great admirer of Christiane Amanapour, their feisty glamorous war correspondent, who popped up at regular intervals from all the world's hottest spots. Yes, Ally was the perfect person. I felt that her life had just been a build-up to this current crisis.

'I don't want you to talk to any journalists. We want to keep them off the scent as long as possible.'

'But the trouble is that they only have to talk to Tim and Mule.'

'Funny how we always say Tim and Mule, not Mule and Tim,' mused Bella.

'Yes, I've often thought that,' I replied.

'So have—'

'Can we get back to the point, girls.' Ally pushed a weary hand through her short blonde hair and rubbed her clear grey eyes, leaving a smudge of mascara around them. 'I suspected it might come to this. Chiara says they've been fielding cancellations all morning. Tomorrow's changeover day and I'm going to have a full coach going to Geneva, but I'm going to have an empty one coming back.' She paused dramatically.

'The long and short of it is that Jolly Holidays have been on the brink of bankruptcy for several months, I had no idea myself, but this is the final straw and apparently they're calling in the receivers. We've all got to pack up our chalets and make our way home.'

There was a stunned silence. I couldn't believe it. Leave Chalet Tiara? It was my home! And what about Ernst? I couldn't just disappear, he'd never be able to find me!

'Have any of you got any questions?'

'Um, Ally, when you last came here, did you notice if I had something on the end of my nose, because it wasn't—'

We were interrupted by banging on the window and sounds of whooping. I looked up to see the Crispinians' scrawny bare bottoms pressed against the window. They reminded me most unpleasantly of a row of raw plucked chickens who had come horribly back to life.

'Ugh, what's that?'

'What are they doing?' The girls' maudlin attention was transferred to the window in horror.

'Oh, don't worry, they do this all the time,' I said crossly. 'But this is the final straw. I've warned them . . . I'm going to have to hose them down.' I made my way quickly and surreptitiously out of the back door and picked up the garden hose, crept round the corner and surprised them with a full onslaught of freezing water. 'I've warned you about doing that! Now GET INSIDE BEFORE I GIVE YOU A GOOD HIDING!'

Unfazed and oddly cheered by my brutal ambush the boys

quickly snapped to attention, pulled up their trousers and dashed happily into the chalet.

'Straight to your rooms without tea!' I yelled as they scooted up the stairs. 'Dinner's at eight *sharp*. I've made apple crumble and homemade ice cream, *so don't be late!*'

I returned to the kitchen to a small round of applause from the girls.

'Gosh, Oriana, when you came out you wouldn't say boo to a goose,' said Bella admiringly. 'What's happened?'

'She's fallen in love, that's what's happened,' said Ally. She gathered up her things. 'I've got to make a move now but I'll ring you all later. Please don't be late back to your chalets. Remember, we're still contractually obligated until tomorrow, so make this last dinner really special. That way at least the punters will give you a glowing report to any journalists sniffing around.'

'Yeah, and pigs might fly,' mumbled the Bolter, to Ally's retreating back. The Bolter had been the victim of a *slew* of complaints from her current punters, who were fed up with eating kebabs and utterly cheesed off with her frequent and inexplicable disappearances. Last week two of them had staged a hunger strike outside the chalet. It had been a musical event with trumpets and chanting. It hadn't worked, though, and the food was as bad as ever.

'And keep your phones switched on, we gotta stay in touch!' yelled Ally from the hall.

Under the circs I thought we could all use a sugar hit and crawled into the Aga to find some sustenance.

'Got anything nice in your magic box to cheer us up?' asked Ambrosia hopefully.

I placed a marmalade cake and a plate of chocolate brownies on the table. 'I told the Crispinians they weren't having any tea, so eat up. I think they've still got some vodka left. Anyone fancy a sharpener?'

Everybody definitely did, so I raided the bar in the drawing room, returning with an interesting selection of alcoholic beverages which the girls laid into with great enthusiasm.

Fortunately the sugar hit had an immediately cheering effect, the alcohol probably helped too, and we were soon looking on the bright side of the situation.

'I'll go on a diet as soon as I get home,' said Ambrosia, licking chocolate off her chubby fingers and adding Baileys Irish cream to the dregs of her hot chocolate.

'I'm sure Daddy will get me off,' said Bella ruminatively, taking a swig of neat vodka. 'After all, you can't sue an egg, can you?'

'Quite. Stupid French egg.'

'Stupid snowboarding French egg.'

'Just as well it wasn't a langlaufing Swiss egg, we'd all have copped it by now,' said Pandora, spooning apple crumble mixture onto her plate. 'Pass me that pear William stuff, s'nice mixed up with this apple-crumble mixture.'

'Better with Calvados,' said Bella, adding a generous swig to the pan and reaching for her cigarettes. 'The great thing is you're never alone with a Whoops.' We all lit up a Whoops slimming cigarette and the room soon built up a cosy fug.

'Coffee, anyone?' I inquired, opening the window to let in some air.

'S'nice with Tia Maria,' mumbled Bella. She was looking a little tired and emotional; I couldn't blame her after the twenty-four hours she'd had.

'I don't know about you but I didn't much care for the Grouts,' said Pandora. 'They always seemed to be a most disagreeable family.'

'Huh, you didn't have to cook for them,' said Ambrosia. 'You know what really irritated me was the way I'd leave them a Mars Bar on their beds then they'd take it and not make their beds.'

'Such a cheek!'

'Sauce!'

'Very poor form.'

'You know, I think if the egg hadn't killed them, something else would have sooner or later.'

'Yeah, all that bad karma and stuff. What goes round comes round.'

'The egg was round. There's got to be something in that.'

We were interrupted by a rustling outside the window and the sound of voices. We peered out; what with the fug in the room and the snow falling outside it was hard to see anything, but we could just make out two scruffy figures, dropping rubbish as they shuffled off down the drive.

'They must have been going through my bins! Fat lot of good that will do them.' I prudently managed to recycle nearly everything. Anything of vegetable origin either went into my stockpot or into the communal compost heap run by a local farmer with scientific Swiss precision. Bottles of water and wine and jars of pickled gherkins were delivered to my door, collected when empty and refilled. My eyes pricked with tears. Oh, how I loved Switzerland!

'Oh God. They look like journalists!' said Pandora. 'You don't think they heard us, do you?'

'OI! YOU! Come back here!' I yelled. But they had hobbled off into the trees.

'Maybe they were vagrants,' suggested Bella hopefully.

Pandora shook her head. 'No, I don't think so. They were definitely journalists.'

'Well, let's just hope they were from the *Mail*. I'm sure they'll be kind to us,' said Ambrosia confidently.

The uninvited guests rather put a dampener on things and the girls soon peeled off unenthusiastically back to their chalets.

'Cheerio.' I waved them goodbye as the deux chevaux, the Bolter at the wheel as she had the most experience of drinking and driving, chugged its way out of the drive, billowing smoke and fossil fuels into the clean alpine air.

Chapter Twenty-four

On Wednesday the Crispinians were due to leave. I know it seems odd to have a changeover day in the middle of the week but Jolly Holidays deluded themselves that their clients, being landed gentry (that was a joke), didn't have to work and could therefore travel at inconvenient times. A bit like very grand people who have weddings on a Friday because they assume all their friends don't have jobs.

I was quite sad to say goodbye to them. The odd thing was that however much one loathed punters on first sight, one always ended up terribly sad to see them go. I think once I passed into nanny mode and started bossing them about things got much easier. They basically did whatever I told them.

'No, I won't give you back your cigarettes, you know how they make you throw up first thing in the morning,' I shouted at Rupert.

'Just one ciggie, Oriana, please?'

'No. Now take your packed lunches, they'll settle your stomach. I've made your favourite marmite sandwiches. Make sure you eat them all up. And are you sure you've stripped your beds and folded up the sheets?'

'Yes, Oriana.' They all nodded meekly. They were reminded of being back at school. If I'd told them to pull down their trousers because I wanted to cane them they would have been in seventh heaven. But I wasn't prepared to go that far. Ugh. No.

'And as you've been so good I've given you each a mini

Mars Bar in your packed lunch, but make sure you eat the marmite sandwiches first.'

I waved goodbye to them cheerfully as the coach pulled away. I was just leaning out of the window, idly musing about the Swiss and wondering if it could be true that they had lost all that Jewish gold when they were so efficient (and fretting about whether Ernst had noticed the blob of apple puree on my nose, I'm pretty sure it was apple), when a smart black BMW pulled into the drive.

Oh no, not more visitors, I thought as a small thin dark girl in her mid-thirties, well-dressed and with a sort of terrier-like expression got out. As soon as she saw me her face softened and she broke into a sweet smile revealing small sharp teeth.

'Hello, you must be Oriana. Ally said I might find you in.' She had the softest, whisperyish voice and I immediately relaxed. 'My name is Emma Batt. I was wondering if I could have a talk to you about recent events.' I stiffened and prepared to shut the window. 'It's OK, I'm from the *Daily Mail*.' She smiled and waved a paper at me.

'Oh, that's all right, you had me worried for a minute.' I went to let her in. I knew Ally had warned us off talking to journalists, but being American she probably wouldn't know that the *Daily Mail* was on our team. And besides, it would be a perfect opportunity to plug my book.

'May I offer you a drink?' I asked hospitably. 'I've just roasted and ground some Kenyan arabica beans, or I have six types of tea specially blended from Whittards, freshly squeezed ruby grapefruit juice, or something from the bar . . .'

'Goodness, chalet holidays never used to be this luxurious. I could *murder* a G and T.'

'Don't talk about murder round here,' I laughed as I tipped the last of the Gordon's over sparkling ice cubes into a chilled glass and filled it up with Schweppes tonic water. 'Slice of lime?' I queried.

'Yes please.' She sipped the drink appreciatively, leaving

a smear of lipstick on the glass. 'Goodness, that's the best G and T I've had in years. Really refreshing.'

'It's the ice cubes. We get water right off the glacier here and it freezes like sheets of clear shiny glass. Plus I squeeze a tiny bit of lemon juice into the ice tray and add a bit of lemon rind. It gives a boost to the drink.'

'Mmm, it certainly does. So how are you all coping with the unfortunate incident? I hear you're all going home tomorrow.'

'Yes, Jolly Holidays have gone bust, which wasn't a great surprise.' We laughed. I took a sip of my G and T (juniper berries are so good for the kidneys, practically medicinal really) and continued, 'But I'm going to stay a bit longer.'

'Have you met a dishy ski instructor then?' she asked confidingly, generously topping us both up with gin.

'Oh no. Nothing like that.' I wanted to promote my Martha Stewart tendencies. Best to leave the *femme fatale* stuff to the others. 'When I came here this place was a wreck and I've just got it shipshape. It would break my heart to leave now. You see,' I said confidentially, 'I'm writing a book about all our chalet girl experiences, and describing Chalet Tiara as it was when I came a month ago and how I've brought it back to life. A beautiful and reclusive heiress used to live here. I discovered her diary when I was cleaning up. It's a very mysterious and romantic place, you know.'

'I can see,' said Emma, sniffing the air appreciatively rather like an asthmatic hamster. 'Super smell. And I love your Aga, but it looks *fiendishly* complicated. D'you know how to use it?'

'Of course. I'm basing my cookery book around it.'

'That's interesting.' She started jotting down some notes. 'Now tell me, did you know the Grout family personally? I hear they were dreadfully unpopular.' She smiled cosily at me.

'Oh no. *Au contraire!* We all adored them. I can't tell you how utterly distraught we are. Several of the girls are hoping to make a career out of chalet girling, and they're horrified that their chances for advancement might be scuppered in this tragic way. Um, shall I show you my book idea?'

'Well, not everyone is *that* unhappy.' Emma didn't seem to have heard my exciting suggestion, and continued smoothly, 'It turns out that Mr Grout wasn't a popular man. He was a vociferous member of the canteen worker union and frankly, speaking *entre nous*,' she leaned towards me intimately, 'Gosh, it's nice to have a girl's chat, you have no idea! Anyway, there's a lot of people who'll wake up this morning feeling quite relieved about Mr Grout's demise. You may have gathered that there's a lot of *Guardian* and *Observer* journalists,' she shuddered, 'sniffing around trying to make political capital out of this story – you know, turn it into some class war thing – but we at the *Mail* want to put the other side of the story across. Besides, our editor is a great fan of Bella's father, Lord Ormsby-Spore of Specklefield. Hero of the right and all that, voice of middle England. Practically hero worships him. Our readers are right behind you gels.'

'Yes, it would be nice to put our side across.' I rifled around for my manuscript which I'd shoved under the table. I'd wait for the right moment then I'd just happen to put it on the table. 'Alpine intrigue, toffs in the Alps poisoning the working class, I can see it's quite a story,' I mused.

'Check out some of today's papers, it'll show you the typical reaction to the story.' She rummaged through a pile of papers in her capacious briefcase. 'Top toffs girl poisons staunch union man in alpine horror.' Typical *Sun* rubbish. The *Mirror*'s just as bad. " 'I'd rather live through an avalanche than face another pilchard dip,' complain starving guests who survived alpine horror!" You get the picture?'

'My goodness. They don't hang around, do they? They must have been rushing round interviewing our punters secretly. I hope they haven't talked to the Crispinians.' I didn't think my brutal discipline would go down well with the media at all. How could I explain the pleasure the Crispinians received from being savagely woken up at 7 a.m. with freezing wet flannels and the naked hosing downs to someone who hadn't gone to a good public school? The average *Guardian* reader would think it utterly perverse.

'I think they'll talk to anyone. These people are quite unscrupulous, you know.' Emma topped up our drinks and lit a Whoops slimming cigarette with a thin nervous hand. 'I've already talked to the other girls and in return for your full co-operation, glam photos and revealing interviews we'll give you favourable publicity and buy you all business-class flights home.' Any doubts were soon dispelled by this delicious prospect.

'And mention the book?'

'What book?'

'I've written this book.' I whipped up the manuscript from underneath the table.

'Oh yes. Yes, of course we'll mention your book. Now what I'd like is to call up my photographer and get him round to take some dazzling shots of you in your beautiful chalet. I'm sure you're terribly photogenic,' she added flatteringly. 'It'll only take a moment.'

A photo op, at Chalet Tiara! How could I resist? I frowned. But what would I wear?

Emma picked up on the frown. 'We'll pay you of course, and it'll only take a moment. Jim's very quick.' I hoped he wouldn't be too quick, it would take hours to show off the chalet to its best advantage, and I would need at least six changes of outfit, hair, make-up. It could take hours.

I agreed, concealing my enthusiasm, and sped upstairs to get changed and perform speedy ablutions.

'She's a cracker, that mate of yours, Rochetta,' said Jim half an hour later. Emma had left to interview Pandora at Chalet Twix and Jim was fixing up his cameras in the kitchen while I carefully stewed his tea on top of the Aga.

'Oh, I could do with this,' he said taking a long gulp.

'First decent cuppa I've had since leaving London. Now, where d'ya want me to snap you?'

Jim unfortunately only had ten minutes so I insisted he take most of his shots with me sitting on the trysting seat in the snowy garden, looking wistfully into the mountains, balancing a tray of homemade shortbread on my lap, scribbling furiously at my manuscript. It was all very proper.

Jim said that the Bolter had demanded to be photographed running naked through the snow. I had considered doing this but forcibly restrained myself. I was changing my karma, becoming a responsible, serious person. By refusing to be parted from my manuscript a publisher might happen to see the article and get in touch!

Once the punters had left we all began to relax and enjoy our last few days to the full. The Bolter, in high spirits and aided and abetted by Pandora, held up the Gstaad Kebab Emporium after one too many at the GreenGo.

'We'd been dancing round our handbags all night,' explained Pandora at Chalet Tiara the next day. 'And we got so hot that the Bolter had to take off her American Tan tights. Then we decided on the way home we were hungry, so I tied her tights over her head and we swaggered up to the counter and said, "Give us a shish and a doner!" The poor little Greek guy panicked and dropped everything. I was trying to tell him it was only a joke but I'd tied the tights so firmly I couldn't get them off.'

'You were lucky you weren't caught, Rochetta,' said Ambrosia seriously. 'The police said they wouldn't give you another warning.'

'We'll be home soon enough,' said the Bolter mournfully.

'Papers!' Bella drifted in, looking even more ethereal than ever in her disintegrating full-length purple velvet coat, her hair loosely caught in a mauve chiffon scarf. She dumped the previous day's papers on the table and we lunged for them excitedly. No one would admit it, but I suspected the girls were rather enjoying the furore. It was quite fun racing around the Co-op with bags placed conspicuously over our heads and being asked personal questions in the street by journalists posing as tourists.

'It's been a bit quieter today,' said Rochetta, pretending to sound relieved. 'I think most of them have gone home. Maybe we've had our fifteen minutes of fame.'

I considered this gloomily for a second. 'Why don't we ring Max Clifford?' I suggested excitedly. 'We could make a pop record. Like the Spice Girls, we could be the Chalet Girls.'

'Ugh, how vulgar,' snorted Bella.

'You must be joking,' added Rochetta.

'I mean it's a bit of fun for a few days, but I should hate it to drag on,' said Pandora.

'I couldn't bear to be known forever as the Swiss poisoner,' agreed Bella.

'My people would never speak to me again,' said Ambrosia.

'Yes, you're right. It would be appalling. Sorry, I wasn't thinking,' I backtracked quickly.

'I'm not looking forward to going home and facing the music,' said Bella grimly, taking a deep breath and picking up the *Guardian* gingerly. The *Guardian* was untrod ground as far as most of us went. Pandora and I used to conscientiously buy it once a week in order to find what the nation's intellectually and sexually insecure were thinking – or being told to think – but had found it so dull that we had soon given up.

'Worst first, OK? "Exclusive report. 'Poisoned punters deserved to die.' Class war rages in millionaires' playground. Fascist judge: my girl did no wrong! Turn to page 19." ' Bella turned the pages anxiously. 'It's written by Emma Batt! But she was from the *Daily Mail*!' She flung the rag onto the table for us all to see.

'It's a set-up,' said Pandora grimly.

'What a wicked trick,' said the Bolter crossly as we scanned the vitriolic piece. 'She lured us into a false sense of security and now she's written these beastly lies. Ugh. Come on, Bella, let's see the worst the others can do.'

Bella reached for the next paper in her pile. '*Daily Mirror*. " 'If we hadn't killed them someone else would.' Toff girls in centre of fascist conspiracy." Oh, please.' Bella dropped the paper in exasperation.

The *Sun* and *The Times* were equally scathing. 'My nights of passion with disgraced chalet girl!' The *Sun* had got hold of the picture of the Bolter running naked through the snow. 'Chalet girls besieged! Sent home without pay or clothes!'

'The cheek of it! I thought they were going to run that in the *Mail*,' said Rochetta crossly. 'That Batt woman has set us up good and proper.'

'At least the *Mail* has been kind,' I commented, glancing over Rochetta's shoulder. 'It's a very supportive piece really.'

'Daughters of Empire Strike Back! Innocent pawns in alpine drama!' Flattering photos of all of us doing our grocery shopping at the Co-op filled the middle pages and the fashion pages were devoted to 'the chalet girl look'.

'And the stuff in the *Telegraph* is good too,' I noted, secretly very chuffed as they had used a picture of me sitting on the trysting seat behind the chalet, pen poised, looking wistfully towards the mountains. The caption read, 'Chalet girl Oriana, a talented cook, takes time out from her duties to pen her first novel, *Chalet Girl Secrets*, based on her extraordinary alpine adventures.'

'You're bound to get a publisher now,' said Pandora. 'People love reading about chalet girls.'

'I'm crossing my fingers. Anyone fancy some more millionaire's shortbread? I've got plenty.'

'Mmm, yes please.' Everyone helped themselves as I went to boil up the kettle.

'So, Oriana, are you really going to stay here by yourself?' asked Rochetta. 'You'll be awfully lonely. You should come with us to Geneva, it'll be such fun.'

The girls had spent the last few days packing up their chalets and were leaving today on the evening train. Ambrosia had invited us all to stay in her uncle's vast flat in Geneva for a few days before we made our way home, but I had declined.

'No, I'm happy to stay here for a bit longer. Ally'll be back soon, and I want to finish my book and do some skiing. And I don't want to miss the Cow Fighting Competition. Frau Perren's best milker is tipped to win.'

'Cow fighting? How cruel. That doesn't sound very Swiss,' said Bella.

'They don't actually fight,' explained Pandora. 'I went once. All they do is munch grass and occasionally push the other cow out of the way when they want to munch in her spot. Sort of like in a supermarket when someone's hogging a shelf, you kind of *nudge* them out of the way with your trolley.'

'Unless you're in Guildford and you try and kill them,' I added.

'The bossiest cow gets a garland of flowers and goes forward into the final next month. The winning cow gets a year's supply of beer. Apparently they love the taste.'

'It all sounds bloody boring,' said the Bolter, fiddling with her curly dark hair impatiently. 'You can't want to stay here by yourself just to watch a lot of old cows.'

'Yes I do. Besides, Ernst is taking me to the Eagle Club for lunch on Saturday. It would be like a tragic movie if he came back to find me and the place was all locked up.'

'You could put that in your novel, it would be terribly dramatic,' mused Ambrosia surreptitiously undoing the top button on her jeans and helping herself to the last of the shortbread. A car pulled into the drive. 'That must be our taxi, it's early. Typical Swiss.' Ally had disappeared with the jeep to Crans Montana. The girls there had gone AWOL and their rep had had a complete nervous breakdown, poor thing.

Bella gathered up the papers. 'Actually I don't want these. Mummy said she's kept six copies of each of the papers. D'you want to hang on to them, Oriana?'

'Yes, they're quite a souvenir really. I wonder if the feng shui had anything to do with all this. Remember, Rochetta, when you said that first week that you wished we could have some drama?'

'God, I never dreamt something like this would happen.'

'We'll stay in touch.'

'Yes, ring me from Geneva, let me know what's going on.'

'Vita lurga.'

I kissed everyone goodbye, feeling choked. We hadn't known each other very long but we'd been through so much together. I felt closer to them than I did to my own family. I almost changed my mind about going with them, but the pull of Chalet Tiara and the lure of Ernst was impossible to resist. I'd waited years to meet someone like him and I was determined to make it work. And the cow fighting sounded interesting too. Frau Perren had been so kind to me; I wanted to support Matilde, her prize heifer. It would mean a lot to her.

Everyone made their way towards the taxi. With unaccustomed efficiency they had all sent their trunks and suitcases on ahead of them to Geneva (Swissair let you do this and it's a life saver) and just had minimal hand baggage.

Pandora hung back for a moment. 'I'm not happy about leaving you here by yourself. Have you spoken to him this week?'

'No, I think he's been travelling a lot. He's floating his company this week or something. He works terribly hard.'

'Well don't break your heart over this guy, OK? It just seems like Tom Gold and Magnus and all the rest of them, all over again. I can't see you flattened by yet another emotionally unavailable tycoony type bloke. None of them seems quite real.'

'I know you think this is like the others, but Ernst is

different. We're really on the same wavelength.'

'Huh, it's just another bloke who reminds you of your father; you're trying to sort out your relationship by falling for people just like him. Look, someone left this book in my chalet.' She handed over a well-thumbed self-help book. 'Will you promise me you'll read it?'

'I promise. I need something to read, but I swear, this is different. Don't worry about me, you've got Jack to fret about.'

'Like I care about him! No, I'm going to devote myself to something a bit more reliable than love, something like corn circles.'

'Come on, Pandora! We'll be late,' Bella called.

We hugged each other tightly, Pandora ran quickly to the car, jumping in and slamming the door behind her. I stood at the door, waving, as the car pulled away with a roar in a cloud of snow, until a moment later nothing remained but a puff of smoke and a heavy snow-soaked silence.

I got up early the next day, full of excitement and trepidation. I put the kettle on and checked my cassoulet which had been slowly cooking overnight. It would be wonderful to surprise him with something delicious for dinner. He hadn't mentioned anything about dinner, but I could see us so clearly sitting down in the kitchen (the dining room was much too formal), sipping wine and laughing about the Crispinians.

By 11 a.m. I was carefully made-up, hair casually secured with a pencil with tendrils of hair escaping (looks very last-minute but takes hours to do), and wearing black ski pants and a white polo neck jersey. The kitchen smelt deliciously of fresh roasting coffee and homemade crumpets that I had left proving overnight in the larder. Ernst's grandmother had included several crumpet recipes in her diary and must have been quite a fan as I'd discovered three crumpet-making pans in the scullery.

I was just pottering around, trying to keep my mind off

the clock – after all, Ernst might have meant a fashionably late lunch at 3 p.m. – when a car pulled up outside. God, after all this he was early! I ran to the window but my heart sank to see the Jolly Holidays' jeep, not Ernst's sleek Merc pull up outside. Ally climbed out slowly and staggered towards the door. It was odd, but she didn't look her usual bouncy self at all. I ran to let her in. At least she would take my mind off waiting for Ernst.

'You couldn't make me one of your chicory coffees, could you, Oriana? It was only the thought of one of them and some of your marmalade cake that gave me the strength to make the journey back to Gstaad.'

I busied myself with the coffee grinder while she eased herself out of her silver anorak and sighed.

'How was Crans Montana?' I asked casually. I thought it might be tactless to ask why she looked so utterly exhausted. There were purple shadows beneath her grey eyes and her shaggy blonde hair looked quite limp. She'd obviously had the most frightful experience, been raped, caught in an avalanche, been mugged, or had a car crash by the looks of her. I cut her a large chunk of marmalade cake. Fortunately I'd marinated it with a 100 per cent proof brandy syrup yesterday. She looked as if she could use it.

She groaned. 'Those girls! I can see why the last rep had a nervous breakdown.'

'Yes, we heard her parents had taken her away by private ambulance and booked her into the Priory,' I said.

'You know, none of them could cook and they could barely ski. They've been there for over a month and they just do the same run called Cri d'err, which is practically flat, over and over again. And they all have these Sony Walkmans that only play Abba so they just ski up and down all day listening to "Dancing Queen".'

This sounded like so much fun I wondered why I hadn't thought of it myself. 'How completely brainless of them,' I agreed feebly.

'But it's not that I mind they couldn't ski or cook, I mean I was used to that, but they'd abandoned their chalets and all moved in with their ski instructor boyfriends. They didn't seem to realize that they were all goat farmers in the summer. I could go on, but I tell you, it was anarchy. Absolute anarchy. It's a relief to be back in Gstaad. Did the girls get off okay yesterday?'

'Oh yes. They're spending a couple of weeks in Geneva while they decide what to do. They're waiting for the furore to die down I think, before going home.'

'You should join them, you know. Chiara was adamant that you had to pack the chalet up and hand the keys to the caretaker. I'm just back myself to finish off an article and pack up my stuff. Then I've got to shoot over to Davos to the avalanche centre to pick up some hot new research they've been doing, and then I'm going to meet Nigel in Paris for a romantic break. Gaaad, I can hardly wait.'

'But I can't leave! Not yet. I've got nowhere else to go. Besides, Ernst is coming this weekend to see me. He should be here by now . . . You know when you met him the other day,' I continued desperately, I had to find out the truth, 'did you notice if there was something on my nose?'

'I'm afraid I don't have a clue, I didn't have my contact lenses in.'

My shoulders sagged with disappointment. I might never find out now.

'Look, Oriana,' Ally continued, 'you mustn't expect anything from a man like that. I know you've taken a fancy to him but, well, I met him, remember?' She put a kindly hand on my arm. 'After all, you don't know anything about him, he might be married or anything.'

'I don't mind. You can't expect a man like that to be single.'

'Oriana, if you were married you wouldn't want some lovely girl pinching your husband, would you?' Ally was very American and puritanical at times, I'd noticed. I could see her point but I didn't have the strength to justify my European *laissez faire* position. It was all right for her to take the moral high ground; after all, she had a boyfriend.

'Did you see the papers?' I changed the subject brightly. 'We had so much fun manipulating them all.'

Ally grinned. 'Yeah, I saw them. There was a great picture of you in the *Telegraph*. I wouldn't worry about Ernst, I should think you'll be getting lots of fan mail from that.'

'I was really hoping that it might help me find a publisher. What do you think?'

'Unlikely. What you need to do as soon as you get home is to order a year's worth of back copies of the *Tatler* and check out their publishing column. That will give you a good idea of the best agents around. Then get *The Writers' and Artists' Yearbook*. That'll have all their addresses, then you can send them a brief but witty covering letter with a few chapters to whet their appetite and sit back and wait for them to contact you.' My heart sank. It sounded terribly complicated.

'But that might take months!'

'I'm afraid that's how the business works. You need the patience of Job. By the way, I did mention it to my agent but she's completely snowed under at the moment.'

'You are lucky to be published,' I said mournfully. 'It must be a great feeling. I can't wait to read your book when it comes out. You could ring the *Mail* and tell them you were our rep, see if they'll do an article on it.'

'Oh no, it'll be quite a while before it's finished. I don't want to jump the gun on the publicity front,' said Ally hurriedly. She glanced out of the window. 'Hey, you've got a visitor. Not Ernst, I'm afraid.' I jumped up and dashed to the window. A tall blonde girl with a swinging pageboy haircut climbed out of an indiscriminate white car.

'Expecting anyone else?' asked Ally.

'No. She's probably lost. I'll go and have a word.'

'Excuse me, are you Oriana Spicer?' The girl spoke with an apologetic half smile.

Another journalist! My fifteen minutes of fame was stretching longer than I expected.

'Yes. That's me. Would you like to come in for a drink?'

'My goodness. That would be lovely. I was rather expecting you to slam the door in my face. You must be sick and tired of all the publicity by now.'

'Yes, it's been hellish.' I ushered her into the hall and into the kitchen.

'G and T, homemade elderflower cordial, cappuccino, hot chocolate . . . ?' Sometimes I think I should be running my own café.

'Elderflower cordial sounds divine,' she replied. 'I better introduce myself. My name is Claire Coquette and I work for Red Duck Publishing.'

I caught my breath. Red Duck were the numero uno publishing house for frothbuster romances. They had recently had an incredible success with a slew of It girl novels. The most successful, written by Anoushka Bird-Whistle, had caused a huge furore when it was revealed that it had actually been written by her Filipino cleaner, Norma Pippolotta, a fact which hadn't hurt sales at all.

'And this is Ally Wheeler who is, or was, our wonderful rep.'

'Hi,' smiled Ally, similarly intrigued.

I placed a glass which I'd frosted round the rim in lemon-scented sugar (marinate sugar for a week in a mixture of lemon rind, vanilla and cinnamon sticks, it's one of Martha's ideas) and poured in some chilled elderflower cordial.

'I've got ice, but it's actually nicer without,' I said.

'Mmmm,' Claire took a sip. 'It's so refreshing. I've driven over from Davos and this is just what I need.' She opened a huge messy handbag stuffed with manuscripts, sweet wrappers, and vitamin pills and drew out the *Telegraph*. 'I was reading this yesterday and was very interested to see that you're writing a book about your, um, experiences out here.'

I nodded brightly, hardly daring to speak.

'I know you've probably been besieged with people trying to sign you up,' I smiled noncommittally, 'but this is just the sort of thing that Red Duck specializes in. I was wondering if you could show me something you've done.'

I reached into the kitchen drawer and pulled out my manuscript. 'This is it. I've been keeping a diary and noting down recipes and household tips and romantic intrigues and sort of tying it all up into a romantic alpine love story.'

Claire flicked through the manuscript intently then glanced at me. I had the feeling she was appraising me. Then she smiled warmly, her blue eyes crinkling at the edges. I liked her very much.

'It looks really interesting, Oriana. Are you talking to any other publishers?'

'Well, actually, I am. But I haven't committed to anything yet.'

Ally snorted. 'Well, she would say that, wouldn't she?'

I glanced up, stunned. Surely she must be joking. But she was stirring her coffee angrily, and avoided my gaze.

Claire continued smoothly on. I hoped she hadn't noticed the bitterness in Ally's voice. 'People always seem to love reading about chalet girls, and this looks like it could be a lot of fun. I had a hunch it might be.'

'So are you on holiday at the moment?' I asked.

'Yes, I had a couple of days owing to me so I went to stay with a friend who's writing a novel in Davos. She's actually the one who showed me the article in the *Telegraph*. What I'd really like to do is maybe meet up with you tomorrow and have a proper discussion about – what's your working title?'

'The what?'

'The title of your book,' said Ally with asperity.

'Oh, sorry. *Chalet Girl Secrets*.'

'Maybe we could meet tomorrow morning. Would that be at all convenient?'

'It would be perfect!'

Claire gathered up her sprawling possessions and scooped them all into her Mulberry bag. 'I'm sorry to just butt in like this.' She spoke apologetically to Ally.

'No, not at all. It's been a pleasure to meet you.' Ally seemed restored to her usual charming self, thank goodness.

'By the way, can you recommend somewhere reasonable where I can stay for the night?'

'Oh, why don't you stay here?' I offered. 'We've kind of shut up shop for the season, I've got plenty of spare beds.'

'Um, actually, Oriana, that's quite out of the question. Chiara would have a fit. I'm sorry, Claire, but you see we're not insured for guests as from yesterday. You could try the Rossli in town, it's a sweet hotel.' Ally gave brief, efficient directions.

'Yes, Hemingway stayed there while he was writing *The Old Man and the Sea*,' I encouraged. I wanted to keep Claire in town as long as possible. Damn Ally, what had got into her. Insurance! Pah!

'It sounds intriguing. Well, Oriana, shall we meet somewhere in town tomorrow morning at about ten?'

'Oh, please come here. I'll make us tea and we can chat,' I offered. The more time Claire spent here the better. Once seduced by Chalet Tiara's enchanted atmosphere and Gstaad's glamorous allure, I felt sure she would be begging me to write for Red Duck. 'Actually, Ally's a writer too,' I went on. 'She's far more experienced than me.'

'Oh, I specialize in nonfiction, in the States,' said Ally casually. 'I do mainly travel journalism at the moment, and I'm working on a book about avalanche control.'

'Oh, that sounds fascinating,' said Claire. 'Travel journalism is something I've always wanted to do. Who do you write for?'

'Oh, *Condé Nast Traveller* and some Canadian magazines,' said Ally quickly. 'I'm sorry to rush you but I'm late for an appointment. If you want to follow me I'll show you where the Rossli is. I'm pretty sure they've got some spare rooms.'

'That would be super. It's been great meeting you both. I'll see you tomorrow, Oriana.'

I waved them goodbye, trying not to jump up and down too obviously on the spot, but a Cheshire cat grin spread across my face, all thoughts of Ernst driven from my mind. I was pulled back to earth by the phone and rushed inside to answer it. It was Ernst, calling from his car phone.

'Oriana, I'm really sorry but I'm not going to get to you in time for lunch. I've missed my flight and I'm still in Paris.'

'Oh, don't worry, things have been hectic here. A publisher dropped in and said she was interested in my book, so I'm busy working on that . . .' I strained my ears; the convivial noise in the background sounded as if he was in a restaurant.

'That's fabulous, Oriana. I'm afraid I can't talk at the moment, I'm in a meeting but I really enjoyed last weekend.'

'So did I, the party was great fun.' Fun wasn't the way I'd describe spending an evening with a bunch of Euro crones, but I wanted to sound positive.

'The good news is that I'll be tying things up in Paris in a few days so I can definitely be in Gstaad for next Friday evening. I can take you out for dinner.'

'I'd love that, but I don't know if I'm going to be allowed to stay. You see, Jolly Holidays has gone bust and—'

'Of course you can stay. It's my chalet, I like the thought of you there.' My heart burned with pleasure. 'Anyway, I better let you get on.'

'Yes. Thanks for letting me know about lunch. Hope your meeting goes well.' The line clicked dead.

I was so relieved that he had rung that I skipped exultantly into the kitchen, examining the conversation again in my head carefully for nuances. After my initial enthusiasm had worn off I cursed myself for being so accommodating. Why had I thanked him for cancelling lunch? Talk about feeble.

Still, I mustn't be too hard on him. Of course it was disappointing that he wasn't coming out, but you couldn't expect a man with his business interests to be able to just drop everything. And he had demanded that I stay in his chalet! Sod Ally and Jolly Holidays, I wasn't going anywhere.

After the brief but none the less meaningful call from Ernst, I spent the rest of the day tweaking my manuscript and updating my recipes onto the laptop.

I then rang Claire at the Rossli and faxed her as much as I felt the hotel fax could cope with. (Hopefully it was industrial sized.) I could have asked Ally, but given her current mood I felt this would be unwise. I just didn't know what on earth had got into her. She had always been so incredibly encouraging. Then I wondered why she'd never shown us any actual evidence of her work. It all sounded terribly high-powered, and there was no denying she was very clever, but her unexpected bitterness at the prospect of my possible success cast doubt over everything.

Chapter Twenty-five

'You're obviously mad about this place,' said Claire, taking her eyes off the gorgeous trompe l'oeil on the ceiling, carefully spreading butter on her crumpet. 'I can't imagine Chalet Tiara without you. How will you ever manage to leave?'

'I'm not going to for a while. Ernst – it's his chalet – says he likes me being here. I'm going to stay until he drags me out.' I glanced into the roaring fire and imagined Ernst dragging me in and out of the chalet. I shivered.

I tore myself away from the throbbing embers and concentrated on Claire who was pulling my mile-long fax out of her capacious bag. At last. She'd been here for ten minutes without mentioning *Chalet Girl Secrets*, and I was beginning to get worried.

'Thanks for the fax last night.' Claire was still pulling the missive, like an endless hanky, out of her bag. It was very cold today so I'd lit the fire and we were toasting crumpets and spreading them with Frau Perren's delicious unpasteurized butter and homemade quince jam.

'I took a good look at it and I rang a colleague for her opinion, and she thought it sounded wonderful. On the strength of what I've seen so far, Red Duck would like to offer you an advance for *Chalet Girl Secrets*.'

I was so astonished I had to sit hard on my buttery hands and take a deep breath. 'An advance! That's very kind.' I wondered if it would be bad form to ask what the advance would consist of. Luckily I didn't have to as she quickly outlined the terms and mentioned a modest sum.

'I know you'll probably want to think about it and discuss it with your agent, but perhaps you could let me know within the week?'

'Actually I don't have an agent. But I can discuss it with Pandora, she's an authoress too. She wrote a book a few years ago called *Pandora's Gold*.'

Claire racked her brains. 'It doesn't ring a bell, I'm afraid.'

'No, it rather sank without trace. She's given up writing now. I think she's taken the J.D. Salinger line, you know, the one-book wonder approach. The trouble is her publisher hasn't even asked her to write a second yet.'

'Well, it's a heartbreaking business. People put their hearts and souls into their manuscripts and they end up in our slush pile at the office. You're incredibly lucky. You don't have an agent, you'll never see a slush pile.'

'I have a feeling that Ernst's grandmother is pushing me on,' I replied lightly. 'You can tell from her diary that she was really passionate about the place.'

'Ahh, the diary! Can I have a look?'

'Of course.' I handed over the heavy leather notebook reverently. 'She was a bit of a Martha Stewart in her time,' I explained as Claire glanced through the densely-written pages.

'What a find!'

'Yes. Till I found it I just saw Gstaad as a Grace Kelly Hermes bag sort of place stuffed with Euro toffs.'

'Which it is!'

'Yes, it is, but reading this helped me look beyond all that, to see the community beyond the froth. This whole part of Switzerland, Saanerland, has a fascinating history. So many of the old houses are still preserved, lots of the chalets have little homilies inscribed on them in seventeenth-century German.'

'Yes, I noticed the inscription on the front of Chalet Tiara. What does it mean?'

'Frau Perren says it means "Seize the day",' I explained. 'And she's written down recipes too. Have you tried any of them?'

'Yes, lots. I've had great fun trying things out.'

She put the book down. 'It's fascinating.'

'Have you been in publishing long?' I inquired.

'Just a year. Before that I was a banker in the city.' She grimaced. 'It was a very different kind of life.'

'I expect it paid better.'

'Talk to me about it. I earn an eighth of what I earned at the bank, I don't travel first-class any more, I sold my swanky loft in Soho, the BMW went back. But the biggest difference is that every day I get up at eight a.m. with a smile on my face. In the old days I got up at five thirty and there was always a knot in my stomach. I lived like that for seven years.'

'But if you hated it so much why didn't you pack it in before?'

'Oh, you know, there's always a big bonus lurking round the corner. You say to yourself, I'll just last another four months, *then* I'll leave. And the two hundred thousand lodges itself in your bank account and you think, hmm, that's nice, I'll have a shopping spree at Joseph and take my family to St Moritz for Christmas—'

'Gosh, that's very generous. They must really appreciate it. My lot would think it was their lucky day if I took them out for pie and mash.' Even pie and mash would be pushing it, what with Siena not eating potatoes and Mum only eating tomatoes, though I suppose she might eat a tomato pie. As for Dad, who knew where he was. 'So what made you actually jump ship in the end?' I asked curiously.

'I'll tell you exactly what it was. I became a Buddhist and started chanting every day. Then I got a terrible ulcer.'

'I thought Buddhism was meant to be relaxing.'

'Hang on. But then the doctor said it wasn't an ulcer and they diagnosed stomach cancer and said I only had three months to live.'

My mouth dropped open. 'It must have been like some ghastly film.'

'So I left work, which was great because I went to stay with my family who I'd never got on with, and they were just so amazing. It brought us all much closer. For the first time in my life I was forced to get off the treadmill. I just chanted, read tons, but the more I chanted the more optimistic and cheerful I became. No one could believe it. It was like whenever I was chanting I was injecting myself with life force.'

'So what happened to the cancer?'

'After six months I was still going strong, and I was having all these foul tests. Then one day the doctor said they'd made a mistake and I'd never had cancer. The lumps in my stomach and colon had disappeared and they thought it might have been something to do with having glandular fever when I was younger.'

I sat looking at the confident glowing girl opposite me. Her clear blue eyes and luminous skin made it difficult to imagine that only a short time ago she had been given just months to live.

'I guess that sort of experience changes everything,' I said humbly.

'It was the best thing that ever happened to me. Big wake-up call. I decided that I wasn't going to waste any more time and that I was going to give up banking and somehow get into publishing. I've always been crazy about books. So I rang an old friend at Red Duck and she gave me some work copy-editing from home, then when I got my health back I went to work for them full time.'

'And this Buddhist chanting. Is it something you could teach me to do here?'

'Of course. We chant Nam Myoho Renge Kyo, which is the title of the Lotus Sutra, the Buddha's most profound teaching. When you chant it you're reciting the Law of Life and drawing it into your life. So you change and become more patient and compassionate, and when you change, your environment changes too and so the world becomes more peaceful and harmonious.'

'And you believe what goes round comes round?'

'Definitely, what you give out comes back to you.'

'Like a boomerang.' I paused. 'So where does that leave the Grouts? I guess they did something pretty wicked somewhere along the line to have been poisoned so horribly.'

'Well, if you believe in the law of cause and effect, nothing is random. But you can't use it as an excuse to justify awful things happening to people. Besides,' Claire continued briskly, 'it's not about worrying about the past, it's more a case of saying yesterday's gone, I can't do anything about that. But I can do something about right now. Because the actions you take now are what will shape tomorrow.'

'Hmm, it's very interesting. If you don't have to leave tonight why don't you stay here for a couple of nights. Ernst won't mind.'

'What about your fierce rep?'

'She's not here. Besides, it's not her chalet, it's Ernst's.'

'Well, in that case I'd love to. I'll ring my friend in Davos and tell her. I'd like to go through things a bit more thoroughly with you.'

'You've got the most lovely job, dropping in on people and making their dreams come true.'

Claire laughed. 'It doesn't work like this very often. It's much more pedestrian usually, not all swooping into gorgeous chalets and signing up glamorous girls. You've come through a very unusual back door.'

'Well, Chalet Tiara's back door really. There's something so magical about this place. Sometimes when I'm locking the place up last thing at night I feel as if everybody's playing grandmother's footsteps, and that as soon as I shut the door, all the secret snowbound creatures, leprechauns, dwarfs, marmots, snow beavers will all start racing around again. You'll think I'm crazy.'

'No, no, not at all,' Claire reassured me unconvincingly. 'Lots of our authors have very vivid imaginations . . .'

'You mean they're all barking.'

'Yes, I mean no, no, of course not.' She glanced outside into the silent garden. There was always a moment between the sun setting and dusk when the sky was a shimmering, icy-clear light blue. It remained this colour for about half an hour before gradually deepening into mid-blue, azure, indigo through to deep, rich cobalt. The mountains remain unmoved, austere, oblivious of the blue subtleties swirling about them.

'You've got the most amazing view. No wonder you've been inspired since you came here.'

'I haven't had a lot of time, to be honest, I've just snatched moments here and there between everything else. But now the girls have left and I've got no one to look after I'm really going to crack on.'

'Well, you've made good headway, some of it's so funny. I just love the bad housekeeping chapter, it had me in fits last night.'

'Rochetta and Bella were very helpful researching that section.'

'But I think the heroine needs to have some kind of love interest – the reader will expect some romance.'

'But why? What's the point of perpetuating this myth of perfect relationships? Every romantic novel always finishes up with the girl getting the guy. As if all the battles have been won and there'll be no more problems. Life isn't like that. If you ask me, it's when you meet the dreamboat that the problems begin. They don't tell you about *that* in Mills and Swoon.'

'Ouch, spoken from the heart,' smiled Claire. 'You sound like you're speaking from experience. Are you getting a hard time from a romantic interest, by any chance?'

'I've got a bit keen on the bloke who owns the chalet. The one whose grandmother wrote the diary.'

'Keeping it in the family, I'm glad to hear.'

'Perhaps the heroine should give up men and fall in love with her chalet. That would be much more original. What do you think?'

'Let her fall in love with a man and the chalet. Hedge your bets.'

'You're probably right. Actually I'm writing quite a passionate bit at the moment. She's just met this gorgeous man who comes charging into her chalet one night. It's going to coincide with lots of unctuous gooey type recipes, like cassoulet and toffee apple ice cream and things . . .'

'Well, keep it fairly realistic, don't get too Mills and Swoony because it all rings very true at the moment.' She glanced at her watch. 'I better ring my friend to tell her I won't be back tonight. D'you feel like skiing tomorrow? I've got my kit in the car and I'd love to do some exploring.'

'Why not? There are some fabulous cross-country trails just outside the door.'

'Ugh, I don't want to do any of that langlaufing stuff. Do I look like a masochist?'

'I'm not sure. I don't know you well enough. But really, it's not hard work at all. English people have got completely the wrong idea, though langlaufing can be quite aggressive sometimes.'

'I thought you said you couldn't ski,' heaved Claire the next day as we clomped into the Wispile restaurant on the mountain.

'I can't usually, but my co-ordination has really improved since I've been skiing to my Abba tape. It's quite dramatic.'

'I'm so glad we skied this side of the mountain, the views are stunning. D'you know which village that is down there?'

'Yes, it's Gsteig.' I peered into the valley. 'I think that's where Frau Perren's farm is. She makes the beeswax polish and the unpasteurized milk and butter. Her daughter delivers it to the chalet every couple of days. I'm going to miss that when I go home.' I gazed at the valley. 'A legend says that God put his hand into the Saanerland and the heel of his hand created Saanen, and his fingers imprinted Saanenmoser, Schonreid, Gstaad and Turbach, you can see it from here. Look, stand up, you can see it better. There's Gstaad, Saanen, Saanermoser . . .' I pointed into the valley.

'Oh yes, I see what you mean.'

'And there's the River Saane which runs through the bottom of my garden. It's named after the Celtic mermaid goddess, Seganne, which means "the powerful". I've got a feeling that the mermaid wood carving on Chalet Tiara's front door is actually meant to be the mermaid goddess. I thought at first it might have been of Beatrice.'

'Either way, it's very romantic,' said Claire as we got up to leave. 'And now I want you to show me where the Eagle Club is. I'm very intrigued since reading about it in your book.'

'But I don't know where it is. None of us ever found out. Bella went there with Tony Louche once. She tried to take us there the next day but we got terribly lost. I'm afraid its exact location will remain a mystery forever.'

'Nonsense. It's a challenge. I'm going inside to ask someone.'

And she did. But though we got it within our sights, it was so late that the chair lift up to it had closed and we had to go home.

'Damn. If I wasn't leaving tomorrow morning we could come back,' said Claire as we undid our skis and boots back at the chalet.

'I'll promise to give you a full rundown after Ernst has taken me there this weekend.'

'I do hope it works out for you, Oriana,' said Claire, rather too doubtfully for my liking. 'You deserve someone really nice. But whatever happens, just keep writing. From now on your readers will want to know *everything*!'

I was sad to see her leave the following morning. The

chalet had been so full of fun and laughter and bad jokes. I'd been looking forward to being alone, but the place just seemed echoing and silent. Still, I only had a few days until the weekend and Ernst's arrival, so I decided to make the most of them and get down to some serious work.

I woke early on Friday, my stomach tied in excitable knots of anticipation. What a week it was turning out to be. Being signed up by Red Duck and now Ernst.

In a triumph of hope over experience I had made another cassoulet (I was becoming a bit of a cassoulet expert), while Chalet Tiara and I were buffed, exfoliated and polished to the hilt, both smelling and looking our best. I had anointed myself liberally with Lust, a bottle of which Pandora had kindly given me before she left, and had marinated my hair overnight in a wildly expensive La Prairie hair pack (the sheep's extracts contained a powerful punch). When I washed it out in the morning I blow-dried it straight, applied a natural-look *maquillage* which took an hour to apply, switched on the laptop and sat down to work at the kitchen table.

Looking back I can see how ridiculous I was expecting Ernst to pitch up, but when you've got a violent crush on someone you don't think logically.

By 7 p.m. after faffing around the chalet all day, I was starting to get cabin fever. I didn't want to go out in case I missed him but I was too feeble to ring him and find out if he was coming. At 8 p.m. I had written all I was going to that day and switched off the computer wearily. I was just going into the larder to find out if my mint jelly had set when the phone rang. I raced through the kitchen and into the hall and fell onto the receiver.

'Is that Miss Havisham?' It was Pandora.

'No. Yes. Yes, it's me.' The link with Miss Havisham, though cruel, was uncomfortably apposite.

'Has he arrived yet?' she asked.

'No, he hasn't. How long d'you think I ought to wait before giving up?'

'Give him till nine,' she advised kindly.

'Nine tomorrow morning?' I asked hopefully.

'Oh, Oriana. I warned you. You're going through the same thing all over again. I've got an idea. Why don't you pack up your stuff and come and join us in Geneva tomorrow? We're having a great time.'

'I can hear.' In the background I could hear sounds of whooping and revelry, and plates being smashed.

'We met this really nice Greek family called the Lubricantococopolis. They've been showing us the sights.'

'Um, yes, they sound very lively.' The plate crashing sounded as if it was getting closer.

'WHAT? CAN YOU SPEAK UP? SHUT UP, YOU LOT, I'M TRYING TO SPEAK TO ORIANA! It's getting a bit crazy in here. Do promise you'll come soon. We'll be here for another week at leaaa—' A plate had obviously landed on her head as the line suddenly went dead.

I wandered upstairs and ran myself a bath. Easing myself into the steaming water, I pushed open the window, enjoying the rush of the freezing alpine air on my flushed face, and the refreshing scent of pine. I leaned out of the window and grasped a handful of pine needles and tossed them into the steaming water. Inhaling the aromatic refreshing scent, I thought fondly of Ernst's grandmother, who had done the very same thing forty years earlier. I wouldn't have thought of doing it if I hadn't read about it in her diary. And for the last month it had become a nightly ritual. When I returned home I would just have to make do with Badedas.

But there was no need to go home for a while. Sooner or later Ernst would come by to check the chalet. I may as well stay a few more weeks. It would be a shame to miss him.

The next morning I decided to ski past the Eagle and check

the place out. I must be more like Claire, seize the day and all that!

It was a wonderful day to be going up the mountain, the little red cable cars contrasted cheerfully with the azure sky, and the stark, gleaming mountains were glossy in the warm sunshine. In the village, snow was packed artfully on chalet roofs, the layers merging and coalescing, like thick layers of white parchment melted together, or uncooked puff pastry, packed so cleanly and tightly, it's a miracle it didn't just slip off.

The weather forecast hadn't been very good for later, but I wasn't going to hang about, this was just going to be quick go see. The Eagle Club would be a nice classy setting for my heroine (could she be called Jemima, or had that name been *done* too much? Maybe Tabitha would be better) so it was important that I see it for myself.

Leaving the cable car I switched on my Sony Walkman, and bombed down the mountain. Several chair lifts later I had the Eagle firmly within my sights. The trouble was it was starting to cloud over and visibility was diminishing rapidly.

I was just taking the Wasserngrat chair lift that led to the club, quietly humming along to 'Waterloo' and trying not to get spooked by the swirling mists that had swept in, when I attempted to lift up the chairlift bar but for some reason it was jammed. The more I panicked the less able I was to lift it. It was even more scary because I couldn't quite make out when to get off.

'Help, help, I'm stuck!' I yelled into the mists, but there was no reply.

Eventually, with only seconds to go before the chair was absorbed into a mangle of machinery before turning round and disappearing down the mountain, I managed to extricate myself, losing a glove and one of my ski poles. By this time I was hyperventilating (not much chance of a brown paper bag up here), but managed to stagger towards the restaurant.

I didn't think I could get down the mountain unless someone helped me.

The place was heaving with glamorous people, laughing and chatting, drinking convivially. Someone looked towards the window, caught my eye, and pointed me out to their companion. They both looked at me curiously, conferred and then apparently lost interest. God, I must look an absolute sight. My mascara wasn't waterproof and I probably looked like a panda. I patted my face gingerly and to my horror noticed blood on my hand. I was having a nosebleed of all things. I couldn't possibly go inside. I'd just have to somehow make my way down alone. And then, to my relief, a figure appeared and I recognized the stony-eyed lady from the Prince of Ruritania's party glide towards me elegantly.

'Oh, hello, hello!' I gabbled with relief. 'We met at Johnny Ruritania's party, I was with Ernst . . .' She didn't seem to recognize me, and looked at me blankly. Then recognition gradually dawned.

'Ernst's little cook! Yes, I remember. How are you?' I was amazed she needed to ask, I must have looked such a fright with mascara and blood all over my face.

'I fell off the chair lift and I've sort of lost my nerve. D'you think you could possibly help me find my way down the mountain?'

She turned to her companion who had just joined her. 'Ectually, we're not going down yet. Desperately need to ski orf our lunch. But all you have to do is ski down to the bubble over there and it'll take you down to Saanmoser. I should think you could probably get a bus back to *Hstaaad* from there. Lovely to run into you again! Ciao!' She clicked on her skis and with a couple of elegantly executed parallels, she and her companion had disappeared from sight.

'Ciao,' I murmured into the mist. I took a deep breath, pinched myself and said, 'Have you tried pulling yourself together?' A handy mantra my parents had been fond of using whenever I had a similarly maddening turn in the past.

I walked back to the chair lift, found my ski pole, though sadly not the glove, and made my way gingerly down to the bubble car, one hand blue with cold. I felt utterly winded. Even the dulcet strains of 'Dancing Queen' failed to raise my spirits as I made my slow tremulous journey home.

The next morning, restored by a good night's sleep and the soothing atmosphere of the chalet, I rang my mother to share my good news about the publishing contract. She'd been in Belgium for a month, finalizing the divorce settlement from Bertie, who had suddenly gone AWOL, taken off in a balloon, hoping to beat the Belgian ballooning record. This was no mean feat, as the Belgians were particularly keen on ballooning, perhaps seeing it as a surreal form of escape from their small but none the less divided country.

I feared negotiations hadn't gone very well as I hadn't caught her in a very good mood.

'Yes, Jolly Holidays has gone completely bust,' I explained. Of course she knew all about the Grouts. No *Daily Mail* reader could have avoided the subject, which had sadly now disappeared from public debate. The rousing term daughters of empire would soon mean nothing at all, unhappily.

'So where will you go now?' she asked worriedly.

'Well, Ernst says he wants me to stay here for a while, but I suppose I can't stay here forever. Maybe I could come and stay with you when I come back? Just till I find somewhere to rent?'

'Oh, Oriana,' she sighed irritably. 'I've just got the house all sorted. Jacob stays in your room now when he comes down. It's full of toys and children's books. There's just no space for any of your stuff.'

'Oh, right.' I paused, hurt and cross. Did she find me so difficult she couldn't bear me to stay for a few weeks?

'There's no need to adopt that tone. You can't just take everyone for granted. You've got to be responsible for your own living arrangements. This Ernst chap, he must think it a bit of a cheek that you're staying on, perhaps he wants to rent it to someone . . .'

'No, he doesn't. He likes me being here. He told me so.' I was very upset. 'Why are you being so horrid? I'm your daughter, for heaven's sake.'

'Because you only ring when you want something. You only come and see me when it suits you.'

'I'm going to ring Dad, he'll put me up.' This was extremely doubtful but had the required inflammatory effect.

'I don't want you to stay. Siena doesn't want you to stay and I'm sure your father doesn't either!'

I slammed the phone down, my eyes full of bitter, angry tears. And I hadn't even told her about my book! Full of indignation, I dialled my father's number.

'Could you tell him his daughter called with some urgent news? He's got my number. Yes, thanks. Be sure to tell him I called, won't you?' I sighed and replaced the receiver.

I felt so angry. It had been an awful day. Maybe I should try the chant Claire had taught me. Damn, I'd written it down but I couldn't remember where. Instead I took some deep breaths. I'd show my mother! I'd make my own way, stand on my own two feet.

I switched on the computer, longing to escape to the Chalet Tiara of my imagination locked away inside it. An easier, softer and more accommodating place altogether.

The following afternoon I took advantage of the unseasonably warm weather to work in the gazebo in the garden, embellishing my visit to the Eagle Club and turning it into a wonderful romantic trysting opportunity for my heroine, Jemima or Tabitha (who had the romantic hero firmly under control and certainly didn't fall off chair lifts or do anything embarrassing at all), when I heard a car pull up in the drive.

Racing round to see who it was, I saw with a sinking heart that it was the middle-aged Swiss lady from the agency that managed the chalet. I hadn't heard from her for a while, she dropped in occasionally to make a fuss about something to justify the no doubt exorbitant fee the agency must charge Ernst (she hadn't liked the picture of Liz Hurley I'd stuck in the relationship corner, or the crystals). I hoped she wasn't going to make a fuss about something today.

'Hello, Miss Spicer. I'm rather surprised that you are still here.' The Swiss lady was stony-faced. 'Jolly Holidays has now terminated their arrangement with us, and I must insist that you leave the chalet and return the keys to us as soon as possible.'

'But Ernst, I mean, Mr Schmitt, was happy that I stay on to take care of the chalet for a few more weeks.'

'Mr Schmitt has unfortunately not instructed us on this arrangement. In fact, we are renting it out again to another family at the weekend.'

'Oh.' I felt an icy wind slice through me. Leave? Immediately? How . . .

'I understand,' I replied, not understanding at all. 'I'll pack up my things today.'

'I shall come tomorrow morning for the inventory check and to collect the keys.' She made her way back to the car.

Even in my numbed state I couldn't help smiling at the logo on the car, 'Competence since 1890.' How Swiss. How efficient. How cold. I must ring Ernst, find out what was going on. There must be a mistake. He was obviously so busy he hadn't told them I was staying on.

I scooted into the relationship corner where Roberto had suggested I leave romantic mementos (like I had so many of them!) where I had left Ernst's card among the wooden flutes, esoteric Venn diagrams, bottles of strange-smelling fluids and pictures of himself that Roberto kept sending me. Cautiously I dialled the number. I was shaking horribly, it was too awful that I was ringing him, I'd always prided myself on being a Rules girl, though fat lot of good that had ever done me.

After being re-routed via various minions I managed to get through.

'Orriannnnna. How lovely to hear from you. How are things?'

'They couldn't be better. I skied over to the Eagle Club yesterday – the snow was fabulous, by the way – and I'm working hard on my book.' I rushed on, 'But I had a visit from the agency today and they said they've rented the chalet out this weekend . . .' I tailed off.

'Oh, darling, I'm sorry. I leave everything about the chalet up to them. Damn, I was going to come out and see you before you left, wasn't I?'

'I guess I'll have to go back to London.' Please, please let him say he'd ring the agency and cancel the guests. But he didn't.

'All good things come to an end, sweetheart. How will I get hold of you when you've gone home?'

'I'm not sure where I'll be . . . but I've got a mobile number.'

'Hang on, I'll just grab a pen. Fire away.'

'0044831645413.'

'When I'm next in London I'll take you somewhere nice for dinner. Doubt it'll be as good as your wonderful boeuf bourguignon but we'll try.'

'Actually it was—'

'Darling, I've got to go. I've got six impatient Swedes waiting to see me. I'll call you soon.' He hung up.

'Actually, it was cassoulet,' I murmured to the white-washed walls. Cassoulet. 'But it doesn't matter. It doesn't matter at all.' But at least he called me darling and sweet-heart. That was nice of him.

It had started to snow and I leant out of the window, loving the feel of the soft whispery flakes melting in my warm hand, enjoying the silence as they drifted noiselessly to the ground. The fir trees dripped with sparkling icicles, the light was dancing and spinning, each one shone as bright as a miniature sun. The beauty had cast a spell over me, leaving would be like tearing skin away from bone. Chalet Tiara, its laughter, its tears and memories of Ernst were worn into every cranny of its timber as well as my mind. I felt as much a part of the landscape as the chalets that had sprung organically out of the mountains and shone at night with the million tiny lights that Julie Andrews had donated to the village.

I glanced around the kitchen numbly. It was all so much part of me: the uneven flagstone floors, the sturdy dresser with its fine collection of blue and white china, the cherry-coloured Aga. I was just the human extension of this pleasing picture. If I left, it would collapse into the shambles it had been when I'd first arrived. Who would care for the place in the same way? Who would love it, and polish it till it gleamed?

If only Ernst could fall head over heels in love with me so we could stay here forever. Why couldn't life just sometimes work out? Why was it easier to get a book published, a feat considered to be elusive and difficult, than have a halfway decent relationship?

My family went to the top of the tree in everything they chose to do. My father turned a business that was in the red into a billion-pound success. My mother had been a top model and was increasingly a leading light in the buttonhook world. Siena had just been promoted to president of Radical Planet, a revolutionary organisation – OK, not everyone's cup of tea but she, too, was a kingpin of sorts. And I wake up one day and get a book contract. All this good luck, but the love thing remained a complete mystery.

'Why is it so complicated?' I asked the mountains. 'Can someone explain?' Nobody could. And so the week of my greatest triumph, the ink barely dry on my dream contract, found me burying my head in my exquisite arrangement of arum lilies on the hall table, hoping the rich sweet scent would provide an answer. It didn't. Neither did my tears as I held my head in my hands and wept.

I was wailing so loudly I missed the first few rings of the telephone, which clicked onto the answering machine.

'Darling. Are you in?' It was Roberto. If he were as psychic as he claimed, he'd know if I was in, wouldn't he? I scooted quickly to the phone.

'Roberto. How nice to hear you. I'm having the most dreadful time.'

'Oh, my poor darling. Are you missing me?'

'No.' Part of my appeal to Roberto was my unrelenting beastliness interspersed with rare moments of enthusiastic flirtation. I was practising The Rules on him with devastating success. Why was the universe so perverse?

'When am I going to see you? I tried to ring Jolly Holidays to arrange another holiday at Chalet Tiara but the phone's been disconnected.' He had rung me a couple of weeks ago to suggest he come to stay as my guest but I had told him forcibly that he must go through the official channels and pay the full whack like everybody else.

'Yes, they've gone bust because of the French egg botulism scandal. It's a disaster because I'm going to be evicted from the chalet. You remember Ernst, who I'm madly in love with?'

'Of course.' Being unable to take his crush on me seriously, I hadn't spared Roberto the Ernst saga in the vague hope that he might come up with a love spell that actually worked. The flute and the red knickers had had no result at all. In fact, they had had disastrous consequences. Could Roberto have been feeding me dodgy information so that my fledgling relationship with Ernst would fail? This had crossed my mind but I felt sure Roberto wouldn't compromise his excellent feng shui reputation for a quick romantic thrill.

'I've just had a horrid row with my mother and I'm literally going to be homeless.'

'My darling, don't be ridiculous, come and stay with me. I'm giving a lecture tour in the States and I'll be gone for at least a month. I was dreading leaving my flat empty. You'd be doing me a favour.'

'Are you giving lectures about love spells?' I asked, much impressed.

'Yes, my book has really taken off over there.' He sighed. 'I'm going to be so busy. So tell me, how are you getting on with your book? All the publicity must have been very helpful.'

'Yes, it was. A publisher turned up out of the blue and offered me a contract. It was quite extraordinary.'

'You see. I told you you had a lucky face.'

'Yes, I'm still amazed about it all really. But the trouble is, as soon as you get something you wanted more than anything, it's easy to begin taking it for granted and to start really wanting something else. I was hoping Ernst would come out to see me, but he got tied up.'

'Have you been playing the flute every night?'

'Yes, religiously,' I replied earnestly.

'You mustn't play it religiously, you must play it softly, like you are playing a dance of lerve.'

'No, by religiously I mean conscientiously.' Roberto's English was so brilliant one occasionally forgot that it wasn't his first language.

'And have you been playing it in your relationship corner – this is most important.'

'Yes, I have. But nothing's happened. In fact, all my relationships are hovering on the brink of total collapse.'

'I've never heard of the flute playing not working,' mused Roberto. 'Your relationship karma must be *intractable*. I shall have to think of something more radical.'

'Oh, would you, Roberto? I'm at my wits' end.'

'So you will come and stay in my flat? The feng shui is excellent. It will really help you.'

'Okay. If you really don't mind, I'd love to.' We made arrangements about collecting the keys from a crippled neighbour and I replaced the receiver feeling much cheered.

Thank goodness for Roberto's kind offer. It was the answer to a prayer. At least I would have a perfectly feng shuied palace to stay in for a few weeks till I decided what to do. I would go back to London via Geneva. Pandora and the others weren't due to leave for a few days.

I wandered outside, gazing intently at the mountains, hoping to engrave each fir tree, each wisp of cloud, and each ray of sunshine into my mind forever. A memory, a talisman to keep me going when I returned to London.

It was a bleak, austere and lovely landscape. Its frozen grandeur and dangerous jagged horizon suited my melancholy. I felt we were as one.

I shut my eyes for a moment and listened to the sound of the river, a million melted icicles trickling their chilly way over a thousand frozen stones. And the birdsong that reached its crescendo at dusk and at dawn. The hooting and yelping of alpine animals, foxes and marmots that I never saw. And the muffled shooting in distant valleys as the Swiss army practised their manoeuvres.

Yes. I would miss it here.

Chapter Twenty-six

It was quite a culture shock to return to Blighty. The five of us arrived at Gatwick one wintry Saturday and it was depressing to face grubby patterned carpets and grey drizzling weather after the bright blue skies and gleaming efficiency of Geneva airport.

Unfortunately none of the escalators was working and it was a great struggle for the girls, who were all partially embalmed in plaster, having slipped on the pavement in Geneva (though they would think up a more *sportif* explanation, I was sure) and utterly disabled when it came to climbing stairs. As the only able-bodied woman on the team I was kept busy running up and down stairs carrying the girls' Louis Vuitton hand baggage.

On the fourth round I stopped for a quick breather.

'You may not be a great skier, old thing,' said Arabella, 'but you'd make a great sherpa.'

'I know it's become fashionable to criticize the Swiss for their war record,' I gasped, 'but at least the country *works*.' I thought longingly of the escalators we had left behind at Geneva airport that were so state of the art that they allowed you to put trolleys precariously stacked with luggage onto them without squashing anybody. The beleaguered Brits thought themselves lucky to find stairs, let alone stairs that actually moved. Stairs, eek, wicked!

'I quite agree. Coming back to Blighty is like coming back to a Third World country,' shouted Arabella in ringing tones. We were all just about to agree forcibly when the entire Pakistan cricket team suddenly appeared from round the corner, took one look at the four of us and our hand luggage scattered about the steps and swept us and it up. They didn't stop until we got to baggage reclaim where they set us up with trolleys and disappeared.

'Very sporting chaps,' muttered Pandora appreciatively once we had recovered from the excitement.

Eventually we collected our bulging trunks and headed off towards customs. Shuffling into the arrivals lounge was a very bleak moment. A crowd of anticipatory eyes passed over me indifferently, searching for the one person they were waiting for. I scanned the anxious, loving faces but I knew no one was waiting for me. Still, you never knew, someone might have found out when we were arriving and come to meet me, it would have been fun to be surprised.

Ambrosia and Arabella's parents were waiting to meet them and Pandora's father had sent a car. I was planning to take a taxi to Roberto's flat – thank goodness I had somewhere to go – but watching Arabella and Ambrosia's parents waving and craning their necks with longing and excitement, I felt tears pricking the back of my eyes. What did one have to do to be so loved? What had I done wrong?

'Hang on, Mummy,' Arabella was saying, 'I've just got to get my *Hello!* before we leave.'

That galvanized us into action; all of one mind, we dumped our luggage and dashed off to W.H. Smith. Hobbling across the airport concourse the Bolter, still wearing huge Jackie O sunglasses for anonymity (she was terrified of bumping into any punters now she was back on English soil), crashed into a posse of Pakistani ladies struggling towards departures, sending the contents of their bulging plastic bags flying.

There had just been a baffling tannoy announcement apologizing for the three-day delay of Air Tonga's flight to Lahore which was the result of an air traffic dispute in New Zealand and stating that passengers now had two minutes to catch the flight.

'They must be rushing to catch the plane that the cricketers came in on,' I said to Pandora as we battled our way through the surge of humanity and plastic bags that were storming towards passport control. 'Imagine being delayed for three days. I've never heard of Air Tonga, they can't be much good.'

At that moment Pandora's head disappeared without trace but before I could search for her I, too, was sucked beneath the swarming crowd. It was terrifying, if I didn't get to the newsagent soon there might not be a *Hello!* left. The new issue came out today and it always sold out quickly.

I eventually made it to W.H. Smith's and met up with the others. Unable to wait a moment longer, we flicked through it hungrily, absorbing the beatific celebrities, many of whom had just given birth, grinning out cheesily from its glossy pages.

'It's been too long,' I murmured, catching up with the antics of various acquaintances. There was a big picture of Peregrine 'sharing a joke' with a grim-looking debutante wearing an Alice band. I sighed with contentment. It was good to be back.

I was interrupted by a terrible squawking and looked up to see Arabella rushing over to say goodbye. The others soon followed, weighted down with armfuls of glossy magazines.

'Look, they've invented another new magazine,' said Pandora, waving a copy of *Celeb-u-like!* in my face. 'I thought that was a baked potato restaurant.'

'No! That's Spud-u-like, stupid,' said Arabella, whose firm grasp on the minutiae of daily life never failed to astonish me. 'I've got to go, my people are getting restless. We'll speak soon.'

We hugged each other affectionately.

'Cross fingers I won't go down,' said Arabella nervously.

'Absolutely, old thing.' The Bolter hugged her.

'Ciao.' And suddenly they were all gone and I was alone. Taking a deep breath, I gathered up my magazines and went to the till. From now on I was on my own. It was a new adventure.

I picked up Roberto's keys as arranged from his crippled next door neighbour and crossed my fingers that he hadn't decided to stay after all and 'surprise me'.

Thank God, he had gone away and I had the place completely to myself.

The flat was stunning but, I have to say, a feng shui disaster. It had wonderful views over Hampstead Heath but his bookcases were *crammed* with feng shui books allowing no room for new projects to come into his life. Taps dripped away in the wealth corner and dusty crystals lay abandoned on the floor where they had dropped off grimy windows.

Conversely, I was quite pleased. I could at least tidy up a bit, stick the crystals back in place and arrange to get the taps fixed. I would start tomorrow first thing. I was too tired now, and was longing to unpack my stuff and luxuriate in a long, hot bath.

I thought nostalgically of the fir tree outside my bathroom window at Chalet Tiara, then pulled myself together. Chalet Tiara was another world. Another life. The sooner I got over it, built myself another, better life, the better. But my whole body *ached* with memories. How on earth would I forget?

The following morning I was woken up early by the sun pouring through the windows. I hadn't been able to find any curtains; Roberto didn't seem to have got round to fixing any – either that or curtains were a feng shui *faux pas*.

I yawned languorously, hardly daring to believe that I was completely alone for the first time in three months. There were no cakes to bake, no breakfasts to make, no beds to change, no nasty shocks in the lavatory to deal with. From now on the only thing I had to concentrate on was my book.

It was hard to break the habits of the last few months just

like that and I decided to do Roberto a favour and tidy up first. Rolling up my sleeves I remembered how much fun I'd had transforming Chalet Tiara into a gleaming palace. It wouldn't take much to lick this place into shape.

Two hours later I had hoovered, scrubbed and re-hung the crystals. Spinning in front of the windows they magically absorbed a million times their weight of wintry sun and reflected it back into the room. Rainbows spun and scattered themselves about the entire flat. The effect was stunning and I felt my spirits rise. It hadn't taken much to create one hundred per cent improvement; the mess was really only superficial.

I looked around with satisfaction and settled down with the latest edition of *Tatler*. I was soon riveted by a potentially useful article about what it took to become a successful micro celeb.

If only I could become a micro celeb around the time my book came out, maybe it would stand a chance in the publishing jungle.

Claire Coquette had rung and recommended I ring Annette, the harassed publicity honcho at Red Duck, for advice, but she was always either at the doctors or 'in a meeting'. Pandora, who had been in a similar situation, advised me to go the whole hog and get a PR agency on board. As this was my first and last chance to make a splash I knew she was probably right. As a small unknown cog in the publishing wheel I was going to need all the help I could get.

Perhaps I would give Petronella Shmooze of Shmooze Associates a ring. I had spoken to her a few times while I was chatelaine of Cheyne Castle, and she had frequently tried to send her celebrity clients to our parties. But that was for the future. In the meantime I had to find somewhere to live very quickly before Roberto returned to claim his 'rent'.

Armed with that week's property listings from the *Evening Standard*, I set to work. Two hours later I had made appointments to see five flats, three of which overlooked the river, the following day.

I ended up taking a small apartment in a purpose-built block overlooking the river in a grimy part of Fulham that was right next door to the Ritzy Marina Club. I loved it. Devoid of any distinguishing features whatsoever, it was clean and streamlined and it reminded me deliciously of living in a hotel. I even had digital TV with a thrilling choice of over one hundred channels. It was heaven. I had always dreamt of living in a hotel.

And best of all it was mine, all mine. But part of me knew that if I could have swapped the calm grey Thames and the view of the candle factory opposite for my magical mystical alpine view and the swirling sound of the River Saganne, I would have jumped like a shot. Besides, I kind of missed being forced to wear full make-up and my skimpiest apron in case Ernst suddenly appeared. Not much chance of him beating my door down in Fulham, though I lived in hope, keeping my mobile charged and switched on twenty-four hours a day. But he never rang.

When I felt sociable I could just nip downstairs to the Ritzy Marina Club where I would occasionally bump into friends and acquaintances. I would swim most days, attend yoga classes regularly but spent most of the time closeted with my laptop.

You see, after several months of intense enforced jollity, I had completely lost interest in socializing. I hadn't even bothered to tell anyone that I had come back from Switzerland. I worked best in the morning so I would get up early and work solidly for two hours before watching a programme devoted purely to beauty tips on the *Hello!* Trivia Channel.

The *Hello!* Trivia Channel was a great indulgence and utterly addictive with its fascinating mixture of celebrity gossip, long documentaries on minor members of the royal family, who were so obscure I was amazed that anyone else apart from me had ever heard of them, society weddings and features about über models' skin care routines and dietary habits.

Occasionally I spoke to the other chalet girls but they were absorbed in extensive husband hunting in Chinless Wonderland and our paths rarely crossed. Pandora was closeted in Devon with her parents and had taken up her painting again. She had hinted at some kind of Lady Chatterley type liaison with a local farmer but she wasn't being terribly forthcoming about it, which was quite unusual for her. Things were a bit complicated because her father owned the whole village, so I guess you could say she was indulging in a spot of *droit de la dame* before she returned properly to London life.

To our considerable relief, it seemed that Arabella's father had not only got her out of trouble, but managed to hold off the showing of the *Chalet Girl* documentary for the foreseeable future.

I finally made things up with my mother. I realized that there had been some truth in what she had said. My phone calls did seem to conveniently coincide with a request for a favour. And I hadn't always been fair to her. I cringed remembering how I had put her off coming to Gstaad because I'd been expecting my father. Served me right that he hadn't turned up after all.

It was misguided to think that it was possible to live happily on bad terms with my family. As Claire had said with her unwavering Buddhist logic, the bad feeling seeped into every other relationship and affected everything. I decided the best thing to do was to put it behind us and start from scratch.

So one day I went the whole hog and invited my mother, Siena, Mary and Jacob to tea. I hadn't seen any of them since coming back from Switzerland, so it was quite a reunion. It was quite difficult to pin Siena down these days, being president of Radical Planet was very demanding and it had recently hit the headlines after being implicated in a bungled plot to blow up Jack Reeves, the dishy government transport minister.

Jack Reeves had caused a national uproar after travelling on public transport for the first time in his life and, on emerging ashen-faced and covered in soot from the bowels of the earth, insisted that he would never do it again because of the frightful people he had been forced to sit next to. He was the green movement's public enemy number one but despite this handicap had recently come top in a poll as the man most women wanted to sleep with, and narrowly beating Prince Philip and P.J. O'Rourke as the man most men would choose as world dictator.

They arrived in a chaotic ramshackle procession. Siena, wearing a scruffy Che Guevara style combat jacket and Doc Martens and Mary swathed in a long Doctor Who style knitted scarf, staggered in bent double under the weight of a huge, unwieldy backpack overflowing with toys, special food (Siena was now strictly macrobiotic), and some of Mary's homemade pots for sprouting grains, which she had started trying to sell. Mummy took up the rear. In her Burberry mac, smooth blonde hair partially covered by a Hermes scarf precisely knotted under her chin and wearing an elegant pair of highly polished leather (eek, leather! What would Siena say!) court shoes she could have come from a completely different food group altogether.

Jacob still had his delightful dimple but his hazel eyes had darkened and his skin had grown quite olive. I was flattered that he seemed to remember me and hugged him affectionately. He seemed so grown up and serious for a child. He was obviously close to Mary and sat very happily on her lap playing with her Doctor Who scarf.

But I was really quite shocked by the change in Siena. She had chopped off her hair to a spiky crop and she was so thin that her combat jacket hung off her tall, skeletal frame.

Her face seemed sad and she appeared to be carrying the weight of the world on her skinny shoulders and they drooped accordingly. Mary, however, was looking very well. She had put on a little weight, her chestnut hair shone and she was glowing rather irritatingly with good health and enthusiasm, having just taken up pottery once more.

'Mary's doing really well, she's incredibly creative,' Siena said, her pale face lighting up with pride.

Mary glowed. 'Yes, my teacher thinks I should be able to make quite a good living from my pots. I actually sold one yesterday. I'm thinking of going to see some store buyers to see if they'll take some. But I don't want to compromise my creativity by becoming too commercial.' In your dreams, sunshine.

'Maybe Oriana might like to buy one,' said Siena, gazing hopefully around my sparsely furnished sitting room. I stiffened. The last thing I wanted was one of Mary's homemade sprouting pots cluttering up my deliciously minimal flat and destroying its exclusive hotel ambience.

'Yes,' said Mary disapprovingly, glancing around. 'You need *something* to brighten the place up with. I know you're only renting but it's just like a hotel. I took a course in interior design once, I'd be happy to give you some advice if you're interested.' Mum and I exchanged looks. We'd had several long chats since I came back and I knew she found Mary as irritating as I did.

'I think Oriana's always wanted to live in a hotel. It's one of her little idiosyncracies,' explained Mum.

'Oh,' replied Mary. Her full mouth tightened. A brief, slightly uncomfortable silence followed.

'Anybody want anything else to eat?' I asked. I had gone to some trouble to concoct a brown rice and adzuki bean risotto. A bit of butter had slipped in but I wasn't admitting to it. I'd also prepared steamed seaweed with a toasted sesame seed dressing and a lightly cooked broccoli salad.

'Mmm, Oriana, it looks simply delicious,' said Mum, not

touching any of it and helping herself to a tomato from the vegetable rack.

'Ugh, Mummy, I don't know how you can bear to eat tomatoes, they're pure poison. You know the pinctatop rainforest Indians won't touch them,' Siena explained earnestly. Apparently tomatoes came from the deadly nightshade family and were forbidden, along with potatoes, aubergines and other totally poisonous vegetables.

'But I'm not a pinca-whatever Indian, am I?' said Mum. 'I don't live in a rainforest, I live in Abinger Hammer. It's very admirable being a principled eater, Siena, but I do hope you're feeding the children properly.'

Siena looked stony-faced and I took a deep breath, expecting An Incident. But thankfully Mary smoothed it over. 'Don't worry, Venetia. The children and I aren't fully macrobiotic, I make sure we have some dairy products and fish and chicken.' She smiled at Siena who visibly melted. 'Get me some of that nice risotto, would you, darling?' she asked, handing Siena her plate.

'I take the children out for a McDonald's every week,' she confided once Siena was out of earshot, 'and Jacob's become obsessed with chicken nuggets ever since he had some on a school trip. But we're living on borrowed time, one of the kids is bound to let the cat out of the bag soon. But not my lovely Jacob, you're far too clever, aren't you, my darling?' She kissed Jacob's curly head adoringly. I had to give her credit, she had my difficult sister right under her thumb and she obviously adored Jacob who quite patently adored her back.

Siena returned, looking earnest. 'Um, Oriana, it's the most delicious lunch, but it's really bad news to serve lots of different things with the same spoon. I couldn't help noticing that you'd served the adzuki beans with the same spoon you served the rice with. It's very unmacrobiotic.'

'Oh, I'm sorry,' I replied, calmly detached. Siena was becoming so loopy one couldn't be cross with her. She was too far gone for reasoning. It was like telling a carrot off for being orange not green. Mummy looked bemused and cut up her tomato.

'And how is the book going, darling?' she asked. 'Isn't it wonderful that Oriana is going to have a book published?'

'Yes, it's extraordinary when you consider how many cookery books there already are. You are clever to persuade them to publish yours, Oriana,' said Mary generously. 'I was thinking about writing a book about pottery but Siena's campaign persuaded me against the idea.' Siena had become heavily involved in a campaign to prevent people buying books and newspapers, to stop paper wastage. She reckoned that if people were really desperate they could read the news on the Internet, but only from solar-powered computers of course.

Mummy shuddered. I knew just what was going through her mind. The thought of being forcibly restrained from reading the *Daily Mail* every day was too horrible for either of us to contemplate. It was the only *Mail* in my life now anyway, if you'll excuse the pun. Since I had given up sex, tabloids and the occasional glass of champagne were my last few remaining pleasures.

'But they use paper from sustainable forests, don't they?' said my mother.

'Yes, it's not that so much, it's the amount of energy wasted in chopping down the trees, making the paper, the trucks used to transport it – it goes on and on.' Siena crumpled at the thought of it, the responsibility for the planet's imminent collapse resting heavily on her scrawny shoulders. We all sighed bleakly.

'Oh well,' I tried to lighten the mood, 'I'll probably only sell about three books anyway.'

'Oh darling, don't be ridiculous. I'll buy at least ten copies, and I'm sure your father will buy one.'

'Maybe,' I said doubtfully. I hadn't spoken to him for months.

'What's the print run going to be?' asked Mary efficiently.

'Um, what exactly d'you mean by print run?'

'The number of books they'll print first go,' Mary patiently explained.

'Gosh, I haven't a clue,' I replied, getting up to stack the lunch plates and feeling ridiculously ignorant. Print run! Of course I should know about things like that.

'I think we're going to have to make a move,' said Siena, gathering up some things and stuffing them into the back-pack. 'I'm protesting at the House of Commons this after-noon, it's going to be quite exciting.'

'That's nice, darling, what are you complaining about this time?' Mummy immediately pasted on an interested expression but I knew that she had had quite enough of the lot of us and was longing to go home and catch up on the *Buttonhook Times*, enjoy quality time with *The Archers* and her frightful cats.

'We're not complaining, Mum, we're *protesting* against Jack Reeves' appalling pro-motorist policy.'

'You know that he's trying to abolish road humps?' Mary was outraged. 'I can't believe that even a *man* can be so irresponsible as to put car suspension before kids' lives.'

'But they do give one such a shock if one isn't expecting them,' said Mummy mildly. 'Colonel Wiggins simply won't have them in the road. He says they upset his hernia.'

'Oh, Venetia! You're such a card!' laughed Mary. 'But we won't be joking if Jack Reeves gets elected as the party leader. You know they think he's got a good chance.'

'Really?' I brightened. 'Politics would be so much more interesting if he won. I know some of his ideas are a little, um, reactionary, but you have to admit he's incredibly attractive.'

'Ugh, Oriana!' grimaced Siena. 'How can you say that! The man's a snob, he obviously loves cars and hates children, he's utterly unprincipled and he's got far too much power, and he's always having affairs—'

'Yum, yum and double yum,' I interrupted irritatingly. I knew I'd live to regret it but I couldn't resist the opportunity to wind Siena up.

'Children, children! Please don't start, it'll end in tears,' my mother implored. 'Just agree to differ. I'm trying to rack my brains, but I'm sure he used to be a great chum of your father.'

'Huh. Surprise me,' said Siena grumpily. 'C'mon, gang. We're going to be late.'

Mary smiled. 'I'm sorry it's such a rushed visit. I'd love to chat for longer but I've simply got to get back to work. I'll have that pot you wanted ready by the weekend, Venetia. We're so looking forward to a few days in the country.'

'Yes, it'll be lovely,' said Mummy doubtfully, abandoning her tomato. 'Though I'm a bit muddled about your latest diet, Siena . . .'

'Oh, don't worry, Venetia, we'll give you a ring tomorrow and explain what we need. It's very simple.'

And then in a flurry of cheek kissing and affectionate goodbyes the three of them were gone. Mummy and I breathed a sigh of relief at their departure.

'I'm thrilled that Mary makes Siena so happy but I find her terribly bossy,' said Mummy as we stood at the window watching their chaotic procession across the street. 'Oh dear,' she added. 'I've got an awful feeling Siena's going to make them walk to the Tube. It's such a long way away and it's raining. I wish she'd let them take a taxi. I had hoped that once she'd got the Canaletto money she might become a little sensible.' The Canaletto had eventually been sold, raising a considerable sum that was to be held in trust, *for years*. But the interest was nice.

'D' you know what she's going to do with it?' I asked curiously.

'Well, I'm a bit worried about that.' She frowned. 'She says she's going to use it to privately educate Mary's children.'

'But they're communists. They don't believe in nice things like private education.'

'That's what I thought. But apparently the local schools are all full up. There is a comprehensive in West Hampstead but it's terrible and India is very bright, she really is. Mary wants her to go to Roedean because it's by the sea which she hopes will help her asthma.'

'I bet she does. Well, India deserves a good start, I haven't seen her for ages but she always seemed bright and helpful. And Siena would only give it to some environmental bomb manufacturing organization if left to her own devices, let's face it.'

'Yes. She is extraordinarily principled. I don't know where she gets it from. Have you had any ideas about what you're going to do with the money?'

In the light of my sister's munificence I decided not to mention the hugely expensive course of rejuvenating facials, the Jimmy Choo mules, and the six exquisite Anya Hindmarch handbags in different shades of pink that I had blown my month's income on in one delicious afternoon.

'Well, if the trustees would release some money,' I said hopefully, 'I thought when I've finished my book that I might go around the world.'

'What a lovely idea. That's the sort of thing you should be doing with it. Of course I admire what Siena's doing, but I'd love to see her do something nice for herself. But she won't listen to me unfortunately.'

'But if she's asking for a lump sum you have the right to refuse it, don't you?'

'Yes, but she's not asking for a lump sum, she's going to pay the school fees in instalments. It'll take up all her monthly allowance.' She sighed.

'Of course it must have been Mary's idea. She can twist Siena round her little finger. I wish I knew why she dislikes me so much. Maybe it's because I wear make-up,' I hazarded.

'Oh, Oriana, really! You're imagining it. I wish you

wouldn't be so sensitive. But I must admit she is very overbearing. Still, she makes Siena happy and that's the main thing. I wish you would find someone nice, darling. You're throwing away the best years of your life, it's not natural for you to be stuck in this empty little flat by yourself. When I was your age I'd been married and divorced and had two children.'

'But I haven't got time to have a social life. Finishing the book seems more important then everything else, I'm afraid.'

'Well, just because it's important to you doesn't mean it's important to everyone else,' retorted Mummy sharply. 'You must keep it in perspective. It's only a book, for heaven's sake.'

I winced and my stomach jolted at the sharpness in her voice, but I said nothing. I couldn't face another argument.

'Oh, I nearly forgot. Daddy rang me because he said he couldn't get in touch with you. He had some idea that you were in New Zealand.'

'Yes, I sent him a card from Switzerland saying I was going to stay in Auckland. I knew he'd be cross about the documentary so I thought I ought to pretend to be as far away as possible when it came out. But now they've apparently put it on the back burner indefinitely and I don't know when they'll show it.'

'Oh well, it's probably all for the best. It sounded a bit chaotic out there.' She sighed heavily and slipped into her Burberry mac. 'Oh dear, it's not that I don't want to see Siena and everybody, but I was so looking forward to a nice quiet weekend. I was going to take the cats to the beauty parlour to be washed but I won't get a chance now. And I'll have to hide all the cat food from Siena because I promised I was only going to buy those vegan Cat-O-Nuggets. I have tried to make them eat it, but they simply won't. Toffles will only eat goose, and I can't let him starve, can I?'

I knew from experience that Siena was a stringent weekend guest, insisting on a strict recycling policy. The latest flashpoint had been triggered over the discovery of an aluminium can in the kitchen bin instead of the recycling skip outside the back door. And it was only a matter of time before she discovered that Mummy still hadn't thrown away her mink coat but kept it secretly wrapped in mothballs in the garage.

After she had left, I sat down at my desk and switched on my computer. But I couldn't work. I thought about what Mummy had said. 'It's only a book.' How could she say such a thing? It wasn't just a book, it was *my* book, it meant everything to me, it was as much a part of me as my right arm. It was my last link with Chalet Tiara, and all that the place had meant to me.

I wondered why what she said so casually had the power to wound me quite so much. The more I thought about it, the more I ached with hurt. It was pathetic. I looked out of the window at the murky grey water rippling gently beneath my window. Normally it soothed me but tonight my body felt waterlogged with sadness. There seemed no division between the water in the river and the water in my eyes. I thought of the law of osmosis – the attraction of a large amount of a substance to a small amount of the same. In my dreamlike state of misery I imagined the river somehow drawn to the tears in my body, filling me up with so many sad grey rippling tears I thought I would burst with the weight of them.

I missed Chalet Tiara so much. It was like a constant dull ache. It was spring now. I wondered what the garden would look like. I imagined primroses poking their way up through the snow, the first buds appearing on the espalier growing up the walls of the chalet. The roar of the river, always the roar of sparkling water rushing towards its source, so many miles away.

Pushing my computer away I gave in to the waves of misery, rested my head on the table and cried.

* * *

The next day I felt hugely better. I must have lost several pounds in water during my paroxysms of weeping the night before and I was feeling emotionally and physically a lot more svelte.

I decided to ring Pandora, a.k.a. Lady Chatterley, for advice on the 'it's only a book' conversation. Her mother was even trickier than mine but it didn't seem to bother her quite so much.

Pandora had a different take on the subject. 'She's probably a bit jealous. I mean look at you, you're beautiful, you're in control – well, sometimes anyway – and you've been offered a jammy deal with the country's biggest publishers. I mean, d'you know how difficult it is to get a book published? People write for years and don't get anywhere. It breaks their hearts. I think our mothers were the last generation that didn't have proper careers and then, whoosh, the world changes and women are all setting up businesses, becoming astronauts, prime ministers. They stay at home, do what they're told, and quite suddenly they realize they've got these talented daughters who are doing incredible things with their lives. It must rub it in a bit.'

'I see what you mean. The comparison between our lives and theirs must just highlight any frustrations. But then again, my mother's never been ambitious, she's as happy as a clam logging her buttonhook collection and looking after her dreadful goose-eating cats.'

'If you think about it, we expect an awful lot from our families, no other species has to put up with their offspring forever. It's only when it comes to humans that it becomes this life sentence thing.'

'So how's your mum? Is she married at the moment?'

'Don't think so. She rang me from Acapulco two months ago saying she was thinking about it, but when I rang her last week she'd disappeared and left no forwarding number. The trail's rather gone cold, I'm afraid.'

'But don't you worry that you can't get hold of her?'

'Oh, I could if I really tried,' said Pandora casually. 'But she's a very rich lady who has a lovely life jetting about and she's just not very interested in family stuff. No, I just accept it the way it is. I'm very close to my father and my step-mother Davina and I've got lots of friends, so I'm very lucky really.'

'I wish I got on better with Siena. Just after she had Jacob we started becoming quite close, but we just irritate each other these days. It's probably too much to expect one's family to be one's best friends.'

'They've given that a name, hang on, I was just reading about it.' I heard her rustle through the paper. 'Here we are. "Singletons have identified a new social phenonomon known as Friends syndrome, named after the hit series, in which real family members are portrayed as difficult intruders".'

I thought of my family's recent visit and shuddered. 'That's bang on. I see my family as difficult intruders. Isn't that awful? Now I've finished *Chalet Girl Secrets* perhaps I'll concentrate on improving my relationships.' I had finally handed in the finished draft and was waiting on tenterhooks.

'Has Claire Coquette been in touch?'

'Yes. She rang a few days ago, but she's being sent to Australia to track down a Spice Girl who is thinking of writing her memoirs. She's been promoted to roving editor, which basically means she travels around signing people up which is the perfect job for her really. I've got a new editor now who's reading it at the moment. She's had it for two days now, she can't like it much.'

'I wouldn't worry. They've got so many manuscripts to get through. It doesn't mean anything.'

'Yeah, I guess you're right. It was odd, while I was writing it I spent the whole time tempting myself with all the lovely things I was going to do when I'd finished it, and now I really have, there just seems to be this big aching void in my life, which is filling up with emotional trauma. I'm sorry to be so boring. Will you distract me with a Lady Chatterley update?'

'That's rather fizzled out, I'm afraid. He kept getting numb from having to stand still for hours while I tried to paint him. We had a bit of a row about it.'

'So no more *droit de la dame* for the moment then?'

'No, I'm not cut out for the sticks. I'm thinking about returning to the big smoke and buying a new flat to do up.'

'Well, if you felt like it you could take this place on when I go away. I'm just about to book my round the world trip and I'll be gone about two months. That'd give you time to find a place to buy.'

'What a great idea, rooms upstairs from the Ritzy Marina Club. When did you say you were leaving?'

The conversation galvanized me into immediate action and I set to work arranging my trip, booking a thrilling itinerary that began in Boston. From there I planned to go to Nantucket. I know it sounds a bit flaky, but Ally had rekindled my curiosity about what the gypsy had said, and I had a strong urge to go there. After that I planned to go to Toronto, Vancouver and Hawaii. From there I would go to New Zealand. Having used it as an imaginary bolt hole when things got too tough to handle at home I thought it might be useful to check the place out first hand for future authenticity. I planned to do a whistle-stop tour of the country, Japanese tourist style, in ten days. From there I would fly to Sydney, Perth, Jo'burg and then home.

One week later I was sitting on the first-class nonstop flight to Boston, New England. I was off to see the world!

Chapter Twenty-seven

'You mean to say you didn't take any photographs of any of those lovely places?' said Arabella disapprovingly two months later as I cracked open one of the bottles of champagne she and Pandora had brought round to my flat to toast my return. We were having a chalet girl reunion to celebrate the eventual scheduling of the *Chalet Girl* documentary, which was to be screened later that evening.

'I've got a nice postcard of Nantucket somewhere.' I rummaged around my handbag unsuccessfully. 'Damn, where on earth did I put it?'

'Talk about a stroke of luck,' said Pandora. 'There's nothing worse than other people's boring holiday snaps.' She took a sip of champagne. 'Not that yours would be at all boring, Oriana,' she added hastily.

'Well, I'm not much of a snapper,' I explained to Arabella. 'And I'm not very good at sightseeing. I spent most of the time in supermarkets and bookshops.'

I thought of the wonderful American bookshops that combined acres of books with delicious cappuccino refuelling stations and sighed. I tried to change the subject from my cultural hopelessness.

'Gosh, it's unbelievably good to be back home.' I looked around my Spartan flat cheerfully. It was a relief to find that although Pandora had stayed here for a month before finding her new flat, she had left absolutely no imprint on it whatsoever. It still retained its characterless hotel ambience, and I felt right at home.

'Did you get to see the Metropolitan and the Frink?' she persevered.

'Um, no, I didn't.'

'Well, you must have got to the Museum of Fine Art in Boston?'

'Um, no,' I said sheepishly. 'I was a bit pushed for time in Boston.'

'But you said you were there for a week.'

'Ten days actually. But I was too busy to go and look at pictures. There was a huge bookshop next to my hotel that did great coffee. But I did get to the Kennedy Museum three times. I couldn't resist getting you this, Pandora.' I handed her a mug with BACK JACK! with a grinning picture of Jack Kennedy on it.

'Nice mug. Shame about the name.'

'I take it things are definitely off between you and Jack then?'

She was prevented from giving what would no doubt have been a very complex explanation by the doorbell.

Ambrosia and Rochetta were flapping newspapers through the letterbox, ringing the bell and knocking on the door in their impatience to come in. 'It's us! We're here! The previews are awful.'

I opened the door and they practically fell on top of me.

'Oriana! Long time no see,' cried Rochetta, wearing an elastoplast of a skirt stretched across her slim thighs which she had teemed with strappy black sandals. 'You're looking gorgeous. And your hair's really grown.'

'It suits you,' added Ambrosia, kissing me affectionately. 'But why aren't you brown? I thought you'd just flown in from Sydney? Didn't you get to Bondi Beach?'

'Of course!' I lied blithely. 'But I've promised everyone not to bore you about my trip.' Oh dear. I was going to have to buy some travel books and swot up on all the sights I should have seen, before the travel police arrested me. 'Anyway, come and have a drink. Arabella and Pandora are here brimming with news, far more interesting than listening to me droning on about my boring old trip.'

'But we're longing to hear about it. How was New Zealand? I've always wanted to go there.'

I grimaced. New Zealand had been a low point of my trip. Sheep, sheep and more sheep interspersed by endless suburbs that went on forever. Maybe it was payback for using the place as an imaginary bolt hole to get away from my father's wrath.

'I had a wonderful time when I went to New Zealand,' mused Arabella, winding a long tendril of blonde hair around her finger. 'So unspoiled. It's just how I imagine England used to be.'

I smiled vaguely and busied myself emptying my home-made kettle chips onto a plate. I had made a huge *crème brûlée* as I knew anything savoury would just get chucked, but at least the chips would raise the nutritional content of the meal.

The truth was I had spent most of the time earmarked for New Zealand in Nantucket. Unfortunately I hadn't met the building tycoon that the gypsy had predicted but had completely fallen in love with the wild, windswept beaches, silvery grey clapboard houses and cranberry fields. As a result I had only had three days in New Zealand, which I spent entirely on a bus with sixty Japanese tourists.

'How's Tony?' I inquired. Bella had sneaked off to Las Vegas soon after returning from Gstaad and married Tony Louche in a clandestine ceremony with a leopard as their only witness.

'Oh, all right. Tony like,' said Bella indifferently, brushing a kettle chip crumb off her ankle length Mulberry coloured velvet skirt. 'Mummy adores him, of course.'

'So does mine,' agreed Rochetta.

'Mine's got all his records,' said Pandora.

'Shall we start with pudding?' I asked, proffering the quivering *brûlée*.

'Yes, I think so,' said Pandora. 'You know, I've been doing headstands every day for a month since someone told me that it stimulates your metabolism by thirty per cent. If I keep my calorific intake the same I've calculated that in three weeks I'll have disappeared altogether.'

'Rairely?' inquired Ambrosia.

'No, quite often actually,' replied Pandora. 'Ha, ha. Oh, I've missed saying that. Shall I show you how to do one?'

'Oh, yes please,' said Ambrosia eagerly.

'We just need a blank wall.' She glanced around. 'That's not too difficult to find. God, Oriana, d'you have a real flat where you actually live? I mean where do you keep your *stuff*?'

'Just chucked it out,' I drawled. I was enjoying my reputation as a free-spirited culturally-challenged hotel-obsessed person.

'Object found in Oriana's flat SHOCK,' mumbled Pandora from an inverted position. She came down flexibly. 'See, it's easy. I'll help you up.' It took some shifting but Ambrosia (she wasn't named after rice pudding for nothing) was soon backed up against the wall, her substantial bosom and large thighs straining against her too tight black jeans and black silk shirt.

'Is Ally coming?' asked Rochetta.

'Um, I didn't ask her,' I admitted.

'Why not? You two were such chums.'

'She just got so funny when you'd all left. Said some really bitchy things about the book. She rings me up every now and then but I just don't want to know.' Ally had indeed rung recently and inquired kindly after *Chalet Girl Secrets*. When I'd revealed excitedly that I was to be featured on the cover, there had been a brief silence before she had spluttered, 'What, couldn't they fork out for a professional model then? They can't think much of the book.' That had been the final straw and I had resolved never to speak to her again.

'Oh, that's a shame. I liked Ally. I wonder if she ever

finished her avalanche book,' mused Rochetta.

'An enemy is only a friend you haven't upset yet,' said Ambrosia profoundly as she stood on her head.

I glanced at my watch. 'Ladies. Ladies!' No one could hear above the din. It was unbelievable how much noise five sensible women could make. At that moment a long-suffering neighbour jumped desperately on the ceiling, causing the *crème brûlée* to quiver alarmingly.

'The documentary's starting now.' I cracked the toffee top and ladled out the pudding. I was feeling terribly apprehensive. What on earth would the public make of us all? Eight weeks in a ski resort and most of us couldn't ski, only two of us could cook and three punters had died from food poisoning. I shouldn't think anyone would ever stay in a chalet again.

The intro was great. Lots of exciting footage of swish skiers skiing down mogul fields at great speed and jumping off cliffs in time to the *Hawaii Five-0* theme tune. There was no footage of them landing, but times were hard and ski bums would do anything for money. I just hoped they had been paid beforehand.

Then the music stopped and there was some footage of a large girl wearing a Jolly Holidays anorak trying to snowplough down what appeared to be a completely flat slope. I peered closely. God, it was Ambrosia. How embarrassing.

'Get me down, please! I'm stuck,' cried Ambrosia desperately, still stacked up against the wall. 'I want to see myself the right way up!'

I helped her down, blocking out as much of the TV as possible. It was too awful that they had been allowed to film practically wherever they wanted. Who knew what frightful footage they had picked up with their hidden cameras? I shivered and settled deeper into the sofa.

'Chalet girl Arabella Ormsby-Spore, daughter of leading high court judge Lord Humphrey Ormsby-Spore of Specklefield, and sixth wife of Tony "the toupee" Louche, who had a string of hits in the fifties with his band, the Louche Limpets . . .'

'Yes, yes, get *on* with it,' muttered Bella impatiently.

'. . . is making the most of her first season as a chalet girl in the exclusive ski resort of Gstaad in Switzerland,' droned the voice as Bella and Tony were filmed swanning around in Tony's Lamborgini. 'And chalet girl Rochetta is feeling a little fragile this morning as she had rather a late night last night.' Terrifying footage followed of Rochetta collapsed, dead drunk on the railway line at 4 a.m., her face obscured by clouds of dark hair, and being scooped up by a stony-faced Swiss official. 'It is reassuring to know that the daughters of empire are as robust as ever,' the voiceover intoned dryly. 'However it's only reasonable to expect these high-spirited gels to let off steam after a hard day's cooking.' Flash to Rochetta hurriedly shoving a frozen pizza into the microwave.

Then there was a clip of Bella completely pissed after too much *glühwein* at the Jolly Holidays cocktail party, throwing some raw liver into the Magimix and switching it on without the lid on, spewing brown liquid all around the kitchen and collapsing with laughter. There followed several clips of disgruntled punters complaining about hygiene and inedible food. 'No one was particularly surprised when three guests died of food poisoning on their second day,' intoned the voiceover pompously. There followed some gripping footage of the contents of three fridges groaning unhygienically with heaving plates of leftovers waiting to be Magimixed into soup. Then a flash to the food poisoning summit in Chalet Tiara where we had discussed the recent deaths.

'It wasn't our fault,' Arabella was saying. 'They obviously had a weak constitution. I mean we can't be blamed every time someone eats a French egg and dies in our chalets. It's ridiculous.'

'They must have been secretly recording us from the bushes outside the window,' spluttered Pandora.

'Yes, remember those vagrants running off? They were obviously Mule and Tim's stooges!' I said.

'The rotters,' mumbled Ambrosia through a mouthful of *brûlée*. 'Absolute stinking rotters.'

We nodded in vociferous agreement as the subject was changed pointedly. 'Intrigue and romance are rife in Gstaad, the resort that never sleeps,' droned the voice portentously. There followed several excruciating minutes of the Bolter snogging an anonymous man wearing an anorak outside a nightclub. You could see tongues and everything. 'It's not fair! They *promised* they'd cut that bit. I bribed them with three weeks' wages!'

'What, you gave them twenty quid?' asked Pandora incredulously.

Rochetta was pink with embarrassment.

But things got worse. We all sat transfixed watching an aerial shot of a bubble car swaying dangerously in a row of stationary bubble cars.

'Oh God . . . which one of us did they catch . . .' Pandora murmured, hardly daring to breathe.

The voice continued, 'Gstaad is known for its high winds, but it is not always wind that makes the resort's bubble cars shake so alarmingly.' Ambrosia and her ski instructor emerged, red-faced and giggling, from the bubble car.

'Oh God,' muttered Ambrosia, setting aside her plate. 'This is *so* embarrassing.'

Joy! A flash to the front of Chalet Tiara, looking wonderfully festive, its windows all lit up and snow banked up against its walls. Then horrors! There was the awful picture of me with my bottom sticking out of the industrial-sized oven covered with nothing but a J-Cloth. It was too awful.

'Chalet girl Oriana, part-time model and society saucepot, is no stranger to ovens as we can see from this exciting picture, but this week she is having a hard time fending off the attentions of the high-spirited lads on an all-expenses-paid trip from Merill Lynch. They've laid a bet on who can get gorgeous Oriana into bed first!'

I cringed. 'That's a lie, none of them were interested in—'

'Shhh.'

'However, help is at hand in the presence of Ernst, German car parts tycoon and owner of Chalet Tiara who has taken a shine to Oriana and who has taken it upon himself to defend her honour!'

'Ahhhh!' I murmured, transfixed. Ernst, looking utterly, gorgeously brutal, was picking up Crispin by the scruff of his neck and slamming him on the table.

'Oriana, you never said he was bald,' said Rochetta bluntly.

'He looks like a bit of a thug,' added Bella. 'Not how you described him at all. I'd say you were better off without him.'

'He's not bald,' I said defensively. 'It's the camera angle.' Thank *God* Ernst had left it at that. Crispin was so thin and enfeebled looking with alcohol it wouldn't have taken much to finish him off completely. Another death would have been just too much.

The documentary continued in this chaotic vein for a bit longer and then ended terrifyingly with an interview in each of our chalets where we had discussed our hopes and dreams for the future.

Ambrosia and Bella said they wanted to marry merchant bankers, live in Gloucestershire and have six children. The Bolter broke the mould and said that she wanted to become a beauty queen and help children. Pandora said she wanted to become a marine biologist and write a book about sea horses, but maybe she'd be an air hostess first, but only in first class.

There was quite a nice shot of me making flowerpot bread and then they had filmed me at my big kitchen table writing up recipes and saying that I was writing a chalet girl diary based on my experiences which I was desperately hoping to get published. When I'd done that, I continued, I hoped to settle down with a man from Nantucket with a seawater swimming pool and devote myself to protecting whales. I'd said that as a joke but it didn't sound very joke like. How embarrassing! It was terribly odd to have one's life, hopes and dreams exposed on national television.

'Thank God that's over,' sighed Pandora, refilling our glasses. 'It's been hanging over me like a sword of Damocles for months.'

'We'll never work again,' sighed Arabella.

'Look on the bright side. We'll be able to spend more time with our families,' said Ambrosia.

'Yes, but will they want to spend more time with us?' I asked.

'You know they said those punters died a slow, lingering death at Montreux hospital. How do we know they actually died? Maybe they just pretended?' In desperation Arabella was clutching at straws. A tear trickled down her cheek. I hugged her affectionately. 'I mean, if they'd seen how beastly they were. I mean, I'm not saying they actually *deserved* to die, but if you ask for packed lunches every day for a *week*, what can you expect?'

'Remember how they ate all the mini Mars Bars and didn't make their beds? Showed very poor form, if you ask me.'

'Disgusting,' added Arabella.

'Outrageous!' said Pandora.

'But the whole family were completely wiped out. They were the last Grouts in the whole of Camberley,' I reminded us sensibly.

This cast rather a dampener on the remainder of the evening and after a desultory damage limitation session during which we came to no new conclusions except that if we hadn't finished the Grouts off someone else probably would have, they sloped off into the night.

Chapter Twenty-eight

We were wrong to think that the public would be satiated after the first media fest in Gstaad. The *Chalet Girls* documentary rekindled interest and the papers couldn't resist the combination of a group of well-connected good-looking girls, sex 'n' skiing, plus the poisoning angle with its delicious Catherine of Medici undertones.

I was woken up early the following morning by an excitable Rochetta. 'Oriana, we're in all the papers, My brother says we're going to be more famous than the Spice Girls! It's simply *too* awful.'

'But we can't sing!'

'Who cares!'

I quickly got dressed and dashed out to the newsagent. The *Daily Mail* had devoted its centre spread to us, praising our spirit and fortitude under punter fire. The right-wing papers were supportive while the left-wing ones were predictably vitriolic. Emma Batt, writing in *The Tit*, had laid into us with spiteful venom. 'Poisoned punters deserved to die, say posh cooks in Swiss resort,' she had written. I rolled my eyes. The television reviews were uniformly bad. The *Guardian* (Emma Batt again! Talk about jackdaw of all trades): 'Grippingly bad, frighteningly watchable. The Sloane Ranger, hoped to be a dying species, was revealed last night in all its glory. Still unable to cook, ski or do anything remotely useful, the species is as arrogant as ever. Oriana Spicer, daughter of tycoon Bill Spicer, and ex-girlfriend of staggeringly wealthy Lord Peregrine Skye-Rocca, is typical.

"I'm writing a novel cum fish-friendly cookery book based on my experiences." With Daddy's money bankrolling his confident little darling's latest interest, and happy to exploit her ex-boyfriend's connections, we predict she will avoid the humiliation of the slush pile that is the sad lot of most real writers.'

I cringed, bracing myself for calls of outrage from my family. When the phone went again I jumped. But it was Annette, Red Duck's publicity honcho. This was very thrilling. I'd been trying to contact her since I returned from my trip to discuss my exciting plans for *Chalet Girl Secrets*, but she had always been in a meeting. While she was 'in a meeting' I had been dealing with sixteen-year-old Emily on work experience, who was charming but inexperienced. But now the meeting had finally finished and the *main man* was returning my call! I steadied myself against the wall and gripped the receiver tightly.

'Congratulations, Oriana. We're all thrilled about last night's documentary, it couldn't have come at a better time. Well done!'

'But the reviews are terrible. All that stuff about me being a daft Sloane Ranger only getting the contract because I dated Lord Skye-Rocca and because my father is a waste-paper tub tycoon.'

There was a short silence. Then she laughed nervously. Rather worryingly she didn't reassure me that I had got the contract on my abilities as a writer rather than my exciting social and family connections. I saved up this nugget of worry to fret over later.

'Don't knock it,' she said. 'All of that stuff will really hook the press interest. I managed to get hold of that fun picture of you in the oven to send out with the proofs.'

'Oh no! You can't! I've been trying to get away from that picture for years.' I had a vision of the J-Cloth reccurring lifetime after lifetime, in different parts of the world, the solar system – forever and ever. There would be no escape.

'Please, let's throw it away. I've got much nicer pictures than that. With me and Lord Skye-Rocca at parties from the back of *Tatler*,' I suggested hopefully.

'Oh dear. It's too late now. They've all been sent out. I know it seems a bit vulgar but it will *guarantee* coverage in the tabloids. Have you any idea how many books come out every day? There are acres and acres of print being reeled out, most of which sink without trace. I really sense we're on a roll with this.'

My spirits rose. She was going to take off sixteen-year-old Emily on work experience and give the book her whole attention, *yes*!

'So I've informed Emily that I want to be kept in touch with events so I can guide her.' She's just failed all her GCSEs and she's feeling a bit low. This is her first big job, and I'm really hoping it will give her some much needed confidence.'

My heart sank again. I had a real opportunity to make a splash with this. I *needed* publicity. The thought of all that hard work sinking under shovel loads of other people's books, well, it was enough to make me weep.

I thought long and hard. I had put my life into this book. If I was lucky, it stood to do very well. It had all the ingredients. It had had a good start, now I needed someone to give it a proper shove.

There was no alternative. I would have to call in Petronella at Shmooze Associates. Picking up the phone gingerly I dialled the number. A very grand-sounding person answered the phone and I took a deep breath and explained who I was. The grand voice immediately defrosted, and to my surprise I was put straight through to Petronella.

'Of course I remember you,' she said at breakneck speed. 'You were the gorgeous green-eyed blonde who had all those stunning parties at Cheyne Castle and broke Peregrine Skye-Rocca's heart. My sister's nephew's ex-girlfriend was mad about him. They went out a few times last year but things just fizzled out. Such a shame. He's probably still nuts about you if he's got any sense.'

I was utterly disarmed. I hadn't expected her to be so friendly; after all, she had a terrifying reputation. 'Oh, you're very k-k-kind,' I stuttered. 'You see, I was sort of wondering if you were taking on any more clients at the moment because I've got a book coming out soon and I really need to get some publicity for it. I was asking who the best person was in the business and your name came up every time.'

'Oh, that's nice to know,' she said graciously. 'Well, why don't you drop into the offices this afternoon and we'll have a chat? Would three o'clock be okay? Bring a copy of your book and your press clippings and we'll go from there!' She thought so quickly and spoke so fast that it was quite hard to keep up with her but I was thrilled that she was interested in taking me on. With Petronella on my side the sky was the limit. Roll on 3 p.m.!

Petronella's offices occupied the penthouse of a stunning white stuccoed house in an exclusive Chelsea square. Elegant vanilla babes who looked as if their names all ended in something designed by Gucci were flittering around like emaciated butterflies. They were all wearing black and seemed forbiddingly soignée. I had stopped wearing black years ago when I was told that it acted like a wall around the wearer and severely reduced exciting social interactions.

Today I stood out in a bright red suit. Roberto had insisted that because of my dangerous Martha Stewart hermit-girl tendencies I must start wearing as much red as possible. Brown was forbidden. 'Only monks wear brown!' he had cried feverishly. It was a shame, I really liked brown.

One of the assistants showed me into Petronella's office. The walls were studded with trophies, awards and hundreds of pictures of Petronella schmoozing with celebrity chums. I felt very intimidated, despite my bright red suit. After ten minutes Petronella steamed in on spiky heels. Even with heels she was much shorter than I'd imagined, barely over five foot, barking instructions alternately to a minion carrying a pad and into a mobile phone. She had black shiny hair, pulled back off her face in a chignon, and very light blue eyes framed by skinny arched eyebrows. Her pale face was enlivened by a streak of expertly applied bright red lipstick while her chic black suit encased a slim but oddly muscular body. I'd read somewhere that she was a devotee of spinning, a form of aerobics so exclusive you had to go to New York to do it. Perfectly manicured nails (rouge noir, I guessed) gave her the appearance of a beautifully groomed bird of prey. She stretched her mouth at me and raised her eyes in amused exasperation.

'Get us two Chai Mai lattes, would you, darling?' she told her assistant between barking into her phone. 'Phew. It's been a chaotic day. We're organizing the *Divorce Guide to Spirituality* book launch for tomorrow night, the whole thing's been an absolute nightmare. But I'm thrilled to hear about your book. I take it you need some help getting the papers interested? That shouldn't be too difficult with your contacts. So when are you planning the launch?'

'In a month. Here's the list of people the publishers have invited.'

Petronella skimmed it and frowned. 'But darling, I don't know any of them! Who are all these people? The books page editor of the *Newcastle Echo*? Puhleese.'

'And this is my list.' I handed over a much smaller one. I had scoured my address book for useful people, Peregrine and lots of his ache-makingly glamorous recusant crowd, plus some very distant grand relatives that I hadn't seen for years and other names that I'd picked out of a hat to impress Petronella.

She whistled appreciatively. 'Now this is more like it.' She sat up and fixed her immaculately made-up icy blue eyes on me. 'Now, Oriana. I don't take on just anybody. Tiffany Strumpet has been ringing me for weeks and she's *desperate* for me to manage her, but I've turned her down.' Tiffany was a glamorous glossy brunette, famous for her vast collection of lurex outfits, who wrote a column in *The Snoop!* about her marathon shopping exploits. 'But you would be an asset to Shmooze Associates, Oriana. You have class and you're a writer. We can market you as an It girl writer! It's a dazzling new concept!' Presumably most It girls couldn't read, let alone write. I smiled happily, hoping that as a dazzling new concept I wouldn't be charged too much money.

I was wrong. Petronella outlined her terms which were also fairly dazzling. I blanched. 'Um, I don't know if I can quite stretch to that kind of money on a regular basis.'

'Can't you just ask Daddy?'

'My father has very strong principles and is very keen that my sister and I fend for ourselves.' I smiled apologetically.

Petrol looked bewildered. 'How amusing. I know it sounds a lot,' she steamrollered on, 'but we'll get lots of press interest, all my clients will come, Nigel Dempster, William Hickey, the *Standard* – but they'll want a good story. What's the news between you and Peregrine these days? They'll want to know all about that.'

'Um, I haven't spoken to him for ages.'

'Well, he's your trump card. I heard that he's just returned from holiday with Lord Rococo and all the royals. Now, if we could get them to come to your book launch, or,' she thought for a split second, 'could you swing it so that we have the book launch at Cheyne Castle? That would *guarantee* huge amounts of press interest. He's got that famous art collection, hasn't he?'

'Yes, he has the largest collection of all-white pictures in England. It's even bigger than the Saatchi collection, and that's saying—'

'Yes, yes,' interrupted Petrol impatiently. 'Ideally, I think you should be romantically involved to maximize press interest. Can you start going out with him again?'

'Um, well, I shouldn't think he's still interested after all this time,' I hedged. Go out with Peregrine again? He was still fond of me, I knew that. And I was so tired of being single, facing life's battles alone. Maybe it was an idea.

The phone interrupted us.

'Oh, hi, Richard! Yes, we're all coming. Of course Anoushka will turn up! OK, OK, 'bye!' She replaced the receiver, looking harassed. 'Are you going to Richard's launch?'

'Um, Richard . . . ?' I groped, feeling foolish.

'You're obviously not if you have to ask. Richard Branson is having a launch party at Nobos. Everyone's going.' Oh dear, everyone except me. 'You see, these are the sort of things you should be going to. You've got to get out and about, sell yourself.'

I smiled amenably. It sounded exhausting. 'Yes. I've got a bit out of touch since I came back from Switzerland, hiding behind my computer, I'm afraid. I'm more of a herm-It girl!' My feeble joke was interrupted by the phone.

'No! You can't fly to New York tonight, I've promised Richard *you will be there*!' She slammed the receiver down. 'Anyway,' she continued calmly, flicking through my press cuttings, 'the best way to get press attention for your book is to get back together with Peregrine.' I grimaced. 'I thought you liked him?' she asked impatiently.

'Yes, I do, he's a great friend, we're very fond of each other but . . .' I could sense Petronella's interest in me waning if I didn't pull this particular plum.

She tapped her fingers on the table impatiently. 'You ended it, right?'

'Yes,' I said doubtfully.

'Well, I've got a hunch that he'd give it another go tomorrow if you just said the word. If I got my girlfriend's sister to put a quiet word in his ear that you were pining for him and that you really regretted splitting up . . . hmm, leave it with me.' She smiled mysteriously. 'It would be the book launch of the year, Oriana. Trust me. We're not talking about warm Chardonnay and smoked salmon pinwheels here.'

I thought of our feasts at Cheyne Castle and smiled nostalgically.

'After our chat on the phone I got one of the girls to do some checking,' she continued, glancing down at a scribbled note. 'I've got written down here that your father is Bill Spicer, wastepaper tub tycoon, and your mother is the ex-sixties model Venetia Mowbray who is a relative of Lord Douche of the Douche sausage skinning empire.'

Petrol had been very thorough in her research, that was for sure.

'Yes, sausage skins and wastepaper tubs,' I said. 'Not very glamorous, I'm afraid.'

'Where there's muck there's brass,' Petrol laughed hopefully. 'Now, what I suggest is that we concoct a little press release with a glam picture of you on it, a brief description of the book – did you say it was quite autobiographical?'

'Um, not really. I mean it's about being a chalet girl which I was—' The phone interrupted us again.

'What d'you mean Corianda Angelica won't talk to *Divorce* on principle? She has no goddamn principles! Who does she think she is? The goddamn Pope! SORT IT! For Christ's sake, IT'S YOUR JOB!' She slammed down the receiver and smiled at me calmly. 'I've just started meditating. You should try it, Oriana. It's working wonders for me, I can't tell you.' She took a deep breath before continuing. 'So your book is autobiographical, isn't it? I think that's a real selling feature. Glam It girl author writes book about her aristo friends and family—'

'Actually it's more about chalet girl Tabitha's love affair with Chalet Tiara and her unrequited love for a Dutch (clever huh!) terracotta tile tycoon who owns the chalet,' I explained.

'Oh, Oriana, that's very tactful of you, but all the papers seem to think it's a *roman à clef*!' Petrol stretched her glossy red mouth and gave a high-pitched tinkly laugh. 'This is going to be easy, it's the sort of thing Shmooze does so well. I'll get onto the Maharanee straightaway.' The Maharanee was a wealthy Indian princess who had recently bought *Divorce!* magazine. 'She's a *great* chum of mine. I know she'd love to give you a big feature. Of course *Harper's*, *Tatler*, *Cosmo* would all be interested, I'm sure, in doing features. We're in constant contact with *This Morning* – Shmooze has contacts with all the major news and TV channels. Because of our impressive celebrity client list, they ring us, not the other way round. If Nigel's short of a story he'll ring and we'll tell him about Anoushka's latest boyfriend or whatever – you get the picture.'

'Yes. Yes, I do,' I replied enthusiastically.

'We're talking blanket media coverage. We'll get you so much puff everyone in the country will have heard of *Chalet Girl Secrets*. Such a sexy title. I'm sure it's very raunchy.'

'Actually, it's not,' I admitted honestly. I wasn't very good at writing about sex, and to be honest, chalet girl Tabitha hadn't got any action at all really.

'I'm thrilled you've come to us, Oriana,' Petronella motored on. 'I want to get on with this straightaway, we haven't a moment to lose. Shmooze can make you famous, Oriana. Are you ready to become a celebrity?'

If I had said no then and there I would have saved myself a whole pile of hassle. But consumed with ego and desire for recognition and success, I put myself willingly into Petronella's experienced hands. I was ready to play the game.

Chapter Twenty-nine

Petrol was as good as her word. The next day my fax whirred out an impressive list of social engagements that she insisted I attend in the run-up to the launch. She'd also included a mouth-watering list of celebs whose attendance she could guarantee if the party was held at Cheyne Castle.

'Please confirm venue!!!!!!!' the fax had ended. 'Time is of the essence!!!!!!!!!'

Petrol was right. Cheyne Castle would provide the perfect venue for the launch, but how could I swing it with Peregrine? If we'd still been going out it would have been the simplest thing in the world to arrange, but as it was, we hadn't seen each other for several months, although we still spoke on the phone occasionally. I cursed myself. Why on earth had I left things so late? Thank goodness I had taken Petrol on board; better late than never, I supposed.

I decided to ring Pandora and see if there was any chance of borrowing the Paddington Palace from her ex-boyfriend, Jeremy. He and his father, a sinister but nonetheless hospitable ex-general of an unspecified country had happily lent her the Paddington Palace, their louche private mansion, for a recent party. Champagne and Bloody Marys had flowed all night, and misshapen black orchids had been flown in from Columbia to provide authentically sinister flower arrangements. It had been quite an evening.

'Of course, the Paddington Palace would be the perfect place for the party,' Pandora agreed, pausing for a moment. 'I'll ring Jeremy straightaway, I'll tell him lots of It girls will come. He'll be thrilled. But what about Cheyne Castle? Why don't you ask Peregrine?'

'I suppose I could,' I said doubtfully. 'I went to see Petronella today and she was keen to hold it there. She's going to get a friend to tell Peregrine I'm still mad about him so that he'll resuscitate our romance and host the party for me.'

'That's a good idea,' said Pandora. 'You should get back together with him to coincide with the launch. It'd be doing you both a favour.'

'Don't you think it's kind of immoral to use him like that, though?'

'No. People go out with each other for all sorts of crazy reasons – because they're rich, good-looking, they've got nice legs, or fun friends. You get on with Peregrine, he gets on well with you. You like his house, he gets a pretty girl on his arm. I'd leave it up to Petronella and see what happens.'

I didn't really feel comfortable about the intrigue, it sounded a bit Machiavellian, but my nervousness about the launch was overriding my better feelings. I decided to let Pandora put the plan into action and just wait and see. I couldn't do anything tomorrow because I was going to Wales for the day to see my father's latest factory. He hadn't seen a copy of my book yet, and I was very excited about showing it to him for the first time.

The train pulled into Llandudno at midday and I rushed outside to meet Dad's ten-year-old Jaguar. I couldn't understand why he didn't replace it with this year's model but I'd just been reading a book called *The Truth About Millionaires* which I'd bought at Paddington, and apparently not buying new cars was perfectly normal tycoon type behaviour.

'Millionaires wouldn't become millionaires if they chucked their money away for the sake of it,' he had always said. 'This is a good motor. If I look after it, it'll see me out.' It probably would, it was in immaculate condition and still smelt luxuriously of polished walnut and leather.

Despite Dad's unhealthy regime of canteen food, no exercise and overwork, he looked surprisingly well. His dark hair was imperceptibly greyer around the temples, but his blue eyes still gleamed with shrewd energy, and his heavyset physique gave off a reassuring robustness.

No matter how much money he now had, a part of him still thought he was a small boy, sharing one room with his mother and three brothers. However much money he made, he never felt rich. It was a shame really.

'I bought you this. It's quite interesting. It explains why millionaires don't buy new cars.' I handed over the book, crossing my fingers that it would distract him from mentioning the *Chalet Girl* documentary.

He glanced at it noncommittally. 'Thanks. I'll enjoy reading that. Now what about this documentary you were in?'

'Um, what about it?' I hedged.

'I've never seen such a bunch of useless prats in my life. And why did they drag that awful picture of you up again?'

'I don't know. You said you were going to get your lawyer to get the copyright back . . .' I trailed off hopefully. It still wasn't too late.

'Did I? Well, it's too late now. Would you like some chocolate?' He proffered some Bournville. I shook my head. I'd hoped he might take me to lunch, but it looked as if this was going to be it. I wondered if I should suggest having lunch out, but glancing at his determined square jaw decided against it. I made a determined effort not to be disappointed.

'Well, here we are.' He stopped briefly at some electronic gates, which lifted to admit us. The operator nodded his head respectfully as we swung through and drove slowly round the massive factory.

'What do you think of it?' he asked proudly.

'It's, um, huge. And all these lorries. Gosh.' We drove past a fleet of gleaming lorries, each embossed with a huge Union Jack and the company logo.

We pulled up outside the office and went inside.

'Good morning, Mr Spicer,' said the receptionist as we entered. Several other minions greeted us. They weren't obsequious or anything, but you could tell that the contact had made them sweat a bit.

Given the size of the place I was expecting him to have an equally impressive office but I was surprised when we entered a small room with several pikestaffs leaning pointlessly against the wall. He kept most of his extensive pikestaff collection locked up in his garage, but liked to leave some dotted about his office. I couldn't understand their appeal, but any hobby that distracted him from his wastepaper tubs could only be a good thing. There was a big desk with nothing on it except a fountain pen and an immaculately stacked pile of paper. He picked up a fax sitting on top of the pile and scanned it. There was another door; maybe that led to his proper office.

'What's in there?' I asked.

'The factory.'

'Can I take a look?'

He nodded distractedly, still skimming the fax.

The door opened straight onto the factory floor, releasing a frightful din of clattering metal and deafening machines. It was like the sound of Dante's Inferno. I shut the door quickly, which immediately blocked out the noise. The door was heavy, but I leant on it just to be sure. I didn't want it springing open suddenly, releasing that awful noise again.

'Phew, Dad, nothing like being on top of the shop.'

'Yes, it's great, isn't it? Means I can keep an eye on things.'

'Yes,' I agreed weakly.

'Come away from the door and sit down. I want to hear about how the book's going. Has it hit the presses yet?' he inquired, leaning back in his chair expansively with his hands interlaced behind his head.

'Um, yes. I brought you an advance copy.' I rummaged in my bag and pulled out the glossy hardback proudly. 'What d'you think?'

'I never thought I'd live to see the day. It's certainly big enough.'

I knew I had to capitalize quickly on this burst of interest. 'You know I'm arranging my book launch in a month?'

'Of course. I'm looking forward to it.'

'Um, well, I was wondering if you'd like to make a contribution.'

He sighed bleakly. 'I'm going to get a sign made up for your next visit. "Do not ask for credit. Refusal often offends." ' It was a familiar joke but I laughed politely, allowing a moment before relentlessly continuing. There was the usual uming and ahhing before the magic words.

'Well, how much do you want?'

'It all depends if I manage to borrow someone's house. If I don't I'll have to hire somewhere. Emily on work experience says I can have it at W.H. Smith's in Brent Cross, but I'm going to need somewhere better than that otherwise none of the micro celebs will come.'

'Can any of them read?'

'That's not the point. If I have a big bash somewhere smart, Petronella Shmooze has promised she'll get Anoushka Bird-Whistle to come with all her friends.'

He grimaced. 'I don't know why you want to be associated with these people.' He pulled out his chequebook.

'Thanks, Dad! I'll be able to have champagne all night and jugglers now! Petronella will be thrilled.'

He grunted irritably. 'Well, it better be worth it. Have you had any reviews yet?'

'No. The book reviewers were all sent a proof copy a few weeks ago, but there hasn't been any feedback.'

'Oh. Can't be much of a page-turner then.' He put the book down but did a double take as he clocked the cover for the first time. 'Is that you?'

'Dad, I *told* you I was on the front. Do you like the picture?' I asked hopefully.

'It doesn't really look like you.' He examined it closely. 'Why are you wearing so much make-up?' A lump came to my throat. I'd so hoped he would be proud of me. It was such a lovely cover.

'Shall we go and have a look round the factory before I go?' I inquired brightly. I had no desire to enter the Dante's Inferno behind the door, but at least the noise would take my mind off what he had just said.

'Yes, if you're interested.' He perked up. 'I'll show you the new paint plant. It's the biggest in Europe.'

He eased his large form out of the chair and opened the door, releasing the volley of noise again. We walked out onto the factory floor, past assembly lines of vast soulless machines, each controlled by a single operator. He stopped to chat with several men, greeting each by name. As he approached each one I noticed that blank expressions were replaced by respect and interest. Curious eyes followed our progress around the factory floor.

We passed the new paint plant, a fearsome place, which resembled a lunar landscape. Men wearing silver space suits directed paint sprays at sheets of metal. It made me claustrophobic just looking at them.

'How can they bear doing that for eight hours every day?' I wondered out loud, watching them as they toiled robotically in huge glass bubbles.

'They don't mind. People write to me every day asking to work in the paint plant.'

'But why?'

'Because we pay the best wages in the country, that's why. Some of them drive better cars than I do.'

'Dad, everyone drives a better car than you do.'

It was quite an education but I was relieved when we slipped through the magic door back into his office. The phone was ringing and he picked up the receiver, frowning.

'He's here already? Well, he's early. OK, I'll be five minutes.' He put the phone down. 'The German rep has just arrived, I'll have to run you to the station now.'

I gathered up my things and we made our way out to the car.

'Thanks for the cheque, Dad, I really appreciate it.' I was silent for a moment, if only he'd say *something* nice about the book, what an achievement it was, anything.

'I really appreciate your coming down, Oriana. I'll see you at the launch.' We had pulled into the station, his engine was still running and he was impatient to get back to work.

'Aren't you at all pleased about the book?' I asked hopefully.

'I can't help thinking that if you'd put your mind to it you'd have written ten books by now, not just one.'

'Oh.' He'd taken the wind right out of my sails.

'I mean, Oriana, I'm your biggest fan but—'

'Oh, that's my train,' I lied, my eyes filling with blinding tears as a train pulled into the station. 'I've got to catch it! 'Bye!'

I climbed out of the car quickly so that he wouldn't see the tears in my eyes and ran towards the platform. Later, when I was sitting in the fortunately deserted compartment grovelling around in my bag for a tissue, I realized that I had picked up my book by mistake. I had been going to make a bit of a thing about signing it for him. I opened it absently, my eyes falling on the dedication, 'To my parents'. I shut it again quickly and squeezed my eyes tightly together. I felt utterly crushed.

A phrase from Mark Twain came into my mind. 'Forgiveness is the fragrance the violet sheds on the heel that has crushed it.' But the poignant image just made me feel even worse. I took a deep breath and clenched my fists.

I am not going to cry. I am not going to cry. But I lied. I'm afraid I cried all the way from Llandudno to Paddington.

* * *

My eyes were a bit red when I got in so it was just as well I wasn't going out that evening. There was a lovely message from Peregrine on my answering machine, which cheered me greatly.

'Congratulations, my darling girl, on your stunning TV debut. Give me a call.' Dear Peregrine. He always knew how to make me feel special. In his eyes I could do no wrong. In an uncertain world he was just what I needed. I rang him immediately. Jenny, his secretary, answered the phone.

'Hellair. Lord Skye-Rocca's office.'

'Hi, Jenny, it's me, Oriana.'

'Oriana! How are you? Peregrine's right here. I'm putting you through now.'

There was a distant sound of a chair scraping and something being knocked over. Oh God, it sounded like the Scrabble board.

'Damnation,' I heard Peregrine saying distantly. 'And I was winning.' After what seemed like an aeon, he picked up the telephone.

'Oriana, darling. It's been too long. How are you?'

'I'm fine. Are you all right? I heard something fall on the floor.'

'Oh, just some papers. We're rushing around as usual tying things up. A touch of the Bill Spicers – your father would understand.' I smiled. 'So when is the book due out?'

'Next month. I'm getting really nervous about it. I was wondering if you might give me some advice about handling the press. You're so clever about that sort of thing.'

'Oh, darling. It's very sweet of you to say. A friend tells me you're in a state because you haven't got a venue for your party.'

'Well, W.H. Smith in Brent Cross is free that night,' I joked hollowly.

'But I insist you have it here. At Cheyne Castle. I don't know why you didn't come to me in the first place.'

It was too good to be true! I hadn't even had to snog him, he'd *offered*!

'Are you free this Saturday?' he continued smoothly.

'Yes, I am.'

'In that case, perhaps I could tempt you to come with me to Glyndebourne? I've got two tickets.'

I shuddered. I'd managed to avoid opera for twenty-seven years, but it looked as if my clear run had come to an end. 'What a lovely treat! Shall I bring us a picnic?'

'Darling, that's very thoughtful, but I'll organize something for us down there. I don't want you to worry about a thing except the colour of your frock.'

Dear Peregrine. He would take care of things. Just talking to him was reassuring.

Peregrine picked me up at 4 p.m. the following Saturday, looking very smart in black tie. His sandy hair was brushed into smooth wings over very clean ears and his cheeks glowed with good health.

'I've just got back from a health cure at the Mayr Clinic in Austria,' he told me. 'I was under so much stress that my doctors insisted I take some time out to really relax.'

'Yes, after all, the graveyard is full of people who thought they were indispensable,' I said sympathetically.

'But it's hard to remind oneself that one is indispensable sometimes,' sighed Peregrine, smoothing back his gleaming hair with a soft white hand and swerving slightly, narrowly avoiding a cyclist who raised a fist and swore at us. Oblivious, Peregrine continued, 'I mean, if I don't take care of things, who will? Jenny is very competent, but she's only a secretary at the end of the day.'

I didn't bring up the Scrabble thing. It wouldn't have been tactful under the circs.

It was lovely to catch up with Cheyne Castle news during the long drive down to Sussex. After an hour Peregrine felt like a break so we pulled into a service station just off the A2. We must have looked a little incongruous queuing up,

Peregrine in his black tie and me in an elegant silvery-green cocktail dress, my blonde hair brushed straight and shining down my back, but the incongruity just added to the adventure. I liked the way Peregrine had no airs and graces about things like service stations. I knew people who wouldn't be seen dead eating a meal in one, but such bourgeois considerations were way over Peregrine's head and we shared a plate of cheese sandwiches and a pot of strong tea – well, true to form, he ate most of the sandwiches, but for once I wasn't irritated. It was relaxing reminiscing about old times and shared acquaintances.

After he had finished gulping down the sandwiches, Peregrine put his hand on mine. 'Darling, I'd almost forgotten how soothing it is being with you.' His eyes misted over. 'Your hair suits you long, and I'd forgotten what a stunning green your eyes are. I'm so proud to be seen with you.' He glanced around the scruffy cafeteria and squeezed my hand. 'I'm afraid this place doesn't do you justice.' I melted. Peregrine did say the nicest things. 'I know you're distracted with your book launch,' he went on, 'but when it's over, perhaps we could have some unpenetrative sex?'

I gazed at him flabbergasted. What on earth was he talking about? I hid my confusion and sipped my tea. Surely I had misheard. 'Yes, that would be nice,' I offered tactfully.

Back in the car I mulled over what he had said. Perhaps it wasn't such a bad idea. Maybe we could have one of those modern no-sex style relationships that you read about in magazines. It would be such a shame to ruin a perfectly good friendship because we were incompatible in bed.

The opera was as grim as expected. How anyone could even think of paying hundreds of pounds to listen to fat people shriek was quite beyond me. It was excruciating enough just having to sit through it, let alone have to pay for the privilege. Of course I kept my estuary opinions to myself as Peregrine seemed to love every moment. After a particularly prolonged bout of shrieking I glanced around the auditorium. Several dowager types seemed to be cringing, but that might be their natural expression, I couldn't be sure. Was everyone really enjoying themselves or was it a case of the emperor wearing no clothes?

Eventually the interminable first act came to an end and it was time for the evening's real highlight, the picnic. There was a faintly unseemly rush for the exits and I distinctly heard some muffled cries as several less well co-ordinated members of the audience tripped up on the ladies' voluminous outfits. People really went to town for Glyndebourne and many ladies were wearing long dresses with trains, which blocked up the exits most inconveniently.

'Wasn't it marvellous?' said Peregrine as we shuffled out into the stunning garden which was full of smart, elderly couples fighting over corkscrews and withered smoked salmon sandwiches.

'Yes, marvellous,' I agreed, painting on an enthusiastic smile. 'The woman in the red dress had such a powerful voice.' It was true, my ears were still ringing from the racket. I hoped I wouldn't get frightful tinnitus.

In the distance I could see more aggressive elderly couples dragging out industrial-sized hampers from tiny, brand new hatchbacks. It occurred to me that minuscule shiny new hatchbacks had suddenly become the province of Sloaney oldies. Handy for hampers but all this lifting looked exhausting. Surely at their time of life they should be taking things easy. I wondered why they didn't just go to the restaurant instead.

Peregrine took my hand and squeezed it. 'I knew you would love Glyndebourne as much as I do.' I smiled noncommittally and followed him enthusiastically into the garden. I was starving, having missed out on most of the cheese sandwiches, and was looking forward to a sumptuous feast.

Peregrine had been impressively organized. He led me to a secluded spot where a grand wicker hamper lay waiting for us. A table had been set with linen and sparkled with silver and gleaming glasses. A bottle of champagne lay chilling in an ice bucket.

Peregrine dived in enthusiastically, lifting out delicacy after delicacy, poached salmon, fresh strawberries, clouds of whipped cream, quail's eggs rolled in celery salt, delicious morsels just kept appearing. He poured champagne into the elegant flutes and made a toast. 'To the future,' and fixed his eyes on me meaningfully. I blushed girlishly and looked away.

'I can't help noticing, Oriana, that you seem a little anxious. Are you worried about the book?'

'I'm worried about everything, I'm afraid, especially the book. I feel I'm at the wheel of this huge great juggernaut without a map or anyone to give directions. I've just hired Petronella at Shmooze Associates at huge expense, so at least I've got someone helping me arrange the launch. I want something a bit different really.'

'Of course. You don't write a book every day, and especially as it's your first, you want to give it a proper send-off. It's like giving birth. Cheyne Castle will be the perfect venue.'

'Darling Peregrine! You're an angel. I can't tell you how perfect it would be. It's impossible to have a bad party at Cheyne Castle. The atmosphere sort of *does* things to people, doesn't it? D'you remember when the ambassadors fobbed off the police with their diplomatic immunity?'

'And when Nars did that headstand and came out with his classic observation, "We Swedes are very supple"?'

'Or when all your doctors started fighting and the urologist had to be wheeled to casualty?'

'Yes. He was never the same after that. His spleen was quite ruptured, poor fellow.'

Reminiscence followed reminiscence, we talked, gossiped and laughed, the champagne flowed, and the strawberries remained uneaten. Then Peregrine suddenly grabbed me and kissed me. Overwhelmed by the unreality of the setting and the champagne, I convinced myself I was enjoying it, but deep down the intimate contact revolted me. I loved Peregrine like a brother, but that was all.

But at least we missed the start of the second act, which was a great relief. I hoped we could just slip off and drive back to London, but Peregrine insisted on waiting for a break in the shrieking so we could edge our way back into our seats.

Thankfully the second act passed much more quickly, my head was in the clouds, and I sat happily making plans for the party which, now Cheyne Castle was the venue, was bound to be the success of the season. Petronella would be thrilled!

We spent the journey back to London busy discussing the guest list. Peregrine placed a white hand carefully on my knee and left it there the whole journey while suggesting many glittering additions to the guest list, so I didn't object. I was overwhelmed with relief to have his emotional and practical support.

Eventually we pulled up outside my flat. Peregrine parked carefully and switched off the engine. Oh God, was he expecting to be asked up to my suite?

'Aren't you going to ask me up?' he asked expectantly.

'Um, maybe another time? I'm absolutely shattered, what with all this worrying. You know what it's like.'

'Oh, all right, darling. I'll ring you tomorrow to find out how you are. You must arrange to see my masseuse every couple of days, and take evening primrose oil. It's very good for stress. I should know.' He laughed ruefully. I reached over to peck his cheek goodbye but he manoeuvred my face round for a full frontal tongue thing. The champagne had completely worn off now, and the whole thing made me feel quite sick. As soon as I decently could I slipped out of the car, blew him a kiss, and ran into my apartment building.

The elderly night porter bid me a respectful 'Evening, miss', and I disappeared with relief into the lift which disgorged me into my flat. I glanced around the crisp white interior, enjoying the extravagant scent of white lilies, kicking off my shoes and peeling off my tights, loving the feel of gleaming wood beneath my bare feet.

I padded into my bedroom, wandered over to the window and watched the Thames swirl grey and murky below and shivered. I was suddenly very tired, my cosy double bed with its mound of lacy pillows and white linen had never looked more luxuriously inviting. I pulled back the cotton coverlet, and sighed contentedly. There was no place for a man here, especially not Peregrine.

Chapter Thirty

I somehow managed to keep Peregrine at arm's length during the run-up to the launch but it was very difficult. I didn't know if his pills were suddenly working or what, but he had developed an alarming habit of grabbing me in public places and trying to kiss me. But on the rare occasions when we had been alone he had suddenly become engrossed in his newspaper. It was utterly bewildering.

Fortunately we weren't able to see much of each other as Petronella kept me very busy by insisting I attend every envelope opening in town.

The It girl writes novel tag, plus the media interest from the *Chalet Girl* documentary, had rather gripped the gossip columns, and I found myself invited to all sorts of bizarre occasions.

Rather embarrassingly I knew that half the time the organizers had invited Anoushka Bird-Whistle, but as she could only manage ten engagements a night, I was often sent along as It girl substitute. This often caused great disappointment and I frequently tried to wriggle out of things, but I was terrified of falling out with Petrol. I didn't think I'd ever been as frightened of anyone.

One one occasion I was sent to judge a very grand interior design competition. The other judges were really famous, and as each of them was introduced there was a small stir amongst the preening posse of interior designers at the front of the audience. When I was introduced, the flurry of interest was replaced with looks of blank indifference. One little man wearing ballet shoes sitting at the front said rather loudly, 'Never heard of her.' I cringed with embarrassment. I recognized Corianda and tried to catch her eye, but she studiously ignored me. She had always been intimidating but had become terribly grand recently, since her new book, a very slim volume called *The Right Shade of White*, had just come out. She had also just brought out an exciting new range of organic white paints, which the cognoscenti had been raving about.

Each designer had dressed up a model with swatches of curtains and fabric. Girls paraded in front of us wearing roller blinds, lino, and dresses created out of carpet samples. Several wore lampshades on their heads.

Corianda had painted her model with different shades of white from her organic paint collection, which was based on herbal stimulants and flower essences. I'd been told earlier that a doctor was on standby, purely as a formality, just in case the model asphyxiated and died, but she certainly looked very perky. She was shivering a bit, but then she was naked. Hopefully the herbal stimulants would keep her warm.

I thought it was a very original idea but Corianda didn't win. The prize went to a model wearing a bikini made of sisal matting. The male judges in particular thought it 'splendidly innovative, reflecting the diverse purposes of this exciting floor covering'.

We all had a nasty shock during the summing-up when Corianda's shivering model suddenly fainted on the podium as she was collecting the second prize. Panic ensued, the chairman shouting dramatically, 'Is there a doctor in the house?' The doctor had pushed off to the pub but he was pulled out to revive the poor girl, but it didn't work and they had to call an ambulance. That put a bit of a dampener on the evening and we all went home soon afterwards.

The next day I had to go into Shmooze's offices to drop off some press clippings with Petronella's latest PA, Citronella, a junoesque black American nightclub singer who was resting because she had lost her voice. While she was waiting for her voice to return she had taken what she hoped was a temporary position at Shmooze. She and I had become allies since we discovered that neither of us particularly liked Petrol, and she was not averse to passing on various juicy nuggets of gossip about Petrol and her celebrity clients.

'She's awful moody today,' whispered Citronella, glancing nervously towards Petrol's door. Luckily she could only talk in a whisper which made it possible for her to exchange intimate confidences without attracting attention from any of the emaciated black-encrusted assistants who hovered noiselessly about the office. They all adored and feared Petrol; I knew any one of them would have laid down their lives for her.

The door was suddenly flung open. Petrol stood in front of us, her glossy black hair cut in an immaculate shiny bob and her skinny frame encased in one of her chic tailored black suits. The effect was that of an elegant bird of prey. I shivered.

'Would you believe it! The bloody girl's only gone and *died*!'

I twigged immediately. 'You mean Corianda's model?'

'Well, I'm not likely to be talking about the Queen of Sheba, am I, darling?' She cast me a withering look.

'Oh, the poor thing,' whispered Citronella, looking shocked.

'Yes, she's absolutely devastated. I've told her she'll just have to cancel the paint party tomorrow night. It's utterly maddening of course, but what can we do?' Citronella and I exchanged bland looks.

'I'm glad you've turned up, Oriana. We need to have a talk.'

I followed her meekly into her white office with some trepidation. I knew she was going to tell me off about something. But what?

'Look here, Oriana. I faxed you a list of parties and events and you haven't been going to them. How are you going to make any impact at all on London Society if you won't go out?'

'But I go out all the time!' I exaggerated desperately. 'Sometimes I go to two parties in one evening. I'm worn out!'

'Two parties! I don't believe you. Take a leaf out of Anousie's book. If she can get to ten parties a night, I don't see why you can't. I mean, she hasn't even got a book to promote, but there she is, out and about every night. She's a real trooper, that girl.'

I looked down at my hands guiltily. I'd begun to pretend to go to parties when in reality I was staying in and cleaning my kitchen cupboards. I was sick of going out to stupid shampoo and deodorant launches.

'You're missing out on the opportunity to meet film producers, journalists, hairdressers, photographers. People who can really help you promote your book!' She was right. I should make more of an effort. The trouble was I just met the same people again and again. Mainly models, actors, restaurant owners, men about town, professional freeloaders and gossip column fodder. They were all politely surprised to find a writer in their midst, but the novelty soon wore off. I was beginning to realize that promoting my book was harder work than actually writing it.

'Yes, you're right,' I agreed. 'I'll make more effort. I met some very useful people last night at the Interior Design Competition. It was a lovely evening – well, until that poor girl died,' I finished lamely. We were interrupted by the telephone. Petronella visibly brightened.

'Coriandy! Yes, you poor thing! Too awful, I know, but long-term the death couldn't have come at a better time. I mean *all* the papers have mentioned *The Right Shade of White* . . . I know, I know. I told the *Mail* that it wasn't the paint that killed her, she was bound to be a drug addict or something . . . being a model . . . anorexic or whatever. The paints are all being tested again? Oh, on monkeys? That's excellent. They can't complain about that.' I cringed. Pandora and I were planning to go on a march to protest about the plight of laboratory animals. It was too awful to think of monkeys suffering for Corianda's stupid paint.

'Yes, she's here now.' Petrol cast me a covert look. 'Okay. Okay. Love you lots. Ciao for now.' She replaced the receiver. 'Poor Corry. But they're going to test her paints on Dutch monkeys so that'll show the public there's nothing to worry about. Now, apart from you being a hermit, things are going surprisingly well. There's a good chance that *Divorce!* will interview you after the launch. Isn't that wonderful?'

'Petrol, that's great! It would be a real coup.' It was true. The *Divorce!* reader was my target audience. *Chalet Girl Secrets'* topical themes of sexual disappointment and lavish recipes would strike a chord with its disaffected readership, I was sure. And with its huge circulation I was guaranteed unprecedented exposure.

'They'll want to photograph you with Peregrine and your parents at Cheyne Castle of course.'

'Oh God. I don't know if I can swing that, they hate publicity. And Peregrine will never agree. He says that being in the gossip columns is bad for his business image.'

Petrol snorted. 'What business image? He's a playboy, for heaven's sake.' She adopted a reverential tone. 'But I can understand your father being cautious, of course. I think it's amazing what he's achieved. Really amazing. How is he, by the way?'

'Oh fine. Fine.' I was still smarting from the 'you should have written ten books by now' conversation.

'But Peregrine's happy to let you have the party at his house, isn't he?' Petrol continued.

'Oh yes. He loves a party, he's just got this thing at the moment about being seen as a lightweight.'

Petrol sucked in her breath in exasperation. 'Well, do you

think you can talk him round? If he won't do it, *Divorce!* will want to know now. I mustn't jeopardize my relationship with the Maharanee.'

'Oh, I'm sure I can,' I lied blithely.

'And that's not the only good—' The phone rang again. 'What d'you mean she's flown to New York? She's meant to be going to the Dalai Lama's fundraiser tonight. Well, JUST FIND HER AND TELL HER SHE'S GOT TO COME BACK!' She slammed the phone down, shaking with rage. 'I had to move heaven and earth to get her an invite and now she's gone and bloody disappeared!'

To my dismay I realized Petrol was weeping. It was very alarming, like seeing a member of the royal family on the loo. You knew they probably went, but you didn't want to be there at the time.

'It's a *disaster!* I so wanted her to go. I'm a very spiritual person, you see. So is Anoushka, deep down.'

I nodded sympathetically, wondering when we could get back to discussing the launch. Luckily she took a deep breath and switched subjects.

'The other good news is that Tiffany Strumpet is now working for Sky. She's doing the *Sloanes at Home* programme. God knows how she got the job, she can barely string a sentence together. We sent her an advance copy of your book and she wants to come to discuss the interior design of your flat tomorrow.' I thought of my empty white flat and frowned. There was nothing in it! What would we find to talk about?

'Could she come next week? My flat's upside down at the moment.'

'Absolutely not. Corianda was originally going to do it, but she's left the country, poor darling. You must do it, I don't know when they might have another slot free.'

'OK,' I agreed weakly. 'By the way, I've organized the caterers and everything and Peregrine's asked some great people. My friend Arabella is bringing her husband Tony

Louche and he'll bring people, so that'll guarantee lots of photographers, I hope.'

The Tony Louche bit was an exaggeration. To my great disappointment Bella had rung to say that he had gone away to have his annual injections in Montreux. She'd been very cagey about it, which was unlike her. I hoped that now that she was privy to the information she would share it generously.

'Excellent, Oriana. Oh, one other thing. I spoke to Nigel yesterday and he's going to run a lead story about your book tomorrow. I think that's everything for the moment, but you simply must get out more, get your picture in the magazines, no one's ever heard of you!'

Thank God the phone interrupted us. I slunk out, feeling completely pulverized. I found Petronella terribly intimidating, she had this way of making me feel the most unpopular girl in the school. It reminded me of the inferiority I used to feel when I was younger when I compared myself to Siena, who was always so much prettier and more popular than I was.

I shut the door to the office and wandered past an emaciated butterfly who was on the telephone. 'No, you can't have Anoushka, but Oriana is available. Oriana Spicer, she's an It girl too, she's just written an *amazing* book about all her society friends. No, I haven't actually read it myself but . . . no, Anoushka hasn't got a spare evening for four months. But Oriana is becoming very well known – *quite* pretty, yes. Okay, I'll let Anoushka know. 'Bye.'

Yes, visiting the agency was a pulverizing experience, I decided, mouthing goodbye to Citronella, who was juggling phones and looking anxious. 'Hang on a sec,' she mouthed back, and put down one phone, murmured soothing words into another. I could hear a volley of screeching coming from the receiver. She raised her eyes in exasperation and then slammed down the phone. 'Oh, sod it.'

'Who was on the phone?'

'Anoushka, who else? I managed to catch her just before her plane took off but she won't come back for the Dalai Lama gig. Hey, you doin' anything tonight? I'll rephrase that. I've seen your schedule – heck, I typed it. But knowin' you I figured that the last thing you want to do is go to the friggin' openin' of some—'

'Envelope.'

'Yeah, that's the name of the place.' We laughed. Well, I laughed and she chortled in a whispery sort of way.

'No, I'm not doing anything important.'

'Well, why don't we have a drink and go see a movie?'

'Citronella, I would love to.'

We met later at the Ritzy Marina Club. Citronella hadn't been before, which surprised me.

'It's a nice place,' she said, casting her eyes around doubtfully, 'but everyone looks the same.' It was true, the club was full of soignée blonde women, sipping diet drinks and exchanging juicy confidences. 'I think I'm the only person here who weighs more than ninety pounds – I mean stones. You know, I just can't get into this British stone thing. If I weigh three stones, are we talking big stones or little stones? I just don't get it.'

'A stone is fourteen pounds,' I said helpfully.

'Sounds like a pretty big stone to me.' I smiled and scooped the froth off my cinnamon latte. Citronella was a breath of fresh air.

'It's just great to see you outside the agency, Citronella.'

'Hey, don't give me this Citronella crap outside the agency, my friends call me C. My brother calls me the Big C, so I don't talk to him any more.' She chortled.

'It sounded like things were getting a bit chaotic at Shmooze today.'

'Christ, talk to me about it. The moment my voice comes back I'm outta that crazy place. It's Petrol. One minute she's your best friend, the next, whoa, you better be lookin' out for yourself. When she gets mad she sure scares the hell out of me.'

It was such a relief to jettison the Petrol is a salt of the earth nice person myth.

'You know, C, she really intimidates me. I feel like the class dunce whenever I go in there. It's like all the other clients are in with the in crowd, and I'm somewhere over there, outside.' I shivered.

'Don't worry about it, Oriana. It's because they all know each other, they go to the same stooopid parties. It's that edge of the jet set scene. But you're in there, you're well-connected. You're dating Lord Peregrine Friggin' Sky-Rocket, for Pete's sake.'

'Yeah, you're right. It's silly to care about that stupid stuff. By the way, I'm not dating Peregrine, we're just friends now. You know, I thought that Anoushka and Corianda might be a bit friendly. It would be nice if there was camaraderie amongst It girls. I mean, Anoushka looks such fun in the papers. But I've bumped into her a few times at envelope openings and she just ignores me even though I've met her at Shmooze a couple of times.'

'You should see the way she treats me. When I first started she tried to get me runnin' around after her, but I soon told her where to go. We don't put up with that kind of shit in Atlanta, I can tell you.'

'I wish I was American,' I smiled ruefully. 'Maybe then I wouldn't worry so much.'

'Honey, if you were American, you'd worry even more. Believe me. Ain't no chalet maids, or whatever you call them, in the States, you'd have t'write about something else. Now wipe that worry frown off your face an' drink your drink.'

I took a sip of my latte obediently. 'I'm relieved that you find Petrol difficult. I thought it was only me. Everyone else raves about her.'

'Well, she can get away with it. She's the best in the

business, she manages all the celebrities that people want to see. If they want them, they gotta get along with her.'

'Wouldn't it be funny if everyone felt the same way as we do but like the Emperor with no clothes they think they're the only ones who feel like that.'

'What's with this Emperor stuff? Is it some quaint English expression I've missed out on?'

We were interrupted by Ambrosia, who bounded up to us excitably. She had just started spinning classes in a desperate bid to look svelte for my book launch. The classes hadn't started working yet and her tight leotard top and stripey blue leggings were under considerable strain.

'Hey, someone else who weighs more than three of your stone things,' whispered C, with relief.

'Oriana, there's a great picture of you in the *Standard*, have you seen it?'

'No, Hang on, there's a copy over there, I'll just go and get it.' First I quickly introduced them. 'Ambrosia, this is C who works for Petronella. Ambrosia and I were chalet girls together.' I grabbed the paper, returned to the table and flicked through it.

'You are lucky working at Shmooze,' Ambrosia was saying. 'Petronella is rairly nice.'

'I wouldn't say that she's rarely nice, I'd say that she's never nice,' whispered C, looking bemused.

'No, rairely is upper-class for really, as in she's really really whatever,' I explained.

'Oh, I see.' C looked even more bemused.

'Oh, don't you like her either?' said Ambrosia, her large brown eyes widening with relief. 'I thought it was only me.'

'Oh, here it is.' I'd made the crumpet corner slot in the Londoners' Diary. I skimmed the short piece quickly. 'Oh God. Oh God.' The piece was very sarcastic.

'What does it say?' asked C nervously.

' "Oriana Spicer, It girl and authoress of *Chalet Girl Secrets*, has sent me some useful information. She is the daughter of wastepaper tub tycoon Bill Spicer and ex-model Venetia Mowbray, a scioness of the wealthy Douche sausage skinning empire. Oriana boasts that her friends include fellow It girl authoress Pandora Black, and that her boyfriend is playboy Lord Peregrine Skye-Rocca. She must be a good writer." '

'I didn't send them anything. What's going on? It's savage, utterly savage.'

'Yes, but it's such a pretty picture of you,' said Ambrosia consolingly.

'I'm afraid it's Shmooze's fault,' explained C. 'Petrol made up this great press pack with your book, all tied up in pink ribbon and stuff. We had it biked round to all the papers yesterday. Look, I know it's difficult, but if you're in the public eye you'll attract a lot of bullshit. It's very tough.'

'Yes, remember how beastly they all were after the docu soap.' Ambrosia shuddered.

'You should see the abuse Anoushka gets. People send her the worst letters; some of them are so bad we don't even show them to her. Once she was sent a turd.'

'Ugh. I know she's a bit snotty, but at least she adds a bit of colour to things,' I said. 'People like that are fun. If it wasn't her, it would be someone else. I mean, who wants to read about politicians all the time?'

'It's jealousy. Pure and simple,' said Ambrosia.

'But I think it's a peculiarly English thing. The press here is much more bitchy than, say, in the States,' I said with feeling.

'Honey, if that girl lived in the States, she would have been shot by now. An' you know who would have pulled the trigger? Me!' She raised her eyes. 'But I know what you mean about the press here. Boy, are they mean.'

'God, is that the time?' Ambrosia glanced at her watch nervously. 'I'm late for a date, I must *fly*!' She smoothed down her unruly dark hair anxiously.

'Anyone nice?' I asked.

'Yes! Rupert from Lucreforole-Rope. I met him at a drinks party last week and I pretended I wanted to sell my flat. He's coming round to value it now. So it's not a date *exactly* . . .' She blew us a kiss and rushed off towards the changing rooms.

'Just so long as he doesn't ask her to cook anything,' I commented.

'Is *she* the one who killed that guy with the egg?'

'No, that was Arabella, who's sort of married to Tony Louche. She didn't really kill him. I mean, she couldn't have known that the egg at the back of the fridge had been there a year. It was a very big fridge, it had lots of, like, cubbyholes. And Jolly Holidays simply *forbade* us to throw anything remotely food-like away. It was in the contract. It was lucky that her father is a high court judge, though.' I sighed. 'It's nearly eight o'clock, I promised Petrol that I'd go to the Tampax launch at the Met Bar. I really don't think I can manage it. D'you think I'll miss out on a life changing experience if I don't go?'

'No.'

'Good. It's my round. Let's celebrate my shameful *Evening Standard* name-dropping debut with some champagne.'

'Congratulations, girl, there's no such thing as bad publicity when you're floggin' a book. Anyway, you made it to Crumpet Corner. That will *really* piss Anoushka off.'

Chapter Thirty-one

We stayed a little too late at the Ritzy Marina Club and as a consequence I was feeling a bit bleary-eyed when I welcomed Tiffany Srumpet to my flat the following morning to film me for the *Sloanes At Home* programme.

I'd met Tiffany at many envelope openings and felt particularly warm towards her because two weeks ago she had described an old Marks and Spencer dress I'd been wearing as a John Galliano, and mentioned my book as well. I had really appreciated the plug.

Tiffany was famous for her extensive wardrobe of lurex outfits and today she was looking particularly snazzy in a black lurex catsuit teamed with spiky black boots and some discreet silver jewellery. She had a glamorous mane of thick black hair and a deep mediterranean tan, set off by lavish application of this season's must have erotic plum lipstick, which was only available in New York, where there was rumoured to be a six month waiting list. As *The Snoop!*'s esteemed shopping correspondent, as well as the Sloanes at Home presenter, she no doubt went to the top of every queue, lucky thing.

'Oriana, thanks sooooo much for letting us come along at such short notice. Could you *bear* to show me round quickly, just so I can get my bearings?'

'Um, yes. This is the sitting room and that's the bedroom.'

'Is that it?' Tiffany looked concerned. 'You see, it's a half-hour programme, we're meant to talk about your furniture and pictures, and knickknacks . . .' She glanced around the empty room hopefully, as if the ceiling might suddenly open up, releasing a pile of clutter. 'Petronella said you had a huge apartment.' I noticed that when stressed her voice lost its well-modulated Sloane-transatlantic intonation and developed a decidedly Midlands timbre. We were both silent for a moment.

'Well, I'm sure it will be fine,' Tiffany continued doubtfully. 'I know! We can talk about your clothes. That would be very interesting.'

I didn't think it would be remotely interesting. I thought of my inadequate wardrobe, which consisted mainly of my mother's old clothes plus Pandora's cast-offs, and shuddered. I knew I would rather be hung naked from an electricity pylon for three months without food or water than allow Tiffany Strumpet, *The Snoop!*'s esteemed shopping correspondent anywhere near my wardrobe.

'I've got a better idea. Let's talk about feng shui. People are very interested in that,' I suggested hopefully.

The doorbell went and I escaped to open it. It was the cameraman.

'Sorry I'm late, girls. This place is a bugger to get to. We'd better crack on. Where shall I set up?'

In the end the interview went very well. Tiffany was intrigued by my feng shui improvements, and we focused for a long time on my relationship corner, which unfortunately was where the waste disposal unit was. It kept getting blocked, recently emitting a foul black liquid from the bowels of the earth. If it hadn't been for the swift attention of Martin and Bill, the Ritzy Marina Club 'wonder plumbers', the whole flat might have been engulfed. Thank goodness it was working today.

I explained that Roberto, my feng shui consultant, always advised the placing of a pair of animals, a romantic picture and a vase of pink peonies here. I had a small pair of cows that Frau Perren had bought for me at the Swiss Cow Fighting Competition. It was difficult keeping them in the waste disposal, but I didn't really have much choice.

'Um, I don't know anything about feng shui,' Tiffany admitted, moistening her erotic plum slicked lips with a small pink tongue and seductively tossing back her luscious dark mane at the camera, 'but wouldn't it be better to put tigers or, well, a more energetic kind of animal here? Wouldn't cows be more appropriate for older people, or room mates, or something?'

I'd never thought of this before. Maybe Tiffany was on to something. 'Gosh. You're probably right'. Now I thought of it, Peregrine did have many bovine characteristics. I would have to give the matter serious thought.

'Although rumour has it that your relationship with,' she peered into the camera for emphasis, '*Lord Peregrine Skye-Rocca* is going great guns. Can we expect an announcement at your book launch, Oriana?'

Good old Tiffany. She'd given me the link. I spent the rest of the programme plugging my book and being mysterious about Peregrine.

To be honest, that wasn't difficult. I'd only seen him once since Glyndebourne and it hadn't been a success. I'd gone round to Cheyne Castle one afternoon to show the party planners around and he'd spent the whole time pawing me. Then they'd left and I'd dashed down to the basement with considerable relief to discuss arrangements with Mrs B.

He'd asked me to stay for dinner but I pleaded stress and slipped off home. He was obviously eager to know if his poultices were working and I didn't know how long I could hold him off. I had a sinking feeling that once the book launch was over he might decide to propose or something even more drastic. Mrs B had veered off the subject at every opportunity to make unsavoury hints about low sperm counts and that ''is Lordship wasn't gettin' any younger', while giving me meaningful looks. The thought of being an incubator for the last of the Skye-Rocca line was too frightful to contemplate in my nervous state, and realizing that Mrs B just wasn't in the mood to discuss arrangements, I gave up. Luckily I had employed excellent party planners who had everything in hand.

I thought it might be amusing to create a chalet atmosphere and had asked the party planners to make the ballroom look as much like Chalet Tiara as possible. Beautiful models and out-of-work actresses were to dress up in Sam De Teran's latest skiwear collection and hand round bite-sized pieces of eggy bread, sponge cakes and tiny baguettes, and trays of authentic alpine tea, while the guests were going to leave with a typical chalet packed lunch with one of Petronella's press packs enclosed.

I was hoping to find an impoverished ski bum to bungee jump off the top of Cheyne Castle. Pandora said Ted Shred, the world-famous ski jumper who hired himself out by the hour, would do it but he had just broken his neck. If it healed in time he'd be willing to oblige but it was unlikely.

I was so consumed with fear about the launch that I didn't have any more energy left to worry about anything else. Peregrine seemed to think that after the party we would somehow get it together. I would face that hurdle when it came. In my dreams I hoped that he might meet someone else, but who would fall for him for the right reasons? His money distanced him from the real world. His eccentricity had always been part of his charm but his behaviour was growing increasingly strange. The grabbing was particularly disturbing.

Fortunately, one relationship that was really improving was with my mother. I didn't think I could ever forgive her for the 'just because it's important to you doesn't mean it's important to anyone else' conversation, and I had avoided her calls. Eventually, after returning to find a particularly sad, apologetic message from her, I knew it was time to clear the air.

I hadn't seen Siena for a while either so as she had once told me that Mary was a great expert in modern art, I invited them round to Cheyne Castle to see Peregrine's renowned collection of white pictures. The painter was extremely famous, although I had never heard of him, but of course I'm not very up on that sort of thing.

Anyway I arranged for them to come round one afternoon when Peregrine was out having his bi-weekly shiatsu scalp massage. Mummy came early so we could chat. She was looking particularly soignée in a mint-green trouser suit, with her blonde shoulder-length hair loosely secured with a matching Hermes scarf.

'I really am so proud of you, darling. I just don't know what came over me. Maybe it made me feel a bit of an under-achiever. You know, I'm fifty,' I tried not to smile, 'and what have *I* done? Not a lot.'

'Yes you have. You've had us, and now there's Jacob. Who knows what he might do? You know, I've always taken it for granted that people have children just like that, but so many people these days find it impossible. It's quite an achievement really.'

'I didn't know you'd given the matter any thought.'

'Well, I don't particularly but every time I go to the Ritzy Marina Club the changing room is full of women discussing IVF, and weeping about their husband's low sperm counts. Maybe that'll stop people insisting on wrapping everything to death in plastic. It's so unnecessary.'

In the ongoing debate about the nation's dwindling sperm count, the *Daily Mail* had recently unearthed scandalous evidence of peculiar and unexplained sexual changes in animals that it attributed to the widespread use of plastic bags.

'In Switzerland everybody takes string bags to the supermarket. If you forget and need one, they charge you a fortune. It's quite a deterrent. They don't seem to have a dwindling sperm count there so the *Daily Mail* is probably right.'

'Life is so much more complicated than it used to be,' she

mused. 'We used to worry far more about getting pregnant by mistake. How is Peregrine, by the way?'

'Well, you know he keeps *grabbing* me, but only when there are people around. When we're alone he's fine.'

'I really think that after the party you should try and meet someone a bit more normal in that department. By the way, darling, I know you weren't going to tell me but I saw a copy of *The Tit* yesterday. Ugh, what a dreadful magazine.' She shuddered.

Unfortunately the oven picture had resurfaced *again*, this time beneath the heading 'Has Oriana got a bun in the oven? Society saucepot turned authoress, Oriana Spicer, daughter of trash tycoon Bill Spicer and Venetia Mowbray, scioness of the Douche sausage skin empire, was recently spotted snogging long-time beau Lord Peregrine Skye-Rocca at Glyndebourne. "They couldn't keep their hands orf each other," complained an elderly dowager who surprised the couple in a bush. "It was disgusting." ' Accompanying the piece was an unflattering picture of Peregrine with his mouth full of food and a close-up of someone's distended stomach. It didn't look like mine at all. I wondered whose on earth it was.

'But Mummy, you don't take *The Tit*.'

'No, but Mrs Crabbs from the Buttonhook Society does and she kindly rang to tell me.' She sighed. 'It's odd how people always ring to tell me when that oven picture resurfaces in the newspapers. I think people really relish telling me. But she wasn't the only one who saw it. Great-Aunts Horatia and Agatha saw it too, and —'

We were interrupted by the front door slamming and the sound of raised voices. I rushed out of the drawing room and peered down the staircase to witness the arrival of Siena and Mary and the gang, who were trailing up, clad in long scarves, woolly hats, fingerless mittens and the prerequisite rucksacks overflowing with bags of cooked brown food. They looked like a family of gypsies who had fallen on hard times. There was no sign of Mrs B anywhere. Fortunately I had primed her, otherwise I knew she would have refused to let them in. Mrs B's very naughty like that. She has this quite unreasonable loathing of gypsies; she's practically phobic about them.

'Ooh, I don't know *who* that *woman* thought she was.' Mary was quivering with rage.

'She's just a bit oppressed, darling,' said Siena crossly.

'Mrs Button? You've got to be joking! She's about as oppressed as Genghis Khan,' I laughed.

'Who's Genghis Khan?' India asked.

They all looked at me. I looked back blankly. 'He was a very brutal . . .' I racked my brains. 'Um, I'm not exactly quite sure who he was,' I admitted weakly.

'He was a very bad man,' Siena explained patiently. 'You know, she even demanded to see my driving licence,' she continued irritably.

'Oh dear. She's never done that before. I am sorry.' Under the circs, that really was spectacularly tactless of Mrs B. I knew she knew all about Siena's anti-car campaigns because she had once drawn my attention to a picture of my sister being dragged away in handcuffs from the Motor Show at Earls Court.

I remembered that conversation in particular because it had led to a long discussion about Mrs B's pride and joy, her Robin Reliant motorcar, which was kept in pristine condition outside the Button HQ in Reigate. Apparently it was now a collector's item due in part to its unbelievably low mileage, the Buttons generally preferring to use their motorbike with attached sidecar for outings.

'Girls, I know it's been an unfortunate beginning, but can we put it behind us now and start again?' pleaded Mummy hopefully.

'Yes, I quite agree, Venetia,' grovelled Mary, which was a bit rich as she'd started the whole thing. 'Oriana, we've been *so* looking forward to seeing the *Collection Blanc* – I believe that's the proper name for the pictures, correct me if I'm wrong?'

'Um, Peregrine just calls them the white pictures. He's put them on the top floor. Shall we go up and look, or would you like a cup of tea first?'

'Ooh, I think after the, um, contretemps, a cup of tea would be lovely,' said Mary. Everyone else nodded enthusiastically, so we all trooped downstairs to the kitchen. I crossed my fingers that Mrs B wouldn't be about, and fortunately she'd decided to make herself scarce.

Providing the team with simple liquid refreshment was a complicated business. Everybody wanted something different. Siena had brought her own bancha tea bags, and Mary had brought the children, who were absolutely forbidden any kind of caffeine or sugar, some freshly squeezed orange juice. Jacob was still being breast-fed, Mary had some decaf organic coffee, Mummy had a gin and six cigarettes, and I had a nervous breakdown. I'm only joking of course.

Given the peculiarities of my family, the children were a delight. India, Conga, Kenya and little Jacob were bright as buttons and seemingly very well balanced. Jacob sat on my lap and tried to eat my hair. But all hell broke loose when I opened the fridge and they spotted Mrs B's supply of arctic roll. Her deep freeze was on the blink so Peregrine's was incubating her and the industrial cleaners' supply of fish fingers and arctic roll, which represented their staple diet, along with the Branston Pickle, of course. That was still kept in the steaming vats in the basement.

'Oh, please, Mummy, please can we have the cold roll?' begged India plaintively. 'We had it at school, it's lovely. Pleeeeese!'

Jacob, Conga and Kenya joined in, and the kitchen was soon an uproar. Mummy poured herself some more gin and lit another cigarette, Siena made ineffectual noises, but Mary, to her credit, stood up and said with icy control, 'Children, *will you behave*, otherwise we *are leaving now*.' She was white with irritation and the children immediately shut up. It was miraculous. 'I'm sorry,' she apologized. 'Oriana, shall we go upstairs and look at the pictures?'

I led them upstairs with considerable relief, wondering what they'd make of the pictures, which were completely beyond me.

The children weren't very impressed with them; they were much more impressed with a Teletubby belonging to one of the industrial cleaners that was lying on the floor.

Mary spent a long time examining the pictures, making several incomprehensible remarks, the gist of which I gathered was that the Saatchis' white pictures were much more 'profound' although Peregrine's pictures were 'not entirely without merit,' due to the interesting and unusual textural detail.

I didn't dare admit that this was entirely due to the industrial cleaners and their enthusiastic scrubbing with various unguents. They were thrilled with the white pictures and took the white concept quite literally. Several times I had caught them red-handed with buckets of their homemade bleach (I had tried desperately to ban bleach and other environmentally unfriendly unguents from Cheyne Castle but to no avail, I'm afraid), and had expressly forbidden them to use anything but a light duster, but I knew they crept upstairs to do their scouring when Peregrine was out. I must say that I agreed with Mary that the scratches in the paint, through which one could glimpse canvas, made the pictures much more interesting.

'We're so looking forward to the book launch,' Mary was saying as we staggered down the stairs in a motley procession. 'I can't wait to read the book. When I get a moment I'm going to sit down and read it from cover to cover. The trouble is, I'm always so busy,' she sighed importantly.

'I'm sure you'll enjoy it,' said my mother kindly. 'It's terribly good. I know I'm biased, but I couldn't put it down.' I glowed with pleasure as we trooped back into the drawing room.

'Yes,' said Siena, smiling. 'Every time I open the papers I see something about you.'

'You must find it frightfully invasive,' said Mary sympathetically. 'Someone insisted on showing me a horrid piece in *The Tit*. I felt so sorry for you.'

'Yes. Great-Aunts Horatia and Agatha saw it.' Mummy raised her eyes. 'Do be careful, Oriana. I do see their point, you are in the papers a lot, and they mention the family connection every time. It's very embarrassing for them.'

'I think it's a bit rich for them to complain about anything considering they make a very nice living off pig bladders, or whatever you use to stuff sausages with,' said Siena fiercely.

'*Skin* sausages, darling. I know it's strange, but I'm afraid it's these sausage skins that paid for your education, clothes and food, and give you the time to pursue your principles,' reminded Mummy sensibly.

'I'm fed up with them both,' I said. 'Until I started being in the papers we all thought they were dead. Now they can't leave me alone. You know they've even started harassing me on e-mail.'

'Oh, yes,' said Mummy absently. 'I'm afraid they bullied me for your address. I couldn't not give it to them.' Mummy had been online ever since she had discovered that the American branch of the Buttonhook Society was on the Internet and was now a regular 'surfer'.

Siena and Mary laughed. 'Go on, Oriana,' said Siena, 'invite them to the party. They'd loved to be asked and it would be interesting to see them.'

'Oh all right,' I agreed. 'They probably won't come all the way from Southwold anyway.' But given the energy of their last e-mail I had an awful feeling that they might. They sounded as if they'd enjoy a good punch-up – that was probably where Siena got her aggression from.

At that moment Peregrine walked in, looking pink-faced and robust, fresh from his scalp massage. His whole head gleamed with expensive hair oil and he glowed with comfortable living. He seemed amazingly thrilled to see us, given that we must have looked like something left over from the Glastonbury Festival.

'Ah, hello, darling.' He kissed me with proprietorial affection. I felt quite proud to be seen by my family in this semi-chatelaine light, with twenty-four hour a day access to Cheyne Castle, the *Collection Blanc* and all its other treasures. I smiled at Peregrine affectionately. He looked quite attractive today. Maybe the sex thing would work itself out. It would be nice to live at Cheyne Castle all the time; there was something so soothing about it really.

'Wake up, darling,' my mother was saying sharply. Peregrine was being introduced to Mary, who was gushing in return. It was odd, considering her liaison, or whatever you wanted to call it, with Siena, who until quite recently had been a fully paid-up member of Class War, but she actually quite enjoyed the whole toff scene. She was gazing up at Peregrine with something like awe. Any moment now I expected her to curtsy, it was very weird.

'Thank you so much for letting Oriana have the party here. It should be quite an evening,' said Mummy politely, doing up the buttons on her Jaeger jacket.

'It's the least I can do,' said Peregrine expansively. 'It's a tremendous achievement having a book published. Now, if you'll excuse me, I must dash upstairs and return some calls.' He gave a half bow and went upstairs. 'Oh, Oriana, you'll come and say goodbye before you go, won't you?'

'Of course,' I smiled. I bit my lip. I was hoping to delay being alone with him until after the party. He only groped me in public these days, but you never knew. My nerves were too fraught to be experimented on before then.

'Oh, but Oriana, could you give me a lift to the station, d'you think?'

I smiled at Mummy gratefully. 'Of course I will. Can I ring you later, Peregrine?'

'That would be lovely. Goodbye, ladies.'

Eventually we all made it onto the street.

'Thanks so much, Oriana, it was such fun,' said Mary as we kissed goodbye. 'And Peregrine was absolutely charming. It's amazing how much publicity you're getting for the book because of him. You know I ran into some friends of yours and they seemed to think that you'd only got the book contract because of the connection. Of course I told them that was ridiculous. It's extraordinary how bitter people can be.'

'What people? What friends said that?' I asked, frowning, but we were interrupted by Siena.

'C'mon kids, time to go.'

'But who said that?' I was trying to kiss the children goodbye and the moment was lost.

'Who d'you think she meant?' I asked Mummy when we were in the car.

'I haven't the faintest idea,' she replied. 'It's really not worth dwelling on. I think she's a bit upset because her pot-making venture flopped. She'd had such high hopes, poor girl. Thank goodness Siena has enough to support them all.' She sighed. 'Now what are you going to do about Peregrine? You can't hold him off forever.'

'I know. Thank goodness you suggested the lift. He's normally fine when we're alone, but if Mrs B or someone is about he'll try and leap on me. It's very stressful.'

'Yes, it's odd how men with his problem overreact like that.' She gazed out of the window distractedly. 'There is something so, oh, I don't know, something almost *too* oily and well-fed about him. It oozes from his pores.'

'It's all the fry-ups Mrs B's been cooking him since I left. He's eating for two at the moment. Perhaps he thinks he's pregnant.' I laughed hollowly.

Later, driving home after dropping her off, I thought how lucky I was that I had a mother I could confide in so readily. None of my girlfriends seemed to confide in their mothers nearly as much, and Pandora didn't even know where hers was. I knew our relationship wasn't perfect, but it was definitely improving. I smiled to myself. Her description of

Peregrine was spot on. The image of rich food oozing through his well-tended pores was one I wouldn't be likely to forget.

Chapter Thirty-two

On the day of the party I arrived at Cheyne Castle in good time to supervise the arrangements. Mrs B had let the party planners in first thing and the house was bustling with florists and caterers. I knew that Peregrine would be out the rest of the afternoon as he was having lunch, so I could supervise the proceedings without interruption.

Petrol had done an excellent job persuading *Divorce!* that they could have sole photo rights for the party, and the planners had not only reduced their fee for a mention, but were really going out of their way to make it the party of the season.

They had taken the chalet theme to heart, spraying snow on all the windows; they had even brought a dry-ice machine plus a huge Christmas tree, decorated with tiny real candles. I'd insisted that they were real even though Gustav, the party planner, had explained that they might be a bit of a fire hazard. I reassured him that it would be fine because I could install one of the industrial cleaners permanently beneath the tree all night, just in case. They'd enjoy being part of the proceedings.

But the *pièce de résistance* was a vast ice sculpture that my mother had ordered in the shape of a chalet! A lorry had set it up in the front garden, as it was too big to get inside the house. It was wonderful and would provide a glistening beacon and talking point for all our guests.

There was really very little for me to do, so I took my suitcase full of clothes and my make-up crate up to the spare room on the top of the house. Mummy had come shopping with me and had bought me a slinky blue dress to wear, but I'd brought along a few other outfits too.

I was just practising my positive thinking mantras when Pandora knocked on the door and came in bearing several cartons.

'I thought you might like some freshly squeezed wheatgrass juice and a latte to keep you going, old thing.' I accepted the cartons gratefully, clutching my nose and swigging down the wheatgrass juice.

'Ah,' I grimaced. 'That will set me up nicely. Thank you so much.'

'They seem to be doing extraordinary things downstairs,' Pandora went on. 'They were attaching icicles to the chandeliers with a spray gun.'

'Oh God, I hope they don't fuse the place.'

'I wouldn't worry,' she said worriedly. 'They seem to know what they're doing.'

We'd both thought that we'd be frantically rushing around before the party, but there was nothing to do except perform a lengthy toilette.

'I must say, whatever one's feelings about Petrol, she's done a first-class job on the puff front, and Emily on work experience has been excellent. She's lined up all sorts of radio and TV things for after the launch. Oh, did I tell you that Ambrosia is going to be on the front cover of *Kitchen Hygiene Monthly*? It's quite a coup for her.'

Pandora snorted derisorily. 'I'm amazed she's doing it. It'll only bring up – excuse the pun – all that food poisoning thing again. You'd think she'd want to live it down.'

'It'll be a very ironic cover, I would imagine. She's got to wear a plastic shower hat and a white coat and wave a syringe about. She's thrilled about it, she says she's always wanted to be a model but thought she was too fat.'

'Oh well, hopefully there'll be lots of photo ops tonight for her,' said Pandora, outlining her full lips carefully with a lip pencil. 'There. I'm done.' She examined herself critically in the mirror. She looked very chic in a short black dress, kitten-heeled shoes and a single strand of pearls. Her fine shoulder-length blonde hair was flicked up at the ends and gleamed in the Cheyne Castle subdued lighting.

'You look very chic, like Audrey Hepburn,' I said admiringly.

'Wrong colour hair. But it doesn't matter what I look like,' she lied fairly convincingly. 'Tonight the focus will be on you and you alone. So,' she paused as I looked through the outfits on the bed for the hundredth time. 'Put something on. You can't go down in your dressing gown.'

We were interrupted by the sound of Peregrine's study door opening. It would be nice to thank him for his support and kindness before the proceedings began in earnest so I made my way out onto the landing. I gasped. Cripes! I couldn't see the carpet at all, just all this dry ice swirling spookily two feet above it. He would be livid.

'My darling girl.' A figure lurched drunkenly towards me in the mist. It sounded like Peregrine. It *was* Peregrine! He *was* drunk! Thank goodness he was drunk, the dry-ice machine was obviously out of control. If it kept churning out at this rate we wouldn't be able to see anything but people's heads! Ambrosia's intensive diet would have been completely wasted – who would see her new svelte form now?

'Shmashing idea, very atmospheric. I've opened a bottle of champagne, my darling, so come down and share a toast. There's not a dry ice in the hice, I mean dry eye in the . . . whatever. Actually, I think I'll just go and have one of my power naps, it's been the most trying day you can imagine. No fish on the menu, and on a Friday. Don't know what Father Hubert will say. Lunch at the Connaught isn't what it was. Most exhausting.' He sauntered off and was soon lost in the swirling fog that was growing thicker by the minute. I dashed back to Pandora.

'Pandora, quick! The dry ice is out of control, we've got

to get downstairs!' I hurriedly dragged on the dress that was at the top of the pile. It was the slinky gold mermaid number that had once belonged to my mother. I'd worn it the night I'd met Peregrine. I smiled. So much had happened since then.

I gave my hair a final brush, secretly thrilled that it hung, thick and gleaming like laburnum halfway down my back. I slipped on my navy blue fluffy mules – black would have been better, but what the hell. An armful of gold bangles completed the ensemble.

'How do I look?' I asked nervously.

'Very slinky,' said Pandora admiringly. She stood back and examined me more critically. 'But maybe you need a smidgen more colour.' She rifled through her make-up bag and pulled out a brush and pencil. 'Try this kohl, it's magic.'

'Why not. I don't want to be overshadowed by Tiffany Strumpet.' I outlined my eyes carefully with the magic pencil and allowed Pandora to brush on some golden blusher. A slick of plump lips lip-gloss and I was all set. Pandora whistled.

'See, that kohl really draws out your green eyes. The lily is now truly gilded.'

It's funny how other people's make-up works so much better than one's own. Perhaps it was the same principle that made food from other people's plates so much more delicious and completely unfattening I thought, as we clattered downstairs.

Pandora was jabbering away about something or other but I couldn't hear her because of the racket of my teeth chattering and my bangles jangling with nerves.

The dry ice had really kicked in now and we had to clutch the banisters for dear life because we couldn't see where we were going at all.

'I think we should go down to the kitchen and see how they're getting on. I gave them strict instructions about the eggy bread, but they've never made it before.'

We tottered into the kitchen on our mules. Fortunately the

dry ice had not made it into the kitchen yet, though it was probably only a matter of time, and the staff from Nosh 4 Nobs were whirring around the kitchen most efficiently. Mrs B was beavering away energetically at the sink and humming what sounded like a Japanese war song, which I knew was her interpretation of the theme music to the *Jerry Springer Show*. I couldn't have risked my life on it, but she was looking quite cheerful. It was probably the anticipation of toff misbehaviour, drunkenness and general fisticuffs of an unspecified and chaotic nature that was revving her up. Historical precedent made this seem very likely, Cheyne Castle soirees had a habit of deteriorating into anarchy surprisingly quickly, but I knew tonight would be different. After all, tonight we were celebrating the Birth of a Book!

Emily from work experience, Shmooze and I had gone to huge efforts to invite the *crème de la crème* of London's literary intelligentsia and several Hollywood mogul types from LA, who were bound not to drink alcohol at all. Luckily I had instructed Nosh 4 Nobs to get in lots of soft drinks to cater for them.

Alerted by the rattle of my bangles, Mrs B turned round.

'Miss Oriana!' There were tears in her rheumy old eyes. 'You look a real picture. 'Ere, George, come an' 'ave a butchers at Miss Oriana.' Mr B shuffled out from behind the fridge. He liked a quiet moment or two to gather his thought before his door duties started in earnest.

'Very nice. A real picture and no mistake.' He stood rather awkwardly, obviously longing to shuffle back behind the fridge. Luckily the doorbell clanged into action.

'Door! Someone's at the door,' twittered Pandora excitedly. 'C'mon, let's get in situ in the ballroom!'

We tottered upstairs as Mr B went to open the door and accepted a glass of champagne from Rufus, the chief honcho from Nosh 4 Nobs. The dry-ice machine was still churning the stuff out like there was no tomorrow and it was now impossible to see anything below waist height.

'Rufus! Can't you find anyone to turn that wretched thing off? The guests are starting to arrive!'

'Everything's under control,' said Rufus tensely. 'The machine will naturally turn itself off in a moment.'

'But you said that an hour ago!' I glanced round the ballroom nervously. 'Where is everybody? And where is Emily on work experience? She promised she'd be here to set the books up early.'

'Don't worry,' said Pandora nervously. 'Everybody will probably come all at once. That's how it normally works.'

Fortunately we were distracted by Max Shyster and a group of his journo chums. Judging from their unsteady gait they'd obviously had a few sharpeners already.

'Dahhling girls!' Max reverted to the plummy tones of his childhood when he'd had a few. 'Shmashing ice sculpture outside the house. A most original touch.' A waiter hovered bearing a tray of authentic alpine tea, exotic fruit juices and champagne. The journos made a sudden grab for the booze. 'No panic, chaps!' said Max languidly. 'This is Cheyne Castle where the champagne never runs dry! Drink up.' I rattled my bangles disapprovingly and helped myself to some authentic alpine tea.

The room was filling up very quickly now, mainly with people I had never seen in my life. Never mind, they were probably all important literary editors and mogul types. I couldn't wait to introduce myself. Max drained his glass and helped himself to another.

'You look gorgeous, doll. Rairly slinky. To think you've actually written a book too. It's marvellous. Bloody marvellous.'

'So you'll give me a bit of puff in *The Snoop!* will you, Max?' I tossed my hair and rattled my bangles in what I hoped was a seductive manner.

'My darling. You are a Snoop Staple. Take it as read. By the way,' he asked innocently, 'has Peregrine seen it yet?'

'Oh no. I did give him a copy, but I think he found the sex a bit offputting.' I was distracted by the sight of Annette, the publicity honcho from Red Duck, staggering in, her ethereal form weighted down with several boxes of books. Her fine blonde hair hung wispily to her slim shoulders and her small pert features were constricted in an anxious expression.

I hobbled over at great speed. It was imperative I catch her before she disappeared. She was famously elusive. I had only met her twice, and each time she had burst into tears and rushed off. When I had tentatively raised the matter with Emily on work experience she had told me not to worry because Annette found meeting authors terribly upsetting; in fact she was practically phobic about them. After meeting Jeffrey Archer she had had to take a whole week off work to recover.

'Hi, Annette! I'm so thrilled to see you!' I was overwhelmed by a warm feeling of sisterly bonhomie. We were united by my book, linked by a deep bond forged by months of blood, sweat and tears crafting this final product!

'Oh! Oriana!' She started nervously and gazed at me with frightened fawn-like eyes. If she hadn't been weighted down with my books she would have scarpered.

'Here, let me help you with those.' I began to load books onto the designated book table by the door. I was to sit here and sign books as everyone went home. We were going to have a till and everything, just like a bookshop!

'Oriana, dahling!' It was Petrol, looking even more frighteningly chic than usual in a tight black suit. She appeared to have made a special trip to the hairdresser and her thin black hair had been so cleverly coiffed that it seemed to disappear into the back of her head. Indeed, it was so tightly wound that it might have been achieved with the key to a sardine tin. She kissed me in what could only be described as an affectionate manner.

'Just love the dry ice, sweetie, but I think it might be a

good idea to turn it off before it engulfs *everyone*, don't you think?'

'But they can't, they switched it off hours ago but it won't shut down! Um, have you met Annette from Red Duck?' I turned round but Annette had disappeared into the mist. Luckily Emily on work experience arrived at last, closely followed by a crowd of slavish men who were helping her carry more boxes of books.

'Sorry I'm late,' she apologized, smoothing down her leather micro skirt and flicking back her long blonde hair. 'Thanks so much. Just put it down here.' She smiled at a small sweating man carrying a cash till who hung around hopefully.

'Just leave me to it, Oriana. I'll set up the books here and stand guard over them all night. We're hoping to sell loads!'

Petrol tapped a small Manolo Blahnik shod foot impatiently. 'Come on, Oriana. Get away from all these fusty books and come along and meet everybody!' She pulled me away firmly and began introducing me to all sorts of useful people.

Photographers were busy snapping away as various micro celebs made their way into the ballroom and were photographed sharing a joke together. Tiffany Strumpet, *The Snoop!*'s esteemed shopping correspondent had eschewed her usual lurex (thank goodness! We didn't want to clash) and was wearing a striking silver chainmail ensemble, whose cunningly spaced holes revealed her considerable embonpoint to maximum advantage. She was making careful notes in a matching chainmail notebook with matching chainmail pen. I hoped my gold lurex outfit would pass muster.

I caught sight of Pandora, Ambrosia and Arabella sharing a joke in the distance but I was sucked into a sea of people who all wanted to talk to me at once. This didn't usually happen at envelope openings where I was just another faceless It girl, so it made a nice change.

I saw my mother arrive and stand around rather forlornly. I wanted to thank her for the sculpture – she'd be amused by my retro cruise outfit – but I was being tugged from all sides by photographers.

'Oriana, come and be photographed with Tiffany,' hissed Petrol, pulling me away from a tedious discussion I'd been having with the literary editor of the *Bexhill Bugle*. 'And then I want to introduce you to the producer of *This Morning*, Lottie Luck from Capital Radio wants a word, and the editor of the *Mail on Sunday* wants a chat about featuring you in their Me and My Shampoo slot.'

I caught sight of my father who must have just arrived, chatting in the corner with Jack Reeves the dishy government transport minister. Where had Jack come from?

'C'mon, Petrol, come and meet my dad.'

'Oh!' she tittered nervously and smoothed her sardine tin hairdo in what could only be described as a potentially flirtatious manner. This was most unlike Petrol. I hoped the authentic alpine tea wasn't going to her head. We managed to make our way over to the other side of the room without being grabbed by anyone. The room was packed, and luckily the dry ice was now down to ankle level, due in part to the industrial cleaners who had been crawling around the floor spraying various substances from their homemade spray guns. Whatever it was, it had worked a treat and the dry ice was down to manageable levels.

I saw my mother, now talking to Siena and Mary, wave at me hopefully as Petrol steamrollered me towards my father. I waved back. Plenty of time to catch up with them later. For the moment I was on autopilot, propelled from one journalist/ photographer/micro celeb to another. I had to make the most of every second.

'Ah, Mr Spicer, I've heard so much about you,' murmured Petronella huskily, once everyone had been introduced. 'You must be *so* proud of your daughter.'

'I certainly am. It's a great day, Oriana.' He beamed at me through misty eyes. 'I'm a very proud parent.'

I gasped. The display of paternal pride was so

extraordinary I was a bit wobbly on my pins.

'I was just saying to my old friend Jack that I was surprised to see him here.'

'Well, I'm surprised to see you,' he said. 'The traffic's at a complete standstill tonight so I decided to walk home from work –'

'Perfect opportunity for agit prop!' I whispered to Pandora who had joined us.

'– and I heard the revelry and just drifted in.'

'People do tend to get sucked into Cheyne Castle when we leave the door open,' I explained, trying to talk in a photogenic kind of way and artfully arranging *Chalet Girl Secrets* to maximum advantage as a photographer whirred around us.

'I'm not surprised.' Jack looked at me appraisingly and gave me a half smile. I felt myself visibly wilt in the force field of his charisma and blushed feebly. I pinched myself firmly. Pull yourself together, girl. This is a perfect opportunity to lobby for the nation's future! But where should I start? Rights for circus animals, an end to vivisection, banning dolphins and whales from ghastly oceanariums, car pollution? Trams? Yes, I would start with trams; he was transport minister after all.

'I'm honoured that you could spare the time to come to our party, sir.' I thought the 'sir' might get things onto a depressingly non-libidinous sensible footing. 'As a constituent, I was wondering if you had read any of my letters about the tram campaign?' Greenpeace had been campaigning to return trams to London streets and I had been firing off letters in support.

Jack's flirtatious attitude immediately became one of gravitas and he frowned in concentration. 'Of course! Oriana Spicer. If I'd known you were Bill Spicer's daughter I would have invited you to the Commons for tea! Yes, I do remember your letters. Very good they are too.'

There! He didn't chuck them in the bin! I knew it.

Someone else probably chucked them in the bin for him.

'Did you know that, Bill?' he said to Dad. 'Your daughter's quite a letter writer.'

Dad smiled indulgently.

'I just wanted to say how much I'm hoping that you'll support the tram bill. London is becoming impossible.'

'Yes, something has to be done about the traffic jams, they've been strongly linked to the dripping, I mean dropping sperm count in London,' Pandora quickly corrected herself. I glanced at her glass disapprovingly. She'd been knocking back the alpine tea with great enthusiasm; she'd be no use agit propping if she was drunk.

'Yes, I always liked trams,' said Dad. 'You should bring 'em back. Then my lorries can get around a bit more easily.'

'In Switzerland, well, in Zurich specifically,' I banged on, 'the trams are marvellous. You don't need a car at all.'

'Trams are, *hic*, most definitely where it's at,' agreed Pandora holding out her teacup to be refuelled with alpine tea. Really!

'I have been giving the matter serious thought,' continued Jack, giving me his undivided attention. (Heaven!) 'But Tony and I –' so impressive being on first name terms with the Prime Minister – 'have been put off by those crazy Radical Planet people. Violence must not be considered a tool for negotiation.' Dad and I exchanged looks of complicity. It was essential to keep Siena away from Jack. It could be too awkward for words.

I was just about to phrase an intelligent reply when Tiffany Strumpet, her chainmail clanking seductively, suddenly materialized at our side. Damn! I rattled my bracelets crossly.

'Ah, *Mr* Reeves,' she purred seductively, running an expensively manicured hand through her mass of raven ringlets, her chainmail pen poised in anticipation of a *bon mot*. 'I'm so *thrilled* to meet you. Could I just take this opportunity to say how much I support your anti-road *hump* campaign.' The emphasis on the word hump was most unappetizing and I tried to switch my attention to the arrival of Peregrine.

'And are you a tram girl too, Miss Strumpet?' asked Jack charmingly, inclining his head towards Tiffany's clanking embonpoint.

'Oh, my goodness, yes. Anything that will get the roads moving. It took me an hour to get from Harvey Nicks to Le Caprice yesterday. Too frightful. If the people could take trams, my driver would be able to get me around so much quicker.'

'Mr Spicer, it's a pleasure to meet you, sir.' Peregrine appeared at our side, gleaming with exclusive unguents and expansive bonhomie. Dad shook his hand cheerfully. I knew he didn't have a clue who he was.

'Dad, this is Peregrine. He—' I stopped mid-sentence in shock. Emily on work experience had abandoned her position at the till, causing a flood of opportunists to seize the opportunity to pinch all the books! One of the rather desperate looking Northern journalists, aided by Emma Batt (what was *she* doing here!) was wrenching open the till with a hammer. It was too awful that the Bat had got in. I had expressly forbidden her entry. The wretched creature must have come in through the window.

I had to find Emily before the Bat and her opportunist chums took advantage of the *laissez faire* security to steam upstairs and pinch something from the White Collection.

I put down my head and made a dash for the door. I needed to find someone from Red Duck to take control. On the landing I caught sight of the elusive Annette, sobbing and running down the staircase towards the door. She couldn't be leaving already. Who else could possibly introduce me to the Northern literary editors and stop them from raiding the till?

'Annette! Wait, it's me, Oriana. Don't go!' She turned, took one look at me and burst into floods of tears. Before I could catch her she had opened the heavy door and disappeared, letting in a stream of glamorous It people who steamed up the staircase whooping, flattening me against the wall.

I grabbed a glass of champagne from a passing waiter. Just one glass of champagne would surely help me see things in a more optimistic light and give me the clarity I badly needed.

On the way down to the kitchen I heard a distinct scuffling and squealing coming from the broom cupboard. No one ever went in the broom cupboard except the industrial cleaners on their pickle breaks and they never squealed, unless they were listening to one of their Jerry Springer videos.

With a flash of intuition I flung open the door, only to discover, *horrors*, Emily from work experience *in flagrante* with Magnus, of all people. I knew I'd encouraged Peregrine to invite all his friends, but Magnus? He was meant to be in prison!

'Ah, Oriana,' Magnus drawled happily. 'Stunning party. Do you want to join us for a quick breather?'

'NO, I DON'T!' Magnus and Emily from work experience, in the broom cupboard. It was horrible. 'Get back into position, girl! Anarchy is breaking out with the Northern literary editors, they're trying to break open the till!'

To her credit, she saw the importance of the situation immediately and hurriedly smoothed down her leather micro-skirt. 'Cripes, Oriana. I'm so sorry, I just nipped in here for a breather and must have lost track of the time.' She dashed out of the broom cupboard, her blonde hair streaming behind her. Good old Emily. She would sort it out.

'Darling, I just love your shoes,' Magnus was saying. 'Are they Manolo Blahniks?' They were. Magnus's knowledge of ladies' accessories was creepy and unnatural. How could I have fancied him! I slammed the broom cupboard shut and locked it firmly. It wouldn't be as comfortable as the Finnish prison but who cared. Phew! I was suddenly exhausted. No wonder. I'd been talking for hours. Maybe I'd take the opportunity to dash into Peregrine's bedroom and freshen up.

I quickly applied a bit of slap, took a deep breath and rushed upstairs, trying to ignore the Finnish, or was it Hungarian swearing coming from inside the broom cupboard. I was immediately grabbed by Petrol's glistening rouge noired talons.

'Dahling, where have you been? Quickly! The *Standard* wants a photo of you and Lottie Longchomp from EastEnders. It's the chance of a lifetime! Hurry!' She dragged me over to a small posse of pouting micro celebs who began air-kissing me frantically while the cameras whirred and promptly ignored me once they stopped.

'Fabulous!' Petrol squeezed my arm affectionately in a vice-like grip.

'Um, Petrol, is Anoushka coming?' I knew that a personal appearance and resulting photos of Anoushka would guarantee puff in all the papers.

'Of course!' She glanced at her watch nervously. 'She's running a bit late, I know she was hoping to get to fifteen parties first, but don't worry, she'll be here! Anoushka won't let you down! Tamara! Sewper to see you, mwah mwah.' I took an opportunity to slip off to rejoin Jack and my father, who were now surrounded by an admiring coterie of my most beautiful girlfriends, including Siena and Mary, of all people.

Siena was hovering next to Dad, engaging him in earnest conversation, while Mary was chatting away with Jack Reeves, fondling the pearls round her neck (pearls!) and throwing back her head with laughter at his jokes. I could see Siena casting cross looks in their direction. Oh dear. Mary flirting with Jack Reeves, green enemy numero uno, was not something I had bargained for. What about the humps and the kiddies' lives? Had she no principles?

The room suddenly went very silent. A celebrity of

gargantuan proportions had obviously just arrived, but who? I jumped up and down on my mules with great excitement, spotting the familiar platinum blonde fluffy hairdo and tall etiolated figure totter into the room.

'It's Anoushka Bird-Whistle,' I whispered to Dad and Jack Reeves. They both groaned. I grinned at Siena who had drifted to the edge of the group but was obviously longing to spend some more time with Dad. I knew that look and felt desperately sorry for her but it was an awkward situation. After all, it was only a few years since she had tried to blow Jack Reeves up. I was saved by the familiar grip on my arm.

'I told you she'd be here!' It was Petrol in a state of great excitement as she steered me towards Anoushka and her large entourage of micro celeb chums who accompanied her everywhere. Everybody was air-kissing everyone else to the whir of flashbulbs.

'Well, join in!' hissed Petrol irritably. 'You're an It girl too, you know!'

But I was transfixed by Pandora, C and various other chums in the distance waving my book at me, and making signing gestures. I looked at the posse of preening celebs and gulped. 'Um, Petrol, I must go and sign my book.'

'Nonsense,' said Petrol, waving at her chums through bared teeth, shoving me with great force into the throng. Her spinning classes had obviously given her the strength of a much fatter woman, and I was sent spinning myself, losing my balance and tripping on an icicle that must have dislodged itself from the chandelier. I picked myself up quickly – so embarrassing! And then I lost control of my mules. Without them I was only five foot four, and stood no chance of standing out from all the other It girls, who due to superior breeding and Jimmy Choo stilettos hovered around the six foot mark. Practically Amazons! As I scrambled up I found myself level with Anoushka's armpit.

'Hello Anoushka. I don't know if you remember me. I'm Oriana, from Shmooze too. Um, I don't mean Shmooze two, there's only one Shmooze of course,' I wittered on as Anoushka peered down at me from a great height. I don't think she recognized me at all. It was *so* embarrassing! I showed her my book. Luckily I'd hung on to that!

'I wrote this book that we're launching tonight, you see . . .'

Anoushka continued to look at me blankly. I had the strangest sensation that when I was looking into her small blue eyes I could see the back of her head. It was very disconcerting. No wonder she wore sunglasses so often.

'Actually, I'm not a great reader,' she drawled. 'I'm more of a people person.'

'Dahhling, it's simply *too* delicious of you to turn up,' gushed Petrol. 'How was Lord Socket's party?'

'Ahtterly ahtterly brillynt.' There was a whoosh of flashbulbs as the photographers began snapping us frantically.

'C'mon, girls, squeeze up a bit closer.' Sensing a photo op, Tiffany Strumpet and Tamara RaRa suddenly appeared while I edged tentatively towards Anoushka's fragrant armpit, displaying my book prominently. Next to them I felt like a midget. But this was what it was all about! This was the social whirl!

At last the flashbulbs stopped and as suddenly as they had arrived the girls melted away. I took the opportunity to get down on my hands and knees to try and retrieve my mules. Unfortunately some idiotic person had switched the dry ice machine back on and it was hard to find anything in the fog that was swirling around the floor. In the mist I recognized Pandora's foot. I pulled it impatiently.

'Mushbe shome mishtake! Someone's let a dog in! Leave my foot, you brute.'

'It's me, you fool,' I hissed up at her. 'Help me find my shoe.'

She collapsed onto her hands and knees and felt around the floor. 'Shmashing party, Max Shyster found the key to the Cheyne Castle gin cupboard and he's selling G and Ts from the loo, and did you know, *hic*, that your shister is slogging Jack Reeves on the balcony?'

'Snogging or slogging?' I asked desperately, though I think I knew what she was trying to say.

'She's shlogging him about, really scary.'

I couldn't bear to think of Siena attacking Jack, but it had to happen sooner or later. 'Oh dear. I'll sort it out but first of all I must find my shoe.'

'And Peregrine's fallen madly in love with your dad, he can't stop talking about him and—'

'Found one! But where's the other beastly one? Damn! I give up. I better go and sign some books now.'

I left her clawing around the floor (hopefully it would sober her up a bit) and hobbled over on my remaining mule (I wasn't letting go of this one in a hurry) to what I had mentally christened the Signing Area, which I had asked Gustav to rope off for me. I sat down with some aplomb and glanced around. Nobody was forming an orderly queue, and what was more, all the books had disappeared. Emily had obviously clocked off for the night.

All around me confusion reigned. Somebody had gained illegal access to the Cheyne Castle CD system. I suspected the industrial cleaners, they were the only people who knew how to work the complex apparatus. If I was right, we were doomed to the Bee Gees, Abba and Barry Manilow all night. Max had abandoned his stance at the drinks cupboard and was teaching Tamara RaRa to salsa dance to the tune of 'Saturday Night Fever,' Pandora was teaching my father how to limbo beneath the drinks table, and all around me people were whooping and hollering with great excitement.

Mrs B was cavorting energetically with Magnus (she must have let him out of the broom cupboard, dammit. I'd always suspected them of some sort of secret rapport). Tiffany's chainmail was clanging away in time to the music while all the other It girls were swaying sultrily to the Bee Gees' wispy wailing.

Well, if you couldn't beat them . . . I got up and joined the swaying throng as Max lurched over with one of his G and Ts which I gulped down in one.

We were momentarily distracted by a massive crash as one of the icicles which had been attached to the main chandelier dislodged itself quite suddenly and hit the floor. Luckily no one was hurt but it did add a frisson of wartime danger to the proceedings, inspiring the guests to even greater displays of energetic and licentious behaviour.

I was pleased to see Mary samba-dancing vigorously into view and waved at her with unaccustomed bonhomie but I don't think she saw me. That reminded me to look for Siena. Swaying towards the balcony, I noticed that she was indeed embroiled in some kind of entanglement with Jack. He was flushed and excited and gripping her fists while she flailed about uselessly. I had no wish to become involved; besides, neither of them looked particularly upset. No, I would leave them to it.

Then somebody came round and topped us all up with the authentic alpine tea mixture, which was tasting much more concentrated than usual, but by now I was past caring. In fact I was so far gone that when someone offered me a Whoops slimming cigarette, I smoked the whole thing, and I never smoke.

The next few hours passed in an ethereal haze of bonhomie and dancing. It didn't seem to matter that the Bee Gees tape was caught on an endless loop (I believe that is the correct term). As Einstein said, time is relative, and I couldn't have said exactly how long we'd been dancing to the swinging strains of 'Saturday Night Fever'. It could have been minutes, seconds, hours, days even. We had become quite used to the crashing as icicles fell from the ceiling, sustained as we were by the alpine tea and Pearl Harbor Explosion cocktails that Mr B was churning out in the kitchen. And what with the dry ice creating a surreal and lascivious atmosphere, you couldn't see what people were doing with their hands and feet at all.

Pandora lurched into view. 'Anoushka's boyfriend, you know that big marine biologist chap, whatshisname is here,' she mumbled, pointing to a corner of the room where Anoushka and a tall, broad shouldered man with a craggy suntanned face and rumpled tawny hair were talking intently. Several photographers were whirring around them snapping. Dan's powerful body seemed too big for the slighty crumpled black suit he was wearing and he looked a bit cross.

'Oh, good,' I mumbled incoherently. 'I'm gonna askim if he believes in mermaids. Heesh a marine bologist, he'll know about shtuff like that.'

'Don't be stoopish, he'll think you're a stoopish bimbo . . .'

I was saved from making a fool of myself by the arrival of a team of firemen, or firefighters as I believe they now like to be known, who charged into the room wielding what looked suspiciously like hoses. I thought at first that they were singing firemen and that they were going to sing me a telegram until somebody shouted 'The tree's on fire!' and from then on pandemonium broke loose, with my guests clambering out of windows and rushing out of the house where they stood wrapped in blankets provided by the industrial cleaners. *They* were remarkably cheerful under the circs, but as I said, there was nothing like a crisis for cheering *them* up.

'No chance of the industrial cleaners needing to take Prozac,' I remarked crossly to Pandora as we shivered outside waiting for the firemen to give the all-clear. 'All they need to do is turn on the news to find a new disaster to cheer them up.'

'I thought one of them was meant to be permanently stationed beneath the tree all evening?' replied Pandora irritably.

'Huh. Probably fell asleep on the job.'

'Who fell asleep on the job? Anyone I should know about?' It was the indefatigable Max.

‘Thought you’d be scooped out by now,’ I smiled nervously. One never quite knew where one was with Max. We were interrupted by Mr Button who had risen to the challenge and was circulating with a large tray of his famous one hundred per cent proof hot toddies. The guests were knocking them back with worrying abandon and warming up nicely, throwing off their blankets and looking dangerously energetic.

I knew it was up to me to take control of the situation. I’d thought the evacuation might encourage the party to break up, but there must have been at least seventy guests in various states of dishabille weaving drunkenly about the Embankment. They reminded me of those motorway madness programmes when wild zoo animals escape and are filmed wandering about unpredictably, causing chaos and multiple pile-ups.

I looked around for my family but couldn’t spot any of them. In the distance I could see Petrol networking furiously with Nerys Nimble from EastEnders, so she wouldn’t be much help.

‘Look, isn’t that your dad?’ hissed Arabella as a chauffeur-driven Bentley edged its way past the house.

I peered into the luxurious interior. Dad had obviously traded in his old Jaguar. ‘Yes!’ I banged on the window. ‘Dad, it’s getting out of control! Help!’

The electric window wound down smoothly. ‘Smashing party, Oriana. I can’t stay because I’ve got a hell of a day tomorrow. I’ve got to be in Amsterdam at nine a.m. You’ll cope, I know you will.’ The window wound up smoothly and he was gone.

‘Oh.’ I was distracted by a roar coming from the balcony and was amazed to see the tiny figure of Mrs B lobbing the remains of the charred tree into the air, where it fell into the ice sculpture, causing it to melt with alarming speed. It continued to melt and steam for several hours, causing considerable traffic chaos from the flooding.

The It girls on the balcony were refusing to leave, insisting the firefighters remove them forcibly. Tiffany refused to be parted from her chainmail outfit and it took two firefighters to airlift her to the ground, she weighed so much.

All this coincided with pub chucking out time. Alerted by the potential of civic unrest and flooding, a disgruntled crowd of what can only be described as 'ne'er do wells' from the Badger Baiter, a public house famous for its punch-ups which frequently ended in death, began to drift over Battersea Bridge. They loitered menacingly, rather lowering the tone of the proceedings. Further book lobbying seemed impossible under these ominous circumstances and I glanced round anxiously.

'Has anyone seen Peregrine?' I inquired of no one in particular. Nobody had, but someone thought he might have gone abroad.

'Oriana! The door's been locked.' It was Pandora, in a state of nervous panic. 'What're we going to do? Nobody seems to want to go home.'

It was true. Our guests, hardened and stimulated by fire, alcohol, crashing ice boulders, flooding and the possibilities of class warfare from the silent gathering crowd on the other side of the pavement, showed no inclination to go home at all.

'Party's over! Thank you for coming!' I cried loudly. 'Super to see you all. *Chalet Girl Secrets* will be available from Harrods and leading bookshops. Or just ring me up directly for a copy. You can always catch me on my mobile, 0831 . . .' My voice was drowned in the whooping and licentious banter, and nobody took the blindest bit of notice.

'*Come on!*' insisted Pandora, pulling me away. 'Let's go home, there's nothing more we can do.'

I glanced around for some shoes – the ground was littered with clothes and shoes from the It girls who had now been airlifted off the balcony. I settled on some rather nice silver mules. I suspected that they may have belonged to Tiffany and I strapped them on tightly.

I kissed Pandora goodnight and hobbled off in the direction of my flat where I collapsed into bed. Thank God it was all over. The last thing I heard was the sound of police sirens wailing in the distance before falling into a deep, sound sleep.

Chapter Thirty-three

The next day I was kept frantically busy. Petrol and Emily on work experience had surpassed themselves in puff opportunities. I was booked for an interview with Acton Radio, which I'd never heard of admittedly, but the nice DJ who interviewed me assured me that they had many listeners in the Ealing area. I was running down Acton High Street trying to find a taxi (as if that was likely) when my phone rang. It was Petrol. I tensed expectantly.

'Dahhhling! Stunning party, you were fabulous!' I began to unclench in the glow of unexpected approval. 'And you should be doubly thrilled because the *Maharanee*, no less, has just rung and offered you *four* pages for the next issue of *Divorce!* You can bang on about your book to your heart's content. The only thing is that they want pictures of you with your father and with Peregrine at Cheyne Castle. I told them that would be fine. It will be, won't it?'

I re-clenched again. It definitely wouldn't be fine. Peregrine was absolutely anti-*Divorce!* and Dad wouldn't agree in a thousand years to that sort of photo op.

'Um, wouldn't it be enough just to have me at Cheyne Castle?'

'No!'

'Even if I was dressed in risqué lingerie?' I asked desperately.

'NO!'

'Risqué lingerie with a photogenic cat?' I pleaded. If I begged, perhaps Mummy would lend me one of her horrible yet spookily photogenic goose-eating felines. They peed on everything and smelt like nothing on earth but they looked great in pictures.

'*No*. The deal is you, with your father and Peregrine. If that is impossible for you to arrange, I must know now.'

'Yes, yes, it's quite possible,' I lied feebly. I wasn't going to let *this* photo op pass me by. I'd work something out, I was sure.

I flagged down a cab (miracle!) and rang my mother to discuss the party and broach the feline issue.

'Oh darling, I just tried to ring you but you were engaged. Last night was a great success, the papers are full of it!'

'I'm sorry I didn't get a chance to talk to you but it was completely frantic.'

'I know, I don't know how you managed. I was very impressed with the way you handled everything, you looked as cool as a cucumber. What did you think of the Chalet Tiara ice sculpture?'

I hadn't thanked her. How awful. 'It was fabulous, Mum, thank you *so* much. Everybody commented on it. Um, I wanted to ask your advice. *Tatler* want to photograph me but only if I have extras like Dad and Peregrine, and they won't agree. So I was wondering if I could borrow the cats? The editor likes cats, they're always doing feline features and this might just swing it.'

I'm afraid I told a little white lie, my family think *Divorce!* is irredeemably naff, but *Tatler* – well, my mother might just approve of a top toff magazine like that. I crossed my fingers.

'I don't know, Oriana. Toffles and Tootles do hate having to leave the house. They're so sensitive to new places . . .'

'Oh Mum, pleeese?'

'Well, all right. But you'll have to come and pick them up and drop them off the same day. They can't be away from home overnight. They'd hate that.'

I hung up with some relief. I wasn't going to tell Petrol that Dad and Peregrine couldn't make it. Once the shoot had been set up I would tell the photographer they'd been unavoidably detained. Cute cats would be better than nothing. And maybe I could persuade Geat-Aunts Horatia and Agatha to visit Cheyne Castle the day of the shoot. After all, Aunt Horatia was a countess and Aunt Agatha was an Hon. A countess, an Hon and two cute cats, surely that would swing it?

The rest of the day was frantic. I had to rush back home as a girl from Oxford University was coming to interview me for a thesis on It girls. I was a little hurt when she let slip that she had tried to get Anoushka and five other It girls, but they had all been too busy. But fortunately, I was able to make several useful points about the importance of bringing back trams as well as the horrors of factory farming. But she seemed far more interested in how I kept my figure on the *canapé* circuit and who my hairdresser was.

Then I was sent by chauffeur-driven car to a photographic studio in Fulham where I spent several hours being coiffed before being stitched into several ski suits. I was to pretend to be a chalet girl making beds for *Country Wife* magazine. I wasn't going to be paid but they had promised to plug *Chalet Girl Secrets*, which was very exciting. And my mobile had been ringing *off the hook* all day with disgruntled guests, several of whom had been arrested after the party for loitering in a public place.

Peregrine had also rung. I'd been dreading speaking to him, but he was thrilled with the party and said he was longing to see me. I thought he might be miffed about the fire and the water damage from the icicles but he said the industrial cleaners had been up since 5 a.m. and the place was as good as new.

So as you can imagine I was pooped when I finally rushed back to the Ritzy Marina Club to meet C and Pandora for a party feedback session. The party had been well covered in all the papers but with hardly a mention that it was actually a book launch and I was keen for their opinion.

As I made my way into the bar to meet them, I have to admit I was secretly thrilled that my arrival created a small stir amongst the svelte lady members, causing them to abandon their champagne and 'lite' complimentary *crudités*.

I waved at C and Pandora in the distance – they were killing themselves with laughter about something and I speeded up, looking forward to sharing the joke. I could do with a laugh after the day I'd had.

'Hi, girls, sorry I'm late.' I collapsed into a chair exhaustedly.

'Um, Oriana, your dress is tucked into the back of your knickers, did you know?' pointed out Pandora helpfully.

'No, I didn't know.' I fished my dress out surreptitiously. 'Damn, I thought everyone was staring at me because they recognized me from the papers.'

'I'm sure that's why,' lied C soothingly. 'You must be thrilled that it was such a success.'

'Yes, you had great coverage, the firemen were the *pièce de résistance*. I loved what they put in the *Telegraph* – 'It girls airlifted to safety—'

'Yes, it's all very well,' I glanced at the picture of Tiffany Strumpet's blissful expression as she was manhandled by six burly firefighters, 'but they didn't mention the book at all.'

'By the way, I don't know if you saw the *Evening Standard*,' said C, 'but Jack Reeves has been caught out in some big scandal.'

'Oh God, not again. I thought everyone knew that he was heterosexual.'

There had been a run of 'outings' in the press recently with many homosexual government ministers being discovered *in flagrante* in public hotspots. In fact it was such an everyday occurrence that the papers no longer even bothered to report such goings on. However, heterosexuals, with their dwindling sperm counts and desperate reliance on helpful aids like Viagra to stimulate performance, were much thinner on the ground, considered even to be a dying breed. A recent sex march for heterosexual rights had attracted just twenty participants, while an equivalent for the other camp had attracted thousands and been declared a national holiday.

Jack Reeves, with his numerous affairs, cheerful, long-suffering wives, mistresses, girlfriends and women claiming to have been harassed by him, often admitting in court that it had indeed been a most agreeable experience, was a source of great fascination to the media at large.

'No, I don't think it's got anything to do with sex,' said Pandora doubtfully. 'He was photographed coming out of the Tube with a terrible black eye and limping.'

'But he doesn't believe in public transport, he's been trying to ban it for years. Hang on, I'll just see if there's anything in the evening paper about it.' I stretched over and picked up a late edition paper from an adjoining seat. Jack was indeed the lead story, which carried a picture of him looking battered and bruised but in apparently good spirits:

'Jack Reeves, the libidinous government transport minister, emerged limping from Westminster Tube station battered and bruised yet eager to discuss the reason for his trip on the Tube. "Several of my lovelier constituents, notably Miss Oriana Spicer the authoress, have used their considerable charm to persuade me to reconsider the government's transport policy (*my goodness!*). This is the second time I have had the misfortune to travel by Underground and I was even more horrified at the state of my fellow passengers, most of whom were grubby and smelt frightful. Do these people realize they are travelling on a train, not a public lavatory? It was even worse than my wife's cleaner had described. Something must be done." Mr Reeves, 46, refused to answer questions about his extensive facial injuries, which he admitted had been caused by "walking into a door late last night." '

'Oh dear. I don't think it was a door. I think your sister had something to do with it.'

'Yes, I spotted them having an energetic discussion on the balcony and she was getting quite emotional,' added C.

'And I distinctly saw her shouting quite loudly and pushing him against the wall.'

Oh dear, I'd hoped that not too many people had noticed the violent altercation. Honestly, you'd have thought that Siena could have abandoned her hooligan impulses at her own sister's book launch. Had she no shame?

'So you think Siena kind of beat him up a bit?'

'I guess she's the major suspect,' said C. 'I doubt that anyone saw him leave because after that the alpine tea began to kick in, we were all dancing away and then the firemen came. It was absolute chaos after that.'

'He could have got one of the industrial cleaners to smuggle him out,' I suggested. 'They love that sort of thing.'

'But you obviously had quite an effect on him, Oriana, if you persuaded him to go on the Tube. Who knows what effect that might have in the long term? He might invest in more public lavatories to stop people—'

'I don't know. If he thinks the Tube is a public health hazard he might close them down completely. It would be all my fault.'

'Siena wouldn't like it one bit,' commented Pandora helpfully.

'She might even blow me up. She's completely obsessed, you know.'

'I wouldn't worry, if there's nothing you can do, there's no point worrying, and if there is something you can do, do it,' reassured C.

'I love this in *The Snoop!* Max has had a field day,' said Pandora.

' "Fisticuffs at top toff's palace!" ' she read. ' "Water cannons, firemen and mounted police officers were last night called out to the home of Lord Skye-Rocca when revellers celebrating the book launch of trash tycoon's daughter and sausage skin heiress, Oriana Spicer, got dangerously out of hand." ' (*Ten more e-mails from the aunts, I thought glumly.*)

' " 'I couldn't believe my eyes,' said Bert Shrimp, 48, who was walking home from a night out at the Badger Baiter pub, with his brother Ted, 41, an unemployed plasterer, later arrested for disturbing the peace. 'All this posh crumpet climbing out of the windows and wandering about the road with no kit on. I'm not a drinking man, if I had been I would have thought my bitter had been spiked.' " '

Pandora and C shook with laughter. 'Top toff's palace! Fisticuffs!' C slapped her ample thigh. 'Bert Shrimp! How d'you get to be called Bert Shrimp? God, I love this country. It's somethin' else!'

'And look, there's a picture of Anoushka and Dan from last night,' exclaimed Pandora, her blue eyes widening as she read out the accompanying article. ' "Anoushka Bird-Whistle and her elusive romantic interest Dr Dan McCloud, Harvard scientist and marine biologist, were spotted on a rare night out together at Oriana Spicer's book launch last night. This morning Miss Bird-Whistle was happy to confirm rumours that the couple are secretly engaged. Watch this space." So come on C, what's the inside track?'

'It's crap,' said C. 'She's crazy about the guy, but they're hardly dating. She did some charity work with him but that's about it. Secretly engaged – in your dreams, honey.'

'I think he does like her,' speculated Pandora. 'I was standing next to them and they seemed to be calling each other darling a lot. I'm sure he's not the sort of man to call people darling unless he really meant it.'

'Pah, what on earth would they have in common?' snorted C. 'He's a Harvard scientist for Christ's sake.'

'That doesn't mean anything. Look at Arthur Miller and Marilyn Monroe,' I rationalized. 'They came from different food groups, too.'

'Well, I'm afraid I was too far gone last night to really work anything out. I think we all were,' said Pandora. 'By the way, has the *Divorce!* shoot been confirmed yet?'

'Sure has,' said C. 'Petrol's thrilled about it. Have you managed to persuade Peregrine and your father yet?'

'Um, no, I'm working on it,' I explained. 'But I've got two cute cats, a countess, an Hon. and Cheyne Castle and a selection of unworn lingerie that I plan to wear against the stunning backdrop of the White Collection. That lot should swing it.'

'Yeah. The great thing is to just do the photos. They're tighter than two coats of paint and hardly ever chuck anything away if they can use it.'

A four-page feature in *Divorce!* It was a dream come true. With a readership that stretched to millions and worldwide coverage it was just the push that *Chalet Girl Secrets* needed to become a big hit. Who knew what opportunities such exposure might lead to?

Chapter Thirty-four

The next day the papers were full of the 'who punched Jack Reeves' debacle. Everybody seemed to think it was a *crime de passion*, and there was much speculation as to who had struck the wounding blows. Jack refused to be drawn into the debate, all he would say was, '*Cherchez la femme*,' but he was obviously loving the intrigue.

I rang up Siena to ask her if she was going to come clean, but she was out. Mum said she had gone to the Isle of Skye where she was organizing an eco rave for Radical Planet.

I must say I loved being in the cut and thrust of media events. The whole thing was quite good timing for Jack because he had just announced that he was lobbying for the coveted post of minister for women. I couldn't blame him for being fed up with being transport minister. Minister for women sounded much more fun, and carried many perks, including fact-finding missions to oppressed places like Barbados, St Lucia and Acapulco, to say nothing of free membership to the Ritzy Marina Club.

There was going to be a referendum (only women were to vote), so he was particularly keen to embrace women's concerns. No wonder he had paid such attention to our opinions at the book launch.

Recent surveys revealed that women rated better public transport (the tram campaign was really gaining momentum, brilliant!), free sanitary protection, better childcare and cheaper organic produce as high on their list of priorities. But Jack had nothing to worry about. Women adored him, and were intrigued and thrilled by his sexual shenanigans. This latest *cherchez la femme* mystery could only enhance his appeal. Just like President Clinton really. The more women came forward to claim to have been 'tampered' by him, the more sexy they found him. Yes, Jack certainly had my vote.

Most people agreed that it would be an interesting departure to have a man as minister for women, especially as the popular actress and beauty Joanna Yummy had just been voted in by the male population as minister for men. This was working very well and her recent spate of party political broadcasts to encourage men to drive responsibly, behave chivalrously and do more housework had the highest viewing figures ever recorded on the BBC.

Her motto, growled seductively after each broadcast, 'Cleanliness is next to manliness', was having a dramatic effect on the country. Scouring was becoming sexy and utilitarian bleaching products were being stylishly repackaged in groovy bio degradable macho grey plastic. Supermarkets were becoming crowded with men whistling nonchalantly around the cleaning product shelves. Normally they only whistle around the freezer cabinets (it's true, look out for it).

It was nice to think that maybe my letter-writing campaigns hadn't gone completely to waste and I was redoubling my efforts. Apart from Emma Batt's brutal review ('Silly silly silly. Should have stayed on the slush pile where it belonged, its author should stick to shampoo launches, don't give up the day job, Oriana') the reviews were surprisingly favourable and I was determined to use any writing ability for the greater good.

If I was going to be *burdened* by being in the public eye, I would use my fame constructively. What was the point of banging on about my beauty routine (far too complicated and obscure to share anyway), when I could stand on my soapbox and say something useful? Talk about Swiss trains monkeys, awful zoos, etc., etc. But the only thing people ever asked me about were Peregrine, my trophy family and what kind of shampoo I used. Still, it was better than not being asked about anything, I supposed.

Siena would be pleased about the trams. It was odd how we both wanted the same things but had such different approaches. Genes were a funny thing.

Recent hints from the Prime Minister that trams were to be reinstated and that cars were to be heavily taxed in the city were making the Greens quite optimistic, as was Jack Reeves' volte-face. But just in case he became too politically correct he soon blotted his copybook: 'There are far too many cars on our road,' he was quoted in the paper. 'I plan to return to the halcyon days of motoring exclusivity by raising road tax by fifty per cent and introducing trams to London. After discussing the matter seriously with a number of experts and my constituents, most memorably the glamorous authoress and public transport expert Miss Oriana Spicer, I have sent for a team of Swiss public transport troubleshooters to fly in from Zurich to advise the government. Something will be done.'

I was thrilled. Troubleshooters, Swiss experts! OK, public transport wasn't that glamorous but it was cutting edge, it affected millions of people. Jack was clever. By wrapping up a serious decision with It people and frivolity, he cleverly avoided the terrible political correctness label. Such a label would be the kiss of death to his campaign to become minister of women. No, the common woman wanted a devil in high office! Way to go, sisters!

London would become livable in. I could put off moving to Zurich. We could take trams from Knightsbridge to the Ritzy Marina Club, thereby saving aeons of time and stress!

Jack continued to blot his copybook when he was quoted off the record as saying that there were too many rustbuckets clogging up the roads and holding people up and that if people couldn't afford to drive a decent motor they were better off on buses anyway. *That* little outburst caused him all sorts of problems. The opposition called on him to stand down from public office, Class War and Radical Planet named him an Enemy of the People and he was given twenty-four-hour police protection. Of course all this made him even more popular and he ended up winning ninety per cent of the votes in the referendum.

Besides, there was no chance of him really resigning because he was a great chum of the Prime Minister and frequently lent him his stunning beachside villa in the south of France. You'd have to be daft to give up free hols like that, and Tony wasn't stupid. No, I felt Jack was safe for the time being.

It was very exciting because the newspapers kept ringing Pandora and me and asking for our views on public transport. We were photographed getting on and off buses, in taxis, trains, even outside the Swiss Embassy dressed up as Swiss train guards and eating Toblerones. We loved it, and it was good for book sales too because I made sure that *Chalet Girl Secrets* was prominently displayed in every photo op.

Great-Aunts Horatia and Agatha were thrilled to have another invitation to Cheyne Castle as they had both had colds on the day of the launch, to view the White Collection and were fortunately free the day of the *Divorce!* shoot. I mentioned that *Tatler* (needs must), might be taking some pictures of Peregrine and me and that I would be honoured if they would appear in several photos 'as a souvenir of the day'.

Predictably, Peregrine was not keen to appear in the photos. 'As a *soi-disant* businessman,' he explained on the phone, 'it would be no good for my credibility. But Cheyne Castle is, as ever, at your disposal.' I understood his reasoning. He was about to sell some land to the notorious 'The Beauty of Concrete' developers. They were public enemy number two (after Jack Reeves), having built a new town on a site of scenic interest outside Aberdeen. Peregrine was keen to stay out of the papers while the transaction took place. He was also becoming more involved with the marketing of Lord Skye-Rocca pickles and was trying very hard to find an outlet for them without much success. You might have thought Harrods would jump at something like that, but not a bit of it.

'What about a nice photo of you holding the pickles? It would be great publicity,' I asked rather desperately.

'Yes, it would, darling, but I need to keep my head down, what with the land just about to be sold.'

I was looking forward to the shoot and had been on a special wheatgrass juice detox program for twenty-four hours beforehand. I don't know why, maybe it was all the toxins rushing out, but I was feeling decidedly queasy when I arrived at Cheyne Castle with Squirrel Nutkin and Peanut, my mother's two Shetland sheepdog accessories. There had been an unfortunate bout of cat kidnappings in London, and Mummy had refused point blank to let me borrow the photogenic felines, which was probably just as well under the circs, given the industrial cleaners' strange eating habits. Mrs B had hinted darkly that one of them had links with a Chinese restaurant in the area, so it was better to be safe than sorry.

Mrs B was up early to let me in (Peregrine would be asleep for hours) and she had prepared some of her home-baked grapenut pellets for my breakfast so I soon felt much restored.

On the dot of 9 a.m. the *Divorce!* team was at the door, eager to be let in. I was very impressed to discover that they had provided a stylist and a hairdresser cum make-up artist do me over, so to speak.

We set up base camp in the kitchen while Mrs B bustled around making coffee for everybody, tut-tutting as Sophie the make-up artist began layering the first coat of slap on my clean face.

'In my day we used to call it gildin' the lily. You'll not

make Miss Oriana look any better than wot she looks like already.' She bustled off with Peregrine's special chicory coffee to run his bath, leaving the team in a state of considerable indignation.

'Silly old bag,' said Sophie crossly.

'Yah. So rude,' agreed Eloise Whisp, the stylist. It was rather a coincidence because her sister, the model Saffron Whisp, had once been sort of engaged to Jack Dudley, Pandora's romantic (dis)interest. Small world!

'Now, girls, let's show some respect,' mumbled Charlie Twiclethwaite-Ormsby-Nore as he fiddled ineptly with his camera lenses. I must admit my heart had sunk when I realized Charlie, whose slightly out of focus snaps I was familiar with from various society magazines, had been assigned to my case. He was actually an impoverished baronet, and was employed chiefly because he was on familiar terms with the people he photographed. It certainly wasn't for his technical skill. He also had a bit of a drinking problem – I'm afraid he wasn't called Shakin' Charlie for nothing.

'Now, Oriana, the Maharanee wanted a sort of tweedy look for you. As the fiancée of Lord Skye-Rocca she envisioned a sort of country lady in town by mistake sort of thing.' *Fiancée!* God, was that what people were saying? The whole thing was getting out of control; Peregrine would be setting a wedding date next. I determined to have a chat with him after the shoot and tell him that he was too good for me, or something like that. And what was it with this tweed thing? I'd never worn tweed in my life! I just wasn't a tweed girl at all.

'Um, Eloise, I don't have to wear tweed, do I? I thought gold Lurex might be more suitable.' I pulled out some exciting retro cruise wear, including the outfit I had worn at my book launch, hopefully. 'And gold would look so great against the white pictures, and match the dogs' fur.' I patted Peanut who was sitting on my lap.

'Yes, I see what you mean,' said Charlie, who prided himself on his colour awareness.

'No, absolutely not,' said Eloise. 'The Maharanee was adamant.' My face crumpled and she relented. 'Well, maybe we'll do a couple of Lurex shots at the end if we have time.'

I spent the next few hours being tweaked, curled and coiffed and then we dashed upstairs to the drawing room where I was to pose in a selection of heavy tweed outfits.

'You don't think I look like Margaret Rutherford, do you?' I pleaded nervously, perching uncomfortably on a shooting stick that someone had found in a cupboard.

Everyone laughed nervously and assured me that I didn't. The bell rang and I looked at my watch. 'Oh, that'll be my aunts for their photograph.'

Eloise looked at her Filofax. 'Oh yes. Countess Horatia Applebee and the Hon. Agatha Roper-Smythe.'

Mrs B appeared at the door with my aunts who coincidentally were wearing tweed too. They are twins and look very similar. Both have long beaky noses, narrow lips and tightly clenched grey curls. They are tall and so skinny that they sew stones into the hems of their coats as they have this quite unreasonable fear of being blown over in strong winds. It's practically a phobia. Mrs B was bowing and scraping a bit, but then she is an appalling snob, I'm afraid.

'Dear Oriana! My goodness, you look just like that actress. Agatha, who is it that I mean?'

'Margaret . . .'

'Margaret Rutherford. That's it. Before she ran to fat of course.' Charlie put down his camera. 'It's Hottie, isn't it?'

'Shakin' Charlie, of course! Are you taking the snaps? How super!'

'I went to school with Hottie's husband,' explained Charlie. 'I must say, this is all very jolly.'

'Well, he's dead now, poor fellow. Been dead for twenty years.'

'Yes, I do seem to remember something . . .' Charlie trailed off vaguely. 'Lungs, wasn't it?'

I thought it was up to me to get things back on track. 'I expect you're longing to see the White Collection, aunts?'

'Not particularly. We were hoping we might catch a glimpse of your beau. We're so excited that you're engaged. Of course, it can't be helped that he's a Catholic, but the one thing no one could ever accuse us of is not moving with the times. Whisper the word, Holyrood Palace?' Two pairs of blue eyes bored into me hopefully.

'Oh, aunts, please. We're not engaged. It was just a wicked rumour in *The Snoop!*'

At that moment Peregrine appeared at the door, gleaming from his morning ablutions and wearing a smart dark suit and tie.

'Um, Peregrine. Darling. I'd like you to meet my aunts, Horatia and Agatha. They've come from Bexhill to be photographed.'

'Yes, Oriana wants us to be in the *Tatler*—' I coughed loudly. If Peregrine and my aunts knew that they were supporting *Divorce!*, a magazine they considered to be utterly scurrilous, we'd be out on our ear. Luckily the moment passed. OK, they might find out afterwards, but then again, they might not. It was a risk I was prepared to take.

'Get a shot of Peregrine before he goes,' I whispered to Shakin' Charlie who knew the situation. He had no desire to return to the Maharanee without at least one shot of Peregrine in the bag.

'Hellair, Peregrine.'

'Good heavens, it's Shakin' Charlie. What a surprise!'

'I was at school with Peregrine's father,' explained Shakin' Charlie, extending a quivering hand in Peregrine's direction. 'Will we be fortunate to have you in our picture too?'

Peregrine backed off. ' 'Fraid not. Unfortunately I'm about to leave for a working lunch. See you later, ladies.' He turned to leave but not before Shakin' Charlie's camera had gone off accidentally in his direction.

'Whoops! Living up to my name!'

Good man!

We spent the rest of the afternoon upstairs taking pictures. The tweed-clad aunts were arranged, perching gingerly on uncomfortable Louis XV chairs, pretending to read my book (I had torn the rude pages out), while I was seated at their bony feet, with the dogs, similarly tweed clad, and looking up at my aunts with a rapt, respectful expression. OK, I know it sounds corny but the Maharanee loves that sort of thing. My aunts soon became impatient, however, and left after ten minutes. There was just time to slip into a sliver of Lurex and perch provocatively in front of the *pièce de résistance* of the entire White Collection, cryptically entitled, 'White paint in the snow', when Shakin' Charlie said, 'It's a wrap. Time for a quick G and T, if you could procure such a thing, Oriana, then I must be orf. Cocktails wait for no man.'

We returned to the kitchen where the team busied themselves packing up the equipment. I was just 'fixing' the drinks, as they say in America, when a nice lady from *Divorce!* arrived to ask me a few informal questions to go with the photos. She seemed to know everyone very well so I 'fixed' her a drink too and we sat down with the others at the kitchen table. It was nice to 'kick back' after the long day.

After a few G and Ts we all loosened up considerably and they began cluing me in about the latest society scandals. There was so much going on, I had no idea.

'Are you quite sure he's gay?' I asked as they discussed a major celebrity.

'Oh, Oriana, where have you *been*?' Eloise laughed superciliously, inhaling her Whoops slimming cigarette elegantly.

'Too busy writing bestselling novels, I should say,' interjected Elizabeth the journalist kindly. 'I hear the book launch was a great success. What a coup to have Jack Reeves turn up. Is he a particularly close friend?' she inquired casually.

'No, I'd never met him before in my life. He happened to be passing and just drifted in.'

'I wonder who really gave him that black eye,' ruminated Eloise.

'Some jealous old tart probably,' said Sophie.

'Actually, it wasn't a jealous old tart, it was my sister, if you must know. They had a disagreement about government transport policy. My sister is a very principled woman.'

'Rairely. You mean your sister biffed Jack Reeves?'

'And there was no sexual motivation whatsoever?' Eloise was incredulous.

'Pah, course there was. Makes the world go round,' grinned Shakin' Charlie, helping himself to some neat gin. I wished he would just dry up but thanks to the gin he was firing on all cylinders.

'My goodness. I didn't realize you had a sister,' said Elizabeth. Oh dear, I'd said too much. If Siena found out I'd discussed her with the media, she'd kill me!

'Um, well, she lives a very quiet life.'

'And does she work?' asked Elizabeth.

'She does voluntary work, for charity.' That was a bit of an exaggeration; since Radical Planet's bungled plot to blow up Jack Reeves had been uncovered, they had not surprisingly lost their charitable status. 'But I'd appreciate it if that could be off the record. You see she's very shy.'

'I quite understand,' said Elizabeth tactfully. 'One doesn't want to antagonize one's family, under any circumstances.' She moved swiftly on. 'You must be very excited about becoming the next Lady Skye-Rocca. As the leading Catholic family in Scotland, the Skye-Roccas traditionally marry at Holyrood Palace in Edinburgh. Is that a possible venue?'

I explained that marriage wasn't on the cards for the

immediate future as Peregrine and my work schedules were too hectic.

Luckily the rest of the team peeled off around then, leaving Elizabeth and me to continue our informal chat. I managed to steer the conversation away from my personal relationships and we enjoyed a stimulating discussion about ecology, how to get the British to break their love affair with the plastic bag, how marvellous trams were, and trying to define Jack Reeves' unique *je nais sais quoi*. You see, I wanted to be seen as more of an intellectual serious sort of person and lose my flibbertigibbet frivolous It girl tag. She gave me the telephone number of her psychic nutritionist, who sounded marvellous, so I promised I'd give her a ring when things were a bit less frantic.

When she eventually left, I carefully stacked all the empty gin bottles (the industrial cleaners used them to grow things in, they're quite eco-minded really), tidied up and wrote a note saying I had a frightful headache, and left the house as soon as possible. I had no wish to see Peregrine as I felt some kind of discussion about our relationship was looming.

I think we were both a little confused about whether we were still going out or not and some sort of clarification was probably necessary. I couldn't face any more emotional upsets and was feeling so muddled I knew that any decision I made in my current state would probably be wrong. I was quite happy to be a virtual fiancée for publicity purposes, so maybe we could drift on like this for a bit longer. And maybe the virtual fiancée situation suited him as well. It seemed that he was similarly indifferent. I mean, if he were remotely keen he wouldn't stand for this half-hearted courtship either.

Wrapping my coat round me I scooted out of the house, trying to block out Peregrine's non-penetrative sex concept which he had recently mooted again. I couldn't get my head round that one at all, but maybe I was just being old-fashioned.

Chapter Thirty-five

Jack Reeves' face had healed miraculously after a day, a fact the papers attributed to the ministrations of one of his mistresses who fortunately happened to be the nurse of a plastic surgeon.

I desperately hoped that my revelations as to the perpetrator of his injuries would not be revealed, but knew that Nigel Demster paid handsomely for such juicy nuggets of information. It did appear as a story the following day, but fortunately a royal scandal had just broken and the media were more interested in that. I knew that Siena would be livid at being described as the daughter of a trash tycoon and as a sausage skin heiress. Fortunately the article didn't reveal the informant; besides, Siena was still at the eco rave in the Outer Hebrides.

Unluckily someone must have shown her a copy because she was on the phone straightaway.

'I'm just really pissed off that this has got into the newspapers, Oriana. I'm trying to do a job, you know, and this sort of thing just stops people taking me seriously.'

'I'm sorry, Siena, but the place was full of journalists, it's impossible to stop them writing anything. Besides, you did hit him, lots of people saw you. You can't go around beating up government ministers and expect people to forget about it.'

She laughed bitterly. 'Yeah, well, he had it coming to him. All that crap about poor people shouldn't be driving cars and the best thing about having money is that it can insulate you from the hoi polloi. You know he's trying to ban rambling altogether? The right to roam is an integral part of our constitution . . .'

'Yes, but you wouldn't like all those kagouls wandering all over your and Mary's garden, would you?'

'That's completely different. We're talking about thousands of acres that are completely out of bounds.'

'But they don't shut gates and they drop hamburger cartons everywhere. It causes chaos. Why can't these people roam around shopping malls or Hyde Park or wherever?'

'Oh, for heaven's sake Oriana! And by the way, Mary has been trying to read your book and she's extremely cross that you've named an unpleasant character after her sister. It's very unscrupulous of you.'

'What on earth are you talking about? I didn't even know she had a sister, for heaven's sake. And what unpleasant character? All my characters are lovely.'

'Charlene from Manchester,' said Siena icily. 'Mary's sister is, surprise, surprise, called Charlene and she lives in Birmingham.'

'Oh, for goodness sake. I don't know anything about her family, except that Mum says she's not on speaking terms with any of them.'

'Well, she is now. The whole family are meeting up this weekend to discuss it.'

'So I've brought them all together. That must be a good thing surely?'

'No, it's not. Mary's been trying to distance herself from them for years and she's dreading having to see them all again. So look what you've done.'

We hung up, both feeling utterly disgruntled. Siena was like a wall. You knew it was there for a reason but you knew it would be utterly pointless trying to reason with it.

Fortunately I didn't have time to dwell for too long on such unpleasantness as Emily on work experience was keeping me very busy doing publicity, interviews and book signings. Although this sounded very grand and ego-boosting, it usually meant being waved to a special table by a harassed, overworked assistant where I was meant to sign piles of books for admiring customers.

Sadly no one ever turned up to these occasions, but I signed the books anyway then, left to my own devices, I would surreptitiously place them in the 'we recommend', 'sizzling new arrivals', 'don't miss this' sections of the bookshop.

Emily went to a lot of trouble to arrange a special signing in Harrods, advertised as, 'An exciting chance to meet It girl writer, *with canapés*!' But nobody turned up to that except my mother and she'd already bought twenty of my books and she doesn't eat, so the canapés were wasted. But at least she bought a book so I made one sale.

I was kept so busy that I was at last able to dispense with Petronella's services. Admittedly she'd done a sterling job on the puff front but I thought I'd rather be a past It girl than have to face any more Shmooze envelope openings. I was flavour of the month since the book launch but I knew it was only a matter of time before I fell out of favour and she started screeching at me again.

Anyway, I was hoping that once *Divorce!* came out, my life would change forever. I imagined *Chalet Girl Secrets* jumping to the top of the bestseller lists and book signings packed out with admiring onlookers. Maybe Ernst would see the pictures and get in touch. Maybe.

It was late November now and the first snow would be falling in Gstaad. I thought with a pang of Chalet Tiara, empty and neglected, and longing to come back to life again. It was odd, but the more time went by, the more I missed the place. Was my memory playing tricks? Had the river really sparkled silvery-grey in the moonlight? Had the sky been such a powdery blue? The sun so bright, the air so still and clear that the sound of icicles melting sounded like glass breaking? I remembered the snow falling so silently and with such stillness you felt yourself to be in another world, a world where mythical creatures and magical things happened.

However much I tried to let go, I was still bound, enmeshed and entranced by Chalet Tiara. It was hard to relinquish the past when it filled the present so completely. After all, it was the inspiration for *Chalet Girl Secrets*.

I'd always loved the quote from Anais Nin: 'Dreams pass into the reality of action. From the action stems the dream again; and this interdependence produces the highest form of living.'

I'd never quite felt what she meant before but now I understood. The dream was Chalet Tiara, the action was the book whirlwind. Now I was waiting, longing for the dream to begin again. But I must be patient. There was still a bit more action left to face, I was sure, and I didn't know how much I was going to enjoy it.

On the morning *Divorce!* came out, I ran down to the newsagent. Too impatient to wait till I got home I stood on the pavement and flicked through it. I gulped.

'The future Lady Skye-Rocca at home with Lord Skye-Rocca at their London seat, Cheyne Castle.' It was followed by an out of focus picture of Peregrine, rushing out of the room looking like a fugitive.

I was frumpily featured, clad in a bewildering array of tweedy outfits over four pages, with dogs, tweed-clad aunts (double gulp, I hoped they'd never find out!), while various gushing captions intersected the pictures. Thank God they'd included two pages of racy 'cruisewear' in between all the ghastly tweed.

'Oriana waiting for Lord Skye-Rocca to join her for cocktails,' intoned one caption. 'Lord Skye-Rocca pursues a successful career in the City' (*hello?*) 'while Oriana spends her free time writing bestselling novels.' *I wish*. The only time Peregrine went near the City was to have lunch in it.

I quickly shut the magazine and rushed home to read the

copy at home. All in all I was quite pleased with it. The pictures weren't too bad, a little out of focus perhaps, and the copy looked anodyne enough.

As long as Peregrine, my aunts, my mother and my sister didn't see the piece, I'd be fine. And if they did, well, it was too late now. It could have been a lot worse, all things considered.

But I was wrong. Things were about to get very much worse indeed.

My mother rang the next day.

'Oriana, your aunts are *livid* with you. They said you'd told them the photos were for *Tatler*. How *could* you have duped them? It's so underhand of you.'

'Oh dear. How on earth did they find out?'

'They went into their local newsagent to pick up their *Telegraph* and were greeted like celebrities.' She imitated Great-Aunt Horatia: ' "Mr Patel waved a copy of the beastly rag under my nose and said, look, you're famous!" '

'Oh dear,' I repeated hopelessly. 'I really didn't think they'd ever see it.'

'I don't blame them for being upset. You know how they hate seeing the family name dragged up every time your book is mentioned.'

'Well, it's my name too. I wish you wouldn't make me out to be some kind of fugitive.'

'Talking of fugitives, I'm very surprised Peregrine agreed to be photographed. He looked most peculiar, like the camera went off by mistake, or something.'

'It did. The photographer shakes a lot.' I shifted uncomfortably. Best not to go into details about *that* wicked subterfuge. 'Honestly, Mum, one might think you'd all be pleased the book is doing so well. It's just made the *Sunday Times* bestseller list,' I finished hopefully.

'Oh, Oriana, I wish you'd realize that there's more to life than your book!' Sounds of canine and feline mayhem suddenly broke out, thankfully bringing the conversation to an end. 'Oh my God . . . I've got to go. Toffles has peed on my lap. Oh dear, it must be the new smoked salmon pâté she's been trying out. Poor, poor Toffles. She so much prefers the sturgeon . . . Oh, and Siena's not at all happy either . . .'

Like, tell me something I don't know, I thought grumpily, replacing the receiver. I dialled my aunts' number and prepared to do some serious grovelling.

'Oh, Oriana, how are you?' inquired Great-Aunt Agatha cheerfully. 'Hoary, come quickly, it's Oriana!'

There was a click as Aunt Horatia picked up the extension.

'I'm so sorry, aunts. I have to admit that my lust for increased book sales completely overwhelmed me, and I'm sorry to drag you down with me.' I took a breath and looked down at my prepared speech before continuing.

'Oh, do stop talking nonsense, girl! We're delighted.'

'Yes, it's very jolly. It shut that dreadful Mrs Crabbit up for once – you know, her son is that actah fellow.'

'Nigel Crabbit, plays that chappie in EastEnders.'

'She's always bleating on about him, you'd think the sun shines out of his ba—'

'*He's* been trying to get into *Divorce!* for years.'

'Yes, we trounced her all right. *Touché*, Mrs Crabbit.'

'And such glamorous pictures. Just think, our niece, an It girl. That'll shut them up at the Red Cross shop!'

'But Mummy said you were livid.'

'Well, we couldn't admit we love *Divorce!* could we? She'd think we were frightfully lowbrow. You know how high-minded she is.'

'She's a frightfully clevah gel,' interjected Agatha.

'We're loving *Chalet Girl Secrets* but some fellah's torn out some of the pages. Pretty poor show. I'm going to ring up your publisher and complain.'

'Oh, I wouldn't do that, aunts,' I said hurriedly. I had torn out several of the trysting scenes as I had no wish to shock them. 'I'll send you a nice new one.'

'Well, we'll let you get along, dear. We haven't started on the *Telegraph* crossword yet, and it's nearly lunchtime.'

Mad mad mad. The whole family were as mad as hatters. Still, it was a huge relief that they didn't mind about the *Divorce!* debacle. If only the rest of the family were as easy.

I couldn't bring myself to ring Siena, but I didn't need to because she phoned me later that day. Mary had seen the *Divorce!* piece (apparently at the dentist, ho ho) and they were both in a state of intense agit prop hysteria.

'How dare you mention me in that stupid article? You have no idea how damaging it is for me to be connected to . . . to . . . this sort of ridiculous It thing,' Siena spluttered. She was so angry she had lost her usual eloquence. It was terrifying.

'But they asked if I had a sister. I could hardly deny it, that would have raised far more attention.'

'Oh, for heaven's sake! It's impossible trying to have a rational conversation with you. Under the circumstances we don't want to see you, or for you to have anything to do with the children. You're a bad influence. And don't you *dare* use me for your stupid book, it's utter *shite* and I don't want anything to do with it. *Get that into your stupid pea brain, Okay?*' She hung up abruptly.

I held on to the telephone, completely shaken, and then my knees gave way and I fell onto a chair, totally winded. The venom in her voice was shattering. She must really hate me.

I was too shocked to discuss the conversation with anyone, but a few days later Dad rang to say he'd heard that Siena and Mary had been burgled but that they refused to call in the police because Siena said they were a fascist right-wing organization which she wanted nothing to do with. 'Well, she's the one who believes in this right to roam stuff. Presumably that applies to burglars as well,' he added wryly. 'Are you all right?' he asked. 'You don't sound your usual cheerful self.'

'It's Siena. An article came out in *Divorce!* about me, and it said I had a sister who worked for charity. It was my fault, but the journalist just asked me out of the blue and I didn't have time to think if I should admit that I had a sister or not. And Mary won't speak to me because she thinks I named one of the characters after her sister and—'

'Yes, I saw that article. Lettuce thought you were wearing far too much make-up. You could have passed for twenty-eight.'

'I am twenty-eight,' I said crossly. 'But I don't know what to do about Siena. She and Mary really hate me now. She's says I'm such a bad influence I'm not to see the children ever again!'

'I'd say that was blessing. You don't want to be around when one of their fathers swings by. Siena will come round. And I wouldn't worry about that bitch Mary, she's polite enough to me because I've got a few bob. Doesn't seem to realize that I've left it all to the lifeboats. Anyway, I've got six Germans outside waiting to see me. You must ring Lettuce straightaway and sort out your flights with her.'

'So we're definitely going to the Kahala Mandarin Oriental for Christmas?' I asked excitedly. This was my father's favourite hotel.

'Of course. Well, I'll let you get on. Look after yourself.'

Over and out! Hawaii here I come. Phew. I was counting the days.

If anyone had said that writing a book was a piece of cake compared to publicizing it, I wouldn't have believed them, but it was true. But as I watched *Chalet Girl Secrets* move up the bestseller list I felt a secret warm glow of pride. I was sorry to have annoyed my family, but every time I saw my book in a bookshop, I felt a rush of happiness. I had really done it!

So I felt I deserved a relaxing week in the sun with the chance to spend time with my father. I saw so little of him during the year that these yearly holidays were the only time we had to catch up and I valued them greatly.

Chapter Thirty-six

Just before Christmas I drove down to see my mother in Abinger Hammer so we could exchange Christmas presents.

Using some publishing contacts I had managed to discover a copy of the *Buttonhook Compendium*, an obscure tome published in 1910, which she had been trying to track down for months.

'Darling, you are so clever to find this!' She held the obscure tome reverently. 'Nanette will be so jealous!' Nanette was one of the big cheeses in the buttonhook world, and she and my mother had a close, if competitive, relationship when it came to buttonhook artefacts.

'So when are you expecting Siena and crew down?' Siena, Mary and the children were descending for a vegan Christmas feast that I knew Mum had been secretly dreading.

'There's been a change of plan,' said Mummy cheerfully. 'They rang yesterday to say that Mary's sister—'

'Charlene?'

'Yes, the one that was so upset. Well, Charlene has invited them all to Birmingham. Honestly, Mary is so self-absorbed. "Oh Venetia, we're so sorry to let you down, I know how much you were looking forward to having us to stay." Of course I had to pretend I was terribly disappointed.'

'But what will you do?' I asked worriedly.

'Well, every year there's a big Buttonhook AGM in Boston which I've never been able to get to because of doing Christmas here, but this year I thought, why not? And when I told Nanette, she asked me to stay with her in Nantucket.

Her daughter's got a house there apparently. You seemed to love it so much, so what do you think, should I go?'

'Definitely! You'll adore there, it's just your kind of place.'

She busied herself pouring out some more coffee. 'I . . .'

'Yes?' I had the feeling she was trying to say something rather awkward, probably about Siena or my book or something, and tensed expectantly.

'Oh, I can't remember what I was going to say. Old age!' she laughed, handing me an exquisite gold-rimmed china cup, part of her treasured wedding set. 'Here, drink your coffee. Are you all packed up for Hawaii?' she asked conversationally.

'Oh yes. I'm counting the days.'

'Is your father flying out with you this time?'

'Lettuce wasn't sure. Probably not. He feels awkward when people find out that he's in first and I'm in economy. It's a bit embarrassing really.'

I always flew out the day before my father. This was to spare him the awkwardness of him being in the front and me in the back. It used to hurt my feelings but recently it had stopped being an issue. All I could think of was how lucky I was to be given a ticket and a week at one of the most beautiful hotels in the world. It was such a relief to slip out of whingeing mode.

'He must realize how hurtful it is for you. And it's not as if he can't afford it.'

'Well, that's just the way it is.'

'Yes, he's not going to change now,' she agreed. 'I do hope you enjoy it this year. Try and stick it out this time.' Last year I had been at Chalet Tiara of course, but the year before, Dad and I had had a horrid argument and I had flown home early.

Siena was never asked on these trips. She would of course refuse as she was rabidly anti air travel, but I wondered if she might like to be asked. Our family seemed to be an endless circle of hurt, with people too proud to admit they were hurt, and misdirecting painful emotional fireworks in each other's faces.

Considering how clever we all were it seemed odd that we still couldn't get something as vital as our relationships sorted out. It was as if we were over-compensated with some genes, and yet missed a chromosome when it came to the nuts and bolts stuff.

Still, armed with an arsenal of self-help books and the telephone number of Honolulu's top tarot card reader, I set off for Hawaii feeling unusually optimistic. I also took the precaution of including *Chalet Girl Secrets* in my hand luggage. If I said I was an authoress, perhaps I might be upgraded!

I arrived in Honolulu in a catatonic state after a very exciting flight. Unfortunately no one had been remotely interested in *Chalet Girl Secrets* at the Air Tonga check-in desk and I was very firmly directed to the back of the plane.

My father's team of assistants had done a sterling job finding the cheapest flight available, which happened to be with the said Air Tonga. 'Still, I'm very lucky to be alive at all,' I muttered firmly.

I tried to block out the memory of being sandwiched between two gargantuan Tongans of Hawaiian descent. One had a bad cold and the other was undergoing some kind of emotional trauma and sobbed constantly.

Fortunately during the stopover at LAX I'd invested in a wonderful book by Wayne Dyer, which put things in a completely different light. He said that concentrating on problems just enlarged them. The thing one had to do was have gratitude for the things one did have. I knew this, but given the horrors of the flight I needed desperately to be reminded of it.

'OK, so we nearly crashed, but we didn't crash. I'm alive and enjoying the beauty of Hawaii.' I wandered onto my balcony which enjoyed a stunning view straight out over the ocean. I had cunningly upgraded myself from my room overlooking the car park. It was a bit more expensive but if Dad complained I'd just say the car park rooms were all booked.

'First class isn't what it was,' my father said the evening of his arrival, looking refreshed after twenty-four hours of first-class airplane pampering. I was still in travelling trauma and compared to him looked pale and wan.

'When I ordered the fillet steak,' he continued, 'they told me they'd only put one on the plane and they'd offered it to someone else. I had to have foie gras instead.' He signalled to the barman for another G and T. 'You're looking a bit peaky, Oriana, you should get some sun.'

'It was the trip. I was squeezed next to these sumo wrestlers on the plane, then I fell asleep and missed my in-flight snack. I didn't eat for twenty-four hours (I didn't mention the Chai Mai latte and bumper pizza I'd scoffed at LA airport), and there was such turbulence we were going to have an emergency landing—'

'In-flight snack?' Dad was incredulous. 'You mean you got a meal? I didn't know that. I'm obviously paying far too much for your flight, I'll have to get Lettuce to shop around for a cheaper airline.' We laughed. It was better to broach this sensitive topic with a light, casual touch.

'Air Tonga *is* the cheapest airline, Dad. I know, why don't I fly back with you in the front? We could change my flight. It would be terribly easy.' I sipped my champagne hopefully.

'No, we won't change your flight. At your age you can put up with it. Now, what are you going to eat?' I gazed at my menu mournfully. He'd strap me onto the airplane wing if that was cheaper than a seat. Grateful thoughts! I must think grateful thoughts.

After the rigours of city life it was heaven to take time out to amble along the beach collecting shells and swim in the sparkling azure ocean. London seemed more than a lifetime away; the worry I'd had about whether my book was selling, whether it was being stocked just melted away. Trying to control uncontrollable market forces was like hoarding sea water in my hands. The more I squeezed and tried to hang on to it, the more it just slipped away. It was time to relinquish ownership of something that was impossible to gain possession of, let go, safe in the knowledge that whatever one gave away would return tenfold. Yes, things were becoming clearer!

Life seemed so much simpler here. The problems of the last few crazy months just melted away in the soft, balmy, fragrant heat and I couldn't understand what I'd been so worked up about.

Sadly the top tarot reader had disappeared but I didn't mind. I was soon addicted to Oprah Winfrey's twenty-four-hour TV news channel, which was full of useful lifestyle hints, as well as being gripped by the slew of self-help books for sale in the hotel bookshop. Americans were great. I loved the way they openly admitted they were utterly confused about life and did their best to get to the bottom of it.

Oprah had suggested studying a new spiritual law every day and discussing it with one's family during the Christmas period. She obviously didn't know my father. But maybe it was worth a try. As they say, where there's life, there's hope. I decided to begin with the Law of Least Effort. Learning to let go, allowing the water and the worry to slip through my hands so they were free to hold more water, which I would again relinquish. Accepting that the void was just part of the abundance and that one couldn't have abundance without the void. OK, I know it sounds a bit muddled but I felt I was getting the gist of things.

I tried to articulate my new philosophical thoughts as we sat having lunch in the open-air restaurant facing the sea.

'Creating money is like breathing. You have to release the oxygen before you can breathe in any more. Giving and eceiving are the same thing, different ends of the same tube. On a spiritual level the fact that you pay people well and look after them comes back tenfold.'

'But I don't do it because I want anything back.' Dad looked bemused. 'Your trouble is that you think too much. What you need is a proper boyfriend. I hope you're not still seeing that Sky-Rocket chap—'

'Skye-*Rocca*.'

'Damn silly name. Surely you can do better than a feeble chap like that?'

'Great-Aunts Horatia and Agatha think he's wonderful,' I said a touch defensively.

'Those old bitches would. They'd encourage you to marry a baboon if it had a title.' This was probably true.

'Oh Dad, I wish you didn't hate them so much. They speak very highly of you, you know,' I lied.

'Do they? Surprising what making a bit of money can do. When I married your mother and didn't have a bean they could hardly stand the sight of me.'

'And I know you think Peregrine's a bit of a drip, but he's mad about you. Every time he tries to do one of his weird business deals he rushes around muttering, "Touch of the Bill Spicers. Your father would understand what this is about." '

'Does he?' He was secretly flattered, I could tell. He had this weird love-hate thing with the establishment. I guess that's why he married Mum.

'Well, the business has had its best year ever, so I can't complain. An American firm made me an offer for it last week actually.'

'How much for?'

He mentioned a stupendous figure. I gasped.

'We've got no debts, the turnover is eight million, we own valuable real estate outright, we've even got ten million in the building society.'

If that was the case why did I have to fly Air Tonga? I longed to ask, but a waiter interrupted us.

'Happy holidays! I thought I'd let you know that the buffet

is closing if you want something else to eat.'

I shook my head. 'I'm fine, thanks.'

The waiter disappeared.

'You mean I'm paying thirty dollars and that's all you're having?' Dad fumed, glancing towards the buffet which was full of robust Americans piling their plates with towering mounds of food. I shuddered. I suddenly thought of Mum and wondered wistfully what she would be having for her lunch. Probably a green tomato. It would be snowing in Nantucket, Main Street would be full of families tobogganing, and the shops would be lit up, festive . . .

The waiter returned and handed my father a leather folder containing the bill. Dad glanced at it, laid some notes inside and handed it to the waiter. The waiter checked the contents and bowed respectfully. 'That's extremely generous, sir, thank you.'

It must have been quite a tip.

'How much did you leave him, Dad?'

'Forty dollars. He only charged you half price for the buffet. And he's a decent chap, can't be easy when you're on your feet all day at his age.'

You see, it's not like he's mean or anything, he's the biggest tipper I know. And although he doesn't like talking about it, he's always giving people 'loans', which he never calls in. His sense of natural justice and integrity is something I deeply admire.

A breeze came off the ocean and I shivered. I pushed my fork away. I'd lost my appetite.

During the following days I avoided meals with my father, going for long walks along the beach and dining on yogurts and apples that I bought from the local supermarket. As everybody else staying in the hotel became fatter, gleaming with good food and sunshine, I noticed that my clothes were becoming noticeably looser.

Dad spent most of the day sitting at the bar, lunching on macadamia nuts and chatting to the barman and various interchangeable old men wearing baseball caps about American football and the American Civil War.

'Had a bit of luck today,' he said as I wandered into the bar one afternoon. 'Jumbo the barman managed to get hold of a *Times* in Honolulu.' He unfolded the paper on his lap and handed it to me. 'There's an article about your chalet boyfriend. I know he's worth a few bob, but he's not much of a looker, is he?'

Indeed, it wasn't a particularly flattering picture of Ernst who was grinning most unnaturally leaning against an Aston Martin holding a tray of his nuts and bolts proudly. In fact he bore more than an unfortunate resemblance to the Michelin man, which was quite appropriate when you think he was the president of Car Fahrt International. It wasn't a very flattering piece either, horribly nudge nudge, wink wink stuff, concentrating on Ernst's playboy image, his homes in Gstaad, Munich and Zurich: 'He admits to cavorting with chalet girls,' *cringe*, and 'his fondness for fast cars and faster women. "The cars are much faster than the women, bearing in mind most chalet girls can't ski," he was quoted as saying.'

The cheek of the man! How many chalet girls had he been out with, for heaven's sake! 'I like the theatre, dining and chasing women,' the quote ended memorably. 'Let me put it this way: I am a single straight billionaire in Zurich. What do you think? It's a wet dream.' Double ugh!

'I should forget all about him if I was you,' said Dad, noting my ashen face. 'You're not bad looking, I don't know why you can't find yourself a decent bloke. I mean, it's a toss-up between this limp-wristed Sky Rocket and this bald Kraut who flogs car parts.'

'Look, it's not that easy to meet people, and Ernst isn't bald, he just looks bald in pictures,' I defended myself hotly

'Have a macadamia nut,' offered Dad. 'That'll cheer you up. Here, Jumbo. Could I have one of your tins? Here we are, Miss Macadamia nut competition. You could enter. doubt you'll win, but it'll give you something to do.'

'I don't want to enter some stupid nut competition,' I muttered.

'Oh, all right,' he replied mildly, eyes returning to an interminable ice hockey game on the TV mounted behind the bar.

'Who's playing?' I asked, feigning interest.

Dad was so absorbed he didn't hear me.

Jumbo smiled at me sympathetically. 'The Pittsburgh Penguins. They're top of the league,' he explained kindly.

At that moment a withered cheer went up amongst the elderly baseball-hatted spectators at the bar. One of the Penguin people had obviously done something extraordinary. Jumbo and Dad did a high five, their eyes glued to the screen. High fives! One of these days I'd come down to the bar and find my dad wearing a baseball hat back to front. Actually, hell would probably freeze over first, but high fives! Really, the sun must have gone to his head.

I wandered back to my room, drinking in the lush green gardens, dripping with orchids, frangipani and bougainvillea and the sound of the waterfall gushing over the shiny grey volcanic rocks. It was so beautiful here; if Ernst was with me it would be just perfect. My tough stance earlier had been replaced by the familiar longing. OK, he'd put on weight and lost most of his hair, but I couldn't forget the way he'd made my heart spin.

I took a deep breath. Dad was probably right. I should be making an effort to meet people. I would go straight to my room and get changed into my best bikini and lie beside the sumptuous pool looking available. Yes, that would be my plan of action.

Feeling more optimistic, I smiled at a man in the lift and made a remark about the weather, but he looked terrified and scuttled out at the next floor. My fragile bubble of optimism immediately deflated and I gave up the bikini idea. Oprah was discussing the Law of Abundance in a minute. That was something to look forward to.

Leaning over my balcony later as the flares were lit at dusk I noticed the same man mooching around the lagoon hand in hand with his boyfriend. I smiled, letting my eyes drift over the waves washing onto the smooth blond sand in the distance. In the light of the moon the waves seemed brushed with silver dust. It was beautiful. It wasn't possible to remain sad amidst this kind of loveliness for long. Besides, there was a double episode of *Ally McBeal* tonight. There was just time for a luxurious bubble bath in the sumptuous marble bathroom before it began.

Sinking into the soft white foam I sighed, enjoying a brief moment of luxurious *tristesse*. I'd spent my life wanting a different kind of father, concentrating so much on the deficiencies of our relationship that I'd lost sight of the good things. But at the end of the day, how could I dare complain? Imagine having a father who was a criminal, a thief, a murderer even? As it stood, I had been blessed. Both Mum and Dad could teach me a thing or two about integrity and honesty.

Thinking back over the troubles of the last few months, I knew that I had no one to blame but myself. I had been so caught up with selling my book that I had lost sight of the bigger picture. I had made a Faustian pact. I had really been prepared to sell my soul down the river, abandon my integrity and mislead people in to thinking I was dating Peregrine to shift as many books as possible.

Yes, my book had been a great success, my dreams had come true, and while I wouldn't deny it had been satisfying, how much more satisfying it would have been if I hadn't antagonized the people closest to me.

What was the point of all those glossy interviews and endless parties? I'd been carried away by the conveyor belt of canapés and the lure of the bestseller lists. And now I was stuffed with canapés and I'd made it into the bestseller list. I wasn't knocking it, I wouldn't have missed it for the world. But now I'd discovered this talent and this energy, how much more powerful it would be if it was driven by something bigger than my ego.

Look at Dad. Deep down I knew him to be driven by something nobler than ego, setting up a fund for his employees, sending the Robinson family to Disney World. I thought of the scrumpled photo of the Robinsons bearing their homemade banner, 'Thank you'. Every time I remembered that, a lump came into my throat.

And Mum. Selling her pride and joy, the Canaletto, to give us security. Selling her Fabergé buttonhook so a cat shelter could keep going for another year. Spending a fortune on that daft ice sculpture of Chalet Tiara and not complaining when I didn't even speak to her at the launch. Remembering the way she had kept trying to catch my eye made my heart fold with shame.

I had been driven by illusions. Clinging on to this illusion of love for Ernst. 'Dinner at home is a wasted sales opportunity.' I mean, what sort of man says that sort of thing? The whole thing was a joke.

It was time to let go of my illusions and create space for something real and new. It would no doubt be hard to force myself to go off someone immediately, but I would begin tonight. I conjured up a picture of Ernst in my mind's eye, but instead of the usual wistful pang I could only visualize the unflattering Michelin man picture from the newspaper. I hummed to myself cheerfully, I hadn't felt this good for months. A missing piece of the jigsaw had subtly slipped into place.

Chapter Thirty-seven

The following morning I was trying to get dressed but was temporarily distracted by the latest juicy tidbits from a President Clinton scandal. The spicy details added to my good mood. OK, I wasn't having sex, but neither were any of my friends, or anyone I knew, and who the hell knew what married people did, they were so damn secretive. You could completely strip off at the Ritzy Marina and none of the chaps would bat an eyelid, and as for the old men at the bar in the hotel, they *certainly* weren't at it. It was therefore extremely reassuring that there was finally some hard evidence that people really were *doing it*, so to speak. Otherwise one might think that sex was entirely an invention of American sitcoms like *Sex in the City* and *Friends* and *Ally McBeal*, where beautiful, marginally dysfunctional thirty-something people were at it all the time.

But yippee! President Clinton seemed to be a real person, and he had been proved to be really Doing It! There were tapes and witnesses and everything. Maybe I should stay in America after all.

I was just about to call room service and celebrate by ordering my favourite breakfast of ripe pawpaw stuffed with creamy birchermuesli (delicious but fattening but okay for special occasions), when the phone rang.

'Oriana, is that you?'

'Mummy! What a lovely surprise! How's Nantucket?'

'It's wonderful, darling. You were right to rave about it.

How's Hawaii and your father? Are you both having a fabulous time?'

'Yes, we are really. Dad's enjoying sitting in the bar talking to Jumbo the barman, and I'm reading a lot.'

'Have you met any nice young people to talk to?'

'Um, not really.' I racked my brains. 'I did try and talk to a man in a lift, but he had to get out.'

'Why don't you talk to people around the swimming pool, or have a tennis lesson or something? You must try to meet people, darling. I don't mean to criticize but you can be very self-absorbed.'

'I know. But I've changed. I'm going to offer my writing skills to the Born Free Foundation, or the Whale and Dolphin Society. Something for the greater good.'

'As long as you don't write about them in a book,' she laughed nervously.

Gosh. That was an idea. But no! The greater good. See what I mean? I have to squash my duplicitous tendencies. 'Perhaps I could help them with their newsletters and pamplets and things,' I said. 'Anyway, tell me about Nantucket.'

'Well, I'm staying in Nanette's daughter's beautiful little guest house by the sea overlooking the lighthouse. It's snowing, and everyone's very friendly, and there's tobogganing in the high street but I rather miss you and Siena. I know I always moan, but I've missed people coming down to stay for Christmas. It's odd being on best behaviour with someone else's family . . .' She sounded very wistful. I felt guilt sweep over me. I couldn't remember the last time I'd spent Christmas with her, I was always so caught up with spending the holiday with Dad I hadn't even considered that she might feel a little hurt at being passed over again and again.

Of course Christmas was only a day, but it summed up everything. All our lives Siena and I had tried to change our father, thinking the relationship would be better if only things were different. All of a sudden I realized with a shock that things were perfect the way they were. And that the relationship I had always longed for had been there all the time, right under my nose, except it was with my mother.

All that time wasted, feeling that we would never be happy until things changed. Once I accepted that things were fine, everything began to fall into place. Next year I would definitely spend the holiday with her if she wanted.

'I'm so glad you persuaded me to come. Nanette's very sweetly put me in the little guest house because she and her daughter have a full house, which is a bit of a relief quite frankly because I can join them for meals but the rest of the time I can come and go a bit. At my age I need a bit of privacy.'

'And when's the Buttonhook AGM?'

'Next week, so Nanette's racing around organizing that. It should be quite a do.' She paused before continuing timidly, 'Actually, I was wondering if you might, well, only if you wanted, of course I'm not as good company as Dad, but perhaps you might think about coming out here for a few days, I mean, only if you're really bored and fed up. It won't be very exciting for you here of course, but if you were desperate . . .'

Nantucket in January. I still had the postcard that depicted the eighteenth-century main street swathed in a blanket of snow, cosy red brickwork partly emerging beneath a thick layer of soft snow, the grey-blue Atlantic swirling in the distance.

I was touched by her self-effacement. Did she really have such a low opinion of herself?

'Oh, Mum, I would simply love it.'

We hadn't been on holiday together since I was a child. Family holidays had always been stressful, with Siena and me getting on each other's nerves. This would be a chance to meet as adults, even as friends.

* * *

I rang the Air Tonga HQ (talk about shambles!) and after considerable difficulty re-directed my flight to Boston. From there I would fly to Nantucket. I rushed down to the bar to tell Dad my plans. Luckily it was a good time, the Penguins were taking some time off from their interminable hockey game and he was able to give me his full attention.

'Nantucket? Where's that? Hang on, let's ask Jumbo, he'll know.' He gesticulated to Jumbo. 'Jumbo, where's Nantucket?'

An involved geographical and sporting discussion followed, during which I learnt far more than I would ever need to know about the state of the Nantucket Reds, an obscure football team. Eventually Jumbo went to shake a cocktail.

'So I think it's quite a good idea that I go to see Mum in Nantucket. I think she could do with some company, it's a bit bleak there in winter.'

'She was a good cook, your mother,' ruminated Dad, reaching for the macadamia nuts. 'Did a good roast beef.'

'She sends you her love, by the way.'

'It's such a shame she couldn't have done a bit more with her life really,' he mused. 'She's a bright woman.'

'She is busy now, with the buttonhooks and everything. She has to do all the cataloging and—'

'In my day she just used to sit around in the sun all day. It was like an addiction.' He sipped his beer. 'Anyway, when are you off then?'

'It's a bit sudden, but Air Tonga only fly to Boston once a month, so basically I have to leave later today. I'll fly to LA and pick up their three a.m. connection to Boston. I do hope the flight's better leaving than it was coming out.' It wasn't too late for an upgrade. Maybe the thought of me sitting in LA airport in the middle of the night surrounded by ne'er do wells might stimulate him into making a gesture.

'Well, if they gave you a hot meal coming out I'm sure you'll get one on the way back.' Obviously not.

‘Yes, I guess. Well, I’ve just got to pack up my stuff and get a taxi to the airport. Shall I come and say goodbye before I go?’ My throat felt constricted with unexpressed emotion.

‘No, I hate goodbyes,’ he said blankly, his eyes returning to the TV which Jumbo had just switched back on. ‘Well, it’s been nice to catch up with you, Oriana. I’ve enjoyed our meals together.’

‘Yes,’ I replied, a strangulated sound emerging through layers of emotionally sodden vocal cords. And then without my approval (I was in the bar, for heaven’s sake! Where men came to escape from this sort of thing!) I was blinded by an unbidden eruption of tears. *So* embarrassing!

Dad patted me on the shoulder awkwardly. He hated emotional outbursts, unless it was because someone had scored a goal or something exciting like that. During his brief reunions with Mum he would disappear down the pub at the slightest sign of female hysteria. These were alarmingly frequent but it’s true about every cloud having a silver lining, because he ended up winning a silver cup for being the pub’s most loyal customer for seven years running. After that they gave up the competition and just let him keep it.

‘You’re too sentimental,’ he said, patting me again. ‘You’ll enjoy seeing your mother again, you mustn’t cry.’

‘No, I’m sorry. It’s such a bore being emotional. And it’s so terribly tiring.’ I smiled weakly.

‘Well, you better run along and finish your packing. Otherwise you’ll miss the plane and then you really will be upset. What time are you planning to leave?’

‘About six o’clock.’

‘Well, make sure you’re on time. I know what you’re like.’

I reached over and hugged him goodbye then scooted out f the bar and past the roaring waterfall. Then it was a rantic rush to pack my case and run downstairs.

The lobby was empty except for a solitary burly figure anging around the taxi rank.

'I thought I better come with you to the airport. I know how chaotic you are about catching planes,' Dad said gruffly, taking hold of my suitcase and weighty hand baggage.

After the quick journey we reached the airport and Dad hailed a porter who stacked a trolley with my luggage and led us to the check-in desk. Dad waited while I checked my bags in.

'Thanks for seeing me off, Dad.'

'It's nothing. I've enjoyed seeing you.' I could see his blue eyes articulating an emotion his voice was unable to express. I hugged him tightly and turned to go.

Just before turning into passport control, I looked round to wave goodbye at his no doubt retreating back. But he was still waiting at the check-in desk and lifted his hand in a farewell wave. He quickly turned to go, but not before I noticed that his eyes were full of tears.

Chapter Thirty-eight

Mum was waiting at the gate of the tiny airport wearing a pair of jeans and a matching blue fleece which was buttoned up very tightly against the cold. Her straight blonde hair was pulled back in a casual pony tail and her small features were set in an anxious expression as she scanned the arrival hall. She looked so thin I felt a gust of wind might topple her over. Her face lit up as she spotted me trundling towards her with my trolley-dolly suitcase, which was astonishingly light due to my careful *feng shui* minimal packing. I didn't know what I was going to do about clothes, all I had was my Hawaiian beach kit, which wouldn't be of any use against the chilly Atlantic.

'Darling, you must be freezing,' she admonished, taking in my skimpy T-shirt and grubby jeans. 'Haven't you got anything warmer to wear?'

'Yes.' I fumbled around my hand baggage and put on a sweatshirt with 'You're a tosser if you fly with Tonga' emblazoned across it that a rival airline had been handing out at LA airport.

As we climbed into the jeep she had hired, I noticed how fragile her wrists had become. They seemed as frail as bird's wings. 'You're looking a bit skinny, Mum, are you eating enough?'

'It should be the other way round,' she laughed. 'I should be asking if you're eating enough. You know me, I eat what I'm given but I haven't managed to find any decent tomatoes yet, so maybe I'm not eating as much as I usually do.' As tomatoes were her dietary staple, she must be eating nothing at all. 'But Nanette is incredibly hospitable. I've been joining her for these huge family meals, which, *entre nous* I do find a little exhausting. But she and her daughter flew back to New York yesterday, so we'll have the place to ourselves, which I must admit will be a bit of a relief.'

I gazed out of the window. Nantucket looked so different in the winter, the cranberry fields, which had been a mass of dark red in the summer, were covered in a smooth blanket of white snow stretching as far as the eye could see.

'I can't bear to think of how cold you must be,' she continued. 'You'll have to borrow some of my clothes.'

'Oh, I'm fine. I'm just so pleased to be here. I mean, Hawaii was lovely, but Dad was a bit depressing really . . .' I trailed off.

'But he's always like that, Oriana, he won't change now.'

'I know. I think I've had a kind of revelation actually.' I paused before proceeding. There was only so much New Ageism that Mum could take and I would have to put my philosophy into plain English. 'You see, I've accepted the way he is, and I'm not fretting because he isn't what I want him to be. He's never going to be the sort of father who helps me move flats or whatever. He is what he is, and that's fine. It's the Law of Least Effort, just going with the flow. After all, he could be a criminal or a rapist or something. I'm really jolly lucky.'

'Oh, darling, I'm so pleased. Your father's a wonderful man, but he's not perfect. Telling you off for not eating enough from the buffet and talking to the barman the whole time – I had to put up with all that for years, it's terribly hurtful.'

She understood what I was trying to say, it was such a relief!

'So I've let go of that dysfunctional blueprint. But it's more than just that, I feel like the slate's been wiped clean somehow . . .'

As we neared Nantucket town, the soft silvery grey shingled houses and cottages were replaced by dignified red brick mansions, built by Quaker whaling millionaires, each cherished garden separated by a white picket fence. The town had barely changed since the golden age of whaling in the mid-nineteenth century. Ironic that something so lovely, that continued to charm many years later, was the result of something as bloodthirsty as whaling. In the near distance lay the wild unpredictable Atlantic. It was even more magical out of season than in high summer.

'You know, the last time I came here it was incredibly hot and everybody was racing round in shorts and T-shirts. It's another place completely in the winter.'

'I wouldn't mind a bit of sunshine. It's been snowing since I arrived, this weekend they had seventeen inches of snow,' said Mum, driving carefully down Main Street. 'It's like something out of a Victorian Christmas card. But I have to say I was never much of a cold-weather person, it seems to go right through my bones.' Her thin wrists shook. 'But luckily the house is very luxurious. You can choose between six guest bedrooms – actually there are more bathrooms than bedrooms. Here we are.'

We pulled up in front of a grey-shingled house overlooking the bay. Sea gulls swooped in front of us; small white sailboats bobbed about the blustery ocean and in the distance Sankarty Lighthouse flickered benignly. I breathed in the fresh salty air as Mum and I crunched our way over the driveway of crushed sea shells to the front door.

'It's so lovely not having to bother about locking anything up,' she said, ushering me in. 'Nanette didn't even leave any keys, I don't even know if she has any. It's amazing when you think how many buttonhooks she's got.'

'I shouldn't think a thief would have a clue what they were,' I said, following Mum through the door with some urgency. The Air Tonga in-flight snack, a curious combination of dried bananas, sherbet and smoked mackerel pâté (at least you could see they were trying), and the bumpy cobbled streets we had just driven over were beginning to kick in with a vengeance and I was longing for the loo.

'I'm so surprised you could tear yourself away from Hawaii,' said Mum later that evening as we sat tucking into clam chowder at a bistro round the corner. Luckily I was completely recovered after a lie-down followed by an invigorating power shower in the sumptuous guest bathroom. 'I know how much these holidays with your father mean to you,' she added.

'To be honest I didn't see much of him. I appreciated having the time to myself really. But it was a wonderful week, I felt that something really clicked into place without even trying. I can't put my finger on it, but I just feel so much more relaxed.'

'Well, it's been a big year for you with the book and everything. I am proud of you, darling. I feel I underestimated you all these years. I always expected you to get married when you were about nineteen and that Siena would end up doing something incredibly high-powered. Still, she seems happy enough these days. Have you spoken to her at all?'

'No.' I put down my spoon and sipped my wine.

'Oh, darling, I wish you would. I know she's been trying to get hold of you. It would mean so much to her if you rang her.'

'Honestly, Mum, what she said to me was so horrible and so insulting I can't get my head round talking to her just yet.'

'But you can't blame her for being upset, darling. I do so wish you could make it up. You know what they say; "to err is human, to forgive is divine." '

'But the way she spat out "your book is shite." '

'I know, it's a horrid, horrid word,' she agreed.

'But the venom, it went beyond the book and everything.' I shivered. 'Just give it a bit more time,' I suggested, seeing Mum's face crumple into a network of fine lines. She suddenly looked her age, sad and vulnerable. 'Are she and Mary getting along all right these days?'

She brightened. 'Oh yes. There's even talk of something called a commitment ceremony. I don't know what your father will make of that. Still, I'm just happy to see her settled. I know Mary's not everyone's cup of tea, but she's a steadying influence on Siena, and Jacob adores her of course.'

'I'm sorry that at the book launch I didn't come and say hello. I feel so bad about that, Mum.'

'Well, I was a bit hurt. Especially as we'd spoken so much earlier in the day about what you were going to wear and everything. Afterwards I went home and had a little weep. I wasn't going to tell you, very feeble of me. But it's all over now, not worth remembering. But thank you for apologizing.'

My heart ached with shame. How could I have been so thoughtless? She hardly ever cried.

'And I can't talk, I've been a bit snappy with you, I know. I guess because I've always felt a poor substitute for your father – it probably makes me a bit hurt and irritable sometimes. Anyway, this soul-searching is all a bit much for me, I'm afraid, but I'm glad we've cleared the air.' She called for the bill. 'You don't want a pudding, do you?'

I shook my head.

'Good, that soup has really filled me up. I'm so glad you made me try it. From now on I'm going to try and be a bit more adventurous about what I eat. I'm getting a little tired of tomatoes.'

Mum was pretty busy cataloging Nanette's extensive collection of buttonhooks which were dotted about the house and was spending a lot of the time in Siasconset, the other side of the island where the treasurer of the buttonhook world lived.

'Do come over to Sconset tomorrow. Petula would love to meet you,' said Mummy a few days later. 'She's got the most amazing collection. You know she even has a Fabergé egg. She says it belonged to Rasputin, though I think she's probably exaggerating.'

'I'd love to, Mum, but I've booked to do the Nantucket ghost walk tomorrow afternoon, and it's market day tomorrow morning so I want to pick up some Nantucket pumpkins. I'll make us a pumpkin pie. You'll like that. I'm looking forward to doing some cooking.'

'But didn't you go on a ghost walk in the summer?'

'Yes, but they might have discovered some new ones, the ghost guide was pretty confident that they would.' I'm a sucker for that sort of thing, and it was great fun wandering around the town being shown spooky things.

The following morning Mum left early to drive to Sconset while I lay in bed idly watching the seagulls hovering outside my window and admiring the way they remained stationary for minutes at a time, as if held by pieces of invisible string. Beneath them the waves ebbed and flowed, merging with the misty sky, a limitless dream of bluey golds, greys and greens. Amidst such beauty anything seemed possible.

I didn't think I had ever felt so happy. When I thought of how things had turned out I felt so grateful I could have wept. Here I was in this lovely place, enjoying the first holiday I'd ever had alone with my mother as two adults, doing our own thing. And somewhere in the world people were buying my book, quite a lot of people if the sales figures were to be believed.

After a leisurely breakfast of grapenut pellets in bed, drooling over the *Nantucket Beacon* property pages (as expensive as London, worst luck, but maybe I should just throw in my lot and move here. Why not? What had I got to lose?), I got dressed and wandered to the market in Main Street.

Local farmers were selling freshly picked dewy vegetables from the back of large muddy Landcruisers. Just like the ones I see being driven around Knightsbridge by beleaguered blonde mothers, with the token pinched infant rattling around the back, rushing to the crèche at the Ritzy Marina Club. I filled my useful Eco-friendly string bag with fifteen small pumpkins, aubergines, fresh sage (perfect with pumpkin pie), and nearly fainted with how cheap it all was. If only I could 'go to market' like this every day. Of course I would miss the trolley rage but I'm sure out here I would find better ways of letting off steam. Meditation or yoga or something. Maybe there was a Ritzy Marina Club on Nantucket.

It was a blustery clear day, with a fresh breeze blowing in off the ocean. Although it was chilly, the sky was cornflower blue, dramatically contrasting with the snow on the grand redbrick houses lining Main Street. Lots of Martha Stewart fans must live here, judging by the gorgeous bright window boxes, which were spilling over with Christmas daisies, red heather and cheerful branches of holly. It was just how I imagined New England to be at Christmas.

I wandered into the Hub, the only newsagent in town, just on the off chance that they might have a *Daily Mail*. Unlikely, but perhaps the ladies attending the Buttonhook Convention had created a demand.

To my delight the uninterested college student behind the counter seemed to think they had one.

'Yeah, we goddit. Top shelf.'

Hurrah, Mum would be pleased. Pumpkin pie for dinner and a *Daily Mail*. What a good daughter I'm being, I thought, stretching up to an overladen shelf stacked with newspapers and magazines. Ridiculous place to keep newspapers but I guess the *Mail* wasn't a big seller in Nantucket. I jumped up and down and tried to grab one of the papers.

'Here, let me help you,' said a voice behind me.

'Thank you, but I think I can manage,' I replied politely. I wanted to see if they had a *Telegraph* up there as well. Mum had been missing the crossword.

I jumped up again, with what I liked to think of as feline agility, but succeeded in bringing down the whole shelf, showering myself with old newspapers and porn mags, which spilled down all over the floor. It appeared that the *Daily Male* was not in fact a family newspaper but an exciting gay magazine with a different man for every day of the week. Sunday's male leered up at me, wearing nothing but a dog collar and large papal ring. I dreaded to think what horrors lay between him and Saturday.

The shelf collapse caused quite a stir, especially as the Nantucket Needlepoint Association bus had just pulled up outside and disgorged a group of ladies into the shop. Eager to prove what good Samaritans they were, they all rushed over and tried to stem the tide of pornography that had spread like a ghastly rash all over the floor.

I busied myself scrabbling around the floor as the needlepoint ladies, under the guise of helping, were examining the magazines in some detail while pretending to pick them up.

'Hey Oriana!' said a deep voice attached to a large pair of Timberland boots. I glanced up furtively from the display of male genitalia on the floor, past a long expanse of faded blue jean clad leg, into an amused pair of heavy lidded grey eyes.

'Dan!' I exclaimed. 'What are you doing here?' I looked around nervously. I hoped to God he wasn't with Anoushka. I really didn't think I could face her pretending not to recognize me again in my current fragile state. 'Hello there, what a lovely surprise,' I continued, keeping one hand poised on an enormous pair of testicles (really, he must be taking some kind of growth hormone, it was disgusting). 'How nice to run into you. They don't seem to take my paper,' I said primly. 'I think I might have to try another newsagent.'

'There isn't another newsagent,' Dan explained seriously, his eyes full of laughter. 'But I was just going to get myself a coffee across the street. Can I tempt you?'

I didn't need much tempting to escape from the Hub, which by now was seething with the shocked and horrified matrons of Middle America.

'Disgusting.'

'Shouldn't be allowed.'

'Think of the *children*.'

'Always thought it was such a respectable shop.'

'Of course we'll have to campaign to have it shut down now.'

'But they can't shut it down, it's an institution,' I wailed as Dan escorted me chivalrously across the cobbled street and held the door of the Espresso Cafe open for me with a capable arm. He was so deliciously tall I was able to slip beneath his broad shoulder quite easily.

'Looks like the place has breathed its last now that lot are on its tail,' said Dan. My face fell. 'I'm only kidding, no one's going to close the place down, it's perfectly legal to sell those magazines. Look at them,' he pointed across the road to where the needlepoint matrons were reconvening on the pavement, chattering like starlings. 'You've made their day.'

'Yes, it's quite important not to get too sheltered from these sorts of realities. I know the pictures were a bit risqué but Mr Sunday, I noticed, had quite a religious theme. At least that's a start. I wonder if the editor is a lapsed Catholic.'

Dan was staring at me with a bemused expression. I realized I'd only seen him dressed in restrictive evening clothes, but in jeans, Timberland boots and a faded old checked cotton shirt – the clothes that American men wear so well – he seemed much more comfortable. His long sturdy legs were stretched out confidently and there was a force field of contained energy all around him. With his thick tawny hair, tanned craggy face and heavy lidded eyes he reminded me of a big contented lion.

'So what brings you to Nantucket?' he asked, taking a sip of coffee. I noticed a heavy divers' watch gleam on his large wrists and was horrified to find myself wondering what it would be like to go to bed with him.

'My mother came for a Buttonhook Conference and I decided to come and join her.'

'What on earth is a buttonhook? Is it some weird British fishing thing?'

'No. It's what people used to use to do up their buttons before zips were invented,' I explained seriously.

'Oh. I'm glad you told me that.' The grey eyes were again amused. 'Many people come along for this Buttonhook Convention then?' he asked.

'Oh yes. I believe it was quite well attended. My mother is the archivist, so she's one of the main honchos in the movement. She also writes long articles for their magazine, *The Buttoneur*,' I said proudly. 'She's writing one now about all the different ways you can display your buttonhook collection.'

Dan looked bewildered. 'She must be a very smart lady.'

'Oh, she is. And they say buttonhooks are going to be the next big thing so she's rather ahead of her time.' I could sense that Dan already knew far more than he would ever need to know about buttonhooks. 'Is Anoushka with you?' I inquired brightly.

'No. I haven't seen her since your book launch, and then only briefly. How is she?'

'I haven't a clue. But I thought you two were engaged.'

He flung back his head and laughed. 'Are you crazy?'

I laughed nervously. 'But the press reported afterward that you'd been canoodling . . .?'

'It was all built up by the papers. I met her at a dance and she said she really wanted to raise money for marine research. And she was great, she really helped out at a fundraiser in New York, got all her mates along, but then she began ringing me up all the time. It got a bit much. Still, I guess I was something different after all those spooky English guys sorry, I didn't mean to be rude.'

I had a sudden vision of Peregrine's bathroom cabinet heaving with Horny Goat's Weed. 'No, you're right, some of them are spooky. I read an article about. Anoushka that sai she'd never been out with anyone who hadn't been to Eton, so I guess you were something deliciously exotic.'

'She'd be hard pressed to find me exotic today. I bought a house here a while back and it's been empty, and now I find there's a darn great hole in the roof. Snow's been dripping on me all night.'

'Oh dear, can you find someone to fix it at short notice?'

'Don't need to, it's an easy job. I like fixing things, it's a kind of hobby.' He stirred his coffee absently. 'I actually came into town to buy a hairdryer.'

I looked up surprised. Dan didn't look a hairdryer type. In fact he didn't look like he'd ever seen a comb, let alone a hairdryer. Ah-ha, *cherchez la femme*. Like I thought, he was bound to have a woman hidden away in his leaking house, dammit!

'Not for me, for the roof,' he explained mysteriously.

'You mean to melt the snow when it comes through the hole?'

'No! I have to line the hole with slate and asphalt. I haven't got a blowtorch, but a hairdryer will do the job just as well. It's not that big a hole.' I hadn't a clue what he was talking about, but it was obviously some delicious male thing that women were excluded from understanding, like the appeal of the Pittsburgh Penguins. You had to be a boy to get it. *Vive la différence!*

'You can borrow mine. I'm staying in a house just over by Child's Beach.'

'Hey, we're neighbours. I'll give you a ride back and pick up the dryer on the way.'

Dan's car/truck whatever was parked outside.

'Is this a Chevy truck?' I asked as we drove over the cobbled Main Street towards the ocean.

'A Chevy truck?' he imitated my accent, laughing. 'Well, it's sure as hell not a Porsche.'

'Thank goodness, awful flashy sort of car,' I lied.

'Actually I quite like them. Unfortunately so does my

ex-wife so I gave mine to her when we divorced.'

'That was nice of you.'

'It was the least I could do really – shit!' The tantalizing conversation was brought to an abrupt conclusion as a weird-looking man wearing an eighteenth-century Quaker costume, and carrying a pikestaff, stepped out right in front of us. It was Mr Moldo, the ghost man! I leaned out of the Chevy and waved hello.

'Hey, Oriana! How y'doin'?'

'I'm bearing up, thank you, but I'm longing to come along for your afternoon tour later. Have you had any more sightings recently?'

Mr Moldo nodded cheerfully. 'A murder, and the victim has been sighted over in Madeket.'

'Oh. Super! We'll catch up later.'

He waved his pikestaff cheerfully and wandered off towards the A and P grocery store.

'How nice of him to remember my name,' I mused as Dan pulled off. 'We had such a nice chat when I was last here.'

'I just don't get why he's carrying that piece of metal around.'

'Oh, that's a pikestaff. My father collects them.'

'Why?'

'Because he's a pikeman. I don't think you have them in America. They're soldiers who carry pikestaffs.'

'Do they use buttonhooks?'

'No!'

'Oriana?' Dan looked over at me, one big hand resting on the wheel, the other on the wound down window.

'Yes, Dan?' He was going to ask me out for dinner, yes

'Are your family for real?'

I laughed hollowly. It was too bad. And I hadn't even told him about Siena. Compared to her the rest of my family were apple-pie normal.

'This is my place,' said Dan, slowing down as we passed a large grey shingled house backing onto the beach.

'It's gorgeous,' I exclaimed. 'You're so lucky being able to live here.'

'Well, I don't know how much time I'll be spending here at the moment. I seem to be travelling all the time. Anyway, where's your friend's house?'

'It's just down the end of the road.'

It didn't take us a moment to reach it and I left him in his Chevy while I raced up to collect the hairdryer. No point in asking him in. Mum had left buttonhooks all over the house as she was having a buttonhook meeting that evening and it all looked a bit odd. Damn, I wished I hadn't mentioned my father's pikestaff collection. I wanted Dan to think I was a cheerful cheerleader sort of girl.

'Shall I come by and return it later?' he suggested when I'd handed it over. 'Or if you're walking past later, why not drop by and I'll show you my Widow's Walk.'

'What's that?'

He pointed to the roof deck on the top of Nanette's house. 'They're called Widows' Walks because the wives of whalers used to go up there to look for their husband's ships.'

'OK, I'll drop by later,' I agreed, waving him a casual goodbye. My heart was thumping. I had a date with Dan on his Widow's Walk!

'd been going to spend the afternoon ringing up PETA!, an nimal charity that was campaigning to release chimps from aboratories in Utah, to see if they needed anyone to help vriting their brochures, but it took me a ridiculously long ime to get ready. I had to perfect a natural cheerleader look nake-up and rifle through Mum's clothes to find a) something that fitted, and b) something that looked fabulous. It's tough call borrowing clothes off your mum when she only veighs seven stone. I mean, I'm considered slim, but seven one! Give me a break.

Anyway, by some miracle she'd packed a gorgeous

sea-greeny blue Versace top, which looked just right with my jeans. I brushed my hair loose, applied some Abba Revival blue eye shadow, washed off the Abba Revival blue eye shadow (too obvious), and applied a light but thorough *maquillage* and a liberal squirt of Antonia's Flowers (very East Hampton). I'd given up on Lust; despite Pandora swearing by it, it had never brought me any lust at all. Besides, knowing my luck, it might work on the ghost walk man, which would be a disaster.

I didn't have time to do anything with the pumpkins, but luckily I'd made a batch of wonders, a melting Nantucket delicacy, which are like doughnuts without a hole. I'd discovered them in an old Nantucket recipe book and was looking forward to doing some experimentation. The wonders would be perfect to take round to Dan's as a housewarming present.

I flung a sheepskin coat over my flimsy ensemble and scooted down the road to Dan's, clutching my warm wonders close to my chest to stop the heat evaporating. When I approached his house I was very impressed to see him doing something mysteriously handy on the roof. I don't know about you, but the sight of a man mending something makes me go a bit weak at the knees. And Dan certainly looked like the sort of man who knew his way round a toolbox.

He spotted me immediately. 'Hey, Oriana, up here. I'd come down but I've just got to hold this tile down for another second.'

'Don't worry, if you haven't finished with the dryer you could drop it by tomorrow if you like,' I yelled up.

'Oh no, no, I want your opinion on something. Just come right up.'

I made my way upstairs gingerly, passing several large airy rooms. Planks of wood and electric cable lay strewn about, and there was no furniture except a huge bed and state of the art hi-fi, which Dan seemed to be in the process of hooking up. But the views from the main rooms wer fabulous, stretching miles over empty sand dunes to the grey-green ocean beyond.

I clanked my way right to the top of the house where Dan had come in off the roof and was writhing around beneath the eaves of the attic, drying bits of the roof with my hairdryer. The checked cotton shirt was rolled up to his elbows and his forearms were tensing and flexing with effort. I couldn't understand how the hairdryer came into it, but it looked terribly impressive.

'Hey!' he switched off the dryer. (I just love the way Americans go 'hey' the whole time, it makes me feel like I'm in an episode of *Friends*.) 'So what d'you think of my place?'

'I love it,' I replied honestly. 'The views are amazing, and once you've got some furniture—'

'What d'you mean? Didn't you see the hi-fi, and what about my new sofa?' He pointed to a huge comfortable black leather sofa. 'See, and I've even got a refrigerator. If I get anything else the place'll just get cluttered. Hang on, I'm coming out.' He slid his way towards the exit, his large Timberland boots hitting the floor heavily. I couldn't help but notice the cotton shirt ride up, revealing a large expanse of muscular stomach. I glanced down modestly.

'I, um, made you these.' I held out the wonders awkwardly. 'As a sort of house-warming present.'

'English muffins!' he exclaimed. 'Mmm, I wondered what smelt so good.'

'Actually, they're wonders. Muffins aren't English,' I said nervously. 'In fact, the only place I've ever seen an English muffin is in America. It's like that Agatha Christie series that's always on the TV out here – *Murder She Wrote* with Angela Lansbury. It's meant to be typically English but it's not at all. I mean Miss Marple is apparently living in a house that's stone-cladded inside and out. It's completely unrealistic.'

Dan was nodding in serious agreement. 'Is that so? Now I've lured you all the way up to my loft, let me fix you a drink.' He wandered over and opened the door of the well-stocked fridge. 'Ah. Here we are.' He pulled out a bottle of champagne from behind a crate of beer and grappled around a cupboard, emerging with some dusty glasses. 'Unless you'd prefer a beer, of course?'

I shook my head.

'Didn't think so somehow.'

He opened the bottle with a flourish, filled the glasses and handed me one. 'If you're chilly, I'll switch up the heating,' he said, gesturing at my sheepskin coat which I hadn't taken off. The flimsy outfit just seemed a bit too, well, flimsy to be alone with Dan in his loft.

'Oh no, don't. I'm really quite warm.' I shrugged off my coat reluctantly. 'So, have you just bought the house?' I inquired.

'No, I've had it for a few years, but my ex-wife didn't like it here so we never got round to doing anything with it. Besides, I was travelling all the time. But now it's going to be my base. I've sold my place in New York, so here I am. For good, I hope.' He lifted his arms behind his head and stretched contentedly. 'It doesn't get any better than Nantucket for me.' He glanced at me. 'I enjoyed your book launch, by the way. But I would have enjoyed it even more if I'd been able to speak to you. You were a popular lady, I couldn't get anywhere near you. That ferocious woman with black hair, Christ, she was guarding you like a Rottweiler.'

'Oh, you mean Petronella from Shmooze. I'm surprised you haven't met her, she's Anoushka's agent, they're very close.'

'I know everyone in Britain thinks I'm practically married to Anoushka, but I swear, I took her out for dinner *once*.'

'But you kept calling her darling. It was in all the papers.' I sipped my champagne casually.

'I didn't call her darling. I was talking about the Darling Institute in Connecticut. It's a big marine biology centre She's thinking about applying to become a marine biologist.'

I snorted. 'She told me she was a people person, she didn't say anything about being a whale person.' Really. Anoushka, a marine biologist? What was going on? It was as unsuitable as nuns using mobile phones on trains.

'Well, she seems pretty set on the idea. I was happy to put her in touch with a few people. Even if she just spends a few months at the institute it'll do her good to get out of London for a while, she's hanging out with a bad crowd. But I want to hear about your book, I bought a copy at Heathrow and read it on the plane.' He frowned. 'I felt sorry for Jemima, she kept dating such awful guys. Thank God it was fiction, you've got a great imagination.'

'Thank you.' Fiction! Thank goodness he didn't know it was my autobiography. That would have been too shame-making for words.

I was longing to bring up the winking incident at Victoria's party but I thought I better not. He probably winked at lots of girls and I didn't want make a thing out of it.

'So what are your plans now you've finished the book?' He refilled our glasses smoothly and helped himself to a wonder.

'Well, I haven't arranged anything for definite. I'm applying to some animal charities to see if they need any help writing brochures and things. I was in the papers a lot after my book came out so I thought I might as well use the press interest for something useful, otherwise what's the point of it all?'

'Is there anything in particular that you'd like to be involved in?'

'Well, lots of things, but I'd particularly like to do something about animals in captivity. The *National Enquirer* are running one of their campaigns to release a whale called Lolita who's been in a tiny pen by herself for *thirty* years just so people can go and watch her do tricks.'

Dan frowned grimly. 'Jeez, what sort of people can do that?' He looked at me for a long moment. 'You won't remember but I gave a talk at a dolphin ball the year before last. I saw you arrive and I was going to ask you for a dance after I'd got my speech out of the way, but I couldn't find you.'

'I had to leave early.' I wasn't going to go into the gypsy thing. It was too weird. 'But I heard your speech. It was brilliant. It made us all really sit up and think.'

Dan looked chuffed.

'Are you still a marine biologist or are you doing more lecturing?' I asked curiously. I realized I didn't have much of an idea what Dan really did, but judging by his house, which due to my perusing of the Nantucket property listings I knew must be worth a few million, he must be doing something very lucrative.

'I studied marine biology and geology at Harvard and then I went on to become a seismologist. You see, certain rock formations reveal if there's oil beneath them. Oil companies will pay a fortune if they get a hit. I just happened to be quite lucky at it. So I did that for a few years, married Madison, got sucked into the lifestyle, his and her Porsches, all that crap.' He grimaced and pushed a weary hand through his hair. 'And then my sister, Anna, was killed in a road accident. She was only twenty-one. We were very close, or we had been very close but my wife, I mean my ex-wife, couldn't stand her and we'd drifted apart. When Anna died we hadn't seen each other for a year – you know, I never had the time, and Madison would have made a row about it. And then it was too late.' He gazed out of the window bleakly and reluctantly continued. 'Around that time there was a spate of oil disasters. I'd devoted my life to making a ton of money with no thought to the consequences. But after Anna died I went to work for the other side, cleaning up oil spills and working for marine conservation. It's ironic, but that's an even bigger business now than discovering oil was then. But I did it for Anna. So that something positive might come out of something . . . well . . . so senseless.'

'What did she do?' I asked quietly.

'She worked for Greenpeace in London.' Dan smiled. 'You might have met her.'

'Actually, my sister might have. She used to work for Greenpeace ages ago.' I really didn't want to discuss my hopeless relationship with Siena. 'So your life now is much more rewarding. It must make the sacrifice of giving up the money much easier.'

'Well, like I said, it's so ironic. I'm earning even more than I did then just clearing up the mess made from the oil I helped discover. The world's gone mad. Hey, your glass is empty.' He picked up the bottle. 'So's the bottle.' He wandered over to the fridge and got out another.

'No really, I better be going . . . I've missed the ghost walk already. I told Mr Moldo I was definitely coming. I hope he didn't wait for me.'

'You can't leave before I show you the Widow's Walk,' said Dan firmly, withdrawing the cork and refilling our glasses. I gave in gracefully. He wanted me to stay! Given the choice between Dan and following the crazy Hungarian ghost walk man around Nantucket wasn't a hard decision, I can tell you.

I followed him out onto the deck. Nantucket harbour spread beneath our feet, a shimmering moonlit carpet of twinkling lights against the deep indigo sky.

'It's a clear night,' said Dan, standing so close I could feel the brushed cotton of his shirt against my skin. 'You can see the Plough if you look over there.'

I squinted vaguely. The champagne hadn't done a lot for my eyesight, which was dodgy at the best of times. 'Where?'

Dan picked up my hand and guided it along the constellation. I have to say I was none the wiser, but it was delicious to be held in the palm of his big hand like that. He began to stroke the inside of my wrist gently. A current of electricity surged through me, it was unbelievably erotic.

'You don't remember but we nearly met at a party a while

back, way before that ball. You had on that amazing gold dress you were wearing at your book launch, and your hair was streaming down your back.' He whistled to himself. 'Jeez, you looked like a mermaid. All these guys were staring at you. I got into a whole lot of trouble because I winked at you and my ex caught me – she didn't talk to me for three days. You probably don't remember. I guess guys probably wink at you all the time.'

'Um . . . yes,' I replied, making a supreme effort to concentrate as his fingers moved from my wrist and played with fronds of my hair. 'But now you mention it I do remember you winking at me. It really cheered me up. I went home that night and I told Pandora that a man had winked at me. She was thrilled too. That sort of thing doesn't happen very often in London. It gave us all a real boost.'

'I really wanted to kiss you then.' He grazed my cheek with warm dry lips. He smelt deliciously of salty air, wonders and champagne. 'You know, when Anoushka rang and asked if I wanted to go with her to a book launch I only agreed because I found out it was yours. I saw you on some television programme with a whole lot of crazy girls, and you said you wanted to meet a man from Nantucket with a salt-water swimming pool. So I thought I'd try my luck.'

'But you're no use, you haven't got one.'

He smiled and looked over the deck towards the ocean. 'Well, I've got access to one. It's not heated but it's pretty private.'

'I was going to ask you if you believed in mermaids but then the firemen came.'

'Yeah, it got a bit chaotic. I was pissed off I never met you though, so I sent you a fan mail letter via your publishers. I guess you didn't get it?'

'No! No, I didn't get any fan mail at all. It was very disappointing.'

'Well, lucky we ran into each other then.' He pulled me towards him, his cotton shirt boring into my flimsy silk top.

I coiled my arms around his neck and drew him to me, shutting my eyes and blocking out the flickering stars above us. And then, in one easy movement, placing strong hands around my waist and scooping me into a fireman's lift, he carried me inside, past the champagne in dusty glasses and the hairdryer abandoned on the attic floor.

'It's chilly out there,' he murmured, but I was too lost for words to reply. As he laid me down on the huge sofa I succumbed to the whisper of his mouth on my skin, oblivious to everything but the feel of his body melting into mine.

A melancholy foghorn boomed in the distance and somewhere a clock chimed. The world gradually came back into view, both of us surfacing for air. I opened my eyes to find Dan watching me intently. A slow lazy grin spread across his face. 'I've been bewitched by a green-eyed girl from London.'

'Guildford, actually.' I stretched languorously. I didn't want to drag myself away from Dan's cosy lair but I knew I ought to leave. It says in The Rules that you must always leave a man wanting more. But then I remembered that there wasn't really any *more* left. I hadn't held back anything for another time, if you see what I mean. It was probably too late to start playing hard to get now.

'What's the matter?' asked Dan, kissing the tip of my nose. 'You look worried.'

I glanced at my watch. 'God, is that the time! I've got to go, my mother thinks I'm on the ghost walk. If I don't come home she'll think I've been abducted by—'

'An alien? Elvis Presley?'

'No! By Mr Moldo, the ghost man. She thinks he's really weird because he never takes his ghost costume off even when he's in the supermarket. She'll think the worst, I know she will.'

'Now he really *is* an alien,' remarked Dan dryly.

'Oh no, I'm pretty certain he's not. On the last ghost walk he was telling us all about his prostate surgery in Helsinki or

Budapest, I can't remember which. I don't think an alien would have those sort of problems.'

I reluctantly extricated myself from Dan's warm embrace and slipped back into my clothes, aware all the time of his watchful eyes on me.

It had started to rain, the sound of it falling onto the skylight made me shiver involuntarily. Dan climbed out of the sofa and quickly threw on his clothes. 'I'll walk you back to your house.'

'But what about the hole in your roof? You haven't finished fixing it, have you?'

'Doesn't matter, I'll stick a bucket under it.'

He kissed the top of my head and bundled me into my sheepskin coat like a child. Despite the intimacy we had just shared I felt a bit awkward. Everything had happened so wonderfully and so instinctively but I didn't know what Dan felt about it at all.

'What are you up to this weekend?' he asked as we clattered down the stairs.

'My mother's leaving so I'll see her off. I thought I'd stay on a bit longer and do some writing. I'm in no rush to get back to London.' That was a bit of a lie, I was quite looking forward to getting back to my flat, but circumstances had suddenly changed.

'Well, if you're at a loose end some friends have asked me to stay with them on the Vineyard this weekend, we've been asked to a party. Come along, it'll be fun.'

My heart flipped. A date! But I kept my cool.

'Martha's Vineyard? I've always wanted to go there ever since I read an interview with Carly Simon. She lives there, doesn't she?'

'Actually, it's her party,' said Dan casually.

Goodness.

'And will the Clintons be attending?' I asked coolly. The President seemed to go to Martha's Vineyard to recuperate between scandals. The place had become quite famous for it, he seemed to practically live there.

The heavens suddenly opened, the rain coming down in slanting lines, crashing over the cobblestones, practically flattening us. We sprinted desperately to my doorstep.

'Damn, I forgot the hairdryer!' exclaimed Dan, caressing the back of my neck. 'I'll drop it round tomorrow.' He stooped down to kiss me and left reluctantly as I let myself into the house. Once inside I rested for a moment against the door, reliving the extraordinary evening and trying to engrave the feeling of Dan's warm body wrapped around me on the sofa, our skin enmeshed, the smell of his tawny hair into my mind forever.

Images flickered through my mind, dusty glasses against the light, the intoxicating sight of Dan writhing around his loft with the hairdryer. I hadn't seen anything as exciting since Steve McQueen nearly made it to the border in *The Great Escape*.

I was soon interrupted from my musings.

'Oriana? Is that you? Where on earth have you been?' Mum came into the porch wearing a dressing grown, drying her sopping hair with a towel.

'I've been looking everywhere for the hairdryer. Have you seen it anywhere?'

To my amazement Dan called round with my hairdryer the next day and he took me to the Vineyard that weekend. I've always thought that The Rules are made to be broken. I feel sorry for girls who take these things too seriously.

Epilogue

On a whim I chucked in everything in London and moved out to Nantucket. Just like that. Sometimes the most radical decisions are the easiest. Of course Dan living here made it a bit easier. But it was my decision, I didn't need to consult my psychic rota or even run it by Mrs Molinari, tarot reader to the stars. I just sat down in a quiet place and listened to my heart. I should try that more often. It's certainly a lot cheaper. I haven't come across any psychics, rune specialists or tarot readers so, as you can imagine, I'm saving myself a fortune.

I thought that once I'd moved to Nantucket I'd take it easy for a while, but Dan's got me on e-mail, so now I can send regular articles to the Whale and Dolphin Society. He's taken me to Harvard, and to the Darling Institute where he was giving some lectures. You'll never guess who we bumped into at the Darling Institute, only Anoushka Bird-Whistle. She really is going to train to become a marine biologist, so good for her. She still didn't recognize me but I didn't mind. The poor thing was understandably jealous that I was with Dan, but she's a few years younger than me so she's probably got a few more frogs to kiss before she meets her Prince Charming.

Things are working out fine. But I need to add something really important. You're reading this and thinking, well, she's got the man, the nice house, enough money, and bloody hell, she's thin too, of course she's happy. I am happy, but the happiness isn't because I have these things, I have these things as a result of being happy, because I took my life by the horns and changed it from the inside out.

I realized I'd been focusing more on what was missing in my relationships with my family than what I had. When I focused more on what I loved about them, those things seemed to increase and relations improved without me even trying.

But it would be misleading to pretend everything is quite suddenly perfect now, because I know Mary still doesn't like me very much. But that will change. I realized how much energy I'd been wasting resenting her and holding a grudge with Siena for rubbishing my book. I started to miss my sister. About a week after I'd made this shift Siena rang me up out of the blue for a chat. I guess you can kind of influence a relationship even when you're thousands of miles away. She said they'd all come down with coughs so I made up a batch of sticky cough syrup from the wild cherries that grow all over the island and sent her a big bottle. Apparently they're a famous cough cure. It didn't help their coughs though. Mary immediately came down with bronchitis, which was a bit embarrassing, but Siena was very touched. I asked her and Mary to stay, but Siena's still on this anti-plane crusade, which is fair enough. Maybe they'll invent a solar powered jet before long.

We had a blazing summer this year so I persuaded Mum to come out for a week. Dan adores her. He says she looks like Ann Margret but talks like the Queen. We (button) hooked her up with Dan's mother in Florida and now she's collecting buttonhooks too. Dad came out this winter on his way back from Hawaii. I stocked up on gin, tonic and macadamia nuts and told Dan to pretend to be a bar tender and they'd get along fine. I have the greatest memories of them both sitting on the Widow's Walk with the sun setting over the ocean, discussing the finer points of the Pittsburgh Penguins (Dan's team!), and arguing about the American Civil war. It makes me quite misty eyed.

Dan spends a lot of time doing fascinating research work in a submersible called the Alvin. It's so high-tech he and his colleagues can explore some of the deepest parts of the ocean which have never been visited before. He comes home full of amazing stories. His enthusiasm is contagious and I've become as passionate about saving the ocean and all the weird and wonderful creatures in it as he is. Who knows what medicines, cures and secrets are yet to be revealed if we respect and protect it.

I'm going to write a novel set in Nantucket (including lots of Nantucket recipes), with a gorgeous marine biologist hero. It's going to be an eco froth-buster. Red Duck have given me an advance for it even though I haven't begun it yet.

I love it when I'm expecting Dan back after a long trip. He'll tell me what flight he's on so when it's expected I'll run up to the Widow's Walk and wave my spangly gold mermaid dress at the sky as the tiny island plane swoops past. There's not much call for gold dresses on the island and it's nice to know I'm getting some use out of it. It makes me think of all the women in the past who might have run up looking in vain for their lovers' ship. *Plus ça change c'est la même chose.*

I didn't think Nantucket could be any lovelier than it was during our first winter, with its freezing clear days and air so luminous that every twig and flower stood out alone. I'd never seen horizons as wide, ships so white. Then quite suddenly the fog, we call it the Grey Lady, would blow in, swallowing us whole and the island became moody and full of atmosphere. Mr Moldo, the ghost man, is in his element then.

The first weekend in spring the whole island lit up as thousands of daffodils burst into flower. It's called Daffodil Weekend and people come from all over to see it. I remember shopping in Main Street and being feted by masses of soft drifting pink confetti from the cherry blossom trees lining the streets. Soon after the picket fenced gardens became a riot of colour and the cottage rooftops cascaded with scented roses.

Summer was so hot we spent most days underwater, with Dan teaching me to dive. Eventually we would surface from the deep and wander into town. I remember it was so hot even the shadows seemed to wilt as they fell softly across the old mellow brick and clapboard houses in the heat of the late afternoon.

Recently I discovered that the flowering almond tree in our garden was rumoured to have come from a Mandarin's garden in Peking. Apparently, whaling ships used to return with seeds and cuttings from distant places, which have bloomed all over the island. They say sea breezes are good for flowers. It sounds whimsical but I feel a bit like a transplanted cutting myself.

Just one more thing. After Dan and I came back from Carly Simon's party in Martha's Vineyard (or the Vineyard as we locals call it) we were sitting outside on the deck enjoying the breezy late afternoon sunshine, and I asked him how the hole in the roof was. Dan had looked unaccountably sheepish.

'There was no hole in the roof. I made it up.'

'But what were you doing with the hairdryer? I was so impressed.'

'Christ knows. When I was at Harvard there were hardly any girls so you had to think laterally. Girls love the sight of guys fixing things so if I liked someone I'd just get up on the roof and pretend to mend it. Worked every time. The hairdryer was an inspired addition. It was the only way I could think of getting you upstairs.'

'That's a frighteningly efficient seduction tool, Dan McCloud,' I replied with mock froideur. 'I think you better get back on the roof and begin practising because I'm going back to England!'

'Oh no, you're not!'

'I rather think that I am,' I replied in my snootiest English accent. He loves it when I talk like the Queen. Of course, I had absolutely no intention of leaving him alone in Nantucket picking up girls from the roof, but I had to get back to England to stock up on Branston pickle. I can't find it anywhere in Nantucket and, though Mum sent me a vat, it exploded in the post.

'*You*, my green-eyed girl, are going nowhere . . . just . . . yet,' Dan murmured, his heavy lidded eyes running over me. A wind was whipping up from the ocean and tendrils of my hair were blowing around my face. Dan caressed a strand off my face with a big brown hand, and played idly with the flimsy strap on my greeny blue silk nightie dress (so comfortable to write in), so that it fell rippling to the deck, a fluid pool of watery silk at my bare feet. He sighed and winding a frond of my hair around his finger reeled me in towards him, kissing me passionately.

'Dan, please, someone might see us!' I mumbled unconvincingly, breaking away for a second and looking beyond the deserted beach into the grey green ocean glinting like a vast sparkling diamond in the distance.

'What're they going to do about it? Arrest me for offences against mermaids?' We laughed into the salty air and fell like playful seals into one another's arms. But as I gazed into the sun to the glittering ocean below, I could have sworn I saw a flash of golden hair attached to a shining crescent of shimmering green, leap from the water, the tail arched and curved as softly as a dolphin's secret smile.

It was just a fancy, of course, and maybe I was blinded by the sun, but I wondered if . . . but, of course, no one believes in mermaids . . .

And Dan kissed the salt from my skin, and soon we joined the roar of the ocean, oblivious to the cries of seagulls melting into the soft sand on the beach below. Sea breezes are good for lovers . . .

The Real Thing

Catherine Alliott

Everyone's got one – an old boyfriend they never fell out of love with, they simply parted because the time wasn't right. And for thirty-year-old Tessa, it's Patrick Cameron, the gorgeous, moody, rebellious boy she met at seventeen; the boy her vicar father thoroughly disapproved of; the boy who left her to go to Italy to paint.

And now he's back.

'You're in for a treat' *Express*

'Alliot's joie de vivre is irresistible' *Daily Mail*

'Compulsive and wildly romantic' *Bookseller*

'An addictive cocktail of wit, frivolity and madcap romance . . . move over Jilly, your heir is apparent' *Time Out*

0 7472 5235 1

HEADLINE

Forbidden

Roberta Latow

Amy Ross, a celebrated art historian, has had many lovers in her lifetime. Again and again she has tasted the sweet ecstasy of sexual fulfilment and erotic depravity. Now, in her later years, she lives as a recluse, blissfully content in her own isolation, an enigma to her friends and admirers.

But Amy has suppressed the memory of her one secret obsession – her love affair with the artist Jarret Sparrow. Their relationship was beyond belief, her love for him dominated her entire life and took her to the furthest limits of carnal desire. Their feelings were too powerful to control – but their love for each other was ultimately forbidden.

Since their separation, Jarret and his manipulative Turkish friend Fee have seduced numerous women in pursuit of their ambition to conquer the art world. And now Jarret is about to re-enter Amy's life. For all those years, Amy had thought it was over. But is she prepared to rekindle the flames of her desire, and at what price . . . ?

'A wonderful storyteller. Her descriptive style is second to none . . . astonishing sexual encounters . . . exotic places, so real you can almost feel the hot sun on your back . . . heroines we all wish we could be' *Daily Express*

'Latow's writing is vibrant and vital. Her descriptions emanate a confidence and boldness that is typical of her characters' *Books* magazine

'It sets a hell of a standard' *The Sunday Times*

'Explicitly erotic . . . intelligently written' *Today*

0 7472 4911 3

HEADLINE